WHAT THE CRITICS ARE SAYING

★ ★ ★

★ *WORLD* magazine says *The Last Days* is "dramatic . . . good entertainment . . . a *New York Times* best seller with the gospel tucked inside."

★ The *New York Times* calls Rosenberg "a Washington success story."

★ **Rush Limbaugh** says *The Last Jihad* is "amazing. . . . I could not put this book down. . . . You have to read this."

★ **Sean Hannity** calls *The Last Days* "riveting to the point you can't put it down—a heart-pounding, edge-of-your-seat roller-coaster ride."

★ **Joe Scarborough, MSNBC,** says, "Joel Rosenberg is almost a prophet. . . . I would recommend you read these books. This is a guy who understands what is going on in the Middle East."

★ *The Jerusalem Post* calls *The Last Days* "a fast-paced thriller, packed with the authentic details and behind-the-scenes tidbits that only a Washington insider such as Rosenberg could know. . . . Screams 'possible' from every page."

★ *U.S. News & World Report* says Rosenberg's novels are so close to reality he seems like a "modern Nostradamus."

★ *CNN Headline News* says, "J.K. Rowling may be the writer of the moment for the young and the young at heart. But for many adults Joel Rosenberg is the '*it author*' right now. Inside and outside the Beltway in Washington, people are snatching up copies of his almost lifelike terrorist suspense novels."

★ **Michael Reagan** says, "*The Last Days* is a gutsy new breed of political thriller—almost prophetically forecasting what you'll read in tomorrow's headlines. . . . Rosenberg is a rising new star on the American fiction scene."

★ *The Tampa Tribune* says, "Predicting the future can be risky business unless perhaps your name is Nostradamus. But Joel Rosenberg hit it in his first political thriller, *The Last Jihad*, written in 2001, in which he predicted a war between the United States and Iraq over weapons of mass destruction."

★ **Steve Forbes** says, "What a timely tale. Rosenberg has written, à la Clancy, one of those rare novels that is riveting to read because it seems too real. A tingling triumph."

★ **Vincent Flynn**, *New York Times* best-selling author of *Separation of Power*, says, "A wild, rocketing read, *The Last Jihad* is Tom Clancy writ large."

★ *Publishers Weekly* calls *The Last Days* "an action-packed Clancyesque political thriller."

★ *Forbes* **magazine** says *The Last Days* is "a rip-roaring, heart-pounding, page-turning, high-octane geopolitical thriller. . . . The action never stops from the first sentence to the last."

★ **FaithfulReader.com** says, "Rosenberg creates the narrative vortex that sucks you in by warping the timeline and populating his story with real people in imaginary places."

THE LAST DAYS

★ ★
★

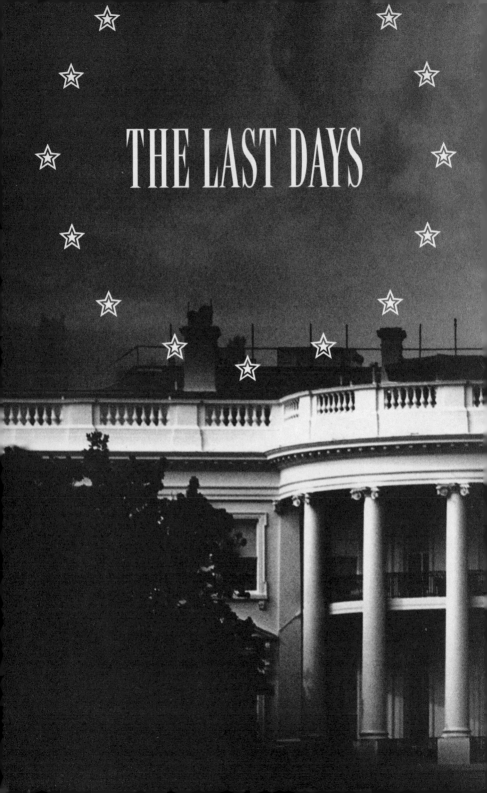

THE LAST DAYS

JOEL C. ROSENBERG

Tyndale House Publishers, Inc., Carol Stream, Illinois

Library of Congress Cataloging-in-Publication Data

Rosenberg, Joel C., date.
  The last days : a novel / by Joel C. Rosenberg.
    p. cm.
  ISBN-13: 978-1-4143-1273-6 (sc)
  ISBN-10: 1-4143-1273-3 (sc)
  1. International relations—Fiction. 2. Middle East—Fiction. 3. Political fiction. I. Title.
  PS3568.O786L36 2006
  813'.54—dc22   2006016233

This book is dedicated to our Arab and Jewish friends
in and around the Middle East
who are pouring out their very lives
for the peace that passes all understanding.

CAST OF CHARACTERS

★ ★ ★

THE PRESIDENT OF THE UNITED STATES
- James "Mac" MacPherson

THE VICE PRESIDENT OF THE UNITED STATES
- William Harvard Oaks

THE PRINCIPALS
- Scott Harris, Director of the Federal Bureau of Investigation
- Stuart Morris Iverson, Former Secretary of the Treasury
- Lee Alexander James, Secretary of Homeland Security
- Marsha Kirkpatrick, National Security Advisor
- Jack Mitchell, Director of Central Intelligence
- Tucker Paine, Secretary of State
- Burt Trainor, Secretary of Defense
- Neil Wittimore, Attorney General

SENIOR WHITE HOUSE STAFF
- Jon Bennett, Senior Advisor to the President
- Bob Corsetti, White House Chief of Staff
- Erin McCoy, Deputy to Jon Bennett and CIA Operations Officer
- Chuck Murray, White House Press Secretary

OTHER KEY ADMINISTRATION ADVISORS
- Marty Benjamin, State Department's Policy Planning Staff Director
- Dick Cavanaugh, Deputy Secretary of State
- Ken Costello, Undersecretary of State for Political Affairs
- Troy Moreaux, U.S. Ambassador to Iraq, Head of ORHA
- General Ed Mutschler, Chairman of the Joint Chiefs of Staff
- Danny Tracker, CIA Deputy Director for Operations

U.S. SECURITY OFFICIALS
- Tariq Abu Ashad, CIA Agent
- Max Banacci, DSS Agent
- Dietrich Black, Late FBI Agent
- Hamid Al-Shahib, CIA Agent
- Sergeant Hunt, Navy SEAL
- Kyl Lake, DSS Agent
- Maroq, CIA Agent
- Donny Mancuso, DSS Agent
- Nazir, CIA Agent

- Bud Norris, Director of the U.S. Secret Service
- George Polanski, FBI Agent
- Eduardo Ramirez, SEAL Team Eight Commander
- Jackie Sanchez, Secret Service Agent
- Robbie Trakowski, DSS Agent
- Neil Watts, FBI Agent
- Jake Ziegler, CIA Gaza Station Chief

IRAQI LEADERS
- Ayad Allawi, Iraqi National Accord
- Mustafa Al-Hassani, Iraqi National Alliance
- Abdel-Aziz al-Hakim, Supreme Council for Islamic Revolution in Iraq
- Masoud Barzani, Kurdistan Democratic Party
- Achmed Chalabi, Iraqi National Congress
- Jalal Talabani, Patriotic Union of Kurdistan

ISRAELI LEADERS
- David Doron, Prime Minister of Israel
- Dmitri Galishnikov, CEO of Medexco, Inc.
- Dr. Eliezer Mordechai, Former Head of Mossad
- Yossi Ben Ramon, Head of Shin Bet
- Avi Zadok, Current Head of Mossad
- Uri "The Wolf" Ze'ev, Chief of Staff of the Israeli Defense Forces

PALESTINIAN LEADERS
- Yasser Arafat, Chairman of the Palestinian Authority
- Abu Mazen (aka Dr. Mahmoud Abbas), Palestinian Prime Minister
- Marwan Barghouti, Fatah-Tanzim Leader
- Mohammed Dahlan, Palestinian Interior Minister
- Jibril Rajoub, Palestinian Security Chief on West Bank
- Khalid al-Rashid, Personal Security Chief for Chairman Arafat
- Dr. Ibrahim Sa'id, CEO of Palestinian Petroleum Group
- Achmed Qurei, Speaker of the Palestinian Legislative Council

AL-NAKBAH LEADERS
- Yuri Gogolov, Russian Cofounder of Al-Nakbah Terrorist Movement
- Mohammed Jibril, Iranian Cofounder of Al-Nakbah
- Nadir Sarukhi Hashemi ("The Viper," "Mario Iabello"), Terrorist
- Daoud Juma, Terrorist

OTHERS
- Akiva Ben David, Founder of the Temple Mount Battalion
- Ruth Bennett, Mother of Jon Bennett
- Solomon Bennett, Late Father of Jon Bennett
- Marcus Jackson, *New York Times* White House Correspondent
- Dorothy Richards, Sister of Ruth Bennett

★ ★ ★

The first page of my first novel, *The Last Jihad*, put readers inside the cockpit of a jet—hijacked by radical Islamic terrorists—flying a kamikaze attack into an American city. As the plot unfolded, the FBI and CIA traced the trail of terror back to Baghdad, and suddenly the president of the United States found himself in a war with Saddam Hussein over terrorism and weapons of mass destruction.

But *The Last Jihad* was written before any of these events actually happened in real life.

When *Jihad* was released on November 23, 2002, I was interviewed on more than 160 radio and TV talk shows in less than 60 days. The questions were less about the novel itself than about the story behind the novel. How could I possibly have written a work of fiction that seemed to foreshadow actual events? Did I work for the CIA? Did I have friends at the Pentagon slipping me inside information? Was it a fluke? Did I get lucky? Or was there something else going on?

In January 2003, my publisher asked if I would like to write another book.

Sure, I thought, *it beats working*. But I felt compelled to caution them that I could not guarantee a second novel would have the same "ripped from the headlines" feel as *Jihad*. After all, I would most likely be writing about events set *after* a U.S.-led war in Iraq, *after* the collapse of Saddam Hussein's regime, and *after* the emergence of a democratic and pro-Western provisional government in Iraq.

None of this had actually happened yet, nor was there any guarantee that it would ever happen. Indeed, there were numerous diplomatic initiatives under way in Europe and the Arab world trying desperately to prevent a war from occurring, and President Bush himself was saying he hoped hostilities could be avoided.

Apparently unconcerned, the publisher gave me a green light to move forward with my second book, the one you now hold in your hands.

On March 19, 2003, the U.S. did, in fact, launch a war against Iraq.

I turned in the manuscript of *The Last Days* in late July. When it was released on October 21, 2003, it quickly became a national best seller.

What intrigued people most was the sense that *The Last Days*, like *The Last Jihad* before it, was somehow telegraphing future events.

As you're about to see, the novel opens with the death of Yasser Arafat and an American president pushing for peace and democracy in the Middle East in the messy aftermath of a brutal war in Iraq. The first pages put you inside a U.S. convoy filled with diplomats and CIA officials heading into Gaza as part of the peace process when it is suddenly attacked by a massive explosion.

On October 15, 2003, fiction seemed to morph into reality. A U.S. diplomatic convoy in Gaza was hit by a Palestinian bomb, and the explosion killed several members of a team sent to oversee the progress of a U.S.-backed peace plan.

There was no way the terrorists could have used my book as a blueprint for their murderous plans. It did not hit bookstores for another six days. But the event triggered an avalanche of media interest. Over the next few weeks, I did hundreds of radio, TV, and print interviews, including *CNN Headline News*, MSNBC, CBN, and the *New York Times*. In its November 3, 2003, edition, *U.S. News & World Report* published a story describing me as a "modern Nostradamus." Paul Bedard, the magazine's political columnist, wrote, "It's getting a little weird being Joel Rosenberg, the *New York Times* bestseller of terrorism thrillers and speechwriter in Steve Forbes's 2000 presidential campaign. First, he wrote *The Last Jihad* about a terrorist's kamikaze attack on a U.S. city and the subsequent hunt for Iraqi weapons of mass destruction. That was well before 9/11. Now he has written *The Last Days*, which opens with a Palestinian attack on a U.S. convoy, just like what happened a few weeks back. And look out, Yasser Arafat: Rosenberg offs you on Page 28."

A year later, Arafat was dead.

It happened November 11, 2004. I remember it distinctly, as I was in Turkey doing research for my third novel, *The Ezekiel Option*, when I got a call from my publicist back in Washington. No sooner had news of Arafat's death hit the wires than he had a stack of interview requests from radio talk-show hosts who had interviewed me when *The Last Days* was published. They were convinced the book was coming true and were curious to know what I thought would happen next.

What would the post-Arafat world look like? Could a moderate, prodemocratic, pro-Western leader now emerge, someone able and willing to make peace with Israel? Or would radical Islamic jihadists seize control of the West Bank and Gaza? Or were the Palestinians doomed to suffer a bloody civil war as various factions battled it out for supremacy?

I spent the rest of the day doing U.S. radio interviews from the phone in my hotel room, noting that any one of those scenarios was possible, but that the first thing to watch for was the outbreak of internecine violence and the emergence of an atmosphere of chaos.

At one point in *The Last Days*, a fictional CIA expert sends a top secret e-mail "Possible Palestinian civil war erupting" to the president. He warns that the "battle to succeed Arafat could be brutal" and urges top administration officials to "watch for PLO factions to mobilize" against each other. As the novel unfolds, the warnings come to pass, top Palestinian officials are assassinated, and the West Bank and Gaza sink into anarchy.

Once again, fiction soon became fact. On November 14, 2004, the Associated Press reported that "militants firing assault rifles burst into a mourning tent for Yasser Arafat . . . just moments after the arrival of the Palestinian leader's temporary successor, Mahmoud Abbas, forcing security guards to whisk him away to safety. The shooting, which killed two security guards and wounded six other people, raised grave concerns about a violent power struggle in the post-Arafat era." By the end of the week, Palestinian prime minister Ahmed Qorei was demanding that the violence cease. But few were listening.

The turmoil continued over the next several years, eventually playing into the hands of Hamas, which took over the Palestinian Authority in January 2006, not long after President Bush decided to make democracy in the Middle East the centerpiece of his second-term agenda.

It has now been almost four years since *The Last Jihad* was first published and three since the release of *The Last Days*. During this time, two more of my novels—*The Ezekiel Option* and *The Copper Scroll*—have been published. Each continues the story and the themes that I began in *Jihad* and *Days*, and each has had an uncanny, sometimes unnerving way of coming true, as well. This led Tyndale House Publishers to ask me to write a nonfiction book, *Epicenter*, to explain the process I use to write books that feel "eerily prophetic" and to explain the next war that will shake our world and shape our future.

Together, these books have sold more than one million copies and have spent months on the national best-seller lists. Such broad interest is, I believe, an indication of the anxious times in which we live. Ours, after all, is an age of kamikazes and snipers, anthrax and suicide bombers, ballistic missiles and nuclear warheads. And while we no longer face Saddam Hussein, now we face a new Iranian regime threatening to wipe the U.S. and Israel off the map. All of this raises troubling new questions: What is coming next? How bad will it be? Where will I be when it happens, and am I ready to meet my Maker if, God forbid, I'm in the wrong place at the wrong time when evil strikes again?

As one of the characters in *The Last Days* says, "To misunderstand the nature and threat of evil is to risk being blindsided by it." We were blindsided on 9/11 by an evil most of us did not see coming. But are we more ready today? Do our leaders truly grasp the fact that the ultimate goal of the jihadists is not to terrorize us but to annihilate us? Are they—and we—willing to take whatever actions are necessary to defend Western civilization from extinction? Or are we going to elevate peace over victory, retreat from the world, and simply hope for the best?

Such questions lie at the heart of *The Last Days*, and they explain, I think, why it has captured the curiosity of so many.

Perhaps you have picked up this book with these very questions in mind. Or maybe you're simply looking for a high-speed adventure ride to sweep you away from your everyday world. Either way, thank you for reading this 9/11 Anniversary Edition. Nothing has been added to the original story. No factual mistakes have been corrected. No dates or details or characters have been changed as a result of events in the actual Iraq war or the actual death of Yasser Arafat or for any other reason. All we've done is a bit of copyediting to clean up the manuscript.

May you enjoy reading this edition of *The Last Days* as much as I enjoyed writing it, and may God bless you as you do.

Joel C. Rosenberg
WASHINGTON, D.C.
MAY 2006

For more about Joel's books—or to read his weblog—please visit

www.joelrosenberg.com.

Then Jacob called for his sons and said: "Gather around so I can
tell you what will happen to you in the last days. . . ."

★

GENESIS 49:1

The real test of a man is not when he plays the role that he wants
for himself, but when he plays the role destiny has for him.

★

VACLAV HAVEL

I
★ ★
★

"YOU REALLY WANT ME to kill him?"

The question hung in the air for a moment, and neither said another word.

The flames crackled in the fireplace of the elegant penthouse apartment overlooking central Tehran. Light rain fell on the clay balcony tiles. Bitter December winds howled outside, rustling trees and rattling windows. Thunder rumbled in the distance. And the room and the sky grew dark.

Mohammed Jibril looked out over the teeming city of his youth, as the haunting call to prayer echoed across the rooftops. He knew he should not feel so tired, but he did. Tired of sleeping in different beds, different houses, different cities. Tired of constantly watching his back, and that of Yuri Gogolov, the man sitting in the shadows behind him, puffing casually on one of his beloved Cuban cigars. Jibril considered his options. There weren't many.

"You understand, of course," Jibril continued, "that you will be unleashing a war that could escalate beyond our control—beyond anyone's control."

A silent, unnerving pause.

"And you're ready for this war?" Jibril asked, perhaps too bluntly.

Instantly regretting the question, he could feel a chill descend upon the room. Gogolov sat motionless in an overstuffed velvet chair. He looked out at the mountains and the minarets and the twinkling lights of the ancient Iranian capital. He drew long and hard on the Cohiba, and the cigar glowed in the shadows.

★　★　★

Air Force One roared down runway 18-36 "Lima."

Flanked by four F-15E Strike Eagle fighter jets, the gleaming new Boeing 747 quickly gained altitude and banked toward the Atlantic. President James "Mac" MacPherson stared out the window. He could no longer see the lights of Madrid Barajas International Airport, or the lights of the Spanish capital itself, just nine miles away. The emergency one-day NATO summit was over. In a few hours, he'd be home, back at the White House, under pressure to answer the question on everyone's mind: now what?

Osama bin Laden was dead. Al-Qaeda and the Taliban were obliterated. And now—just three and a half weeks after it began—the war in Iraq was effectively over. Saddam Hussein was dead and buried under a thousand tons of rubble. His sons were dead too. His murderous regime had been toppled. His henchmen were being scooped up by U.S. Special Forces, one by one, day by day. But the president had never felt more alone.

Rebuilding Iraq and keeping it from blowing apart like Bosnia would be difficult enough. But that wasn't the only thing on his plate. Wars and rumors of wars dominated the headlines. New threats surfaced constantly. North Korea was just months away from building six to ten nuclear bombs. Iran would soon complete a nuclear reactor with Russian assistance, capable of producing two to three nuclear warheads a month. Syria and Iran appeared to be harboring top Iraqi military officials and scientists. NATO was badly divided. The U.N. was a mess. Democrats threatened to filibuster most of the White House's major legislative priorities. And now this: the FBI and Justice Department were recommending the death penalty in *United States v. Stuart Morris Iverson*, one of the most chilling acts of espionage in the nation's history, not to mention one that involved one of the president's closest friends and a man who had been, until a month ago, secretary of the treasury.

Saudi Arabia, meanwhile, was insisting that all U.S. forces leave its soil immediately. And OPEC—outraged by the U.S. strikes against Iraq—was threatening an all-out oil embargo unless war reparations were made to the Iraqi people and pressure was brought to bear on Israel to allow the creation of a Palestinian state. The president recoiled at the thought of an ultimatum from countries he had just saved from nuclear, chemical, and biological annihilation. He wasn't about to submit to blackmail, but he was painfully aware of the risks he was running. Even now, his handpicked diplomatic team was on its way to Jerusalem.

MacPherson—feeling quite vigorous at sixty until a team of Iraqi assassins nearly took his life the month before—was beginning to feel his age. He swallowed a handful of aspirin and washed it down with a bottle of water. His head was pounding. His back and neck were in excruciating pain. He needed sleep. He needed to clear his head. The last thing he needed was an oil price shock reminiscent of '73. So much of the road ahead was foggy. But one thing was painfully obvious: the horrific battle of Iraq wasn't the end of the war on terror. It was just the beginning.

✯   ✯   ✯

When ordering a hit, Jibril preferred the anonymity of an Internet café.

No one would bother him. No one could trace him. And at less than twenty-five thousand rials an hour—about three U.S. dollars—it was far cheaper than using his satellite phone.

Tehran alone boasted more than fifteen hundred cyber shops, which had exploded in popularity ever since Mohammad Khatami was elected president in 1997 and gave the fledgling Internet sector his blessing. The hard-line religious clerics continued to be wary. In 2001, they'd forced four hundred shops to close their doors for operating without proper business licenses, breaking Islamic laws, and trafficking in "Western pollution." They'd insisted that the government deny anyone under the age of eighteen from entering the shops. But that just made the idea of an electronic periscope into the West all the more alluring, and Web traffic shot up faster than ever.

The bulletproof sedan eased off the main boulevard. Mohammed Jibril told his driver to drop him off at the Caspian Cyber Café on Enghelab Avenue, across from the University of Tehran. A moment later he logged on and sent a half dozen cryptic e-mails. Next, he pulled up the home page for Harrods of London and quickly found what he needed. *Harrods Chocolate Batons with French Brandy—twelve individually wrapped milk-chocolate batons filled with Harrods Fine Old French Brandy. Made from the finest Swiss chocolate. 100g.* He hit the *Buy Now* button, typed in the appropriate FedEx shipping information, paid with a stolen credit card, and left as quickly as he came. Now all he could do was wait, and hope the messages arrived in time.

★ ★ ★

The eyes of the world were now on Jon Bennett.

A senior advisor to the president of the United States, Bennett was the chief architect of the administration's new Arab-Israeli peace plan. The front-page, top-of-the-fold *New York Times* profile the day before—Sunday, December 26—had just dubbed him the new "point man for peace." The media was now tracking his every move and the stakes couldn't be higher.

The president was eager to shift the world's attention from war to peace, to rebuilding Iraq and expanding free markets and free elections in the Middle East. The Pentagon and CIA insisted the next battles lay in Syria and Iran. But the State Department and White House political team argued such moves would be a mistake. It was time to force the Israelis and Palestinians to the bargaining table, to nail down a peace treaty the way Jimmy Carter had with Menachem Begin and Anwar Sadat at Camp David in '77, and the way Clinton had tried to with Barak and Arafat in the summer of 2000. "Blessed are the peacemakers," they reminded the president. And the president was listening.

Bennett wasn't so sure it was the right time, or that he was the right man. He hadn't asked to be named "point man for peace." He hadn't wanted the job. But the president insisted. He needed a deal, he needed it now, and Bennett couldn't say no.

At forty, Jonathan Meyers Bennett was one of the youngest and most successful deal makers on Wall Street, and a guy who had everything. An undergraduate degree from Georgetown. An MBA from Harvard. A thirty-eighth-floor office overlooking Central Park. A forest green Jaguar XJR, for business. A red Porsche Turbo, for pleasure. A seven-figure salary, with options and bonuses. A seven-figure portfolio and retirement fund. A $1.5 million penthouse apartment in Greenwich Village near NYU, for which he'd paid cash. Closets full of Zegna suits. And Matt Damon good looks.

Few people on Wall Street knew much about this shadowy young man, but he was the talk of all the women in his office. Six feet tall with short dark hair and grayish green eyes, he had a picture-perfect smile after a fortune in dental work as a kid. He'd once been voted the office's most eligible bachelor, but only part of that was true. He was a bachelor, but not all that eligible. He dated occasionally, but all his colleagues knew Bennett was married to his work, pure and simple. He typically worked twelve to fourteen hours a day, including Saturdays. None of that had changed at the White House, and now he was at his desk by ten-thirty on Sundays, too, watching *Meet the Press* and planning for the week ahead.

Before coming to Washington, Bennett had been the senior VP and chief investment strategist for Global Strategix, Inc., one of the hottest firms on the Street. Part strategic-research shop, part venture-capital fund, GSX advised mutual and pension funds, as well as the Joshua Fund, which had $137 billion in assets under management. Over the years, GSX had become known as the financial industry's "AWACS"—its airborne warning and control system—able to alert money managers of trouble long before it arrived. GSX also had a reputation of finding "sure things," early investments in start-up ventures that hit the jackpot and paid off big. Most of the credit went to Bennett. He had a sixth sense for finding buried treasure, and he loved the hunt. The plaque on his desk said it all: "I'm not the richest man in the richest city in the richest country on the face of the globe in the history of mankind. But tomorrow is another day."

Then "tomorrow" threw him a curveball. Suddenly he was off the Street, out of GSX, working for the White House, and on the secretary of state's 757, headed for the Holy Land. It was surreal, to say the least, but the package came with one big incentive: the chance to cut a deal they'd be writing about for decades. And Bennett was determined to see it through.

"Hey there, Point Man; we there yet?"

Erin McCoy rubbed the sleep from her eyes. She put her seat back in its upright position and prepared for landing. A senior member of Bennett's team for the past several years, she'd been teasing him about the *Times* profile for the last twenty-four hours, and enjoying every minute of it. After takeoff from Andrews, she'd persuaded the pilot to welcome the entire American delegation, including "our own Jon Bennett, the esteemed point man for peace." She'd even plastered the interior of the plane with big red, white, and blue signs asking, "What's the point, man?"

"You kill me, McCoy."

"Don't tempt me, Jon." She smiled.

Bennett stared back out the window, trying to ignore how good McCoy looked in her ivory silk blouse and black wool suit. She really was beautiful, he thought. Why hadn't she become a model instead of joining the CIA? She was five-foot-ten with shoulder-length chestnut brown hair, lightly tanned skin, sparkling green eyes, and a picture-perfect smile that hadn't required any dental work at all. All that, and she was ranked an expert marksman with six different kinds of weapons, including her favorite, a 9 mm Beretta, which she carried with her at all times. How could this girl still be single?

"Just give me a copy of the schedule, would you?" Bennett asked.

"You got it," said McCoy as she pulled out a few pages from her briefing book. "Point Man touches down at 0700 local time, Monday, December 27th; meets with the Palestinians, then the Israelis; saves the world; spends New Year's in Cancún; then cuts large check to beautiful deputy for saving his life, and his job."

Bennett fought hard not to give her the satisfaction of a smile. But it wasn't easy.

"I don't know what I'd do without you, McCoy," he said, snatching the pages from her hands. "But believe me, I'll think of something."

* * *

The webmaster in London instantly recognized the e-mail address.

This was no order for chocolate. And she knew it was urgent. She quickly e-mailed a copy to Harrods' shipping clerk downstairs for immediate processing, then logged on to AOL and IM'd a gift shop on the Rock of Gibraltar.

* * *

Thirty minutes later, they sped along Highway 1 toward Jerusalem.

Through driving rains. Past huge green road signs in Hebrew, Arabic, and English. Past the rusted shells of armored personnel carriers destroyed in the 1948 war. Past roads that would lead them, if they wanted, a few miles and a few thousand years away to ancient biblical towns like Jaffa and Bethlehem and Jericho.

Two blue-and-white Israeli police cars led the way. Two more brought up the rear. In between were a jet-black Lincoln Town Car carrying the advance team from the embassy, two bulletproof Cadillac limousines, two black Chevy Suburbans carrying heavily armed agents from the State Department's Bureau of Diplomatic Security, and four vans of reporters who would beam the historic words and images to a global audience desperate for some good news from the war-torn Middle East.

The first limousine—code-named Globe Trotter—carried the secretary of state and his aides. Bennett and McCoy rode in the second limo—code-named Snapshot—joined by two old friends upon whose wisdom they now greatly counted. The first was Dmitri Galishnikov, the hard-charging CEO of Medexco, Israel's fastest-growing oil-and-gas company. The second was Dr. Ibrahim Sa'id, the soft-spoken, Harvard-educated chairman of PPG, the Palestinian Petroleum Group, which had made a fortune in the Gulf and now had everyone in the West Bank and Gaza buzzing with excitement.

"Miss Erin, I must say, you look like an angel—like my wife on our wedding day," Galishnikov boomed. "As for you, Point Man, you look terrible."

That got a laugh from everyone, even Bennett.

"Seriously, how are you feeling, Jonathan?" Sa'id asked. "We were worried about you. It's a miracle that you're alive, much less here."

It *was* a miracle. The last time they'd been together, they'd been under attack by Iraqi terrorists. Bennett took two AK-47 rounds at point-blank range. He'd practically bled to death before being airlifted to Landstuhl Regional Medical Center in Germany. Three weeks of recovery and rehab later, he was still not 100 percent.

"Good days and bad, you know." Bennett shrugged. "But it's good to see you two again."

"You too, my friend," Sa'id agreed. "And your mother? How is she?"

McCoy watched Bennett shift uncomfortably.

"Well, she's not exactly thrilled about me coming back, that's for sure. Dad's heart attack, the funeral, what happened to me—she's been through a lot. But she's hanging in there. I'll head down to Orlando to see her for a few days when we get back."

"That's good." Sa'id smiled. "You're a good son, Jonathan."

Bennett wasn't so sure about that, but he said nothing.

* * *

An e-mail arrived in a small gift shop on Gibraltar.

It was quickly forwarded to a wood-carving shop in Gaza. Soon it drew the attention of an immaculately well-dressed young man by the name of Khalid al-Rashid. To anyone but him, the message would mean nothing, just an old family relative sending greetings for the holidays. But to the third most powerful man in Palestine, it could mean only one thing: his date with destiny had arrived.

* * *

The motorcade began to climb the foothills leading to Jerusalem.

Tonight, the U.S. delegation would take up two entire floors of the King David Hotel, overlooking Mount Zion, the stone walls of the Old City, and the Mount of Olives just beyond them. Tomorrow they'd have a long working lunch with Israeli prime minister David Doron. But soon they would actually be sitting in Gaza City, overlooking the stormy Mediterranean, drinking coffee and eating baklava with Palestinian Authority chairman Yasser Arafat and his hand-chosen, silver-haired successor, Prime Minister Mahmoud Abbas, better known by his nom de guerre, Abu Mazen.

It would be a long day. Diplomatic formalities and endless pleasantries would likely take until lunch. They'd eat lentil soup and lamb until they couldn't stuff down another scrap of pita. Then they'd get down to business.

At the heart of the proposed treaty was the discovery of black gold deep underneath the Mediterranean—a massive and spectacular tract of oil and natural gas off the coasts of Israel and Gaza that could offer unprecedented wealth for every Muslim, Christian, and Jew in Israel and Palestine. And the American message they were about to deliver was as daring as it was direct: Both sides must put behind them centuries of bitter, violent hostilities to sign a serious peace agreement. Both sides must truly cooperate on drilling, pumping, refining, and shipping the newly found petroleum. Both sides must work together to develop a dynamic, new, integrated economy to take full advantage of this stunning opportunity. Then—and only then—the United States would help underwrite the billions of dollars of loan guarantees needed to turn the dream into reality.

Bennett's "oil for peace" strategy was controversial, to be sure. It shifted the discussion from simple "land for peace"—long the central premise of fruitless diplomacy between the Israelis and Palestinians—to a shared vision of economic growth and wealth creation. Secret polls commissioned by the White House found 63 percent of Palestinians in favor of the idea, though 71 percent opposed U.S. military action in Iraq. More troubling, 14 percent of Palestinians—the hard-core Islamic militants— vowed to stop the American peace process at all costs.

The key was Yasser Arafat. He'd repeatedly hailed the discovery of petroleum off Gaza as "a gift of God to our people" and the basis of "a strong foundation for a Palestinian state." But the big question remained: was the isolated and aging Arafat—at eighty-one, now in the cold, cruel winter of his life—finally ready to make peace with the Jews? On that, the jury was still out. But that's why Bennett and his team were there.

★ ★ ★

Khalid al-Rashid was born on June 6, 1967.

It was the day the shooting started, a struggle the Jews called the Six Days' War and the Arabs called Al-Nakbah—"The Disaster."

Raised in an apartment over a woodworking shop on the outskirts of Gaza City, al-Rashid was no maker of tourist trinkets. That was his father's work, before he was gunned down by Israeli soldiers during the first intifada, the Palestinian uprising against Israeli occupation, in February of 1988. The son had risen through the ranks of Force 17—Arafat's *Fatah* security apparatus—first as an errand boy, a driver, then a bodyguard, and now Arafat's personal security chief.

It was al-Rashid who now ensured the survival of Arafat from all threats, foreign and domestic. It was al-Rashid who handpicked Arafat's security team, grilled them, trained them, and either rewarded or punished them for their loyalty to him and to the cause of liberating all of

Palestine from the river to the sea. And though the Israelis and Americans were not yet able to prove it beyond a reasonable doubt, it was in fact al-Rashid who for years had personally selected and then paid the family of each suicide bomber who slipped across the Green Line into an Israeli coffee shop or pizza parlor or bus station or elementary school to blow themselves up, kill as many Jews as possible, and deliver themselves into the arms of Allah.

But this was different. Now, with the secretary of state and U.S. delegation en route from Jerusalem and the whole world watching, al-Rashid sat in his father's home, thinking the unthinkable.

★　★　★

Ahead of the motorcade lay the Erez checkpoint.

The Gaza Strip. No-man's-land.

Here in a sliver seven miles wide and twenty miles long lived more than a million souls—half under the age of fifteen—and the population would double over the next decade. Six in ten men were unemployed. Most families lived in refugee camps amid unimaginable squalor. The Strip was a breeding ground for radical Islam and volcanic hatred of Israelis and Americans that could erupt in a firestorm at any moment—without warning—and often did.

The motorcade slowed. Bennett's heart beat a little faster. Jittery Israeli soldiers, their M16s locked and loaded, opened the steel barricades and guided them past concrete bunkers, guard towers, searchlights, and barbed-wire fences. Border guards in Humvees and army jeeps mounted with heavy machine guns watched their every move. It was an eerie experience. For they were leaving Israel proper and entering the most dangerous and densely populated 140 square miles on the face of the earth.

★　★　★

Secretary of State Tucker Paine took Bennett's call.

Bennett wanted to brief him on his conversations with Ibrahim Sa'id, and Paine needed to sound interested. Paine didn't appreciate the *New York Times* profile that made Bennett, not Paine himself, appear the mastermind of this deal. He felt quite sure his unattributed quotes had done their appropriate damage, reminding Bennett who was in charge. But he also had to watch his step. The president trusted Bennett a great deal, and the last thing Paine needed was more trouble from the Oval Office.

Indeed, Tucker Paine had been dispatched for this delicate mission precisely because he could truthfully tell Arafat how vehemently he had opposed the president's decision to attack Iraq. Who better to win a hearing with Arafat than a secretary of state who'd almost been fired for his heated opposition to the president's policy of "regime change," a policy that had left Baghdad in ruins and the Atlantic alliance in tatters.

★ ★ ★

Time was running out.

But al-Rashid couldn't think clearly. He knew what they wanted. It was something he'd considered for months. But the implications were enormous.

The American, after all, was bringing a death sentence for the Palestinian revolution. Did he think they could be bought off? Had the Americans no idea what this revolution was all about, what fueled these fires? Why not simply destroy this infidel and send the world a message? Surely that was a cause worth dying for, was it not? And yet, who was more culpable—the infidel, or the betrayer?

How could he do it? How could he even consider this meeting? How could he even consider cutting a deal with these devils? How could he betray the martyrs—the blood of al-Rashid's own father—now, of all times, with their brothers decimated in Baghdad? For what? To make the Palestinians rich? To let their sons become fat and happy? To let their daughters grow up to drink Starbucks and listen to Britney Spears and shop at Victoria's Secret? Again al-Rashid glanced at the e-mail. He knew what the answer must be. He could not merely send little girls to do the cause of justice. It was time to be a man. It was time to do the job himself.

★ ★ ★

The motorcade roared through Beit Lahiya.

Uniformed policemen of the Palestinian Authority—commonly referred to as the PA—manned checkpoints at every major intersection. But it hardly made Bennett feel more secure. The PA was arguably the most dysfunctional pseudogovernment on earth. It remained Yasser Arafat's private fiefdom. The security forces operated at his pleasure. If Arafat said you were safe—and meant it—you probably were. If not, you'd be advised to stay as far away as possible. So "supplementing" the Palestinian police presence were heavily armed American DSS agents, strategically positioned along the way. Not since President Clinton's visit to Gaza in December 1998 had security been this tight. Anti-American sentiment was running high. But so too were hopes that a Palestinian state might not be so far off.

★   ★   ★

They gathered in the White House Situation Room.

National Security Advisor Marsha Kirkpatrick and White House Chief of Staff Bob Corsetti drank coffee and watched the live coverage. From a FOX camera positioned on the roof of a hotel near the PLC headquarters, they could see the motorcade coming down Salah El Din Street, packed with crowds spilling into the road despite the metal barricades and hundreds of Palestinian security forces set to work a double shift. A moment later, they could see the motorcade turn onto Omar El Mukhtar Street, past the Great Mosque on the right and the Welaya Mosque on the left.

Just past Jamal Abdel-Nasser Street, the motorcade finally turned into the gates of the PLC's executive compound, past a dozen Palestinian flags snapping in the winter winds. A CNN shot from the roof of the Rashad Shawa Cultural Center across the street showed the vehicles pulling into a huge courtyard. Two new five-story glass-and-steel administrative buildings stood to the left and right. Each was connected to an impressive three-story legislative headquarters upon which towered a thirty-foot gold dome. The entourage pulled into the compound's semicircular driveway and parked behind huge, waist-high concrete barriers designed to minimize—if not fully prevent—the prospect of Israeli tanks driving straight into a cabinet meeting and obliterating the Palestinian Authority. DSS agents jumped out of the last Suburban. They took up positions around the secretary's limousine and ran a sector check.

"Globe Trotter is secure," lead DSS agent Doug Lewis told his team.

"Blueprint, secure."

"Foghorn, secure."

"Perimeter One, secure."

"Perimeter Two, secure."

"Rooftop team leader, we're secure."

"Snapshot, secure."

"Roger that; we're good to go."

* * *

Agent Lewis stepped out of the lead limousine.

He opened the door for Secretary Paine, code-named Sunburn for his nearly albino complexion. The secretary was immediately greeted by a blinding flurry of flashbulbs and questions. The secretary simply smiled and waved. Bennett got out of his car and watched Paine button his Brooks Brothers coat, straighten his red-silk power tie, and begin walking across the courtyard to center stage, trailed by Lewis and two more DSS agents. It was quite a walk—almost forty yards to the front steps of the legislative building, past three marble fountains and a huge bronze replica of the Dome of the Rock in Jerusalem.

Following strict protocol, Bennett, McCoy, and the others would hang back and wait for the statesmen to shake hands and go inside before joining them. Over the hood of the limousine, Bennett could see Arafat emerging from the front door in a wheelchair, flanked by Prime Minister Abu Mazen with his distinctive silver hair, silver mustache, and wide-rimmed glasses.

Arafat's wheelchair was being pushed by his ubiquitous security chief, Khalid al-Rashid. What struck Bennett first was how small Arafat looked—just five foot four—and how old he looked, even from a distance. His thinning gray hair was combed back over his head, but largely covered by his trademark black-and-white-checkered kaffiyeh. He'd lost weight. His pale, gaunt face wore a day's worth of stubble—why bother shaving for the Americans?—and his lower lip and his hands shook slightly from the onset of Parkinson's disease.

Forbes magazine said Arafat was worth a cool $1.3 billion. It seemed hard to believe. For the first time, Bennett was actually glad to be here. He found himself fascinated by this feisty, frail, strange little man in olive army fatigues, a man who for five decades had captured headlines the world over.

Mohammed Yasser Abdul-Ra'ouf Qudwa Al-Husseini.

Aka Yasser Arafat.

Aka Abu Amar.

Born August 24, 1929, in Egypt, or—he claimed—in Jerusalem.

Founder of Fatah in 1959.

Head of the PLO since 1969.

A 1994 Nobel Peace Prize winner who somehow had never actually made peace.

* * *

With Abu Mazen at his side, al-Rashid gently lowered Arafat's wheelchair.

He maneuvered down the front steps and reached inside his coat pocket to make sure it was still there, hidden by his stocky build and thick Italian leather coat.

It was an odd moment—indiscernible to anyone but a professional—but even from a distance it caught the eye of Erin McCoy and Donny Mancuso, Bennett's lead DSS agent. *Why would a security chief of al-Rashid's stature be pushing his principal's wheelchair? Why not let a bodyguard do that job while al-Rashid stayed a few steps back, surveying the scene? And why take his hand, even for a moment, off Arafat's wheelchair as he lowered it down a few steps?*

Al-Rashid quickly withdrew the hand from his pocket and again placed it back on the handle of the wheelchair. A chill rippled down McCoy's spine. Instantly suspicious, she glanced over to Mancuso, wondering if he'd seen the same thing. *But then, what exactly had she seen really? And what was she supposed to do about it? Was the secretary of state and their team really in danger of being shot at by Yasser Arafat's personal security chief? Here? In front of the international media? The whole notion was ludicrous.* She was becoming a little paranoid on her first trip to Gaza, McCoy thought—too much history, too many briefings. She tried to drive it all from her mind and stay focused.

But she couldn't. It wasn't a rational thought she was processing. It was instinct, and hers were rarely wrong.

* * *

It was gray and wet and cold.

Yet beads of sweat were forming on al-Rashid's forehead and upper lip. *Do I wait for the secretary to cross the courtyard? Do I wait until after Arafat greets him? Or would that just provoke a devastating U.S. attack against Palestine? Look what the Americans have just done to Iraq. Is now the right time? Is this the legacy I want to bring upon my family, my people? And yet . . .*

Arafat began coughing violently in the damp air.

Al-Rashid stopped pushing the wheelchair and again reached into his coat pocket.

McCoy and Mancuso tensed as the secretary finished crossing the huge courtyard, though for some reason each hesitated to say anything to the lead DSS agents up ahead.

It was a false alarm. Out of al-Rashid's pocket came a white cotton handkerchief, which he handed to his leader.

A moment later, the secretary reached the portico, draped with Palestinian and American flags. He stood in front of Arafat and Mazen, smiled, and reached down to shake the old man's trembling hand. A hundred cameras snapped a thousand pictures.

McCoy began to breathe a sigh of relief—but suddenly al-Rashid plunged his hand back into his coat pocket and pulled out a long red wire with an ignition switch.

McCoy and Mancuso reacted immediately—*"Get down, get down!"*— tackling Bennett, Galishnikov, and Sa'id and trying to cover them with their own bodies. The secretary and his two DSS agents just stopped and stared, frozen for a fraction of a second in utter disbelief. Like the herd of international journalists watching in horror, they were unable to move, unable to react as al-Rashid screamed out, *"Allahu Akbar"*—*"God is great"*—and pulled the trigger.

The massive explosion ripped through the courtyard. The sound was deafening. The entire facade of the legislative building began to collapse. Blood and body parts showered down from the sky. In the blink of an eye, in a fraction of a second, on live worldwide television, the two highest-ranking Palestinian leaders and the U.S. secretary of state were obliterated in a massive fireball.

Bennett landed hard on the cold, wet pavement and felt McCoy slam down on his back. They were largely shielded from the full effects of the blast by the limousine beside them. Now they tried to shield themselves from the falling debris. Fire and smoke seemed to suck up all the oxygen.

Bennett couldn't think, couldn't breathe. Underneath the car, through a gap in concrete barriers, he could see the hailstorm of rubble and glass crashing down on the open courtyard—a grisly scene unlike anything he'd ever witnessed.

And then, in an instant—as quickly as it had happened—it was over. It was quiet. Only then did the irony begin to dawn on Jon Bennett.

Yasser Arafat was dead . . . at the hands of a Palestinian suicide bomber.

2

★ ★
★

"CODE RED, CODE RED—Sunburn is gone, I repeat, Sunburn is gone."

Donny Mancuso shouted into his wrist-mounted microphone. He was now the special agent-in-charge. Most of the secretary's detail lay dead or dying. The rest lay on the ground, weapons drawn—a combination of Uzis, MP5 submachine guns, and Sig Sauer P228s. They scanned the scene and tried to make sense of it all. Neither he nor they had any idea what had really just happened, or what other threats they might face. But it was Mancuso's job to make sure they didn't get blindsided again.

By motorcade—even at high speeds—it would take nearly an hour to get the wounded back to medical facilities in Jerusalem. Tel Aviv would take at least ninety minutes, maybe more. Some might not make it that long. Several had third-degree burns. Others faced massive loss of blood.

★ ★ ★

Lightning flashed across the dark sky.

Thunder rumbled overhead and the winds were picking up. Another torrential downpour was coming any moment. McCoy began to stir. She shook glass off her back and out of her hair, then leaned inside the open limo door beside her. She reached under the driver's seat, and grabbed her Uzi. She popped in a thirty-two-round clip of 9 mm ammo and stuffed two others in her jacket pocket.

Bennett could feel his heart racing.

* * *

Mancuso grabbed his MP5.

He crawled forward—around McCoy and Bennett—to open the front door of Snapshot and grab the satellite phone off the front seat. He speed-dialed the State Department's Operations Center back in Washington—code-named Black Tower—and connected with Agent Robbie Trakowski, the night-watch officer.

"Black Tower, this is Snapshot," said Mancuso. "We are Code Red. I repeat—we are Code Red. We have extensive casualties. Requesting immediate air support and extraction. Acknowledge."

He began to hear sirens in the distance.

"Roger that, Snapshot. We've got you on a live video feed from the Predator over your location. Let me check on air support and extraction. Stand by one."

* * *

It sounded like a few firecrackers, at first.

Then three machine-gun rounds exploded into the open limo door above him. Someone was firing at them from the street. Eight or nine more rounds riddled the engine block just a few feet away from him. The crackle of automatic-weapons fire was getting louder, and closer. Crowds were running in all directions. People were screaming. All around them, DSS agents and PA policemen were dropping. Bennett suddenly felt someone pushing him under Snapshot's chassis. It was McCoy, trying to shield him from the gun battle erupting around them.

A man in a red kaffiyeh was sprinting toward them—toward McCoy. He was screaming something in Arabic and firing a 9 mm automatic pistol. McCoy's body blocked most of Bennett's view to the street—but not all of it. He saw McCoy click the safety off her Uzi and spray repeated bursts of return fire. The man dropped to the pavement not far from the open gates. Bennett tried to breathe again. That's when it hit him—he had no weapon.

Suddenly—a flash—a puff of white smoke—then he heard the sizzle.

"*RPG*," McCoy shouted.

It was too late. From a darkened window across the street, a rocket-propelled grenade streaked across the top of the crowd, through the wrought-iron gates, and into the open door of the secretary's limousine. Globe Trotter erupted. The explosion blew out the windows and ripped off the roof. Glass and shrapnel were flying everywhere. Flames and thick black smoke poured from the wreckage.

Bennett saw six more DSS agents incinerated in front of him. He'd have slipped into shock, but everything was happening too fast. More machine-gun fire erupted from windows across the street as McCoy, Mancuso and his assault teams from the Suburbans behind them fought back.

☆ ☆ ☆

"Black Tower, this is Snapshot. We are now under fire."

"We acknowledge, Snapshot. You need to stand by for a moment and we'll—"

"Negative, negative. We are taking heavy fire from unknown assailants. Machine-gun fire and RPGs. Sunburn's gone. Globe Trotter's gone. We're taking heavy fire. We need close air support and extraction teams *immediately*—acknowledge."

The sky was getting darker. The winds were getting stronger, whipping through the courtyard, fueling the raging fires all around them.

"Snapshot, this is Black Tower. Air support from the Med is a no go. I repeat—"

"Why not?" Mancuso shouted. "What are you talking about?"

"Calm down, Snapshot."

Mancuso let out a string of obscenities. *"Don't tell me to calm down.* We're out in the open and you're telling me you guys won't send us air support?"

A deafening crash of thunder shook everyone. Bitter cold driving rains began pelting down on them. Bullets ricocheted off the pavement all around them. Now shots were coming from a smashed open window on the third floor of the PLC administrative building towering over their position.

Mancuso ducked closer to the limo and unleashed several bursts toward the windows. "Rooftop Three, Rooftop Three, this is Snapshot— we're taking sniper fire. Third floor. Window eight."

"Got it, Snapshot."

A U.S. countersniper agent on an opposite roof pivoted hard, aimed his Remington 700 sniper rifle, and fired twice. The shooter's head exploded. Mancuso, however, had no time for thank-yous. Washington was trying to get his attention again.

"Snapshot, you need to execute Alpha Bravo."

"Negative, negative. You don't understand. We're pinned down. Taking sniper fire. *We cannot move.*"

"Snapshot, listen to me—*listen*. There's nothing we can do right now. Nothing. The storms over you are even worse out in the Med. Flight ops onboard the *Reagan* and the *Roosevelt* are completely shut down. They can't risk sending in birds right now. You guys are going to have to shoot your way out of this thing until we can get you some help. I'm sorry."

Crack, crack, crack.

The shots echoed through the courtyard. Mancuso instinctively looked up to the roof—only to see Rooftop Three falling through the air and smashing onto the pavement. He cursed and threw the phone back into the car in disgust. How exactly was he supposed to get Bennett, Galishnikov, and Sa'id to safety? How was he supposed to get his own men out?

★　★　★

Three men now rushed their position from across the street.

McCoy was out of ammo. Bennett was unarmed. So were Galishnikov and Sa'id, pinned down behind him. The three gunmen—their faces covered in black hoods—were running hard, unleashing bursts of AK-47 fire from the hip as they came.

"*Donny!*" McCoy screamed.

Mancuso looked left and unloaded an entire clip. Two attackers went down. The third kept coming.

McCoy went for her spare clips.

Bennett could see she wasn't going to make it. This guy was no more than twenty yards away and coming fast. He cleared through the gates, and came up the driveway. Bullets whizzed past him, but didn't stop him. He raised his machine gun. Bennett stared at his eyes. They were wild with rage. Bennett froze. He couldn't move. Couldn't think. Couldn't run. Everything seemed to go into slow motion.

Then he heard it: three loud cracks from a rooftop. *Crack, crack, crack.* It was another American countersniper. The third attacker crashed to the ground. His AK-47 skidded across the bloody pavement. It came to a stop just a few feet away from where Bennett lay. Bennett hesitated for a moment, then strained to reach it from under the limo. He couldn't. It was too far away. He glanced over at McCoy. She seemed momentarily paralyzed. He'd never seen her like this and it rattled him. He looked back at the gun; then suddenly, without looking, without thinking, Bennett scrambled out from under the car, into the cross fire, grabbed the AK-47, and brought it to her.

"Here—you might need this," he shouted over the gunfire.

The gesture seemed to snap her back into the moment.

"No, you keep it," she said, wiping soot from her eyes. "I'm okay."

McCoy reloaded her Uzi, then swiveled around, reached inside the car, and grabbed several more ammo clips from a drawer under the driver's seat. She stuffed them in her pockets and turned back to him. "Okay, Bennett. Back under the car."

"No way, Erin. We've got too much—"

"Shut up, Jon, and get under the car. You're the only game in town now. It's my job to keep you alive, and I haven't got the time to argue."

Her glare was intense. She wasn't kidding. Bennett did what he was told. McCoy turned and began firing at militants outside the gates. Bennett got under the car and looked to his right. What remained of the front section of the PLC building was now engulfed in flames. The searing heat was unbearable. He could smell the burned flesh. He could taste the acrid smoke filling the courtyard. But he could barely breathe and his eyes were stinging with soot and dust.

★ ★ ★

"Snapshot, this is Rooftop One. Over."

Mancuso could barely hear over the gunfire. But it was the head of his countersniper unit. He had something urgent. Mancuso took the call. He stopped firing for a moment and engaged his wrist-mounted microphone.

"Rooftop, this is Snapshot—go."

"Snapshot, we're taking heavy fire up here. But something's going on over in the courtyard of that mosque across the street. Can't see much from here. But there's a crowd gathering down there—around the corner and down the street about a block from your location."

"Roger that, Rooftop. Any PA cops over there?"

"Negative, Snapshot. Regular PA police have taken heavy casualties. They seem to have scattered. The radios are filled with chatter that they're bringing in reinforcements. But I don't like the looks of things from up here."

"You think the mob's headed here?"

"Can't say for sure. But yeah, that's my guess."

"Roger that, Rooftop. Keep your eyes open and stand by."

Mancuso tried to process the situation. They'd all been through years of intense training for an array of worst-case scenarios. They'd all been thoroughly briefed on the possible threats they could face on this trip—specifically the threat that radical Islamic groups opposed to the peace process might stage some kind of an attack or disruption. Perhaps a car bomb along the motorcade route to delay or cancel the secretary's meeting with Arafat. Perhaps a suicide bombing in Jerusalem or Tel Aviv or Haifa to distract attention. Perhaps Molotov cocktails thrown at the motorcade, or a skirmish with Israeli border guards, or an angry anti-U.S. march through the streets of Gaza City or one of the refugee camps. All these had been thoroughly analyzed and war-gamed.

But no one in ITA—the Bureau of Diplomatic Security's Intelligence and Threat Analysis Center—or the Tel Aviv field office had talked about, much less planned for, a scenario like this: an inside job by an Arafat loyalist and a coordinated, multilevel attack from forces loyal to . . . to whom? Who was behind this? Whom were they really fighting? They knew Palestinian frustration against Arafat had been intensifying for years. Anger among many Palestinian Islamic leaders at the U.S. for the war against Iraq was to be expected. And in the past few days, Israeli electronic intercepts had been picking up all kinds of chatter of dissent against the resumption of peace talks. But neither the Israelis nor the Americans had picked up any serious evidence of internal threats against Arafat himself, certainly not from within the PA's security forces, much less from within Force 17.

Even "outside" Palestinian threats were extremely rare. In 1998, Arafat's security forces had cracked down on Islamic militants and put

Hamas leader Sheikh Ahmed Yassin under house arrest. At that point, a Hamas faction known as the Izzedine al Qassam Brigades issued a pamphlet in the territories. They warned the PA to back off or risk igniting the "fires of revenge" against Arafat and "the horrors of civil war" in the West Bank and Gaza. Arafat did back off and other top Hamas leaders publicly distanced themselves from the threats. Nothing happened, and the incident was largely forgotten.

In the fall of 2002, a series of death threats forced Abu Mazen—then serving as Arafat's top political deputy in the PLO—to leave his home in Ramallah and seek safe haven in Jordan. Some said the threats came from Islamic factions because Mazen had publicly denounced the practice of suicide bombing and called the intifada's use of violence against Israel a disastrous mistake that set back the Palestinian cause by years. Others said the death threats came from PA factions close to Arafat after rumors that Mazen might be plotting to overthrow Arafat. Mazen heatedly denied the rumors, but it was clear someone was trying to take him out. Suddenly Mazen was on an extended trip to Jordan, Egypt, and the Persian Gulf—anywhere but the West Bank and Gaza.

A few months later, though, Arafat kissed and made up. Instead of having Abu Mazen arrested for allegedly plotting a coup against him, Arafat named him prime minister of the Palestinian Authority. It seemed a bizarre turn of events. In fact, it was a scene straight out of *The Godfather*: "Keep your friends close, but your enemies closer."

But the move spooked radical Islamic leaders. They openly worried Abu Mazen might cave in to U.S. pressure to end the armed struggle against Israel and crack down on the Islamic militant factions. They called Abu Mazen's appointment evidence of a conspiracy to destroy the Palestinian "resistance to occupation." Abdallah al Shami, a senior Islamic Jihad leader, told the *Gulf News*: "We will continue our resistance to the Zionist enemy with all possible means and we will not be stopped by a Palestinian or a Zionist." Abdel-Aziz al-Rantissi, a senior Hamas operative at the time, warned Arafat and Mazen that jihad against the Jews was the "sole solution" to the occupation of Palestine. "Hamas does not believe in political negotiations," he said, adding that the appointment of a Palestinian prime minister was completely unacceptable because the position would have the singular mission of "stopping the uprising."

The message was clear: Arafat and Mazen had better watch their backs.

But that was all years ago. Neither the CIA nor ITA had any warning of this, and now the house of cards was collapsing all around them.

FLAMES SHOT OUT of the gutted limo.

Thick black smoke made it hard to see. Mancuso again speed-dialed the Op Center in Washington and went to a secure frequency.

Mancuso actually knew Rob Trakowski—not well, but well enough to know he was just doing his job. Trakowski was a decent guy, and loyal. If extraction teams could be sent from either of the U.S. aircraft carriers steaming across the eastern Mediterranean—the USS *Ronald Reagan* or the USS *Teddy Roosevelt*—there wasn't any doubt in Mancuso's mind that Trakowski would have dispatched them immediately. Something really was wrong. Weather, politics—it didn't really matter. What mattered was that Mancuso needed to get his team out before it was too late.

"Black Tower, this is Snapshot. You still got that feed from Predator Six?"

"Affirmative—what do you need?"

"Can you get a shot of the Great Mosque down the street?"

"Roger that. What are we looking for?"

"Just tell me what you see."

"All right, hold on."

Mancuso reloaded his MP5. It was only a few moments—but it felt like forever.

"Son of a—"

"What? What is it?" Mancuso pressed.

"Sir, you've a militia of some kind lined up at the back of the mosque. Someone's handing out machine guns, RPGs, ammunition— you name it."

"Who?"

"A bunch of mullahs—I can't tell for sure. They've got a bucket brigade going—they seem to be bringing up weapons from the basement and handing them out the back door, as fast as they can."

"How many are we talking about—a few dozen?"

"Actually, sir—it looks like hundreds."

✳ ✳ ✳

They were only forty yards away and coming fast.

Their faces covered in red kaffiyehs, they poured out of two guard stations in either corner of the compound. *Who were these guys? Whose side were they on? Were they coming to help, or finish them off?*

McCoy was pretty sure they were members of Force 17, Arafat's elite bodyguard unit. All these guys knew for sure was that their leadership had been blown away in the last few minutes. Arafat was dead. Abu Mazen was dead. So were half the cabinet and most of the top legislators. But did any of the Force 17 guys know how or why? Did they know it was one of their own guys? Maybe not. Most had been manning posts inside the legislature or the adjacent buildings when the motorcade had arrived.

Likewise, all the DSS agents knew for sure was that the secretary of state was dead. Many of their own were dead. Now their entire detail was under fire from multiple directions. Palestinians of some kind were doing the shooting. *What did it all mean? Was this a one-man coup, or a larger conspiracy? Did the armed men rushing at them work for Arafat, or his killers? Should they trust them, or shoot them?*

Bennett assumed they were good guys. He was wrong. At thirty yards, they began firing from the hip. Glass was cracking but not shattering above him. Round after round was hitting the limo's doors and windows, but so far, none had broken through.

"McCoy—behind you!" Bennett yelled, unable to get a clear shot.

McCoy and Mancuso wheeled around and returned fire. They cut down eight or ten men in the first few bursts. Mancuso's assault teams took out a dozen more. They also watched their teams' backs, providing covering fire against threats from the front gate and Omar El Mukhtar Street. Mancuso passed the word that more trouble was on the way.

★ ★ ★

"This is an NBC Special Report. Now from Washington, Brian Williams."

It was Monday morning, barely a few minutes after 3:00 a.m. Washington time—just after ten in the morning Gaza time. Most of America was asleep, but each of the cable news networks was already covering the mushrooming crisis live. Now, one by one, each of the major U.S. broadcast networks began covering the gun battle in Gaza as well. NBC simulcast its feed from the MSNBC crew on the ground. ABC and CBS had more difficulties. Without a cable news channel of their own, and without any plans to do a live broadcast of the arrival of the secretary of state, they were caught without exclusive footage. Soon whoever was up at that hour watching ABC began seeing a feed from Al-Jazeera, while those watching CBS saw a combination of feeds coming in from Israel's Channel Two, the BBC, and an Abu Dhabi TV crew.

A mob of Palestinian militants was now working its way up the main street and several side streets, shooting wildly into the air. A wounded CNN cameraman was on the roof. He and his crew broadcast the scene to the world. Their presence caused the U.S. sharpshooters to think twice. Should they wait until they were fired upon directly? Or should they be systematically picking these guys off, one by one, before the rest of the U.S. team was ambushed and outnumbered?

★ ★ ★

Only a handful of U.S. officials had ever heard the name Jake Ziegler. To most of Washington—and all of the Arab and Islamic world—he didn't exist. As the CIA's station chief in the Gaza Strip, it was Ziegler's job to be invisible. And he was good. In a covert operations center along the Mediterranean coast known as Gaza Station, Ziegler watched the nightmare unfold via satellite feeds from three U.S. networks, as well as from live video images provided by the unmanned aerial reconnaissance vehicle—Predator Six—hovering over the crime scene. His mind reeled. The images were horrifying. But what did they mean?

The death of Arafat had the potential of triggering all kinds of scenarios. Few of them were good. The most serious: a Palestinian civil war, as various faction leaders mobilized their forces and tried to seize control of the power vacuum left in Arafat's wake. Ziegler should know. As far back as the spring of 2002, he'd written the CIA's National Intelligence Estimate on what could happen when Yasser Arafat one day passed from the scene. Even now—eight years later—he could still recite from memory key findings from his report.

"Who would be the likely successor to Arafat as head of the Palestinian Authority?" the chairman of the Senate Intelligence Committee had wanted to know. Ziegler's answer—factored into his report—was blunt, and grim. "PA and PLO Chairman Yasser Arafat has no clear-cut successor," he wrote, "and any candidate will have neither the power base nor the leadership qualities necessary to wield full authority in the PA." Ziegler went on to note that, "Mahmoud Abbas (Abu Mazen), Arafat's principal deputy and secretary-general of the PLO Executive Committee, and Ahmad Qurei (Abu Ala), speaker of the PA's Legislative Council, are poised to assume preeminent roles after Arafat. Security chiefs like Mohammad Dahlan (former head of the Gaza Preventative Security Forces, now in charge of all PA Security Forces), Jabril Rajub (the longtime head of the West Bank Preventative Security Forces), and Fatah Tanzim leader Marwan Barghouti are likely to play important supporting roles in the succession." He also pointed out that "according to PA laws, after Arafat's death, Ahmad Qurei, in his role as speaker of the PA's Legislative Council, would assume the duties of PA president for no more than sixty days, during which time a new president would be elected."

The problem, Ziegler warned then, was that the prospects for a peaceful transition were slim to none. The worst-case scenario—a full-blown civil war—was also the most likely. At one point in his top-secret report, Ziegler cited a prediction by Israeli academic Ehud Ya'ari, who'd publicly warned that Arafat's eventual departure from the scene would likely result in "the creation of regional coalitions" resembling some kind of "United Palestinian Emirates" but "not necessarily in a peaceful alliance." Any figurehead that emerged to try to take Arafat's place, Ziegler argued, would need to possess "some of Arafat's credentials and prestige in order to obtain international recognition." But, he added, there was a strong possibility that there could be "violent infighting among the competing security services vying for supremacy."

The bottom line: no one in Washington had listened, and now Ziegler's worst fears were coming true.

* * *

So far, the Americans were holding their own.

Their armor-plated vehicles and the cement barriers nearby were giving them a decent measure of protection. But McCoy knew it wasn't going to be enough. So did Mancuso. They looked at each other quickly. Both knew they needed an exit strategy—fast.

"Jon, can you get me more ammo?" Mancuso yelled. "I'm almost out."

Bennett could hear the fear in Mancuso's voice. It shook what little confidence he had left. Mancuso wasn't panicking. The anxiety in his voice was controlled. It was measured. But it was real. It was palpable. The man was a professional. He was an experienced security agent, trained his whole life to deal with danger. But if—with all that—*he* was still worried, what chance did Bennett have? He could hear Mancuso shouting to him. He knew Mancuso's life depended on what he did in the next few seconds. He wanted to get up. He wanted to help. But he couldn't. He was terrified—afraid to fight, afraid to move, afraid of death and what might be on the other side.

Suddenly, someone called to Bennett through the gunfire.

"Jon, I've got it."

It was Galishnikov. Desperate to do something to help his friends, the Russian scrambled out from under the car. He jumped into one of the open passenger doors and rummaged around the backseats.

"Where is it?" Galishnikov yelled. "Where's the ammo?"

"*I'm out,*" Mancuso yelled.

"I can't find it," Galishnikov kept screaming. "*I can't find it.*"

Mancuso ejected his last spent clip and rushed in behind Galishnikov. He opened a second ammo box concealed under the passenger seats, reloaded, and came out firing.

Crack. Crack.

Bennett pressed his face against the wet pavement. He couldn't see where the shots were coming from, but they were close—too close—and he didn't dare move. He looked over at McCoy, terrified that she might have been hit. She wasn't. She was fine, and fighting back. Bennett began to breathe again. Then he heard it again. Two bursts—*crack, crack—crack, crack.* Mancuso wasn't more than two feet from McCoy. Bennett saw Mancuso's head snap back. Then he dropped to the ground. Bennett watched him fall. He watched a pool of blood begin to form around him.

A flash of lightning stung his eyes. Time stood still. Bennett could feel himself slipping into shock, and it all came rushing back. Jerusalem a few weeks before. The "four horsemen of the apocalypse." The gun battle that left Dietrich Black dead and Bennett bleeding to death on the floor. He could still see the Iraqi terrorist—the black hood, the fire pouring from the muzzle. He could smell the smoke, the gunpowder, the rancid stench of death. He could still feel both rounds—the excruciating pain, like his body had been set on fire—one grazing his right shoulder, the other tearing off a chunk of his left forearm.

But somehow he'd survived. Mancuso was dead. The man had a wife. Four kids. He'd worked for the State Department for sixteen years. He'd been handpicked by the president to protect Bennett and McCoy, and now he was gone. Why? It didn't make sense. What made a husband and father put himself in harm's way for complete strangers? What possessed any man to give up his own life to save others?

A shudder rippled through Bennett's drenched body. Waves of guilt washed over him in the rain. He was paralyzed by fear. He couldn't move, couldn't think, and shame began to consume him. He'd give anything to be back in New York, crunching numbers, cutting deals. *What was he doing in Gaza? What made him think he could cut a deal with the devil?* The stupidity of it all suddenly hit him—a Wall Street strategist in a world where money couldn't help him. It didn't walk, didn't talk, couldn't shoot an AK-47, and neither could he.

The rules here were different. There weren't any rules at all.

Maybe Dr. Mordechai was right, thought Bennett, suddenly oblivious to the gunfire all around him. "The problem with you Americans is that you don't believe in evil," the former Mossad agent had told Deek Black in the summer of 1990, just before Iraq invaded Kuwait. "You guys at the CIA and the FBI—and definitely the guys at State—don't properly anticipate horrible, catastrophic events because you don't really believe in the presence of evil, the presence of a dark and wicked and nefarious spiritual dimension that drives some men to do the unthinkable."

Bennett hadn't known what to make of that before. It went against everything he'd been brought up to believe.

"I believe Saddam Hussein is both capable of and prone to acts of unspeakable evil, and you don't," Mordechai had added. "I'm right, and you're wrong. It's not because I know more than your government. I don't. I know less. But I believe that evil forces make evil men do evil things. That's how I anticipate what can and will happen next in life. That's how I got to be the head of the Mossad, young man. And why I'm good at it. It's going to be a horrible August, and my country is going to suffer very badly because your country doesn't believe in evil, and mine was born out of the ashes of the Holocaust."

Bennett looked around him. Bullets whizzed over his head. Fires raged. Explosions were erupting all around him. Mordechai *was* right. He hadn't believed in evil. Not really. Not until this. Now he could feel it in the air. He could smell it, taste it. The radicals had to be stopped. Suicide bombers and the groups and states that funded them—they weren't misguided or misunderstood. They were controlled by evil. Pure evil. And evil couldn't be negotiated with. It could only be hunted down, captured, or destroyed. Like a cancer or Ebola. Ignore those possessed by evil and they'd kill you. Fast or slow, it didn't matter. Remove some but not all traces of the virus and it would still kill you. Fast or slow, it was just a matter of time.

Bennett could see it clearly now. *To misunderstand the nature of evil is to risk being blindsided by it. For evil, unchecked, is the prelude to genocide.*

It wasn't all Muslims. Most gave their religion mere lip service. But radical, fundamentalist Islam required jihad, a war of annihilation against Christians, Jews, and Western culture and modernity. It was a lethal virus in the global body politic. It was an unholy war, and it was winner take all. There could be no truce, no cease-fire, no *hudna*, as it was known in Arabic. You were either on offense, or you were losing. Fast or slow, it didn't matter, and time was not on your side.

Bennett couldn't just lie there and do nothing. Friends of his—men and women willing to put their lives on the line to protect him—were being slaughtered. Last time it had been Deek Black. This time it was Mancuso. But it could have been McCoy. It could have been him. At least the last time he'd gone down fighting. At least the last time he'd tried to fight back. Bennett could feel his heart racing. His hands were trembling. His face felt hot. A surge of anger so intense and so foreign that it scared him even more began forcing its way to the surface.

The thoughts rushing through Bennett were alien to everything he'd been taught to believe. They smacked of the very intolerance and judgmentalism he'd been so relentlessly warned against back at Georgetown and Harvard. But what was "tolerance" in the face of terror? Wasn't it surrender? Wasn't it social suicide?

Suddenly—without warning—Bennett began to move. He grabbed the machine gun, scrambled out from under the limousine, and took aim at the two hooded men who'd just shot Mancuso. Now they were charging at him. It was kill or be killed. It was winner take all, and he could see fire coming from the barrels of their AK-47s. He'd been here before. He'd looked into a killer's eyes. Bennett raised the AK-47, pulled the trigger, and didn't let go. In a fraction of second, he emptied the entire clip, riddling the two men with dozens of rounds until they collapsed just fifteen or twenty yards away. They were screaming and thrashing about in pain and rage. And then, their bodies and screams went silent.

McCoy was stunned. She just stood there, mesmerized by the two lifeless bodies, taken off guard by Bennett's sudden engagement.

"Erin, we can't stay here—we've got to move out now." Bennett wheeled around. He saw two men sprinting through the flames at the other end of the courtyard. Then he heard the incoming sizzle.

"Get down—get down—RPG."

Bennett hit the deck, bringing McCoy down with him. He covered her body with his own as the rocket-propelled grenade came whistling through the gates. It missed McCoy's head. It missed his own by no more than a few inches, and barely missed the limo as well. Bennett could still see the smoke of the RPG's trail slicing the air above them, across Snapshot's hood. The missile hit the PLC building. The ferocious explosion sent another massive shock wave through the compound. But it was the image of McCoy almost having her head blown off that changed everything.

"You two, in the car—now," Bennett demanded, pointing to Galishnikov and Sa'id. Then he turned to McCoy. "Get them in—everybody—let's go."

Bennett pulled Sa'id and Galishnikov out from under the car. He shoved them into the backseat of the vehicle that now had to save their lives. Then he looked down at Mancuso's crumpled body. He checked his pulse—just to be sure—but it was too late. He was gone. He and McCoy lifted Mancuso's body. They carefully set it inside the car, along with his MP5 and the Sig Sauer pistol inside his jacket pocket. McCoy climbed in beside him, slammed the door behind her, and covered Mancuso's body with coats.

Bennett grabbed Mancuso's earpiece and radio, put them on himself, jumped into the driver's seat, pulled the door closed behind him, and hit the automatic door locks.

"Halfback, this is Snapshot—can you hear me?"

Max Banacci—six foot three inches tall, former Army Ranger turned lead DSS agent for the assault teams—responded immediately. "Bennett, that you? Where's Donny? Where's McCoy?"

"Mancuso's dead. McCoy's with me. I've got Galishnikov and Sa'id. We've got to get out of here—*now*."

"No, no," Banacci insisted. "We can't just leave these guys here. We've got to—"

"Banacci, it's over. We've got to get out of here—now."

"No way. If Mancuso's down then I'm in charge now and I say we stay until—"

"Until what? We're all dead? Forget it. I work for the White House. You work for me. Now get us out of here before the rest of the peace process goes up in flames."

"You're out of your mind, Bennett!" Banacci shouted. "We don't leave until we get the last man out. No one gets left behind. That clear enough for you?"

Bennett fought to control his anger. "Everyone who's alive is coming with me," he shot back. "If you've got a problem with that, bring it up with the president. I'm taking these guys home."

4
★ ★
★

AIR FORCE ONE shot across the Atlantic at forty-three thousand feet.

Among those aboard were Defense Secretary Burt Trainor, Deputy Secretary of State Dick Cavanaugh, Press Secretary Chuck Murray, and a cadre of senior officials from the Pentagon, the National Security Council, and the State Department Policy Planning Staff. Those who weren't working were sleeping or watching the in-flight movie system. Events on the ground were moving fast, and word of what had just happened in Gaza would reach the president any moment. But it hadn't yet.

MacPherson sat alone in his airborne office, sipping a cup of coffee and reviewing the latest intel from Iraq. The Persian Gulf port city of Umm Qasr was controlled by the Marines. Navy SEAL (Sea, Air, and Land) commandos were almost finished clearing mines from the Tigris and Euphrates rivers. Basra and Nasiriyah were largely secured by army units in the south, as were Mosul and Kirkuk in the north. There were still sporadic skirmishes in Karbalā' and Al Kut. Holdouts from the Republican Guard were booby-trapping cars, and fedayeen snipers took potshots at night. But that was to be expected. He had no doubt the entire country would soon be secure.

All things considered, civilian casualties in Tikrit, the birthplace of Saddam Hussein and Saladin—Muslim conqueror of Jerusalem in AD 1187—were much lower than he'd feared.

Baghdad was not so lucky. American spy satellites had found the smoking gun the world had been demanding. Saddam had been minutes away from launching a nuclear ICBM—code-named The Last Jihad—

against New York or Washington, or perhaps Israel or Saudi Arabia. His nuclear forces had been hidden in a children's hospital in the heart of the city, not far from Baghdad University. The president hadn't had a choice. It was kill or be killed.

MacPherson knew he'd done the right thing. But that didn't make it easier to sleep at night. It didn't make it easier to see the latest bomb-damage assessments, or read the latest intelligence updates, or listen to Paris, Bonn, and Moscow denounce him at the U.N. This was the price of being the world's only superpower, and it was high indeed.

★ ★ ★

Banacci was a Ranger.

He couldn't bear the thought of leaving behind the bodies of his fallen comrades. And as a senior DSS agent and team leader, he was supposed to take over after Mancuso. But Bennett was right. There were bigger fish to fry here and they didn't need to be fighting each other. Banacci needed to get the president's "point man" out of this hellhole and back to Washington. His job was to provide security for Snapshot and its occupants, so that's what he'd do, like it or not.

"Fine, hold on," he shouted into his microphone. "We'll give you guys cover."

Banacci cranked up the air-conditioning and directed the team in the Suburban ahead of him—code-named Halfback—to take the point. His Suburban—Fullback—would bring up the rear. Agents in both vehicles locked their doors, popped in new ammo clips, and sucked down bottles of water.

McCoy scrambled into the front passenger seat, next to Bennett. She pulled out a map and quickly tried to assess their options, navigating a way of escape. Bennett looked in his rearview mirror. *What was this guy waiting for?*

Bennett gunned the engine. He was determined to get his team out alive. But if Galishnikov or Sa'id asked him what their chances were, he'd be tempted to lie. Yes, he'd raced his Porsche Turbo down hairpin turns in the Colorado Rockies on weekends. He'd floored it on country straightaways in Connecticut. But he'd never been trained by the CIA's school for defensive driving, or the Secret Service's. And yes, he'd reviewed some maps and logistics on the flight from Washington. But he didn't really know where he was. He hadn't driven this team into Gaza. And he knew one wrong turn was a death sentence.

Maybe he should have let McCoy take the wheel, but things were happening so fast. They'd be moving in a second—they'd be moving *now* if Bennett were leading. He couldn't say it out loud. He could barely say it to himself. But the fact was that even a bulletproof, armor-plated limousine wouldn't be enough if they were stopped and surrounded. Eventually, the mob would break in, the four of them would be yanked out, and, if history were any guide . . . it was a thought he couldn't finish.

★ ★ ★

Yuri Gogolov held the satellite remote in his hand.

He was transfixed by the coverage from Gaza. He was watching on four different television sets, while checking the latest updates from AP, Reuters, and Agence France-Presse on a laptop. The images of fire and death were mesmerizing. Thus far, the operation was going far better than expected. But these were just the first, early minutes. The world had no idea what still lay in store.

★ ★ ★

MacPherson's thoughts turned to his own Judas Iscariot.

Stuart Morris Iverson—held in isolation under a twenty-four-hour-a-day suicide watch at a federal maximum-security prison—wasn't talking. He refused to cooperate unless the Justice Department—and the president himself—promised to take the death penalty off the table. The man wasn't asking for a pardon, or immunity. He knew such inducements were out of the question. He was simply negotiating for his life, and he was a world-class negotiator.

Unless MacPherson spared his life, Iverson—the man who'd served as president and CEO of the Joshua Fund and GSX, who'd served as the national chairman of then-governor MacPherson's campaign to succeed George W. Bush as the forty-fourth president of the United States, who'd been approved by the Senate ninety-eight to nothing to become MacPherson's treasury secretary—would simply refuse to talk. He'd refuse to divulge what he knew about a terrorist conspiracy whose tentacles reached from Moscow to Tehran. He'd refuse to tell the FBI the inside story of Yuri Gogolov—the shadowy Russian ultranationalist—or his Iranian operations chief, Mohammed Jibril.

FBI Director Scott Harris and Attorney General Neil Wittimore didn't care. The case against Iverson was solid. They didn't need a plea bargain. They needed to fire a shot heard round the world. The president had to send the world a message: terrorists would be hunted down and brought to a final justice. To send Stuart Iverson, a personal friend of the president, into the gas chamber—or order him to receive a lethal injection—would do just that. Yet to show even the slightest bit of leniency—especially with Iverson—would be devastating to the country's war-on-terror efforts, Harris argued. It was a compelling case, even to a president who could generally be described as willing but ill at ease with enforcing the death penalty.

"Mr. President, you've got an urgent call from the Sit Room."

Was there any other kind?

The president looked up from his reading. "Which line?"

"Line three, sir."

MacPherson picked up the phone and found his national security advisor on the line. Marsha Kirkpatrick quickly briefed the president on the crisis in Gaza. She explained that Bennett and his team were pinned down, and a torrential electrical storm made it impossible to send in a rescue team by air—not yet anyway.

MacPherson tried not to betray the emotions suddenly forcing their way to the surface. But it wasn't easy, and for a few moments, the line was silent. He was numb. He'd never even considered the possibility of Arafat being assassinated. Certainly not by a fellow Palestinian. And certainly not by Arafat's own personal security chief. It was unthinkable. Abu Mazen, maybe. Mazen didn't have Arafat's stature in Palestine, much less throughout the Arab world. He might never develop it. But Arafat *was* Palestine. He was the face, the voice, the spirit of the Palestinian revolution.

Most of MacPherson's top advisors considered Arafat a major obstacle to peace. Jack Mitchell's guys at the CIA were adamant that MacPherson should refuse to even acknowledge Arafat's presence or give him a role. The Clinton team had courted Arafat aggressively, constantly inviting him to the White House. But what had they gained? The most violent phase of the Palestinian intifada began during the Clinton years. So did the suicide bombings against Israeli civilians. And the evidence was compelling—the vast majority of those suicide bombings (Mitchell called them "homicide bombings" to put the emphasis on the fact that their purpose was murder, not self-sacrifice) were encouraged, paid for, and/or explicitly or tacitly approved of by Arafat and his henchmen.

The Bush team had reversed course. They'd refused to deal with Arafat directly. They'd isolated him internationally. They'd given Israel the green light to invade the West Bank and Gaza and rip up Saudi- and Iranian-backed Hamas and Islamic Jihad terrorist cells. And they'd pressured Arafat and the Palestinian Legislative Council to appoint Abu Mazen as a new, "moderate" prime minister, someone the United States, the West, and Israel just might be able to deal with over time.

Everyone knew the Islamic radicals felt threatened by Mazen's rise to power and by even the slightest prospect that Arafat and Mazen might consider accepting the new American peace plan. But could anyone have predicted this level of carnage? MacPherson began to reconsider his own strategy. He'd tried to combine Clinton's willingness to deal with Arafat with Bush's insistence on dealing with Abu Mazen. Had he moved too fast? Had he pushed too hard?

★ ★ ★

They made a good team, thought Bennett.

McCoy was smart and gutsy and she had great instincts. Based in the GSX London office—overlooking the Thames and the British Parliament—at one point she'd been jetting back and forth across "the pond" several times a week, a Virgin Atlantic preferred customer. She'd often met with Bennett in New York or the Denver headquarters until the wee hours of the morning, mapping out strategies, crunching numbers, debating best- and worst-case scenarios. The two had traveled all over the world together during the last eight months—Davos, Paris, Tokyo, Cairo, Riyadh, and Jerusalem, to name a few—always business, never personal.

McCoy had earned his trust over the past few years—not an easy thing to do—and he'd twice promoted her. When he'd hired her, he'd known she was the best-qualified woman who had applied, and the best-looking. She had an economics degree from UNC Chapel Hill, an MBA from

Wharton, and a license to make money from the Securities and Exchange Commission. What he hadn't known was that she also had a license to kill from the CIA. She'd worked for Bennett for almost three years, but only in the last month had he discovered who she really was: a mole in his operation, planted by the president and the director of Central Intelligence to watch his back and clear him for government service. Any way you sliced it, she was a mystery, and the longer Bennett knew her, the more he wanted to figure her out.

McCoy adjusted her earpiece and buckled her seat belt. She still couldn't get a bead on what was happening. The mobs on the streets now couldn't be the "silent Palestinian majority." These couldn't be people who Ibrahim Sa'id claimed were exhausted by the intifada, longing for peace, and willing to accept a two-state solution with Israel for the sake of their children and grandchildren.

These had to be "Mohammed's mobs," drawn from a small but highly radicalized subsection of Palestinian society who saw themselves as hardcore Islamic loyalists. They despised Israel *and* were deeply committed to jihad, a "holy war" against the "Zionist infidels" and their conspirators from the "Great Satan" known as America. They weren't the vast majority of Palestinians. They weren't even a plurality. They weren't "nominal" Muslims. They were true believers, and—though she'd never admit it to anyone in this car—what they believed terrified McCoy.

They were "Islamists," and during America's long war on terror a lot had been learned about the financial, technical, and ideological links between the purists of Islam. The mob closing in on them now had bitterly fought in the streets and in the Palestinian Legislative Council for the imposition of the *shari'ah*, an Islamic legal system not unlike the one the Taliban had imposed on the poor souls of Afghanistan. Like the Taliban, they wanted a world where women couldn't be educated, couldn't work, couldn't show their faces. A world where women couldn't wear nail polish, couldn't smile or laugh in public, couldn't listen to Mozart. Indeed, they could be flogged or stoned or killed for trying. They wanted a world where children couldn't play with toys or dolls or watch *Sesame Street* or have birthday parties. They wanted a world where men ruled and ruled ruthlessly, just like the Taliban.

These were kindred spirits with the Iranian-funded Hezbollah of

Lebanon. They'd been supporters of Hamas and Islamic Jihad. But wherever they lived or whatever they called themselves, the mission of the Islamists was the same—to conquer in the name of Mohammed. They'd danced in the streets when the Ayatollah Khomeini led the Islamic revolution in Iran and took Americans hostage for 444 days. They'd danced in the streets when Osama bin Laden and the Saudi-funded Al-Qaeda attacked the World Trade Center and Pentagon on September 11, 2001. And in the subsequent U.S. war in Afghanistan, they'd joyfully sided with their "Muslim brothers" in the Taliban.

One Reuters headline McCoy had come across before leaving Washington now came flashing back: "Hamas Backs Taliban, Urges Muslim Unity." The article was dated September 14, 2001, just three days after the terrorist attacks that left three thousand Americans dead. Cited prominently in the story, Abdel-Aziz al-Rantissi of Hamas couldn't have been more clear: "I join the cause for Muslims to be united in order to deter the United States from launching war against Muslims in Afghanistan. It is impossible for Muslims to stand handcuffed and blindfolded while other Muslims, their brothers, are being attacked. The Muslim world should stand up against the American threats which are fed by the Jews."

There it was, in black and white. The dots were connected. Radical Muslims in Gaza and the West Bank were soul mates with their brethren in Afghanistan, not to mention those in Tehran and Riyadh. They saw the world the same way. They fought for the same objectives. They'd supported each other in the same struggles. This was an alien world into which she and Bennett had just been submerged. It was an alien world out of which they now had to fight.

McCoy fought back a flood of emotions. Her own father had died fighting radical Islam. Was she destined to do the same? Sean McCoy had worked for the CIA. Now she did too. He'd been a senior advisor to the president of the United States. Now she was too. Despite his strong marriage, he'd struggled with putting his career ahead of love. Wasn't she doing that too?

"There are only two places for a woman," a Taliban leader once said. "In her husband's house and in the graveyard."

Erin McCoy had no husband, and she didn't want to die.

Not here. Not yet.

5
★ ★
★

MACPHERSON'S HEAD was pounding.

He hung up the phone and shut his eyes. In a few minutes, Jackie Sanchez of the United States Secret Service would be knocking on his door. She'd move him into the next room, where he'd be patched through to the National Security Council via a secure satellite videoconferencing system. But there were too many questions to answer. Could they mount a rescue operation? Should they ask the Israelis to? Could all this really be the work of one man? Why, then, the gun battle? And were these attacks isolated to the Palestinian territories? Or were they likely to see new terrorist attacks unleashed throughout Israel, and/or against American interests all over the globe?

★ ★ ★

The motorcade was ready.

Now all they needed was the vice president. Special Agent-in-Charge Steve Sinclair—head of the VP's protective detail—was edgy. His orders had been clear: get Checkmate to the Situation Room quickly and without incident. Most of the principals were already on their way to the White House. The NSC meeting was scheduled to begin in less than ten minutes. Given that the VP was supposed to chair the meeting in the president's absence, it wouldn't do to be late. Not tonight.

★ ★ ★

MacPherson simply couldn't believe it.

He and Secretary of State Tucker Paine had hardly been kindred spirits. But they'd known each other for more than a decade, and they'd become useful to each other.

MacPherson couldn't really remember exactly how they'd met, but he was pretty sure it had been in Denver. A middle-class kid, MacPherson had grown up in Lakewood, Colorado, graduated from Harvard, then joined the navy, gone to Top Gun school, and headed to Vietnam. When he'd come back to the States, MacPherson moved to Manhattan, made a fortune with Fidelity, then moved back to Denver, where he made quite a name for himself—and an even more impressive fortune—as founder and CEO of Global Strategix, Inc., and the Joshua Fund, two of the premier institutions in the financial-services industry.

Somewhere along the line, he'd met Paine, an old-money gazillionaire whose family seemed to own half of Colorado and who wanted to run for the state's open U.S. Senate seat. Paine wasn't the sharpest knife in the drawer. He was a bit too moderate for MacPherson's liking—good on taxes and growth, bad on education and the life issue, horrible on defense and national security issues. But if Hollywood were going to make a movie about a crusty old patrician senator with a penchant for French wine and a good pipe after dinner, Tucker Paine was direct from central casting.

GOP control of the Senate hung in the balance at the time, and it wasn't a tough call. MacPherson was nothing if not a loyal Republican, and even then he'd had his own political ambitions. He was planning a run for governor, and his chief political advisor—Bob Corsetti, now the White House chief of staff—made the case succinctly: to blow through the primaries and win the nomination in a landslide, MacPherson needed to find a way to unite the state's conservative and moderate factions. It wouldn't be easy.

As a pro–flat tax, pro-life, former navy fighter pilot, MacPherson could count on strong support from the conservative political base in and around Colorado Springs in the south, Fort Collins in the north, and the more rural congressional districts in the mountains and on the plains near Kansas.

But Denver itself, MacPherson's hometown, would be tougher. Republicans there tended to be wealthier and more moderate, and though his Wall Street successes had helped him build inroads among the country-club crowd, Corsetti concluded that if MacPherson strongly backed Tucker Paine, it certainly couldn't hurt. And it hadn't.

MacPherson took Corsetti's advice. He helped Paine raise more than $2.5 million in less than six months, as Paine was too cheap to spend his own money. Unfortunately, Paine went on to lose the Senate race—though he soon was named U.S. ambassador to the U.N.—but MacPherson picked up a boatload of goodwill and a pocketful of chits. A few years later, he went on to win the GOP nomination for governor without opposition, winning Paine's much-desired endorsement along the way. And in the process he'd laid the groundwork for two successful terms in the governor's mansion, and a storybook run for the White House in 2008 after two Bush terms.

Paine wasn't MacPherson's first choice to be the secretary of state, nor his second, though thankfully the press hadn't ever picked up on the behind-the-scenes intrigue surrounding the selection process. Paine didn't have Colin Powell's military experience or international stature. But with several years at the U.N. under his belt, he was certainly a safe choice, and MacPherson knew he wasn't going to run foreign policy out of the State Department anyway. He and the VP and Marsha Kirkpatrick would take the lead from the White House.

Paine had chafed at the arrangement from the beginning. But he wanted the job and didn't want to be left out of the administration. He'd tried to negotiate for more power. But MacPherson never budged. The president wanted a Rockefeller Republican at State for political cover. But he simply didn't trust the bureaucrats at Foggy Bottom, and he certainly had no intention of giving them free rein over the future of U.S. relations with a rapidly changing world.

Still, despite their sometimes prickly alliance, Paine and his wife, Claudia, had just spent Christmas Day at Camp David with the First Family. MacPherson smoked a cigar. The secretary smoked his pipe. The two talked about Bennett's Oil for Peace strategy and reviewed the blowout they'd had over going to war with Iraq.

Now he was gone.

* * *

Agent Sinclair stood on the porch of the Residence.

Agents were positioned around the lead limousine, in the lead Suburban and the two that would follow. Vice President Bill Oaks was still inside on the phone with Israeli prime minister David Doron. The motorcade would wait, as would the NSC meeting, if need be. Doron had just ordered the IDF to prepare for a massive ground invasion of Gaza and the West Bank. It would take a few hours to get all the men and machinery in place. But the Israelis were offering to rescue the Americans and begin to restore order. All they wanted was a green light from Washington. Would they get it?

Oaks was an old Washington hand. He'd risen through the ranks of naval intelligence, then gotten out, made some money, and gotten into politics. He'd once been the governor of Virginia, then served four terms in the U.S. Senate from the Old Dominion, much of that time as the chairman of the Senate Armed Services Committee. He knew the game. He knew what Doron wanted. He just wasn't convinced the United States should say yes.

* * *

MacPherson took off his reading glasses and rubbed his eyes.

The phone rang. It was Kirkpatrick again.

"Mr. President, we're picking up indications that the Syrians are going on full military alert. Air-raid sirens are going off in Damascus. One of our Keyhole satellites is showing all kinds of activity at their forward air bases. Military radio traffic is picking up. I'll have transcripts of some of our intercepts soon."

"What are the Israelis doing?"

"They're mobilizing as well, sir. The VP just got off the phone with the prime minister. They're putting their forces along the northern borders with Syria and Lebanon on full alert. They're also preparing for a massive ground invasion into the West Bank and Gaza. They're offering to rescue our people. They've just put their best counterterrorism units on high alert. The Sayerat Matkal and Ya'Ma'M will be ready to move within the hour. Doron would like to talk with you as soon as possible."

"Does he think the Syrians are behind this?"

"He doesn't know what to think, sir. None of them do. Seems Shin Bet was completely caught off guard as well."

"What about you?"

"I don't know, sir. Bashar Assad doesn't have much use for Arafat. But there's no reason I can see why he'd kill him. Assad isn't a religious man. Khalid al-Rashid was. I can't see how Syrian intelligence could have persuaded him to blow up Arafat and Mazen and Paine and himself for the glory of the Ba'ath Party. It doesn't add up."

"God help me, Marsha," said the president, "if Assad is behind this . . ."

"Mr. President, I know what you're saying, and I feel the same way. But things are very early. It's far more likely that there's a religious angle here than that this is the Syrians."

"Who then—Iran? the Saudis?"

"It's just too early, sir."

MacPherson tried to refocus. "All right, here's what I want you to do. Put CENTCOM on alert. Start moving air and ground assets toward the Syrian-Iraqi border. Watch for more Iraqi officials trying to flee for Damascus and make Assad feel the heat. Then tell our ambassador over there to get this message to Assad—quote—'The president advises you to stand down your forces. The U.S. will not tolerate Syrian interference in the crisis in Palestine. Any attempt to exploit the situation or provoke hostilities with the State of Israel or any regional player will be considered a hostile act against the United States. On these points there can be no misunderstanding. The U.S. will protect our vital national interests, and the interests of regional peace and security.' End quote. Got it?"

"Yes, sir."

"Then get me the VP right away."

"What about Doron, sir?"

"What do you think?"

"For the moment, I'd tell them to get their forces ready for ground operations in the West Bank and Gaza. But I'd recommend you advise Israel not to actually move in—or engage in any armed contact with the Palestinians—until we gather more facts and you can get back to the White House."

"All right, have the VP call Doron back and give him that message. Have him tell Doron that as soon as I land in Washington, we'll talk by phone. Then have the VP call me."

"Roger that, Mr. President. By the way, not that you need anything else on your plate right now, sir, but we've gotten word that there have just been two massive earthquakes in the past hour. The first was in southern Turkey, about forty-five minutes ago. Looks like a 6.9 on the Richter scale. Death toll already appears to be over a thousand, with the number of wounded closing in on three thousand."

"My God."

"I've spoken twice with Ambassador Rebeiz in the last few minutes. He just called the Turkish foreign minister to offer our sympathies and full support. Our military forces in the country—including our base at Incirlik—all appear unaffected so far. But I should be getting an update at the top of the hour from DOD."

"Good. Get Rebeiz back on the phone. Have him call President Sezer and Prime Minister Gul and give them my personal condolences. Let them know I've authorized the full resources of our government to provide anything he and his people need—search and rescue, medical facilities and personnel, the Army Corps of Engineers—whatever."

"Yes, sir."

"And make sure the Red Cross and other groups are doing whatever they can."

"We'll get right on it, sir."

"What about the second quake?"

"It happened in northwestern India, near Kashmir, about eighteen, maybe nineteen minutes ago. That one hit 8.1—casualties are mounting fast but we don't have any solid numbers yet."

Kirkpatrick could hear the president gasp.

"We've just established an open line with our embassy," she continued. "I haven't had a moment to talk with Ambassador Koshy yet, but same drill as Turkey?"

"Absolutely. Get State involved right away, and get somebody on the horn with the Pakistanis. The last thing we need is a humanitarian rescue operation near Kashmir to be perceived as provocative by General Musharraf or the ISI."

"You got it, sir. Anything else?"

"Just tell me Bennett and McCoy are safe."

"I can't, sir. Not yet."

★ ★ ★

The president couldn't get his mind off them.

McCoy was practically a third daughter. MacPherson and his wife, Julie, had known her all her life. They'd known her father since Vietnam. He and Sean McCoy had been close friends. MacPherson was flying F-4 Phantom fighter jets off the decks of aircraft carriers in the Sea of Japan. McCoy was a SEAL team commander and one of the most decorated commandos in the navy. He'd eventually joined the CIA and worked his way up to the deputy director of operations.

When Sean married Janet, the executive assistant to the secretary of the navy, MacPherson had been the best man. When little Erin was born, he and Julie had been at the hospital with flowers. When Sean was killed, it was MacPherson who'd given the eulogy. When Janet died of ovarian cancer in '91, he'd done so again. Now, as he put his head down and clenched his fists, he prayed to God he wouldn't have to do so for Erin, their only child.

And Bennett? He was the son the MacPhersons never had. He was a little too old for the MacPherson twins—they were half his age—and that was too bad. But it felt like he'd been part of their family forever.

Bennett was an only child, and his parents had always been traveling. He'd rarely spent holidays with them and almost seemed without a family. So the MacPhersons took him under their wing, inviting him to birthday parties and cookouts and Christmas and political conventions. The girls loved him. Julie loved him. And why wouldn't they? Bennett always seemed to have time for them. Or to make time. He brought them gifts, helped the girls with their homework. He teased them about their latest boyfriends and always enjoyed playing basketball or volleyball. His favorite, of course, was Monopoly night, with pizza and popcorn and root-beer floats. Every fourth Friday, for years, it had been a family tradition, until the MacPhersons moved into the White House and everything changed.

Bennett's first real job after Harvard had been as MacPherson's personal assistant. Along the way, he developed great sources and great instincts. His Rolodex was a who's who of the wealthiest people on earth, and their personal secretaries, assistants, drivers, and caddies. He ran his network of corporate spooks with the zeal of the KGB. And he'd made MacPherson a very wealthy man.

It was Bennett who'd insisted in 1998 that the tech-averse MacPherson take a major position in America Online at $7 a share. AOL had just shot past 15 million subscribers and was gobbling up CompuServe and ICQ, pioneers of instant messaging. Bennett's sources told him this was just the beginning.

At first, MacPherson resisted. He worried AOL was just a fad. CEO Steve Case was a new kid on the block. "You've got mail"? What kind of slogan was that? But Bennett practically begged him to take the company seriously. Then the stock shot past $10 a share. Suddenly MacPherson was ready to get in the game and play big. The Joshua Fund scooped up 50 million shares at an average of $11.47 a share.

Bennett had been terrified. It was one thing to work your sources, trust your gut, and make a recommendation. It was another thing for your boss to place a half-billion-dollar bet on *your* advice. What if he was wrong? What if the stock sunk like a rock . . . and his job with it? Bennett became a man obsessed. He made it his mission in life to know every detail he possibly could about AOL, Steve Case, and anyone and everyone connected in any way, shape, or form with the company.

In the spring of 2000, AOL's stock hit a high of $72 a share, giving the Joshua Fund a pretax profit of over $3 billion. MacPherson wanted to bolt. Bennett said no. They were just getting started. Then the tech crash began. AOL stock plunged to $47 a share in just a few months. MacPherson was furious. He prepared to dump all of the Joshua Fund's AOL holdings, but Bennett urged him to hang on for a little while longer. They were still $36 above their purchase price. AOL was still acquiring good companies at bargain prices. They'd just nabbed MapQuest. They were launching new divisions in Argentina and Mexico. ICQ had just hit 85 million members.

Bennett was on to something hot. His sources were telling him Steve Case was plotting to take over media giant Time Warner. The news hadn't yet broken publicly. But it would soon, and the stock would skyrocket. MacPherson wasn't so sure. Time Warner was a strong company, but the whole market was overpriced. The Fed was trying to burst the bubble, and the Joshua Fund couldn't afford a massive loss. True, Bennett argued, but why not let the AOL–Time Warner merger news begin to leak and then see what happened? If the stock began to drop, they could dump it all. If it rose, they could hold on a bit longer, then cash out and take the whole company to the Bahamas, all expenses paid.

MacPherson had to smile. He liked this kid's moxie. Fine, he said, let it ride for a little while longer, but under no circumstances could they let the price drop under $40 a share. Deal? Deal, Bennett agreed. And the merger news leaked.

By Christmas of 2000, AOL stock hit $74 a share. When it slipped to $72, Bennett and his team began selling off. When it was all over, the Joshua Fund had sold 50 million shares at an average of $70 each, scoring a pretax profit of just under $3 billion. A pretty nifty chunk of change, MacPherson had to admit. And he had Jon Bennett to thank for it. Which he did.

MacPherson promoted Bennett to senior VP. He named Bennett chief investment strategist. He put him in charge of a staff of more than a hundred. And he asked him to begin helping him on an entirely new project—MacPherson's bid to enter elective politics. Sure, he was a Republican and Bennett wasn't. But so what? Bennett was a Kennedy Democrat—Jack, not Ted—and MacPherson could live with that. It was a match made in heaven.

Quietly, under the radar, Bennett recruited a few friends to form Democrats for MacPherson—first for MacPherson's gubernatorial campaigns, then again for the run for the White House. From the Iowa caucuses through the convention and right up to the inauguration, Bennett was there for MacPherson every step of the way. He did so enthusiastically, without pay, without expecting anything in return. He'd never asked to join the administration. He'd never wanted a fancy-sounding Washington title. Bennett didn't care about politics. He wanted to make money—lots of it. And why shouldn't he? He was good at it.

The president had no doubt that Bennett would have been on the *Forbes* 400 list in the next five years. But events had conspired against him. Suddenly—inexplicably—everything was different. History was taking a turn for the worse. Jon Bennett's destiny was being recast. MacPherson had asked him to give up everything to serve "at the pleasure of the president," to figure out a way to nail down a deal between the Israelis and Palestinians, a deal that now seemed impossible to achieve. And the kid said yes. As a personal favor for his onetime boss and mentor, Bennett had walked away from staggering wealth, and his dreams. And now MacPherson second-guessed himself. Had he really given Bennett the opportunity of a lifetime, the chance to be part of history—or had he just handed him a death sentence?

6
★ ★
★

"WE DON'T STOP for anything or anyone—is that clear?"

Bennett's voice was icy cold. "I don't care what happens. We keep moving until we're out of the hot zone. No exceptions. We stop, we die—you got it?"

Banacci gunned the engine. He didn't like taking orders from this guy. But he couldn't argue with the logic. Bennett was right, and every DSS agent listening knew it.

Jagged streaks of lightning flashed across the sky and it began to rain, slowly at first, then harder and harder. The storm was picking up steam. They needed to move quickly.

Bennett flipped on his headlights and cranked up the windshield wipers to the fastest speed. Then he turned to McCoy and nodded. "You ready?" he asked, as gunfire exploded all around them.

"Let's do it," she said confidently.

The lead black Chevy Suburban—Halfback, riddled with three or four dozen bullet holes and driven by DSS agent Kyl Lake—peeled out in front of Snapshot, blue-and-red lights flashing, sirens blazing. Bennett jammed the limo into drive and peeled out with him. Special Agent-in-Charge Max Banacci's Suburban brought up the rear as a colleague unlocked a black-leather legal briefcase filled with classified contingency plans and maps marked with multiple escape routes and extraction points.

Bennett could see the leading edge of the mobs coming at them from their right, from the direction of the Great Mosque and the Sayed Hasem

Mosque. So as the motorcade roared out of the gates, they turned left and shot up Omar El Mukhtar Street through a blizzard of bullets and smoke. They didn't get far.

Away from the epicenter of the gun battle, huge crowds now jammed the streets around the Fras Market, despite the intensifying rains. People were chanting something. Some were burning American flags. Some began firing pistols at the convoy, or in the air. Others started heaving rocks at the American vehicles and swinging at the windows with baseball bats.

"Halfback, take the next right," Banacci shouted into his microphone.

"What? Say again, say again," Lake yelled back, barely able to hear above the rain, the deafening chants, and the continual bursts of gunfire.

"Right—break right—at the next street. *Go, go, go.*"

The lead Suburban was only moving at maybe fifteen or twenty miles an hour. In a few seconds, they'd be completely engulfed by the mob and unable to move.

"Let's go, let's go!" Banacci screamed. "Run them down if you have to, Halfback. Let's get out of here. Step on it."

Lake glanced up at his rearview mirror. Had he just heard right?

"We're not gonna make it!" Bennett yelled.

"He's right, Kyl, gun it," Banacci demanded. "Move it. Let's go."

They didn't have a choice. If he hesitated, they'd be dead.

As he approached the corner of El Mukhtar and Bor Saaid streets, Lake stepped on the gas and plowed through a half dozen militants. McCoy grabbed the handle over the passenger-side door as Bennett tried to follow the path that Lake was blazing. He could hear screams outside. He saw the metal trash can just before it smashed against the passenger-side window. Snapshot rocked violently as they hopped the curb, smashed the rear end of a taxi, and blasted through a glass bus stop in their way.

⋆   ⋆   ⋆

The first story flashed on the Reuters wire at 10:19 a.m. Gaza time.

"Paine, Arafat Dead; Gaza Erupts."

AP's story moved one minute later: "Suicide Bomber Kills U.S. Secretary of State." The first update posted three minutes later: "Palestinian Security Chief Blows Up Peace Process; Dozens Feared Dead, Wounded."

Still, none of the wire-service stories matched the imagery beamed around the world by the television crews still alive at the scene.

★ ★ ★

Marsha Kirkpatrick studied the eyes-only e-mail from State.

She didn't quite know what to make of it. Most state-run television networks throughout the Arab world—including Al-Jazeera—had been covering the secretary's arrival live when the suicide bombing occurred. None of those networks had pulled the plug on the transmissions from Gaza. They were still broadcasting the live, horrifying images.

The implications of that intrigued Kirkpatrick. Millions of Arabs had just seen Yasser Arafat's own security chief assassinate the father of the Palestinian revolution. They'd just seen dozens of Palestinians slaughtered by a fellow Palestinian. No matter what kind of conspiracy theories Arab state-run newspapers might write tomorrow, people were seeing the truth right now.

What did that mean? What kind of effect might that have? There was too much else to concentrate on for the moment. But Kirkpatrick made a mental note and stuffed the report in a file. There was something there, something she was missing. She was just too tired, too busy, to figure out what.

★ ★ ★

"*Look out!*" screamed Ibrahim Sa'id.

Through the pouring rain and fogging windows, Sa'id could see a masked gunman in a black hood—fifteen, maybe twenty yards ahead— raise an AK-47 and open fire. He screamed, sure they were all dead. But he couldn't look away. Round after round came straight for their faces and smashed into the front windshield. The bulletproof glass splintered wildly but didn't shatter.

Beside Sa'id, Galishnikov's heart was racing. His hands were clammy. The air-conditioning was on full blast to suck out the rapidly rising humidity. But Galishnikov could still feel the sweat running down his back.

Bennett didn't blink, didn't flinch. He gunned the engine and headed straight for the guy. Flames and smoke were pouring from the barrel of the machine gun, but none of the rounds were penetrating their mobile fortress. Bennett's skin turned cold. He saw the gunman's bloodshot eyes go wide, then disappear under the hood.

Lake focused on the road ahead of him, quickly becoming a river of rain. It was almost impossible to see now. Thunder kept crashing over-head and lightning ignited the skies like a strobe. Lake sped down Bor Saaid Street, looking for a way to outflank the mob and cut left, back toward the Mediterranean. That was escape plan Alpha Bravo—the plan they'd mapped out back in Washington.

✷　✷　✷

The first flash traffic didn't move until 10:27 a.m. local time.

It was Jake Ziegler's job to nail down precisely what was going on and feed a continuous stream of data and analysis back to CIA headquarters at Langley and the White House Situation Room. But that was easier said than done.

They were experiencing the classic fog of war. Reports were pouring in from his slim but growing network of agents and informers. But every-thing was so chaotic. What was real? What was reliable? It was hard enough to establish hard facts in these first few minutes of the crisis. Es-tablishing what any of it meant was nearly impossible. And the clock was ticking. Headquarters had already called twice. The DCI would be brief-ing the president soon. They needed something fast.

Thirty-seven, fluent in Arabic, and the father of a four-year-old daughter, Ziegler had been working undercover in Gaza for only eighteen months. The work was brutal. Long hours, low pay, high stress. But it kept his mind off the searing pain of his divorce.

Technically, he was an analyst, reporting to the CIA's DDI—deputy director for intelligence—not the DDO, the deputy director for opera-tions. But just before his wife had filed for divorce—a divorce he angrily maintained was not his fault and was fighting in family court back in Montgomery County, Maryland—he'd been assigned to slip into Gaza incognito. His mission: to bring coherence to a heretofore woefully inept CIA intel-gathering and analysis operation.

For years, Langley had simply relied on Israeli and Egyptian intelli-gence, to the extent that it was provided, to understand Gaza. But the president and the DCI had insisted that if a serious Israeli-Palestinian peace process was to ever really get under way, they'd need a far better ground operation and listening post than they'd had up until then. That certainly meant ELINT, electronic intelligence. So nearly $25 million had been covertly invested in outfitting Gaza Station as a state-of-the-art joint CIA-NSA operations center underneath an abandoned hotel just outside of Gaza City.

They also needed a far better network of HUMINT, human intelligence—i.e., agents and informants. That would take time. Lots of it. But it had to start somewhere.

So Jake Ziegler—the agency's best Palestine analyst—was given less than seventy-two hours to kiss his wife and baby girl good-bye and hook up with a Navy SEAL insertion team that would slip him unnoticed into the Strip in the dead of night to establish a beachhead and start feeding Langley information it could really use. It was the assignment of a lifetime, and he threw himself into the work.

For eighteen hours a day for the past three and a half weeks, Ziegler and his brilliant but miniscule and overworked team had been working to get ready for Bennett's trip. And they'd blown it. They'd completely missed the attacks that were coming. They'd been blindsided, and the cost was incalculable. Numb didn't even begin to describe how Ziegler felt at the moment. His career was over. But he still had work to do.

What was coming next? What did his superiors in Washington need to know that they couldn't learn simply from watching television? How could he justify a $25 million operation if he didn't have the foggiest notion what was happening around him? Ziegler was still scrambling to synthesize everything he and his team were seeing and hearing. But he had to get something to Washington fast.

```
102710L DEC 27 2010
FLASH TRAFFIC
FROM: Station chief, Gaza Station CIA-OPS
TO: DCI, CIA-Langley, Washington DC DIR
DDO, CIA-Langley, Washington DC OPS
DDI, CIA-Langley, Washington DC INTEL
NSC, Washington DC DIR
White House Situation Room OPS
```

```
              SecState, Washington DC OPS
         SecState-Black Tower, Washington DC DS
              CJCS Washington DCOPSPA
              HQ USCENTCOM, Tampa FLOPS
              HQ USEUCOM, VAIHINGEN GE OPS
              Joint Staff Washington DCOPS
              Clas—EYES ONLY—PRIORITY ALPHA
          SUBJECT: Possible Palestinian civil war erupting
```

Initial assessment from the ground: attacks appear premeditated, well planned, and coordinated. . . . Possible Palestinian civil war erupting. . . . Battle to succeed Arafat could be brutal. . . . Watch for PLO factions to mobilize.

At least 150 dead so far. . . . 23 DSS agents confirmed KIA. . . . Status of other DSS agents—those not with travel package—unclear at this moment. . . .

Other agents off the air. . . . Caution: casualties could mount. . . . Numbers not final.

Travel package attempting to execute Alpha Bravo evac plan. . . . But resistance heavy.

Mediterranean chopper extract impossible due to weather. . . . No U.S. ground forces available to go in. . . . Israeli ground rescue package available—but advise caution due to political risks. . . . Repeat: advise caution due to political risks.

More TK.

                    JZ GS-SC

                  ★   ★   ★

To their left, every street was blocked by burning cars.

So the motorcade kept zigzagging to the right. Word of the bombing was out. News of Arafat's death spread through the city and refugee camps like wildfire. Angry crowds were pouring out of their homes. Teenagers were setting tires and Dumpsters on fire.

Lake and the team worked their way toward the beach. It was simple, direct. It was a landmark they knew and could follow most of the way out of the city.

They were driving through wretched, filthy slums. Bennett had never seen poverty like this. None of them had. Crumbling cinder-block tenement buildings. Bombed-out shops. The scorched remains of cars. Empty playgrounds. The stench of uncollected garbage. The farther they moved from center city, the farther they seemed to plunge into a wasteland of human misery.

The road ahead would only get worse. They'd still have to make it through or around the Shati Refugee Camp—then through or around the Jabalya Refugee Camp—before racing north for the Erez checkpoint and the relative safety of Israel. Both camps were Islamic strongholds. But there weren't a whole lot of options. If they weren't dead, they should be on Ahmed Orabi Street along the Med in less than ten minutes. Where they'd go after that, Bennett had no idea.

★　★　★

Lake suddenly slammed on his brakes.

But not in time.

From out of nowhere, a massive green garbage truck pulled out in front of the lead Suburban and cut it off. Lake's team plowed into its side at almost forty miles an hour. The SUV burst into flames. Bennett turned the wheel hard to the left and skidded to a stop. All they could hear was the crash of metal and glass.

Lake—not wearing a seat belt—smashed against the front windshield, then back against the driver's-side window. The air bags never fired. He was dead. The interior quickly filled with smoke. An engine fire engulfed them. Panicked, Lake's team burst out the side doors, gasping for fresh clean air.

They didn't even see them.

Two men, dressed as garbage collectors—except for the ski masks over their faces—pulled out AK-47s and opened fire. They emptied their entire clips into the bodies of Lake's security detail.

For a split second, no one in Bennett's vehicle or Banacci's could comprehend what was happening. It all seemed like slow motion. They saw the shooters. They saw Lake's team fall. Then they saw a beat-up black Mercedes pull up to the scene and watched the two masked men toss their weapons and themselves inside and speed off. And then—their minds still trying to process the hideous scene—they watched in horror as the garbage truck blew up right in front of them.

The fireball engulfed the lead Suburban. There was nothing they could do. More of their team was dead, and their killers were gone.

7

★ ★
★

MCCOY GRABBED her satellite phone.

She punched a button. The line crackled with static. *Come on, come on,* she silently screamed.

A moment later, the garbled voice cleared up. "Prairie Ranch, go secure."

"Secure, go—it's McCoy—who's this?"

"Erin, it's Marsha."

"Paine's dead—so are Arafat and Mazen."

"We know."

"We're taking heavy fire. We're in a convoy headed west to the water. Jon's driving. We've got Galishnikov and Sa'id. We've just lost another team of DSS agents."

"We've got you on video from the Predator. . . ."

Bennett swerved around a corner and hit his high beams. The rain was coming down so hard that visibility was becoming a serious problem. Still, they could see a jeep of some kind—fitted with a .50-caliber machine gun on top—racing toward them. It wasn't firing yet, but Bennett kept glancing back through his rearview mirror, sure the jeep saw them now.

"*Hold on!*" Bennett screamed.

McCoy dropped the phone and grabbed for something to hold on to as Bennett turned the wheel hard to the left, plowed through a chain-link fence, and raced through an open-air vegetable market. No one was around, thank God, because of the storms. Bennett was leaving a trail of destruction in his wake. Weaving through row after row of wooden stalls, he smashed through most of them while making Snapshot a tough target to pin down. The .50 caliber was blasting away at them now, and as he came to the far end, Bennett slammed on the brakes and turned the wheel hard to the right, fishtailing into an alley draped with PLO flags and clotheslines.

The limo felt like a tank. Its engine was powerful. Its body was almost indestructible. But their bulletproof windows were so badly splintered from multiple rounds of gunfire that Bennett wasn't sure how much more they could take. Behind them, DSS agents opened the back windows of Banacci's Suburban and started firing M16s at the jeep bearing down on them. With so many curves and turns, it was tough for either side to get a clear shot.

"Erin, Erin—you still there?"

Again the voice was garbled. It was Kirkpatrick.

"Yes, I'm still here," said McCoy. "Can you hear me?"

"Barely—listen—you're about to spill out on the main beach highway."

"Right."

"When you get there, turn left, head south, and floor it—got it?"

"I got it."

The heavy machine gun behind them was red-hot. Even amid the raging storm, everyone in the car could hear the rounds striking Banacci's Suburban behind them. McCoy covered the mouthpiece of the phone and relayed the instructions to Bennett.

"*South?*" said Bennett, incredulous. "Is she crazy? We need to go north, back toward the Erez checkpoint."

McCoy relayed Bennett's concern.

"Just tell Jon to trust me—I'm going to get this jeep off your tail," Kirkpatrick shouted over the roar of the storm and the gunfire.

Two minutes later, they broke out of the alleyway and were suddenly facing the violent, crashing waves of the Mediterranean. Bennett slammed on the breaks, spun out onto Ahmed Orabi Street, and broke left, headed south. He'd given Kirkpatrick the benefit of his many doubts. But they didn't have any margin for error. Six seconds later, Banacci's Suburban spun out on the main beach road and raced to catch up with them. A few moments later, the jeep—guns still blazing—followed suit.

Kirkpatrick had better be right.

* * *

She punched the button marked "Langley."

Kirkpatrick's eyes were glued to the images of the chase scene in Gaza, fed from Predator Six, the CIA's unmanned aerial vehicle. The jeep was gaining fast. Bennett and McCoy might make it, but she wasn't so sure Banacci's team would. Someone picked up on the first ring. She expected the watch officer in the Global Operations Center. She got CIA Director Jack Mitchell instead.

"Mitchell, go."

"It's Marsha—you guys ready?"

"Almost, hold on."

"Come on, Jack."

"I know, I know—just tell Bennett and Banacci to floor it and hang on."

* * *

The dimly lit war room was high-tech and state-of-the-art.

The whole place looked a bit like NASA's Mission Control Center in Houston. But this was the CIA's Global Operations Center. This was where the agency's secret war on terror was run—24/7/365—in a command post less than a hundred people in the world had ever seen. No press had ever been allowed in. No official photos had ever been let out. Entry required the highest possible security clearance, a retina scan, a voiceprint, and authorization from the director of Central Intelligence himself.

Danny Tracker—the CIA's deputy director for operations—was six foot three, 223 pounds, and forty-one years young. A former Navy SEAL who'd fought in the '91 Gulf War, he'd specialized in blowing up Iraqi command-and-control centers. Tracker's father had been a top counterterrorism specialist who'd worked extensively throughout the Middle East. In 1968, during a two-year stint at the Pentagon, his father met and married a gorgeous coed from Beirut studying mechanical engineering at Georgetown University. Danny was born a year later—dark hair, dark eyes, dark skin—and grew up all over the world, learning army life and Arabic.

By the post–Gulf War 1990s, Danny was not only one of the precious few Arab-language specialists in the operations division, he was the agency's most decorated field agent. And its most eligible bachelor. Twice voted by the women in the operations division as the guy they'd most like to do a "covert op" with, rumors about his love life were legendary. So were the rumors of his mission history. Hunting down Al-Qaeda leaders in Pakistan and Afghanistan. Assassinating an Iranian arms courier supplying Hezbollah in southern Lebanon. Flipping a senior Saudi intelligence operative working at the Saudi embassy in Washington to work as a double agent for the CIA. Even—allegedly—bugging the Al-Jazeera newsroom in Doha, Qatar.

All anyone really knew for sure was that quiet but high-octane Danny Tracker had risen through the ranks faster than anyone else in the CIA's history, and that those who worked with him and for him in the Operations Division not only loved him, they were willing to risk death to catch his attention and make him proud.

Jack Mitchell now caught Tracker's eye—this mission was a go.

* * *

"Gun it, Jon," McCoy shouted.

Sa'id crouched on the floor in the back of the limousine. He held his head in his hands and kept praying to Allah. He was terrified for their lives, and filled with shame for what his fellow Palestinians were doing to the Americans, and to themselves.

Galishnikov wasn't nearly as scared. He'd grown up as a Jew in Stalin's Siberia. As a child, he'd seen his father and his father's two brothers, all prominent refuseniks, shot execution style in his parents' living room. He'd seen his mother taken away that same night by the secret police, never to be heard from again. He himself had spent three years locked away in Lefortovo, the KGB interrogation prison in Moscow, where he'd survived on cockroaches and rats. He'd seen evil firsthand, and now he felt almost numb to its shock value. Fear wasn't an emotion he readily identified with. But rage was.

He was furious. Furious at the Palestinians for this culture of barbarism. Furious at himself for getting sucked into a business deal with a Palestinian. "Oil for peace"? There wasn't going to be any peace. This was war—pure and simple. The Americans had better get used to that. You couldn't just swagger in like John Wayne and remake the modern Middle East. It didn't work that way. There was too much hatred. The place was an endless cycle of vengeance and retribution. How could he have ever let himself believe for two seconds that Yasser Arafat and Abu Mazen could make peace? Or that the Muslims would let them? They were on a fool's errand, trapped, and about to die.

Galishnikov was glued to the back window. Amid the driving rains and blinding flashes of lightning, he could see Banacci's Suburban weaving back and forth across the street at forty, fifty, now sixty miles an hour. He could also see the much lighter jeep picking up speed and closing the gap. Two hooded men were in the back of the jeep now, soaked to the bone and trying to reload the .50-caliber machine gun. It wasn't going to be easy, but Galishnikov could tell they were professionals. It wouldn't take more than a few seconds. That's all they had.

✵ ✵ ✵

Tracker barked orders to his team.

They were doing all they could, but he wanted more. One of the CIA's own was in a race for her life. They all knew the stakes, and they'd do anything to bring her home safely. But no one was more serious about that mission than Danny Tracker. He adjusted his headset and snapped a command at a specialist sitting just a few yards away.

The biggest coup of Tracker's impressive career was recruiting Erin McCoy into the CIA's Operations Division. It was Tracker who'd first heard about a college-age daughter of the late Sean McCoy from MacPherson. It was Tracker who'd obtained access to Sean McCoy's file and begun poring over it. It was Tracker who'd cleared Erin to learn what her father had really done for all those years and why she'd rarely seen him. It was Tracker who helped her understand for the first time how her father had died, and why. And in time it was Tracker who'd persuaded her to join his team, and eventually to infiltrate GSX and watch Jon Bennett's back.

McCoy's foray into Global Strategix hadn't gone precisely as Tracker had hoped. There'd been complications that he hadn't foreseen. Still, he regarded it as a coup for many reasons, some professional, some personal. But now all of it was in jeopardy. McCoy's life was on the line, and he wasn't entirely sure their plan would really work.

* * *

Galishnikov could see the jeep catching up to them.

He knew they were running out of time. This wasn't random. This was personal. They were coming after him—to kill him, to send a message to the president to stay out of their war with the Jews. Why weren't the Americans and Israelis on offense? Why weren't Bennett and McCoy calling in air strikes? Where was the IDF? Why weren't they sending a strike force? This was out of control.

If the Palestinians were going to start blowing up their own leaders, how could Israel ever make peace with them? Why should they? Maybe Ariel Sharon had been right. Jordan *was* Palestine. Sixty percent of the country of Jordan was Palestinian. Why did they need the West Bank and Gaza too? All of the Palestinians should just be deported to Jordan, Galishnikov thought. Let King Abdullah take care of them. God had promised all this land to the Jews. They were willing to share some of it. He certainly had been. But enough was enough. No one could accuse him of being a hawk. He wasn't an extremist. He wanted peace. He'd worked for peace. But a peace treaty without real security guarantees for Israel was a suicide pact, and he wasn't going to be part of that. Not anymore. Not after what he'd seen today.

Galishnikov told Bennett to get off the road and find a way back. They needed to be heading north, not south. They needed to be getting out of Gaza, not going deeper into it. They were rapidly heading toward the Strip's most dangerous stronghold, the Khan Yunis Refugee Camp, where radical Islamic forces were especially strong. What were they supposed to do then? How were they supposed to survive with no DSS agents to protect them, and no air support to extract them?

"What are you doing, Jonathan? Get us off this road now—now!"

* * *

Snapshot blew down the straightaway so fast that it was beginning to shake.

The engine was heading into the red zone. Bennett was pushing this car beyond its limits, but the jeep was still closing the gap. He couldn't slow down now. He certainly couldn't get off the road or turn around. At the rate they were going they'd just flip the car and roll until they blew up or the jeep got a clear shot at their gas tank.

Banacci continued to swerve back and forth across the road, trying desperately not to provide a clear shot, while two of his agents lay on their stomachs in the back, laying down M16 fire, hoping to take out a tire, if not the driver behind them.

★ ★ ★

Bennett's eyes were locked on the road.

McCoy tried to keep hers from locking on Bennett. She knew he loved his Porsche. She knew he loved flooring it on the open road. But she'd never seen him like this—in total command at a hundred miles an hour, bullets whizzing by their heads.

Suddenly, both of them heard the .50-caliber machine gun unleash—again. Rounds began smashing all across the back of Banacci's already badly damaged Suburban. Then, the unthinkable—two rounds penetrated just to the left of the license plate. They ripped their way forward, into a reserve fuel tank. The force of the explosion lifted Banacci's Suburban into the air and flipped it two or three times before the flaming wreckage crashed to the pavement and skidded off the road onto the front steps of a rain-drenched apartment building.

McCoy whipped around, trying to see exactly what was happening, then instinctively shielded her eyes from the intensity of the blast and the heat. Bennett fought to keep control. The jeep veered to the right to avoid a crash, smashing out onto the beach before the driver clawed his way back onto the main road and jammed the accelerator to the floor. Banacci and his team were gone. The Palestinian gunner now had a clear shot at Snapshot.

Bennett was out of options.

8

★ ★
★

THE JEEP was gaining on them.

Mitchell and Tracker couldn't believe what they were seeing. At these speeds, the slightest mistake by either driver would be fatal. They still had no way to get friendly forces to them. Whoever survived—if any of them did—might still fall into the hands of Islamic extremists, and then all bets were off. They might be executed on the spot. But that would be the most merciful scenario. More likely they'd be held hostage—tortured, brutalized, without mercy and without much hope of the U.S. or Israelis finding them, much less rescuing them.

★ ★ ★

Bennett fought to maintain his composure.

He didn't want McCoy to know how he felt. How could she stay so calm under fire? Sure, she was trained. She did this for a living. But it was more than that. She didn't seem scared. She didn't seem to fear death—not like he did.

Bennett's shirt was soaked with sweat. He struggled to breathe normally. Adrenaline coursed through his veins. Fifty-caliber rounds sliced past their windows. Snapshot was moving now at well over 120 miles an hour. They were heading deeper and deeper into enemy territory, and he was scared.

Terrified, actually—he was terrified of dying. So many people in his life had died violently. It wasn't just now, or in Jerusalem a few weeks back. During the September 11 attacks, twenty-three people he'd known well had perished in the inferno. Several dozen more he knew in passing had died as well. All of them were colleagues in one way or another. All of them worked in the financial-services industry. Like Bennett, they typically got to work at five-thirty or six o'clock in the morning. Like him, none of them ever missed a day of work. They didn't take sick days. They didn't take personal days or mental health days or vacations. They were driven, like he was. They were obsessive, like he was. The difference was where they worked. Their firms rented space in the World Trade Center. They worked in the towers. He did not.

GSX could have easily afforded space there, and Bennett would have loved to have an office somewhere north of the eightieth or ninetieth floors—the commanding heights, he called them. But at the time they were looking, the Trade Center hadn't had any space available that high, and Bennett didn't want to consider anything lower. He eventually found the thirty-eighth floor of a high-rise office building overlooking Central Park. It wasn't as high as he wanted. It didn't have views as spectacular as those of some of the guys he'd gone to business school with. But something in his gut told him to take it. So he did. And now his friends were all dead.

* * *

Like a bolt of lightning, the message hit the satellite.

It flashed to Gibraltar. From there, it was cross-linked to the angry skies over Gaza and was instantaneously received by the Trojan Spirit II SATCOM system on board Predator Six. It was decrypted and fed into the hard drive. Unseen at four thousand feet up and five miles out, the electro-optical, infrared Versatron Skyball 18 immediately engaged its spotter lens, then its zoom lens, then ran a cross-check.

A fraction of a second later, Predator Six put the jeep squarely in its sights, fired a laser at its engine block, locked on, and fed the image and targeting data back to the ground station on Gibraltar, where it was shot back to Langley. All systems were green.

Tracker made his recommendation. Mitchell concurred.

* * *

The AGM-114C Hellfire launched clean.

Screaming toward its prey at Mach 2, the six-foot-long, twenty-five thousand dollar missile was nearly as big as the men it targeted. It left no trail. It made no sound. It was essentially invisible to the naked eye. Seventeen seconds later, it slammed unannounced through the front windshield and turned the jeep into a death trap.

★   ★   ★

The explosion stunned them all.

The jeep was gone. A moment later, convinced they faced no other immediate threats—at least for a few moments—Bennett slowed down and pulled the limo over to the side of the road. When they were safely stopped on the shoulder, he turned and stared at the burning remains. He was grateful to be alive, but couldn't speak. It didn't make sense. What had just happened? His enemies had been consumed by fire—but how? It was a miracle. That's all he could think of, and he didn't believe in miracles.

Galishnikov also stared out the back window. They were safe; that much he knew. But he badly wanted to be back in Jerusalem, at home with his wife and a good bottle of vodka.

Sa'id lifted his head. He got up off the floor and sat back on the seat, staring at the fires behind him. He, too, wanted to be home with his wife and four sons. This was more than he'd bargained for. Perhaps he'd made a terrible mistake. Perhaps he'd been wrong to go into business with Galishnikov, or get mixed up in the peace process. He was sure Galishnikov felt that way. He'd always suspected that just under the surface his Russian Jewish friend despised the Palestinians and thought of them all as terrorists, just as he suspected most Israelis did.

But that really wasn't fair. Galishnikov couldn't have been nicer to Sa'id and his family and those who worked for Sa'id's company. But didn't all that was happening just prove that the Palestinians couldn't be trusted, that they were a bloodthirsty and barbaric people, that they wouldn't be satisfied until they drove the Jews into the sea?

It didn't prove that at all, of course. This wasn't the work of all Palestinians. It was the work of a few extremists, hell-bent on destroying any prospects for peace. Sa'id knew that. He knew it all too well. But did Galishnikov? Did Bennett or McCoy? How could they all have come so far and achieved so little? Actually, it was worse than that. Maybe their vision of Arab-Israeli peace and prosperity was naive, even dangerous.

It was now clear to Sa'id that they'd be lucky just to make it through the day.

* * *

A cheer went up inside the war room.

Mitchell got back on the line with Kirkpatrick. "You see that?" he asked.

"Sure did," said the national security advisor. "I've been giving the VP a play-by-play. He's on the other line—about to call the president and give him the good news. How soon can you get here from Langley?"

"Twenty minutes?" said Mitchell.

"Make it fifteen."

* * *

McCoy glanced at Bennett.

She knew what he was thinking. After all these years, she could read him like a book. And he knew she could, which made him uncomfortable. So she didn't say anything. He'd talk when he was ready. Until then, it was better to leave him alone with his thoughts.

She looked back at the wreckage and silently said a prayer of thanks. They were all still alive, and she knew why. She knew exactly what had happened. She knew what Marsha Kirkpatrick had just authorized, what Jack Mitchell had just ordered, what Danny Tracker had just orchestrated. It wasn't exactly fire from heaven, the kind that had destroyed Sodom and Gomorrah, not that far from where they now were. But it was certainly a miracle. Of that, she had no doubt.

* * *

Andrews was dead ahead.

MacPherson could see the snow- and ice-covered trees of Prince George's County, Maryland, as *Air Force One* approached the home of the 89th Airlift Wing, the 89th Security Forces Squadron, and some twenty-four thousand military and civilian personnel who lived and worked on the country's premier air force base.

The call from the VP was certainly good news—but now his thoughts were shifting back to Stuart Iverson's fate.

Bennett and CIA director Jack Mitchell were taking a completely opposite position from Justice and the FBI. What message did it send if people with information that could lead to the arrest and conviction of terrorist cells became convinced they couldn't cut a deal with the U.S. government? Of course Iverson deserved the chair or worse. But this was no longer about one man. It was about the fate of a nation in the fight of its life with a terrorist network about which the CIA obviously knew far too little.

"Andrews control, this is *Air Force One*. Over," radioed the pilot.

"Go ahead, *Air Force One*; this is Andrews."

"Request permission to land. Over."

"Roger that, *Air Force One*. You're cleared for immediate landing on runway One-Lima. We're at ThreatCon Delta. The base is locked down, ready for your arrival."

"Good to hear, Andrews. Gambit's wings ready when we get there?"

"That's affirmative, sir. *Marine One* is fired up and ready to roll. Apache security package is also on the tarmac and ready when you are."

"Thank you, Andrews. ETA, four minutes."

"Roger that, and welcome home, *Air Force One*."

"Thanks, guys—it's good to be back."

☆　☆　☆

At Langley, rivers of information were now pouring in.

It came in from Gaza Station, from the U.S. Embassy in Tel Aviv, and from the consulate in East Jerusalem. It came from Cairo Station in Egypt and Beirut Station in Lebanon. Reports were also beginning to flow in from Damascus and Amman and Riyadh, and they were threatening to overwhelm the agency's ability to sort, process, and analyze it all in a timely, effective manner.

CIA operations officers in the field were pressing their informants hard to give them any scraps of hard data or rumors or whispers—anything at all—that might help explain how this could have happened and what else might be coming. At the same time, NSA and CIA analysts were simultaneously trying to track all kinds of electronic intercepts, as well as Arabic radio and television coverage of the mushrooming crisis.

The problem was that this was a classic case of drinking from a fire hose. They had too much information and it was coming in too fast. The buzz on the Arab street and among foreign embassies and intelligence services and terrorist factions—what the CIA typically called chatter—had become a deafening roar. Theories and threats and counterthreats were being bandied about throughout the region. But what was real? What was true?

✶　✶　✶

"Snapshot, this is Prairie Ranch. Do you copy?"

Kirkpatrick's voice startled Bennett and McCoy. There'd been no traffic on the Black Tower wireless radio system for the last few minutes, just an eerie silence, a silence that spoke volumes about just how alone in Gaza they really were.

"Prairie Ranch, this is Snapshot—go ahead," said McCoy.

"You guys okay?"

"We are—just trying to catch our breath. Thanks for the help."

"Hey, what good is a forty-million-dollar toy if you can't take it out for a spin?"

Bennett jumped into the conversation. "Now what?"

"You're wondering why I sent you south?"

"You got it."

"It's pretty simple, actually—do you know where the Bat Cave is?"

"What are you talking about?"

"The Bat Cave," Kirkpatrick repeated. "McCoy knows what I'm talking about."

"Look, we haven't got a lot of time to chitchat down here."

"You mean Gaza Station?" McCoy asked.

"Exactly—the guys in the field call it the Bat Cave."

"I've spoken with JZ," said McCoy, regaining her bearings. "But no, I don't know where it is."

"Stay put. I've got a guy coming to get you. Let me check his ETA."

The line was silent. They were on hold.

McCoy opened the glove compartment and fished out a pair of high-powered night-vision binoculars. She scanned the roads, apartment buildings, and storefronts around them. She could see a VW van about a mile and a half away down the coastal road. It was approaching without headlights or lights of any kind. The night-vision technology picked up the heat signature of the engine, and McCoy used the binoculars to zoom in. No license plate. No markings of any kind. But it was coming up fast.

Was it hostile or friendly? They were about to find out.

9

★ ★
★

"MR. PRESIDENT, you've got a call from the vice president."

"Put him through. Bill, that you? What have you got?"

"Looks like Bennett and McCoy may be all right—we're trying to get them to Gaza Station. I'll let you know the minute they're secure."

"Good. I want Bennett and McCoy on the NSC videoconference."

"Yes, sir. Also, I talked with Doron. The Israelis are finalizing their mobilization. They're willing to hold off until they hear from you unless the fighting spills over. If Israelis start getting killed, Doron said they'll go in immediately."

MacPherson didn't know quite how to react to that yet.

"We're getting reaction in from around the world," the VP continued. "Morocco's king was the first to call. He's furious at the extremists and offered any assistance we might need. Also, President Aznar called from Madrid. Most of the NATO leaders are still there. We did a conference call with them. They sounded quite shaken up, actually, even the French. Paine was well liked, as you know. They're all ready to help. They just want us to hold back the Israelis from doing anything rash."

"I bet."

"That was echoed by President Mubarak. He's in Cairo until this evening. He's supposed to fly to Geneva tonight for a U.N. conference. King Abdullah called from Jordan. He's in Amman, also supposed to go to Geneva, but said he's going to cancel his trip and monitor the situation. Like Doron, he's worried the fighting could spill over. Both he and Mubarak condemned the attacks and offered intelligence and medical assistance. But both of them also insisted in very strong terms that we keep the Israelis from going in. They said an Israeli invasion of the territories would cause irreparable harm to the peace process."

"What peace process?" asked the president.

"I know."

"Fine, anything else?"

"Just condolences from the rest of Europe, Asia, Latin America. Russian president Vadim wants to talk as soon as you've got a spare second."

"Set that up for my return. That, and a call to Doron."

"You got it. Oh, I also just got a call from Achmed Chalabi in Baghdad. He said the new interim government is going to hold its first official news conference tonight. They'll probably do it from one of Saddam's palaces. Anyway, as you and I talked about at Camp David on Saturday, the interim government is ready to declare itself open for business, announce its members, its mandate, and its structure, and ask for a continued coalition presence to help stabilize the security situation, get the oil flowing, and begin to establish civilian control. They're also going to denounce these attacks in Gaza and call for an immediate Palestinian cease-fire."

"Really? That's a change."

"Hold on—Kirkpatrick is e-mailing me something. . . . She says Bud Norris at Secret Service is worried about possible attacks inside the U.S., particularly Washington, in the next few days."

"Anything solid?"

"No, sir, just lots of chatter. But he's concerned about a possible larger operational concept at play here."

"What does he recommend?"

"Threat Level Orange."

"What does Lee think?" asked the president, referring to Secretary Lee Alexander James of the Department of Homeland Security.

"The e-mail says Secretary James is in full agreement, sir."

"Then do it," MacPherson said. "And put all U.S. forces at Threat Condition Delta. The last thing we can afford is to get blindsided again."

* * *

He was known simply as Nadir, aka the Viper.

Mohammed Jibril had heard a great deal about the gaunt little man, all of five feet six inches tall. But the two had never met. Nor would they. It wouldn't be proper, much less safe. Jibril knew that Nadir was one of the most effective black-ops specialists in all of Saddam's fedayeen forces and one of the most fearsome killers on the face of the planet. He knew Nadir was thirty-nine, born just outside of Baghdad, the son of Palestinian refugees. He also knew that Nadir had been personally trained by Daoud Juma as an expert in the use of C4 plastic explosives. That much he knew for sure.

What he did not know—what Jibril wanted to know but couldn't seem to find out—was how the Viper had escaped detection, much less arrest, for so long. Practically speaking, of course, it didn't really matter. But it would be nice to know his secrets.

If he was only a fraction as good as Jibril's sources said he was, the Viper would be well worth the $150,000 in U.S. currency just wired to his father's Swiss bank account. He'd better be.

Nadir stared out the window of the Air France Boeing 777. Inbound to Mexico City from Berlin, after a transfer in Paris, he'd already been traveling for more than thirteen hours. It was dark and early and he was exhausted. But at thirty-five thousand feet over the Caribbean, he found himself restless and unable to sleep. Soon he'd be on the ground; he'd secure a rental car and stay for a night. He'd figure out how best to cross into the U.S. and reach his strike point on time. Theoretically, it couldn't be simpler, and in a few days it would all be over.

★　★　★

Air Force One landed amid airtight security.

Three F-15s circled overhead. Humvees blocked each base entrance. Soldiers patrolled the perimeter. Bomb-sniffing dogs worked their way through the hangars and administrative buildings as Secret Service sharpshooters, SWAT teams, and surveillance teams kept a watchful eye over the tarmac and the woods nearby. News crews were asked not to broadcast the arrival live, though they were allowed to videotape the landing.

Surrounded by a phalanx of Secret Service agents, Gambit—the Secret Service code name for James MacPherson—soon boarded *Marine One*. Still recovering from the terrorist attack that had nearly taken his life less than a month before, the president was confined to a wheelchair. He'd quickly grown tired of it, but remained too fragile to do without it. Special

Agent Jackie Sanchez directed her team to lift Gambit and his wheelchair and slide him into place through the side door of the gleaming green-and-white military helicopter and make sure he was secure. With the president were Press Secretary Chuck Murray, Defense Secretary Burt Trainor, and "Football," the military aide carrying the nuclear launch codes.

The short hop from Andrews to the South Lawn of the White House would take only a few minutes, but it would be bumpy. The weather was rapidly worsening, and having just read the latest forecast from the National Weather Service, Sanchez was anxious. An ice storm was descending from the northeast. In New York and New Jersey, temperatures were plunging into the teens and could drop to single digits overnight. Ice and snow were making airports and roads treacherous. Across the mid-Atlantic, temperatures were hovering just around the freezing mark, but were expected to drop precipitously overnight. For now, a nasty freezing rain was battering much of the coast, beginning in Delaware and extending as far south as Richmond. Road crews were already spreading salt and sand on the roads to keep them open, and Virginia Power was bracing for falling limbs, downed lines, and possible blackouts.

It was time to get Gambit out of harm's way.

★　★　★

"Prairie Ranch, this is Snapshot."

Bennett revved the engine again.

"Go ahead, Snapshot," Kirkpatrick responded.

Bennett watched McCoy reach down on the floor by her feet to pick up her Uzi and check its clip. It was full. She clicked off the safety and set the submachine gun on her lap. Then she reached under the seat and pulled out a spare Uzi, double-checked the clip, and handed it to Bennett.

"Prairie Ranch, we've got a dark brown VW bus approaching at twelve o'clock," McCoy radioed to the Situation Room. "Can you see that from your angle?"

"Roger that, Snapshot," said Kirkpatrick. "It's the Batmobile."

Bennett looked at McCoy but said nothing. The Bat Cave? The Batmobile? Maybe it all seemed clever to Kirkpatrick and her world, but Bennett was in no mood for kiddie code names and James Bond wannabes.

For her part, McCoy couldn't care less what Bennett thought at the moment. She'd done her job. She'd kept him safe this far. And she was glad for backup, whatever it was called.

She turned away from Bennett and looked back at Galishnikov and Sa'id. "Saddle up, gentlemen. Our ride is here."

A few minutes later, the driver knocked on Bennett's window with the butt of a loaded pistol. He was young, twenty-five-ish, clean-shaven, muscular, and wearing jeans, dirty white sneakers and a Bir Zeit University sweatshirt. He was soaked to the bone in the torrential downpour that still refused to let up. His dark face and eyes were suddenly illuminated by several intense flashes of lightning, and more thunder boomed overhead. He and McCoy talked in Arabic. The only thing Bennett caught for sure was the driver's name—Tariq—and a palpable sense of urgency.

A split second later, McCoy was out of the limousine, helping Tariq open the back doors. Together, Bennett, Tariq, and McCoy moved Donny Mancuso's body into the back of the van and covered him with a sheet. Then, apologizing to Sa'id and Galishnikov that they were not authorized to see the place where they were going next, McCoy handed black cloth hoods to both men, and directed them to move quickly into the van. McCoy then asked Bennett to guide the two older men and make sure they got there safely while Tariq got into the VW's driver's seat and cranked up the heat for his shivering guests.

With a nickname like the Batmobile, Bennett was half hoping for some kind of state-of-the-art spy vehicle right out of a Hollywood special-effects shop. But as he glanced around at the shabby interior, it quickly became clear that nothing could have been further from the truth. The VW had no bulletproof shields, no front-mounted machine guns. It had no ejector seat or night-vision front windshield. There was no satellite dish on the roof, or racks of high-tech weaponry to play with. It was just an ugly old van, strewn with recent Arabic newspapers, empty soda cans, a rather generous supply of cigarette ashes, and four new passengers, all of whom felt hunted and alone.

Galishnikov and Sa'id stayed low in the back, unable to see a thing even if they'd been allowed to. Bennett got in the front passenger seat. His eyes were riveted on McCoy, still outside. She was gathering all the weapons, ammunition, and electronics gear she could and transferring them from the limousine to the van. She popped the limo's trunk and opened a steel box. Bennett saw her grab several small objects, stuff them in her pockets, and then back away several yards from the car. Then she gave Tariq a signal and he revved the VW's engine.

Bennett glanced back down the road. No one was approaching, but time had to be running out. What in the world was McCoy up to?

* * *

"Let's go; let's do it!" Sanchez yelled.

"You got it, ma'am—we're out of here," the pilot shouted back over the *thwap, thwap, thwap* of the rotors and the chopper's three-thousand-horsepower engines.

MacPherson knew full well that *Marine One* was virtually impregnable. It bore a stunning array of cutting-edge combat avionics—all of which were highly classified—including protections against the electromagnetic pulse of a nuclear blast and against attacks by multiple surface-to-air missiles. But it wasn't missiles that gave him pause. It was the ice building up on the rotors. Nevertheless, he saw the pilot give the thumbs-up to the ground crew, and the Sikorsky Sea King lifted off and headed northwest.

* * *

McCoy held up her right hand.

Five, four, three, two, one.

She plunged her left hand into one of her pockets, pulled out what looked like a hand grenade, pulled the pin, and tossed it into the open side door of the limo. Then a second. Then a third. Then she jumped into the side door of the van and slammed it shut. Tariq floored it and they were gone.

Perhaps they weren't typical grenades. Perhaps they were on a timer or a delay of some sort. Bennett had no idea. Nor did he ask. He was just grateful that the VW was picking up speed. It had opened up a distance of at least a few hundred yards. Then they heard it. The first explosion blew out the limousine's windows. It blew off the doors and the roof. It sent glass and shrapnel flying in every direction. A fraction of a second later came the second explosion, louder than the first. This one engulfed Snapshot in a fireball that could be seen for miles.

Flames roared from the chassis, from the engine block, as billows of thick smoke poured into the sky. Tariq braked hard and spun the VW to the left, down a side street and out of visual range of Snapshot. Then came the third explosion, louder than either of the other two. It shattered windows a block and a half away. They could hear it echo up and down the coast.

McCoy didn't look back. She fiddled with her wireless radio gear and tried to connect with the DSS agents still pinned down. Nothing. She kept switching frequencies. Still nothing.

"Snapshot to DSS agents. Snapshot to DSS agents. Please respond. I repeat, please respond. Can you hear me?"

She strained to pick up even the slightest sound. There was nothing but static and hiss. McCoy feared the worst. Was it really possible that the entire protective detail from the State Department's Bureau of Diplomatic Security had been captured or killed? Were they so badly wounded that they were unable to respond to her messages? How could that really be true? What about the undercover guys? Why weren't they responding? She'd covered every frequency. So had the Black Tower command center. But the fact remained—no one was responding, and there could be only one reason why.

*	*	*

Tariq turned down another side street, then raced into an alleyway.

He screeched to a halt behind an abandoned five-story, boarded-up hotel known as the Hotel Baghdad. A broken neon sign out front read Vacancy in Arabic and in English, though all of the letters were long since burned out. They could hear the wail of approaching sirens. They could see crowds of young men running for the beach road to see if the Americans had finally been caught and killed.

But in the rush for safety, what Tariq didn't see—but should have—was the fifteen-year-old boy in the fourth-floor window of the apartment building across the street. He was peering out at them from behind some tattered blue curtains. He was holding a cell phone, and he was dialing.

10

THE EARTH POURED forth fire, as the demons below found their way of escape.

It was noon, but there was no sun. It was winter, but it was not cold. Into the thick, black, midday sky climbed the howling, raging, deafening firestorms. Up, up into the darkness—thirty, forty stories high—shot the flames of fury.

Daoud Juma was no longer twenty-six. No longer was he commander of Saddam's fedayeen. No longer was he on the run, escaping a wounded Baghdad in a stolen French Renault—packed with dozens of cans of extra fuel, bottles of water, and boxes of food and other supplies—racing west toward the border of Syria, surrounded by oil well fires, burning wild and deadly.

In his mind, in his heart, Daoud was suddenly back in the desert sands of Kuwait. His thoughts raced back in time, to April of 1991. He was a child, just seven years old, and he was standing over the charred bodies of his mother and father. His eyes welled up with tears and he began to weep. Through his tears he was staring out at hundreds of oil-well fires, Saddam Hussein's parting gift to the people of Kuwait and her neighbors.

At over 2,200 degrees, the great furnaces were quickly turning the desert sands into glass. They consumed more than 5 million barrels of oil a day, and already the infernos had been raging for nearly a month.

In an instant, in the blink of an eye, Daoud was transported back to the nightmare of his youth. Not so long ago, he and his family had all been together, peaceful and content. They lived a sparse but decent life. His father managed oil wells along the Iraqi border, not far from Basra. His mother raised him and wrote letters to Daoud's three older brothers, conscripted into the military. Then came August 2, 1990—the beginning of Saddam Hussein's "liberation" of Kuwait. Then came January 16, 1991—the beginning of the air war, the beginning of Operation Desert Storm. Then, early in the morning of February 24, 1991—the thirty-eighth day of the bombing campaign—came the start of the one-hundred-hour ground war. The Americans and their allies invaded. They polluted the Iraqi motherland, and in retaliation Iraqi forces set fire to more than six hundred Kuwaiti oil wells . . . and changed Daoud Juma's destiny forever.

All three of Daoud's brothers died in combat operations that spring. So had his mother. So had his father. Suddenly, Daoud was an orphan in a firestorm. In time he would search out the history of those days, trying to learn more details, trying to make some sense of it all. It had taken some ten thousand personnel from forty countries more than nine months and $1.5 billion to fight and extinguish all those fires. It was an enormous, expensive, exhausting challenge. But left alone, those fires could have raged on undiminished for another hundred years.

No amount of time or money or historical perspective could bring back his mother or father or three older brothers. Nothing could bring back the innocent life he'd once known. Ashes to ashes, dust to dust, they were gone forever.

Never again would he hear his father regale him with colorful tales of his parents and grandparents and ancestors battling the Israelites and the Persians, the Greeks and the Egyptians, the Ottomans and the British. Never again would he hear his mother tell him bedtime stories of growing up in Palestine, running through the olive groves, hiking through the rugged hills, napping under the cool breezes sweeping in off the sparkling Mediterranean, sparkling like the most brilliant diamonds in Hammurabi's vaults. Never again would he hear his brothers' infectious laughter, or wrestle with them in the yard, or play pranks together on the neighbors across the street. Never again would he hear his mother's voice, singing him to sleep on hot summer nights with songs of the Great Revolution, while she scratched his back and gently stroked the perspiration away from his eyes and forehead.

The more he thought about his mother, the more Daoud Juma wept. She'd been born in Jericho. Her family had escaped through Transjordan and made their way to central Iraq during the 1948 war, when the Jews announced their new State of Israel. So, while they were ethnically and legally Iraqis because of their father, the Juma family sympathized with the plight of their brothers and sisters in Palestine, and the Juma boys had grown up hearing stories of a Holy Land they longed to see one day, stories of a holy war they someday longed to win.

Daoud refused to blame Saddam Hussein for the death of his parents. He blamed the Great Satan. He blamed the Zionists. He certainly did not blame the man who'd given his family a home and a heritage.

* * *

Tariq hustled Sa'id and Galishnikov into the back entrance.

Bennett and McCoy grabbed the luggage and supplies and followed them inside. Then they went back for Mancuso's body and set it down in a corner of the lobby. The whole transaction took only a few minutes, but Tariq insisted they move faster. If they were seen, if they were caught, he couldn't guarantee their safety, or his own.

Once everyone and their things were safely inside, Tariq shut and bolted the door behind them. He'd worry about the VW later. He'd stolen it the day before. No one could trace it to him or his team, and with chaos engulfing the Strip, it wasn't likely the police would be tracking down stolen goods for the next several weeks, if ever. If the van was gone in a few hours, who would really care? Tariq would just steal another and dub that the new Batmobile, and it could certainly serve as his new mode of transportation—for a while anyway. That was the first law of Gaza: there was no law in Gaza. The sooner Bennett and his team understood that, the better off they'd be.

* * *

Daoud remembered his father as a proud, gregarious man.

A native-born Iraqi, he constantly boasted of being able to trace his family's roots back to the days of King Nebuchadnezzar and the glories of ancient Babylon, though as Daoud grew older he doubted this could literally be true.

His father was not a Tikriti. He'd grown up in a small, dusty town not far from Tikrit. He loved his country and he worshiped Saddam. Literally. Every morning, early, before daybreak, before he left for the oil fields, Daoud's father would face Mecca, kneel down on his small rug, bow his forehead to the ground, and say his prayers. Then he would kiss Daoud and his brothers and his mother good-bye, and then kiss the framed black-and-white photo of Saddam that hung in their living room. Every day, year after year. It was a ritual, a way of life, and it made an impression on Daoud.

Once, in the marketplace, a shopkeeper—the man sold bread, or maybe meat—Daoud was only seven at the time so couldn't remember for sure—anyway, the shopkeeper cursed Saddam for the food shortages their town was experiencing. Daoud's father was not a large man, maybe five foot seven, maybe five foot eight. He weighed only about 150 pounds. But Daoud would never forget how enraged his father became. His face had turned deep red, almost purple. He'd shouted at the man. He cursed him to his face. He said the man was a Zionist, a lover of Israel. He demanded the man recant or die.

The shouting match came to blows. A crowd was gathering, chanting and shouting. The scene was getting uglier by the minute. Daoud feared for his father's life. Then a shot rang out. People screamed and scattered. Daoud ran to his father. He saw the blood on his father's hands and face and started sobbing uncontrollably. But after what seemed like a few minutes, he wiped the tears from his eyes and realized his father was not wounded. His father was holding a smoking pistol. The shopkeeper was lying in a pool of his own blood. His father had killed him, and Daoud now feared for his father's safety.

But he needn't have worried. Three days later, his father received a signed letter of commendation from President Hussein himself, a promotion to foreman, and a sixty-dollar-a-month raise. Daoud couldn't believe it. Neither could his father. That night they slaughtered a lamb, roasted it over a spit, invited the entire neighborhood over, and celebrated throughout the night. It was one of the happiest days of Daoud's life. Then the war came. Four days later his brothers left for the front. Two weeks later, his entire family was dead.

What made Daoud—the baby of the family—so loyal to Saddam and his regime was not simply that the Iraqi leader had been a great friend of the Palestinian people, though he certainly was. He'd given them jobs and opportunities in the oil fields and in his paramilitary forces. He'd funded their war against the Jews, and given them weapons and training. But it was more than that. Saddam Hussein had given the Juma boys the chance to wage jihad against the Jews and against the Americans. He'd shown favor to Daoud's father; he'd honored them—kept them from public humiliation and shame—and in so doing he had won the allegiance of the Juma boys forever.

To Daoud, Saddam was an Arab savior. It was the sheikhs of the Gulf who were ruthless and corrupt. At best, the Kuwaiti and Saudi elites treated Palestinians like second-rate citizens. At worst, his relatives working in the Gulf states were treated like slaves, like the Jews under the pharaohs. The Palestinians built the sheikhs kingdoms of splendor by the sweat of their brows, but never tasted the fruit of their endless labor. Why should such despots be rewarded in this life? Why shouldn't Saddam have been allowed to claim what was rightfully his—the oil fields of Kuwait? Why should such wealth and power remain in the hands of the thieves and prostitutes?

Daoud grew up listening to the preachers in the Sunni mosques and to Saddam Hussein on Iraqi state radio. He loved the fiery speeches, the unflinching resolve to liberate Palestine and create a great, unified, prosperous Arab nation from the Persian Gulf and the Euphrates River to the shores of the Mediterranean. From the earliest days he could remember, he'd been inspired by the Great Revolution led by Saddam and Yasser Arafat and the imams of his youth. And from the time his parents were killed, he'd been ready to give his life for a cause greater than himself. He was willing to pay whatever it took to avenge his parents' deaths and see Palestine rise again like a phoenix from the ashes. This was Allah's will, Daoud's eternal destiny, and he was ready.

But for the moment, Daoud was engulfed in a lake of fire. Only a madman would be out here alone. Only a pitiful soul—a man with absolutely nothing to lose—would take such risks, driving through a hellish landscape, risking death by an American smart bomb. Yet a magnet was drawing him forward. Senior Iraqi officials and Ba'ath Party members and advisors had a standing—if covert—offer of safe refuge from Syrian president Bashar al-

Assad, son of the late president Hafez al-Assad, one of the most feared of all modern Arab dictators. So here he was, on the road to Damascus. He had come this far, and he could not go back.

Amid the scorched earth of a forward Iraqi military outpost, he could see only charred bodies, melted wreckage, and utter carnage all around him. Now—here—staring out at this ghastly, incomprehensible vision of destruction, his eyes burned. His throat burned. His skin blistered as it baked. His filthy black T-shirt, covered in sand and dried blood and drenched in his own sweat, reeked with the stench of fear and fatigue. The heat was unbearable. He could smell the cooked flesh. He could taste the acrid smoke. But he could not breathe. He could not speak.

And then Daoud began to vomit. He vomited again and again and again, until he was down on his knees, doubled over in excruciating pain. His body convulsed in dry heaves, until he nearly collapsed, exhausted and dehydrated. His systems began to shut down. Yet he knew he could not stay out in the open. He had to keep focused. He had to keep moving. Or he would be hunted down and killed, and his vows would go unfulfilled.

✻ ✻ ✻

Tariq handed out flashlights and clicked on his own.

He headed to the lobby of the Hotel Baghdad, motioning Bennett and McCoy to follow him closely and to guide Galishnikov and Sa'id, each of whom still wore the black hood. Torrents of rain poured through a large gash in the far left wall, in what looked to be an old dining room. There were no tables or chairs in the room any longer, but shards of porcelain and glass dishes of some kind were scattered all over the wooden floor. It appeared as though that corner of the building had been hit once by a mortar round or RPG and had never been repaired. Now it was wet, cold, and covered with mud.

The hotel's foyer and main lobby were around the corner from the dining room—damp, not soaked, but also quite cold. Bitter winter winds howled through the building, sending a chill down Bennett's spine, if no one else's. The place was eerie, to say the least. Bennett scanned the shadowy, cavernous rooms. Apparently built in the late 1940s or early 1950s, the hotel had once been quite beautiful and ornate. But everything about the place suggested it hadn't been used or inhabited in any way for at least a decade, if not more. A glass chandelier dangled overhead, barely connected to the ceiling by a fraying wire and completely covered with cobwebs and dust. Tattered old cloth-and-wood furniture lay scattered about the room—three couches, two coffee tables, and four overstuffed chairs whose stuffing had long ago disintegrated.

An old Coca-Cola machine stood plugged in but not working in one corner. A stack of yellowed newspapers, all in Arabic, lay beside it. Badly mildewed Egyptian and Iraqi carpets covered sections of the floor, though several other large carpets were rolled up and leaning against the base of the once-grand staircase that led up to a balcony on the second floor and then continued winding up to the third, fourth, and fifth floors. Hideous green-and-yellow drapes covered all the windows, and everything was covered with thick layers of dust and chunks of plaster falling from a damp, rotting ceiling.

Something inside Bennett wanted to explore a little with his flashlight and his Uzi. He wasn't entirely sure why. A few minutes earlier he'd been cursing the fact that he'd ever stepped into this godforsaken hellhole known as the Gaza Strip. Now, so long as no one was gunning for him, he suddenly had the urge to do a little exploring. Who knew what secrets this place might hold?

AIR FRANCE flight 1039 touched down in Mexico City.

A few minutes later, Nadir Sarukhi Hashemi disembarked with the other passengers and cleared through customs. Not with his given name, of course, and certainly not with his nom de guerre found anywhere on his passport. No one here knew him as the Viper. Nor did anyone here know that he was really a Palestinian.

He had no previous arrests, no outstanding warrants, no information of any kind on file with the Mexican authorities, Interpol, or the FBI. As far as the international law-enforcement system was concerned, Nadir Sarukhi Hashemi was Mario Iabello, an Italian citizen traveling on an Italian passport, a senior computer programmer working for Microsoft and in Mexico City for a small business management conference. They gave him no hassles. Indeed, they barely noticed him at all.

Nadir rented a Ford Taurus and drove to the Sheraton Maria Isabel Hotel and Towers, where he paid the valet with a crisp American fifty-dollar bill to park his car overnight. Next, he headed inside to reservations, then upstairs to a corner suite. He set up his laptop, checked his e-mails, and took a long hot shower. He watched the news from Gaza. The Americans were reeling. The world was stunned. The Israelis were preparing to move. It was going better than expected, and this was only the beginning.

One e-mail worried him, though. It was supposedly from Antonio Cabrera, one of his Microsoft clients in Moscow. It was actually from Mohammed Jibril. The timetable had just been sped up. Rather than having a leisurely seven days to reach Atlanta and Savannah, he now had only four. Nadir wasn't sure it was even possible. But what was he going to do, write back and say no?

★ ★ ★

It was 4:37 in the morning in Washington, 11:37 a.m. in Gaza.

Marine One touched down on the icy South Lawn as the freezing rains intensified and the National Weather Service began issuing severe winter storm warnings for the District of Columbia and most counties in Maryland and Virginia. A moment later, the backup chopper landed as well, and Agent Sanchez breathed a sigh of relief.

"All units, Gambit is secure at the Ranch," Sanchez said into her wrist-mounted microphone, once they were in the Oval Office and beginning to dry off.

Sanchez turned to the president, on the phone to the Residence to check in with his wife. The First Lady had been up for hours, tracking developments on television, getting regular updates from the Situation Room, and working the phones to alert family and friends to pray for the wounded and for the families of those who'd been killed.

"Mr. President, the vice president is on the way," Sanchez said, catching MacPherson's eye. "Where would you like everyone to gather?"

Bob Corsetti and Marsha Kirkpatrick entered the room. A few seconds later, Defense Secretary Trainor and Chuck Murray joined them.

The president told Sanchez to have the vice president meet them in the Situation Room in ten minutes. The rest of the group began going over a list of questions Corsetti had worked up. Had any of the DSS agents survived? Were Bennett and his team safe? How were they going to get them out? Should Murray hold a press conference? Should the president? What would they say? What *could* they say?

★ ★ ★

No one said a word.

Bennett felt sorry for his friends Galishnikov and Sa'id. They were businessmen, not criminals or commandos. They deserved better than this. They were used to the Plaza and the Ritz and the Waldorf-Astoria. They were used to five-star hotels, not no-star hotels, and they certainly weren't used to being treated more like fugitives than like trusted allies—not since Galishnikov had emigrated to Israel, anyway. Still, neither had much of a choice, and they knew it, so they kept quiet.

Tariq stepped behind the huge wooden registration desk and pointed his flashlight down at a filthy red throw rug. Then, as Bennett and McCoy watched closely, he pulled back the rug and lifted away several loose wooden floorboards, revealing a steel doorframe. He punched a nine-digit code into an electronic keypad built into the door, and a lock clicked open. Tariq quickly slid open the thick, rectangular, steel blast door, easily moving it sideways to the right as though it were a sliding glass door leading to someone's back porch or deck.

Behind this door, set several feet down in concrete, was a round steel hatch, like one found on a submarine. To the left was a small, palm-sized glass pad onto which Tariq placed his left hand. The pad lit up fluorescent green, highlighted each of his fingerprints and his palm print, digitally scanned them, and fed them into a mainframe computer database somewhere down below, then emitted a series of muffled beeps as it processed the incoming data. A few seconds later, satisfied that the complete handprint really was that of Tariq Abu Ashad, aka Robin—Jake Ziegler's senior watch officer at Gaza Station—the hatch electronically unlocked.

"What about Mancuso?" Bennett asked.

"I'll send some guys up for him in a few minutes," Tariq answered. "We've got a morgue down below."

Bennett just looked at him. They had a morgue?

Sporadic machine-gun fire could now be heard outside. Soon the entire coastal area would be swarming with militia members, firefighters and medical personnel, and crowds eager to know the Americans' fate. Bennett offered to go down the hatch first. McCoy went down next. Then Galishnikov and Sa'id. Tariq brought up the rear, pulling the rug back in place, closing both doors above them, sealing the hatch, and rearming the alarm system.

It took a moment for Bennett's eyes to adjust. Though the main room before him was dimly lit, the technology was spectacular. It reminded him of the safe house underneath Dr. Mordechai's house in Jerusalem, the house where he'd almost died, and then it hit him again—in the Middle East, nothing was ever what it seemed.

"Mr. Bennett, I presume?"

Bennett stood there silent for a moment, stared Jake Ziegler in the eye, and took his measure. They were both about six feet tall, but the similarities stopped there. Where Bennett had short dark hair, Ziegler's bleached-blond hair was tied back in a ponytail. Bennett was an ethnic mutt, Scotch-Irish on his father's side and Greek-Italian on his mother's side. Ziegler was 100 percent German. Both of his grand-parents had escaped the kaiser's regime just before the First World War, made their way to Ellis Island, and settled just south of Pittsburgh. Bennett had his mother's olive skin, giving him a year-round look of be-ing slightly tanned though he was hardly ever outside. Ziegler couldn't have been paler. He too was rarely in the sun, but with him it showed. Bennett had perfect twenty-twenty vision. Ziegler wore thin, round, silver wire-rimmed glasses from a life spent in front of computers of all kinds and in unnaturally dark rooms in Washington and all over the Middle East.

Ziegler put out his hand. Bennett didn't shake it.

"Are the blindfolds really necessary?" Bennett asked, a bit too bluntly.

"I'm afraid they are," Ziegler said.

"These are friends," Bennett continued. "They don't deserve to be treated like criminals."

Ziegler lowered his hand, but didn't flinch. "As for saving your lives, Mr. Bennett, you're welcome. As for your friends, I will have them es-corted into a secure room where they can clean up. They'll have clean beds, hot food, plenty to drink, access to satellite television. They'll have a phone they can use to call out of the room—just within this facility, not lo-cal or international. And, of course, you'll be able to see them whenever you'd like. Beyond that, I can't help you."

Ziegler was careful not to give away his name or any information that could help Galishnikov or Sa'id identify where they were or whom they were with.

"But they're basically prisoners?" Bennett pressed.

"No, they're foreign nationals without U.S. citizenship or top-secret clearances."

"They're with me," Bennett said, his voice a bit louder. "That should be enough."

"Please, please, it's okay, Jonathan," Sa'id offered. "You've got work to do—go do it. don't worry about us. We'll be fine."

"First of all, it's not okay," said Bennett. "Second—"

"Jonathan, really," Galishnikov interrupted. "We understand. Really we do. It's okay. Ibrahim is right. Don't worry about us."

"I appreciate that," Bennett said "But like I said, it's not okay."

"It's going to have to be," Ziegler said, his placid demeanor unchanged. "Gentlemen, I appreciate your understanding of the unique situation you're now in, and your willingness to make the best of it. We'll get you all out of here just as soon as we can. But right now I've got a job to do and I need to get back to it."

Bennett took a step forward and stared hard into Ziegler's eyes. McCoy tensed. She wasn't sure what he was going to do, or how she should respond.

"If you'd been doing your job," Bennett said in a whisper, "we wouldn't be here. So now you work for me. You got that?"

Ziegler wasn't sure how to respond. Bennett was right. Moreover, he knew Bennett outranked him by a factor of ten. So did McCoy. But did that mean he was really supposed to let them take over his operation? Marsha Kirkpatrick had personally called him from the White House. She'd ordered him to give Bennett anything and everything he needed, and to set him up for a videoconference with the president that was supposed to start in just a few minutes. Ziegler was already in enough trouble. His career was already on the line. Did he really want the first thing out of Bennett's mouth when he got on the line with the president to be that Ziegler was guilty of insubordination?

"I'll need to run this past my boss," Ziegler insisted.

"*I'm* your boss," said Bennett. "Now get these guys taken care of."

Ziegler nodded. So did Galishnikov and Sa'id. Ziegler took Tariq aside and whispered something to him in Arabic. Tariq excused himself and led the two out of the main room, through a double set of soundproof doors, down a dark corridor, and out of sight as Ziegler introduced Bennett and McCoy to the rest of his team and started directing them to "seal the cave."

Ziegler's three duty officers, it turned out, were all American-born Palestinians. Each was a fluent Arabic speaker, and all were veterans of the

CIA's Directorate of Operations with at least five years' experience. Their love of the United States and willingness to die to defend her principles and values stood in marked contrast to the horror show unfolding above them, and Bennett couldn't help but be impressed with their professionalism as they moved quickly through a series of emergency procedures.

Nazir worked the computer systems, sending a new flash traffic e-mail to Langley—Code Red, Priority Alpha—backing up files and data systems, and doing a systems check on all of the myriad telecommunications systems to make sure they were still working and hadn't been compromised in any way—shut down, rerouted, or tapped, for starters. Hamid worked the physical plant, double-checking the purity of the air and water coming into the facility, firing up the auxiliary power generators, and preparing to take Gaza Station off the local power grid. Maroq unlocked the weapons vault, giving everyone instant access, if needed, to flak jackets, gas masks, and fully locked and loaded M4 submachine guns.

Only then did Bennett offer his hand.

"Jon Bennett," he said, though there was still an edge to his voice.

Ziegler eyed Bennett, then McCoy, then shook Bennett's hand. "Jake Ziegler," he finally said. "Welcome to the Bat Cave."

12
★ ★
★

BENNETT PUT his arm around McCoy's shoulder.

"My guardian angel," he said. "You guys know each other, right?"

"Just over the phone," Ziegler replied, shaking McCoy's hand. "Good to finally meet you in person, Miss McCoy."

"Thanks, JZ. Please, call me Erin—it's nice to finally put a face with the voice."

"I agree. Welcome to Gaza Station."

"Glad to be here, thanks."

"You're welcome. You guys have had a harrowing morning, to say the least."

"You could say that," said McCoy.

"I'm sure you'd like to grab some showers and some rest. But here's the deal. Mr. Bennett, in about fifteen minutes you've got a videoconference with the president and the NSC. Erin, the president wants you in on that as well."

"That's fine," she said. "I'd just like to throw on some dry clothes, but all of our luggage is at the King David in Jerusalem. We don't have anything with us."

"No problem, we'll take care of everything," said Ziegler, directing one of the guys on his team to get clothes and towels for Bennett and his team.

"What's the deal with this weather?" Bennett finally asked.

"Happens every now and then. You may be with us for a bit."

"Wonderful," said Bennett, lying.

"Any word on the DSS agents?" McCoy asked.

Ziegler looked down. The news could hardly have been worse. Thirty-four DSS agents were confirmed KIA, killed in action. Thirty-one others were missing and presumed dead. He'd just tasked one of his Predator UAVs to monitor the emergency rendezvous point, a coffee shop six blocks from the PLC building run by a CIA informant. Any DSS agents who had survived the initial series of attacks would know to head there immediately and reestablish contact with Black Tower, Gaza Station, or what might be left of the joint operation command, at PLC headquarters. Thus far, the Predator hadn't picked up any signs of life, but Ziegler wasn't giving up hope.

★ ★ ★

The president looked around the Oval Office.

His senior team huddled around him, around the desk where the Kennedy brothers had managed the Cuban missile crisis, where little John John had played hide-and-seek, where Reagan had stared down the Evil Empire. They needed to start making decisions.

First, MacPherson decided to address the nation at 7:15 a.m. EST. Two hundred seventy million Americans were about to wake up to a horror show. They didn't need play-by-play and color commentary from a bunch of network anchors and armchair analysts. They needed to hear from him directly. They needed to understand what was at stake, and know that someone was in charge. He'd condemn the attack and praise the victims, and he'd vow not to let extremists deter the American government from working for a just and lasting solution to the Arab-Israeli conflict. White House Chief of Staff Bob Corsetti took detailed notes, as did Press Secretary Chuck Murray.

It was a good start, but every point generated more questions, some practical, some conceptual. Should it be an address from the Oval Office? a statement in the briefing room? With questions? Without? For now, the president said, it was enough for Murray to put the press corps on notice and ask the networks for airtime.

Second, the president directed Murray to hold his first "gaggle"—an off-camera, background briefing for White House correspondents—promptly at 6:45 a.m.

All the major morning shows—*Today, Good Morning America, FOX & Friends,* CNN's latest incarnation, and whatever CBS was calling their show this week—would begin at the top of the hour with the shocking footage of the suicide bombing or its aftermath, whatever the network executives thought the country could stomach over cornflakes and English muffins. Then they'd cut to the White House for a preview of the live address that was coming. It was critical, therefore, for the correspondents doing their live "stand-ups" out on the North Lawn to be up to speed on the latest details, to understand precisely what the president was thinking and what was likely to happen throughout the day.

The White House needed to get ahead of this story, to shape it and mold it before someone else did. It would be up to Murray—"Answer Man"—to make that happen.

Third, the president told Corsetti to page "Shakespeare"—the president's chief speechwriter—at his home in Old Town Alexandria and get him into the West Wing immediately. The NSC's two speechwriters should also be brought in ASAP. By no later than 6:00 a.m., they'd need to have a solid draft of remarks the president could make to the country. The speech-writing team should look to Corsetti and Kirkpatrick to coordinate the message. They should aim for an address no longer than seven to eight minutes, but it had to be just right, and they had to be done by six so the president could edit and practice it, or, if need be, throw it out and start over.

★　★　★

Bennett scanned the room again.

If he was going to be pinned down in Gaza for a few hours or a few days, Bennett figured this was the place to be.

Ziegler pointed to the five large, flat-screen plasma video monitors on the walls and explained that each displayed live feeds from Predator and Global Hawk UAVs hovering over Gaza, the West Bank, and Jerusalem, or from U.S. spy satellites operating overhead. ThreatCon maps offered visual displays of the latest regional intelligence assessments from the CIA's Global Operations Center at Langley, CENTCOM's main headquarters at MacDill Air Force Base near Tampa, Florida, as well as the most up-to-date intelligence on the situation in Iraq via CENTCOM's forward command center in Doha, Qatar. A bank of state-of-the-art note-book computers tracked the latest regional intelligence feeds and periodic updates from the Mossad (Israel's equivalent of the CIA), Shin Bet (their equivalent of the FBI), and Aman (Israeli military intelligence).

A half dozen high-definition, twenty-seven-inch color televisions gave Ziegler and his team the ability to track local and regional news channels. Each was hooked up to a digital recording system that burned DVDs twenty-four hours a day, seven days a week, 365 days a year, just in case any of the material was found to be needed somewhere down the line.

Meanwhile, a dozen smaller black-and-white monitors showed a ro-tating series of images from tiny security cameras positioned all over the hotel and grounds upstairs. These images were also digitally recorded, though only kept for twenty-four hours at a time before they were erased and rerecorded. A bank of radio receivers, scanners, and digital recorders simultaneously provided Ziegler and his team the ability to listen to and store local and regional radio broadcasts, as well as intercept, monitor, and record cell-phone calls and other wireless traffic.

The Batmobile upstairs couldn't have been less aptly named. The Bat Cave Bennett was now in couldn't have been more so. There were multi-ple, independent, and redundant communications, power, water, and HVAC systems. Bathrooms. Showers. A fully stocked kitchen. A weapons and ammunition room, complete with gas masks and NBC—nuclear, bio-logical, and chemical—gear. And a medical bay, with two operating rooms, twelve hospital beds, and lifesaving equipment and supplies worthy of the best urban trauma units or mobile medical triage centers.

Only a half dozen people worked here, Ziegler said, and thus far, less than three dozen people had ever been in these rooms, including those who'd helped build it. All of them were Americans. All of them worked for the CIA. And all of them held the highest possible security clearances, plus written authorization from the president of the United States. Gaza Station was one of the most closely guarded secrets in the U.S. intelli-gence arsenal. It was expensive, and virtually irreplaceable. And that, Ziegler explained, was why he was so nervous about an Israeli and a Pales-tinian knowing anything about where they were or why.

"Israeli prime minister Doron doesn't know where we are," Ziegler ex-plained. "And the Palestinians certainly don't know. Arafat didn't. Neither did Mazen. They all figure we've got intelligence assets on the ground, and some kind of headquarters. But for obvious reasons, the less they know about my team the better."

Bennett agreed to take Ziegler's case under consideration. But he needed to change for a videoconference with the president. Everything else would have to wait.

★ ★ ★

The president moved into the Situation Room and took the call.

Israeli prime minister David Doron was on a secure line from Jerusalem. He knew the president was busy. He just wanted to reinforce what he'd said to the vice president: express his condolences and offer his full cooperation for whatever steps the president might be contemplating next.

The situation on the ground was worsening. Various security forces loyal to Arafat and Abu Mazen were on the move, beginning to engage pockets of Islamic militants in fierce gun battles. The president explained that he was about to meet with his National Security Council. He also explained the diplomatic pressure that was building from various Arab and European countries to keep the Israelis out of the crisis. He asked Doron to hold off on any military options at least until the NSC concluded its meeting. The two agreed to talk again in a few hours.

Next came a call from Russian president Grigoriy Vadim.

An NSC staffer provided simultaneous translation from Russian to English and then back again. Vadim was also calling to offer his condolences for the tragic turn of events in Gaza. He too pledged his government's help in any practical way possible. But then he too went a step further. As a member of the "Quartet"—the self-appointed guardians of the Arab-Israeli peace process made up of the United Nations, the European Union, the United States, and Russia—Vadim urged the president not to let the peace process be derailed by this act of savagery. Too much was at stake, especially after the U.S. actions in Iraq, which they both knew all too well had caused no small degree of strain between Moscow and Washington.

MacPherson was noncommittal, but promised to keep in touch with the Kremlin throughout the crisis.

✱ ✱ ✱

Tariq now led Bennett and McCoy down a hallway.

He unlocked Ziegler's private quarters, and showed them inside. There were no guest bedrooms in Gaza Station. There was no visitors' suite. So for now, Tariq explained, this was where Ziegler wanted them.

The boss had the nicest digs of anyone in the bunker, and he wanted them to be as comfortable as possible. For living in a safe house under Gaza eleven months of the year, it really wasn't bad—two leather couches, a glass coffee table, a top-of-the-line entertainment system (with TV, VCR, DVD with Dolby surround sound), bunk beds, an office chair and a desk built into the wall, a brand-new laptop, and three separate phone systems sitting side by side.

Through the walk-in closet, there was a bathroom and shower. Tariq gathered fresh towels and washcloths for each of them, and dug out some new toothbrushes, still in their boxes. For Bennett, he grabbed a white T-shirt, a thick gray fleece from the Naval Academy—Ziegler, it turned out, was an Annapolis grad—a pair of jeans, and some white athletic socks, and tossed them on the lower bunk. For McCoy, he promised to return with something similar but smaller, though he wasn't sure exactly what he'd be able to scare up. When they were ready, he'd bring them some hot soup and fresh pita, just out of the oven. He knew they had only a few minutes before the NSC meeting began. He knew they needed to get ready. So as quickly as he'd gotten them there, Tariq left the room and closed the door behind him.

Bennett and McCoy were suddenly alone.

The room was quiet. Too quiet. The only sound was the hum of the fluorescent lamp over the desk. From the moment he'd arrived in Washington, it seemed like there'd been back-to-back, wall-to-wall meetings and briefings and strategy sessions, except for Christmas Eve. They'd been at the White House, Langley, and the State Department, working from six or seven in the morning until ten or eleven at night. There'd been piles of memos to write, and piles more to read.

There were so many questions he wanted to ask her, but didn't know how. She intrigued him, and confused him, but he admired her. He wasn't sure if he'd ever really noticed it before, or acknowledged it, but he did now. She had something he wanted. She knew something he didn't. It gave her a quiet strength, a sense of purpose and confidence he found incredibly attractive. He'd thought about her a lot over the last month, but now they were finally together with no one else around and he didn't know what to say. The silence was awkward.

McCoy looked over at the dry clothes waiting for Bennett on the bunk bed. "Why don't you go ahead," she finally said, brushing away wet bangs from her eyes. "You can change in the bathroom first. I can wait."

The two were standing just inches apart, soaked to the bone.

"No, no, I'm fine," Bennett insisted. "You go first."

He stared into her eyes. She looked cold and sad. He wanted to touch her. He wanted to kiss her.

"You gonna be okay?" he asked.

"Hey, you don't have to worry about me, Jon Bennett. I'll be fine."

He knew. He just couldn't help it.

13

THE MEETING in the Situation Room had now begun.

Everyone was present and accounted for. MacPherson sat at the head of the polished mahogany table. The seal of the president was mounted on the white wall behind him, illuminated by a small lamp recessed into the ceiling. To the president's right sat Vice President Bill Oaks. White House Chief of Staff Bob Corsetti was next to him, followed by CIA Director Jack Mitchell. National Security Advisor Marsha Kirkpatrick sat directly across from the president.

To her right was the chairman of the Joint Chiefs of Staff, four-star general Ed Mutschler, with Defense Secretary Burt Trainor next to him. Then came Attorney General Neil Wittimore. The seat traditionally belonging to Secretary of State Tucker Paine was filled by Deputy Secretary of State Dick Cavanaugh, fresh in from the emergency NATO summit in Madrid.

Along the wood-paneled walls sat a senior aide for each principal; several NSC Middle East experts; Ken Costello, the undersecretary of state for political affairs and the department's senior crisis manager; and Marty Benjamin, director of the State Department's Policy Planning Staff.

"Let's get started," the president began. "First of all, I've just asked Assistant Secretary Dave Rogers to head over to Great Falls to Secretary Paine's house. As soon as there's a moment, I'll go over there myself. Bob, let's make sure all government flags are at half mast and that notifications start going out to families of the DSS agents."

"Yes, sir," Corsetti agreed, taking notes on a yellow legal pad.

"Perhaps right now," the president continued, "we could take a few minutes to pray for Claudia and the kids and the agents and their families—and, of course, for Jon and Erin and their team. Bill, would you mind leading us in prayer?"

"It would be an honor, Mr. President," the vice president said, and everyone bowed their heads and closed their eyes.

★　★　★

Yuri Gogolov was not just a chess player.

He was a Russian grand master. He seemed to see around corners and through walls. And he did not play to win. He played to conquer and humiliate, and thus far he had never lost.

Born July 2, 1949, the only son of a highly decorated Soviet colonel—the grandson of politburo members who traced their heritage back to the czars—Gogolov grew up in a gilded Moscow flat. He talked of a glorious future in the Red Army, but he secretly dreamed of a double life as the man who would destroy Bobby Fischer.

When Fischer won the U.S. Junior Championship in 1956 at the age of thirteen, he captured international headlines and the imagination of Gogolov, then a seven-year-old chess novice. Gogolov became obsessed by the world's youngest and most dangerous player. In time, he would become obsessed with the fact that the world's greatest player was not only an American but an anti-Semite from Brooklyn.

Fischer had a hatred of Jews that mirrored Gogolov's own. Fischer called the Jews "filthy, lying bastard people." He raged in public against his enemies as "Jews, secret Jews, or CIA rats who work for the Jews." He attacked the U.S. government as a "brutal, evil dictatorship." He studied *Mein Kampf*, slept under a framed picture of Adolf Hitler, and once told a friend that he admired Hitler so much "because he imposed his will on the world."

And Fischer didn't just destroy the Soviet grand masters; he crushed their will to play. In 1972, at the tender age of twenty-nine, Fischer came from behind—two games to nothing—to annihilate Boris Spassky, one of the great Soviet champions. "Now he feels like a god," Spassky fumed at the time. "Fischer thinks all his problems are over—that he will have many friends, people will love him, history will obey him. But it is not so. I am afraid what will happen to him now."

What would it feel like? Gogolov remembered thinking when he'd read that quote. *To be a god? To make the world love you and history obey you, not because you could determine the fate of little marble statues, but because you could truly command the fate of real kings and kingdoms?*

Gogolov had never liked speed chess. His game was careful and quiet. He would bide his time, plan his moves. He would follow his father's wishes, rise through the Soviet military ranks, and emerge as a *Spetznatz* special forces commander. But that would be only the beginning. Deep down, in places he never spoke of, Yuri Gogolov wanted to live the reckless, ruthless life of Bobby Fischer, perhaps the greatest chess player to have ever lived. To be him. To transcend him. To destroy him, and the country of Fischer's birth.

Now he found himself thirteen stories above Tehran—alone with his thoughts, transfixed by the coverage from Gaza. Thus far, the operation was going far better than expected, and these were only the early stages.

Gogolov soon found himself on the *New York Times* home page and began scrolling through America's newspaper of record. The lead headline: *"President Denounces Gaza Attacks; Israeli Forces Go on Full Alert."* He clicked on the story and scanned through it quickly to see if there were any tidbits he didn't yet know. And there, in the last paragraph, he hit pay dirt. *White House Press Secretary Charles A. Murray refused to comment when asked who the U.S. suspected was behind the multiple assassinations. But he confirmed that senior presidential advisor Jonathan M. Bennett escaped from the scene unharmed and is being kept in a secure, undisclosed location until his safe return to Washington can be arranged.*

Jonathan M. Bennett.

The name jumped off the screen at Gogolov. He knew very little about him, and neither Jibril nor any of the rest of his team seemed to know much either. But his name kept popping up on the radar again and again. Gogolov muted the television screens for a while and thought about that. A "secure, undisclosed location." What did that mean? Could Bennett have already gotten out of Gaza? The weather didn't permit a helicopter extraction, either by the Americans or the Israelis. The only way out of the Strip was in a car or truck or vehicle of some kind. But Al-

Nakbah operatives either controlled or were monitoring most of the major roads in and out of Gaza, though neither the Israelis nor the Americans knew it.

There'd been no word of Bennett's limousine getting past his men. It was still early. Was it possible that Bennett had eluded them and slipped out before Jibril's noose had tightened? Possible, but unlikely. More likely, thought Gogolov, was that Bennett was still inside the Strip. But for that to be true, for the White House press secretary to say that Bennett was in a "secure, undisclosed location" would mean, by definition, that the U.S. had a secure, undisclosed location inside Gaza. That would be news to Gogolov. A facility of the United Nations Relief and Works Agency? That might be undisclosed—for the moment—but it would hardly be secure. Same with the Red Cross and Red Crescent facilities. None of them were secure against Palestinian military forces, and the U.S. had to know that, particularly given the current conditions. What could possibly be a secure location inside of Gaza for a White House advisor on the run?

He would keep pondering that thought. But for now he wanted to know more about Bennett. Linked to the current story was a lead headline from the *New York Times*'s Sunday edition. Gogolov had read it a few days before, when it first came out. But now it intrigued him even more. *"Point Man for Peace: Can Wall Street Wizard Really Cut Elusive Mideast Deal?"* Gogolov took a sip of his piping hot Russian *chai*, and double-clicked to read it again.

> *The eyes of the world are on Jonathan Meyers Bennett, a Wall Street strategist turned senior advisor to the president, as he and the U.S. secretary of state head to the Middle East Monday to meet Israeli prime minister David Doron and Palestinian chairman Yasser Arafat. The mission is to jump-start peace talks in the bloody aftermath of the recent war with Iraq, but many questions are being raised about the man behind the mission.*
>
> *Bennett who? It's a reasonable question, admit senior administration sources, all of whom spoke on the condition of anonymity. At forty, the New York City native may be one of the nation's savviest and stealthiest financial deal makers. Colleagues say Bennett has an uncanny*

ability to find "buried treasure," obscure or low-profile companies whose products and stock prices are poised to explode in value. The story of how he was drafted into a White House job just last month, then seriously wounded in a hail of terrorist gunfire in Jerusalem, is told here exclusively for the first time.

Gogolov took another sip of *chai.*

But White House colleagues concede that the president's new point man for peace is inexperienced in the art of Washington politics, much less global diplomacy. Still, the president has tapped Mr. Bennett to be the chief architect of a dramatic and potentially historic peace plan about to be unveiled this week.

Gogolov kept reading.

Bennett's father, Solomon, had died of a heart attack just a few weeks ago. Gogolov hadn't known that. Nor that Bennett's mother, Ruth, now lived all alone in Florida, in a retirement community just outside of Orlando. Interesting, Gogolov thought, and his mind began to wander. Orlando. How far was that from Savannah? It couldn't be more than a few hours. He mulled the idea over for a few minutes, then logged off the Internet, clicked off the TVs, and closed his eyes.

They've sent a rookie to challenge the grand master, Gogolov thought to himself. *Better yet, they don't even realize what kind of game they're actually playing.*

★ ★ ★

Changed into dry clothes, Bennett was ready.

He sat down in the small conference room off the main control room and sipped a cup of freshly brewed coffee as Tariq gave him a microphone to clip on, set up a digital video camera, and prepared to make the video feed to the White House go live.

A few moments later, McCoy entered Gaza Station's main control room. Bennett saw her through the doorway and did a double take. She hadn't had a chance to take a shower yet, but she was drying her hair with a towel, and even in borrowed navy blue sweatpants and a white cotton

T-shirt, she looked incredible. Fortunately, she didn't catch Bennett's startled reaction, and for that he couldn't have been more thankful.

"Can I borrow that?" McCoy asked Ziegler.

"Be my guest."

She grabbed a rubber band off his desk and put her hair up in a pony-tail. Then she spotted a Yankees baseball cap sitting on a file cabinet. She snagged that, too, adjusted the plastic straps to make it smaller, put it on, and thanked Ziegler and Tariq for their hospitality. Then she came into the conference room and sat down next to Bennett. "Ready when you are, Point Man."

Ziegler had sensed something in the air between these two the moment they'd arrived. He'd seen how McCoy looked at Bennett. He'd just caught Bennett's reaction when McCoy came into the room. It didn't take Dr. Phil to know something was going on here. They didn't get many visitors at Gaza Station. Certainly not White House VIPs like Jon Bennett. And certainly not Uzi-toting, Arabic-speaking CIA supermodels like Erin McCoy. Ziegler couldn't help but find himself curious, or wonder if Bennett was really McCoy's type.

Like everyone on his team—like everyone else in Washington and governments in two or three dozen other capitals around this region and the world—he'd read the *New York Times* profile on Bennett. He'd read the quotes by Bennett's colleagues and former college roommates. He knew Bennett's MO—big money, big temper, and absolutely no experience in the Byzantine political world of the Middle East. Was McCoy really drawn to this guy? Was she really interested in someone almost ten years older than her? Maybe. But maybe not. Ziegler knew better than to assume anything. Who knew? Maybe he had a shot.

Suddenly, Ziegler's face turned ashen. The man seemed transfixed on the bank of video monitors in front of him, but Bennett couldn't see a thing. His view was obstructed, and he was about to be patched through to Washington.

"What's going on?" Bennett yelled.

"Oh no," Ziegler said, his eyes darting from one screen to the next.

"What is it?" Bennett pressed.

But for a moment, Ziegler just stood there, shaking his head, unable to speak. He punched a few buttons. The TV monitors in the conference room where Bennett and McCoy were flickered to life. The images were unbelievable. A bloodbath was under way, but neither Bennett nor McCoy understood exactly what they were seeing. Phones started ringing. Ziegler's team was moving quickly now, scrambling to get on top of the situation. E-mails started coming in from field operatives scattered throughout the West Bank and Gaza. Adrenaline was flowing and the tension in the room was palpable.

"JZ, what in the world is going on?" Bennett demanded. "I'm on with the president in less than three minutes. I've got to—"

"We've got a little situation here. We've got a huge gun battle erupting in Khan Yunis. But it's not just Khan Yunis. It's Gaza City. Hebron. Jericho. Nablus. We've got huge battles starting in most of the major Palestinian population centers."

"With who? Israelis?"

"No, that's just it—it looks like the top Palestinian security chiefs are mobilizing their forces and squaring off against each other."

"What are you talking about?" Bennett asked, trying to process what Ziegler was saying.

"I'm talking about the worst-case scenario, Jon. I'm talking about a full-blown Palestinian civil war."

14

★ ★
★

SOMETHING EVIL was moving through the streets of Gaza.

Bennett stared at the monitors in front of him. Through pouring rain and thick clouds of smoke, he could see a raging firefight under way. He could see cars overturned and consumed by flames.

Tracer bullets crisscrossed through dark alleyways, and though it was only approaching noon, it was as though an oppressive darkness had fallen over the rain-soaked city. It was impossible to assess accurately the extent of the carnage, at least by watching it from the vantage point of a Predator drone. But men, women, and children were dying. Their blood was running through the gutters.

All hell was breaking loose. That much was clear. Bennett felt severe pains shoot through his stomach and abdomen. McCoy saw him wince and hold his side.

"Gaza Station, this is Prairie Ranch."

It was Marsha Kirkpatrick in the Situation Room. The video-conference was live.

"You are now connected to a National Security Council meeting already in progress. Please authenticate."

Ziegler and Tariq scrambled to secure the connection and patch Bennett through.

"Jon, it's the president. Can you hear me?"

Bennett straightened up and tried to ignore the intense pain he was now in. He fumbled with his IFB earpiece, but after a moment or two—with McCoy's help—he was finally connected.

"Yes, Mr. President, I can—finally—and I can see you guys as well on the monitors here. Sorry for the delay."

"Are you and Erin okay?"

"We're good, sir—lucky, I guess."

"Luck had nothing to do with it, Jon. Someone's looking out for you, and it's not just our friends at Langley. What about Dmitri and Ibrahim?"

"They're okay, sir—shook up, like all of us. But physically, yes, they'll be fine."

"I understand there's been some confusion over how much access they can have?"

"Well, yes, that's true, sir."

"Let me spell it out for you, Jon, so there's no confusion. I know you've got the best of intentions. Dmitri and Ibrahim are good men— friends of peace, and of this administration. But they're not American citizens. They're not cleared. And we can't just let them go roaming around in there. You and Erin are sitting in a twenty-five-million-dollar foxhole and we can't afford to let anybody know what it is or where. You got that?"

"Yes, sir."

"Good. Now make sure those boys are well taken care of, and put them to work. Get Dmitri on the phone with Dr. Mordechai and all his pals at the Mossad. Get Ibrahim on the horn with his buddies inside the Palestinian Authority. Tell them to press their sources. Find out what they know. Find out who's behind all of this. Anything they can find out, the better. Tell them it's a personal request from me, and I won't forget their help."

"I'll do that, sir."

"Good. And how's your mom holding up? She knows you're okay?"

"No, I haven't called her yet, sir. It seemed too early, but—"

"No, no, no. As soon as we finish up here, you give her a call. You're all she's got now. You hear me?"

"Yes, sir."

MacPherson never ceased to be his surrogate father, Bennett realized, nor would he, especially now. He'd taken the young whippersnapper under his wing when he was only twenty-two. He'd taught him how to become a world-class strategist. He'd praised his successes, gently warned him about his weaknesses, and was always offering Bennett friendly advice on everything from finding good restaurants in New York to finding good ski slopes in the Rockies. And given that MacPherson had achieved every goal he'd ever set for himself—and then some—his advice was something Bennett took seriously.

"Now look, I just got off the phone with Prime Minister Doron," the president continued. "Here's the situation. State says all their DSS agents are dead. With this storm, we have no way to get you out of there right now. Doron's offering to send in ground forces to extract you. We'd have to get you all out of Gaza Station, of course. We can't let the IDF know where you are right now. But if all things go well, you could be home by tomorrow. We've all been talking about it, and most of the NSC thinks we should accept Doron's offer."

Bennett sensed MacPherson wasn't quite finished with his thought, but perhaps it was just a second or two delay in the satellite transmission.

"What do you think, Jon?" the president asked.

Bennett hesitated. He knew how much the president was investing in this Medexco deal, and it was hard for Bennett to imagine that he didn't see or understand the implications of what he was asking. The last thing Bennett wanted was to be voted down by the NSC on the first question put to him. There were a lot of other issues ahead for them to deal with. But his heart was racing. It felt as though every molecule in his body was shaking. His gut told him not to get the IDF involved. But was he really about to tell the president to turn down Doron's offer?

* * *

Merkava, in Hebrew, meant "chariot."

But the sixty-five-ton Merkava Mark 4 was more than a chariot. It was the IDF's premier battle tank. With a 120 mm smooth-bore cannon, three 7.62 mm machine guns, an internal 60 mm mortar, and dual smoke-grenade launchers, it turned a four-man crew into a death machine. Add night-vision and thermal-imaging capability, a twelve-hundred-horsepower air-cooled diesel engine, automatic fire-suppression equipment, and the most advanced nuclear, biological, and chemical protection on the face of the planet, and the Merkava was the most sophisticated weapon in the Israeli ground game. It owned the night and could smash through enemy lines at sixty kilometers an hour.

And now, while MacPherson and his National Security Council debated the merits of an Israeli ground operation, 150 Merkavas were taking up positions on the Green Line. They were preparing to sweep into the West Bank—into Nablus, Hebron, Ramallah, and Jenin, backed up with fifty more armored personnel carriers and an array of bulldozers and close air support from Apache attack helicopters, each with rapid-fire front-mounted cannons and sixteen Hellfire missiles.

At the same time, forty-five more Merkava and American-made Abrams M1 battle tanks and armored personnel carriers were also moving into position. They were preparing to blast their way into northern Gaza through the border town of Beit Lahiya, supported by two squadrons of attack helicopters and six F-18s carrying laser-guided missiles. At the southern point of the Gaza Strip, twenty more Israeli battle tanks and troop carriers were poised to cut off the main road to the dusty little Palestinian refugee town of Rafah, the last checkpoint before the Egyptian border and the vast Sinai Peninsula.

A decision needed to be made. Prime Minister Doron wasn't at all convinced he *should* send forces into the territories, or that it would serve Israel's national interests. His Security Cabinet was actually sharply divided. But all of Doron's senior advisors agreed that Washington was about to ask them to move, and they needed to look cooperative. They needed to give the American president cover by offering to go in before they were officially asked. So that's what they were doing. By sundown, everything would be set.

★　★　★

Bennett took the plunge.

"Mr. President, with all due respect to my colleagues, it would be my strongest possible recommendation that the IDF stay totally out of Gaza and the West Bank."

Everyone was stunned by Bennett's intensity, including McCoy.

Was this one of the fringe benefits of having $9.6 million socked away in the bank after years of high-stakes poker on Wall Street? she wondered. He could certainly speak his mind. He trusted his instincts, his experience. It wasn't arrogance. It was clarity and conviction, though to a competitor it might be hard to make that distinction.

"Go on," the president said, also taken aback.

"Erin and I will be fine. Sa'id and Galishnikov will be fine. We're all safe. We don't need to be taken out of here right now. What we need to do is think strategically, not tactically. Let's keep our eye on the ball. What do we know? Arafat, Mazen, and the secretary are dead. But the peace process isn't. What's just happened is horrible, but it's not fatal to the process. Just the opposite. This could be an opportunity—not one we'd want, or plan for—but let's not kid ourselves: this changes everything."

"How so?" asked the president.

Bennett's voice was gaining strength. "Sir, a week ago, we were gathered in the Oval Office arguing over whether we should be dealing with Arafat at all. Jack, you and your guys at the CIA argued that Arafat was a terrorist who'd never change his ways, didn't deserve his Nobel Peace Prize, and shouldn't be elevated by a meeting with a senior U.S. official. Marsha, you made a rather eloquent case that Abu Mazen—if he were really a potential partner for peace—could never amass enough authority to lead unless we dealt only with him, and sidelined Arafat. Secretary Paine, of course, argued that sending a delegation to Gaza and not meeting with the father of the Palestinian revolution would be so insulting that Arafat would work against us to undermine the entire peace process. He insisted that we *had* to work with Arafat, or risk shaming him in front of his people and the world."

"And?" the president pressed.

"And now they're gone. A Palestinian extremist has just assassinated the leaders of the Palestinian revolution. This is no longer about whether the U.S. refuses to deal with one or the other. It's no longer about whether the Israelis want to deport Arafat and try to prop up Mazen. They're gone. And every Palestinian—every Arab, everyone—knows it wasn't us, or the Israelis. Now they're watching this nightmare on TV, Palestinians attacking each other."

McCoy wasn't entirely sure where Bennett was headed. But her initial fears were quickly dissipating. She was fascinated to watch his mind work and wondered where all this was coming from.

"Mr. President, as you know, the confidential polls we've taken over the last few weeks show the vast majority of Palestinians are already tired of all the fighting," Bennett continued, his sentences coming quickly and with passion. "A strong majority thinks Palestinian violence has become counterproductive. They *want* the intifada to end, and they *like* what they've started to hear about our Oil for Peace deal. They're tired of the killing, the poverty, and deprivations. Sure, when we asked if they'd love to wipe out Israel and control all the land if they could, of course they said yes. But when we asked if they think that's ever really going to happen, most Palestinians said no. When we asked if they were ready to settle for a little less land in return for a share of huge oil-and-gas revenues, a significant majority said yes."

"So long as they still get part of Jerusalem," Mitchell added.

"That's right," Bennett agreed. "They still want part, if not all, of Jerusalem."

"So what's your point, Jon?" Kirkpatrick asked.

"My point is that all of our polling was done before this violence today. I guarantee you if it were possible to poll again tomorrow, we'd find the majority of Palestinians horrified by what's just happened and sick of what they're doing to themselves and the way they look to the rest of the world. I think we'd find the vast majority finally, firmly resolved to end this generation of violence once and for all."

"And . . . ," Kirkpatrick pressed.

"And we need to seize on that sentiment before it fades or changes. Mr. President, when you address the nation later this morning to mourn our losses, speak directly to the Palestinian people—offer condolences for the loss of their leadership and then ask them if this is what they want for their children and grandchildren. Tell them that 'he who lives by the suicide bomber dies by the suicide bomber'—more artfully than that, of course. But appeal to the better angels of their nature. Are they angry at Israel? Yes. And they have a right to be. Do they want to be free from occupation? Of course. Acknowledge all that. But use your line you're always quoting to us, that there's 'a time to kill and a time to heal, a time to tear down and a time to build . . . a time for war and a time for peace.' "

"Ecclesiastes, chapter 3," MacPherson said, betraying the hint of a smile.

"Right—tell the Palestinians that the time for killing and tearing down is over. Enough is enough. Tell them that tomorrow has to be a new day, a time for healing and building and making peace. Appeal to them to support new leadership that will lead them in a new direction, and lead them to the state they've always wanted but never had. But whatever you do, don't tell them that the Israelis are about to invade the West Bank and Gaza. Don't tell them that IDF tanks and helicopter gunships are going to start killing Palestinians all in the name of rescuing Jon Bennett and Erin McCoy."

The president leaned back in his chair and looked around at his senior advisors. Bennett could sense he was gaining ground, but the argument wasn't won yet.

"Jon, it's Jack Mitchell again from CIA. Can you hear me?"

"Yes, sir."

"Look, I hear what you're saying. But you're sitting on a volcano, son, and it's erupting. We've got a civil war on our hands. Three different Palestinian security forces are out there trying to butcher each other, trying to seize control of the post-Arafat environment. Somebody's got to clamp down, provide some order, and do it pronto."

"I understand, sir," Bennett cut in. "I do. You're absolutely right—we can't just sit back and ignore what's happening here. The world can't turn a blind eye. *Somebody* has to go in and do the dirty work. But it cannot be the Israelis. An Israeli invasion would destroy everything the president is trying to achieve."

"Then who's it going to be, the U.N.?" Mitchell snapped. "Come on, Jon, wake up. People are killing each other over there and your polls don't mean squat. That 'silent majority' you talk about—all those Palestinians you say want peace—first of all, I'm not sure I buy the premise. But second, none of this so-called silent majority is going to lift a finger to take on all these security forces. So a whole lot of innocent people are going to die, and who's going to get blamed? Not Arafat. He's dead. Not Mazen. He's dead. Not the E.U. They're not there. *We're* going to get blamed. Why? Because we sent the secretary of state to stir up a hornet's nest. And if the Israelis don't go in with an overwhelming show of force, and if we just sit back and watch thousands of Palestinians get slaughtered on the evening news, I don't see how that exactly furthers the cause of peace. Do you?"

No one said a word. Mitchell had a point, and it was obvious most of the president's senior team agreed, or were certainly leaning that way.

McCoy didn't know what to say. She'd seen Bennett in hundreds of meetings and negotiations over the years. She'd seen him speak his mind and play hardball when necessary. But this was completely different. She was used to hearing him make utilitarian arguments based on economic and financial considerations. She was not used to him making moral arguments based on right and wrong, good and evil. Bennett wasn't exactly known for waxing philosophical in strategy sessions of any kind, least of all closed-door sessions of the National Security Council, and given his newcomer status to the team and its standard modus operandi, it was risky. He was rocking the boat in a storm and about to be thrown overboard.

Bennett knew he was outgunned. The CIA director was, after all, one of the president's best friends and closest confidants. Moreover, even half a world away, he could feel the mood turning against him. It wasn't a sensation he was used to, and he didn't know quite what to do next. He finally looked away from Mitchell and found Kirkpatrick, then looked to the president, hoping to find a bit of reassurance. But Kirkpatrick was staring down at her notes. The president looked around the table at the others gathered with him in the Situation Room and tried to gauge their mood.

Bennett knew he had to say something. Leave no charge unanswered. It was the cardinal rule of brinkmanship, business or political. But what exactly was he supposed to say? He was already sinking fast. Was he now going to recommend that the president send ground troops into the West Bank and Gaza instead of the Israelis? Was he insane? Why not just play Russian roulette with every chamber loaded?

The silence was unnerving. He had to speak. If not, the case would be closed. He'd lose by default. The peace process would be finished for decades to come, and all these deaths would be for naught. Bennett cleared his throat and shifted in his seat. But before he could speak, the vice president suddenly stepped in and cut him off.

"Mr. President, with your permission, I'd like to say a few words."

That was it. He'd waited too long.

"Please, Bill, go right ahead," said the president, almost visibly relieved.

"Thank you, Mr. President. I'll be brief."

McCoy quietly slid a piece of paper across the conference table, out of camera range. Bennett opened the note, read it to himself, then crumpled it and looked back at the VP, now beginning to speak.

"I've been listening to this conversation with great interest."

Bennett braced himself. Oaks was about to lower the boom.

"I must say that with all due respect to my friend Jack Mitchell, for whom I have the highest regard, I'm afraid I find myself with Jon on this."

Bennett looked up. So did McCoy.

"Look, all of us know our Edmund Burke—'The only thing necessary for evil to triumph is for good men to do nothing,'" the VP continued. "We have to do *something*. But the more I look at the situation, the less comfortable I am with the Israelis going in. Not because I don't trust them. I just think Jon's right."

No one was more surprised than Mitchell. His stony expression said it all.

"An Israeli invasion," the VP continued, "even if it's called a rescue operation, will simply inflame an already terrible situation and make peace efforts all but impossible. The Jordanians and Egyptians want to be helpful, but won't be—can't be—if the Israelis invade. Russia is offering intelligence assistance. But that's off if Israel moves in. And given what else is happening in the region, the risk of a wider war is too big. I'm not saying I've got a perfect solution. I'm not saying I've got *any* solution at the moment. But, Mr. President, I'm pretty clear on what *not* to do."

McCoy reached over and squeezed Bennett's left hand. It was trembling. He'd just gained a major ally. But would it be enough?

15

CHECKPOINTS WERE UP on all roads and bridges leading into Washington.

It was still dark, still well before morning rush hour. But the Secret Service and D.C. Metro Police were taking no chances. The security perimeter was rapidly being expanded. Concrete barricades were being put into place in a five-block radius around the White House, Capitol, Supreme Court, and other major landmarks. SWAT teams began taking up positions on the roofs of key buildings. Counterterrorism assault units armed with Stinger missiles were being deployed throughout the city. Avenger antiaircraft missile batteries surrounded the Pentagon. Police reconnaissance helicopters patrolled the skies—spotlights and thermal-imaging cameras looking for any signs of trouble—while U.S. Air Force F-16s armed with Sidewinder missiles roared overhead.

The White House itself was in total lockdown. Even staff members with West Wing clearance would be subject to extensive searches, metal detectors, and questioning by the Secret Service.

Jack Mitchell regrouped. He wouldn't argue with the VP directly. He'd simply focus the president on the facts. He introduced Jack Ziegler, his man in Gaza, then fired a series of questions at him, each more difficult than the one before. What did he make of all the horrific video images they were seeing flashing across their screens? What exactly was happening on the ground? Who was doing what to whom? And, more important, were Jon Bennett and the vice president right? Should the Israelis stay out of the territories, or was it essential for them to move in immediately, before the situation really got out of hand? And if the Israelis did move in, what were the prospects that such a move could trigger a wider conflict in the Middle East, drawing in the Syrians, or the Egyptians, or Hezbollah forces in southern Lebanon, backed by the mullahs in Iran?

Jake Ziegler was about to get caught in a political cross fire. He began on safe, neutral ground, explaining that the stakes couldn't be higher. There was no question the region was a powder keg, and the fuse was already lit. They did need to be careful of how to proceed. But there was no clear right or wrong answer.

Iraq, of course, was in shambles, and Palestine was going up in flames. More than a million Iraqi Shi'ites were expected to take to the streets in the next few days in southern Iraqi cities such as Karbala and Al Kut. Iran was adding fuel to the fires. The latest satellite photos and reports from sources on the ground indicated that Iranian Shi'ite intelligence agents and volunteer agitators were infiltrating southern Iraq. Using smuggling routes dating back for centuries, routes that ran through Baluchistan, Halabja, and the island of Abadan in the southwest corner of Iran, these provocateurs were stirring up the local populations against the United States and calling for an independent, pro-Iranian state. Sixty percent of Iraqis were Shi'ites, after all, and shared not just a religious affinity with Iran but a mutual hatred for Saddam's regime.

Tehran also seemed to be opening up lines of communication with Damascus, encouraging the Syrian regime to continue accepting senior Iraqi military officials and to resist any and all American pressure to the contrary. And Hezbollah did appear to be moving militia units and Kaytusha rocket forces from the Bekaa Valley in eastern Lebanon, along the Syrian border, southward toward the border with Israel.

How would it all play out? Ziegler thought to himself. How was he supposed to answer that? He had no idea. He was a station chief, not a god. The director of Central Intelligence was asking him to predict the future. But the events of the past few hours had rattled him. How could he predict the future when he could barely understand the past? He and his team had missed all the signs of an assassination plot against the secretary of state, Yasser Arafat, and Abu Mazen. What right did he have to speculate on what else might be coming?

But the president was waiting for an answer, so he plunged in. "What does all this mean here in the West Bank and Gaza? Well, sir, I think the best way to understand what's going on right now is to take a step back and think about *The Godfather*."

"*The Godfather*?"

"Remember in the first movie, when Marlon Brando—Vito Corleone—has a heart attack in the garden while playing with his little grandson?"

"Of course."

"Remember what his son Michael worries might happen?"

Ziegler let the question hang in the air for a moment, then answered it himself. "Michael worries that now that his father is dead, someone close to him—perhaps one of his own bodyguards—will conspire against him, even while claiming to set up a meeting to talk about a peace deal. That's what the Godfather warned Michael about shortly before his death, right? 'The one that comes to you to set up a meeting, he's the rat, he's the Judas, he's the betrayer,' right?"

"Right."

"Okay, and that's exactly what happens. The Corleone family is betrayed by one of their bodyguards."

Ziegler had the president's attention now. He had all their attention now.

"I'm with you," MacPherson said. "Continue."

"Okay, next, Michael worries that the result of the betrayal will be that other crime families in New York will try to have him assassinated. Why? So they can take over the operation and consolidate their power base. And it's not an idle concern, is it? Again, that's exactly what happens. The Corleones' enemies are, in fact, plotting to move into the power vacuum created by the death of the Godfather to seize control and wipe out Michael and his family. But that's not all. Third, Michael worries that one of his own brothers—someone he loves, someone he thinks he can trust—will sell him out, maybe for money, maybe for power, maybe for a little respect from someone, somewhere. It's not really important why. It's not the motivation behind the betrayal that worries Michael so much as the act of conspiracy and betrayal itself. So remember what happens next?"

The president didn't. Neither did Bennett.

"Coolly, methodically, mercilessly, Michael sends his thugs to hunt down and kill his enemies, one by one," Ziegler continued. "He has competing crime bosses killed. He has his brother-in-law killed. He even has his own brother killed after that whole thing in Cuba. The point, sir, is that we're watching the same thing play out right in front of us. We're watching a series of mafia crime families battle for control. The big question isn't whether they're all going to fight to the death until someone gains total control. That's a given. The question is, which one of the Palestinian faction leaders is actually Michael Corleone? Who's the real heir to the throne? Who's thinking strategically? Who's thinking ahead? Who's playing speed chess, and which one of these guys can see five, ten, fifteen moves ahead? The war to succeed Arafat—the Godfather, the last don of Gaza—is under way, Mr. President, and things are going to get far bloodier."

Ziegler took a drink of water, in part to catch his breath and think about what he needed to say next, and in part to let the grim truth of what he was saying sink in. A moment later, he cleared his throat and continued. "In Gaza, troops controlled by Interior Minister Mohammed Dahlan—basically the overall head of security for the Palestinian Authority—appear to be squaring off against Marwan Barghouti's Fatah-Tanzim faction. Dahlan's forces are also being activated in the West Bank. My team just intercepted a flurry of calls from Dahlan's headquarters to his commanders in Ramallah, Hebron, and Jericho, all on the West Bank. They're mobilizing every fighter they've got and vowing not to leave any enemy standing. Still, that said, for the moment, Dahlan's forces—strong as they are—will have to play catch-up on the West Bank."

"Why? Who's in control there right now?"

"On the West Bank, Colonel Jibril Rajoub's forces seem to have the upper hand. Now, technically—legally—Rajoub and his West Bank security forces are supposed to report to Dahlan. But it's not playing out that way. Most of Rajoub's forces are loyal first and foremost to Rajoub himself. He's commanded them for years. And now comes the moment of truth. What's interesting is that the moment Arafat was assassinated Rajoub personally got on the phone and started mobilizing his troops. We picked up that call. They hit the streets immediately. They're seizing PA buildings. They're seizing radio stations and newspaper offices. They've begun moving into Hebron, where an intense gun battle is under way, one of the bloodiest anywhere in the territories. Marwan Barghouti's Tanzim forces are fighting back. But early indications look as though they're being overrun by Rajoub's guys."

The vice president cut into the conversation now.

"JZ, it's Bill Oaks."

"Yes, Mr. Vice President."

The two had known each other for several years, having met during a Senate Intelligence briefing on Capitol Hill some time back.

"JZ, what's unclear to me is whether one of these factions set all this into motion. I mean, is it possible to tell who started all this? Did this al-Rashid character, Arafat's personal security chief, do all this on his own? That's hard to believe."

"The lone-gunman theory does seem suspect, I agree," Ziegler answered. "My initial sense is that al-Rashid was told to do this suicide bombing. I don't know by whom. Was it one of the faction leaders—one of the sons, as it were? Or was it by someone from the outside? I don't know. There were obviously others planted in nearby buildings, armed with AK-47s and RPGs, who were told to move in and attack our guys once the initial suicide bombing occurred. So who was controlling them? I'm afraid all we have right now are questions, not a whole lot of answers."

"I know I'm asking you to guess," said the president, "but what I want to know is whether there's one suspect in your mind that emerges out of the pack."

"Any one of these guys—Dahlan, Rajoub, Barghouti, you name it— any of them could plausibly be responsible. They've all had their blowouts with Arafat. They've all had reason to hate him, and each of them is poised to benefit enormously by his death, if they can wrestle control from the others. The only thing for sure right now is that nothing's for sure."

★ ★ ★

It was getting dark and he had no choice.

Daoud Juma flipped on his headlights and pushed the Renault to its limits. Along a highway hugging the contours of the Euphrates River, he raced westward across the desert at almost eighty miles an hour. But with all of the sand and dust, he was terrified of clogging up the car's systems and breaking down in these godforsaken wastelands. The last thing he could afford was to be stranded in western Iraq while U.S. Special Forces were still on the hunt.

His last set of instructions couldn't have been more clear. He needed to be in Damascus. Syrian intelligence would be waiting for him in the Iraqi frontier town of Al Qa'im, if he could make it that far, then smuggle him across the border into the Syrian village of Abu Kamal. They would then hide him in the trunk of a car and head north, taking him to a mosque on the outskirts of the capital. He'd meet up with an Al-Nakbah control agent and receive food, cash, new clothing, new passports, and a green light to carry out his mission.

He'd been studying English for almost two years now. But he'd never actually set foot in the United States. He would soon. This was it, he told himself. The moment for which he'd been training—and for which he'd been training so many others—was almost here, and he could hardly wait.

Suddenly, up ahead—near the junction of the ancient town of Annah—Daoud saw two vehicles pulled over on the side of the road. One looked like a Range Rover. The other looked like a minivan of some kind. Daoud began to worry. He couldn't turn around now. They'd already seen him, and where was he supposed to go? He turned his high beams on to get a better look. A number of men were milling about, and two were standing in the road pointing rifles at him. He glanced into his rearview mirror. There was no one behind him. Should he gun it and plow through these guys? The chance of making it through alive seemed remote, at best. He slowed down and pulled the Renault onto the shoulder, trying to be as careful and nonconfrontational as possible.

The men's faces were covered by kaffiyehs. At first glance, they didn't appear to be Americans or Brits, but one couldn't be sure. He considered reaching under his seat and grabbing his 9 mm, but thought better of it. He could now see four more men aiming rifles at him. He'd never survive a firefight under these conditions. He was alone, without his "followers."

One of the men rapped on his window with the barrel of a pistol. He spoke Arabic, with a Tikriti accent. Daoud rolled down the window and felt the gun press against his left temple. The men were shouting at him now, cursing and waving their guns. When they told him to get out of the Renault with his hands in the air, he complied without a word. When they told him to lie down in the middle of the road, spread-eagle, he did that too without a sound. Now a cold steel barrel was pressed into his right ear. A man was standing over him, his foot on Daoud's back, barking questions.

Yes, he had extra cans of fuel, Daoud answered. Yes, he had enough to get to the Syrian border. Yes, he had supplies of food and water and cell-phone batteries. But when they asked him his name, Daoud refused to speak.

The man standing over him asked him again. But Daoud refused to say anything. He didn't know who they were. He couldn't afford to trust them. He had his mission and he wasn't about to compromise it now, so close to the goal. He heard the bolt action of several rifles. He could see men inside his car, opening up boxes and rifling through his papers. A few seconds later, one of the men shouted out his name. Was that fear in his voice, or just surprise? Daoud's entire body stiffened. He closed his eyes and said a silent prayer to Allah. He wasn't ready to die. Not yet.

"Are you *the* Colonel Daoud Mohammed Juma?"

Daoud said nothing.

"Are you the commander of Saddam's elite fedayeen forces?"

"Are you actually the head of Q1?"

Daoud's mind began to race. He tried to understand what was happening. How could they know him? None of the papers he was carrying with him identified his name, much less his rank or mission. He didn't have a driver's license. The car was stolen so the registration couldn't give him away. His credit cards were stolen. The cash he had with him was untraceable. The 9 mm was standard issue by Iraqi intelligence, the Mukhabbarat, without serial numbers. Half the men on this road had to have the same kind of weapon with them.

The desert night was cold but Daoud felt nothing. And then, a command went out in Arabic for all the men to put down their weapons. Everyone obeyed immediately. The cold steel barrel came off Daoud's ear. The steel-toed boot came off his back. Daoud was quickly helped to his feet and dusted off. Then another command, and all the men bowed down to him.

"We are Q5," said one man, his voice trembling ever so slightly.

For a moment, Daoud had trouble accepting what was happening.

"We are Q11," said another, still bowing but taking off his kaffiyeh. Daoud still couldn't believe it. These were fedayeen under *his* command. These were *his* men carrying out *his* orders—on their way to Syria, then to Germany and France, then on to Canada and the United States to complete the mission for which they had been hand chosen and relentlessly trained.

All of them knew who Colonel Daoud Juma was. He was nearly a legend within Saddam Hussein's special operations directorate. And now here he was, in person, standing in front of them. It had to be the divine intervention of Allah. These men wouldn't kill him. They would kill *for* him.

Daoud tried to shake the confusion from the edges of his mind, and began giving orders. Ten minutes later, all the vehicles were refueled. The men ate some of his food and were back on the road, heading to the Syrian border. Together.

✴ ✴ ✴

Ziegler finished speaking.

It was a grim assessment, and Bennett thought it left them right back where they had started. If the president accepted Doron's offer, the Israelis would move in by nightfall and any chance for some kind of a peace deal being struck during the MacPherson administration would be lost. Moreover, the Israeli action could in fact trigger a wider war. But if the president refused Doron's offer, and Palestinians slaughtered themselves on worldwide television and the U.S. did nothing, wouldn't the result be the same? Wouldn't the U.S. be condemned around the world? Wouldn't other Arab and Islamic forces be tempted to take matters into their own hands? Wouldn't the prospects for peace suffer the same fate as Arafat, Mazen, and Paine?

The U.S. couldn't exactly trust the U.N. to go in and restore order, and Congress would go ballistic if the president was even perceived as contemplating such a move. The U.S. itself had plenty of forces in the region, in Iraq and in the eastern Mediterranean. But they couldn't use them in Palestine. They were already occupying one Arab country. Invading the West Bank and Gaza wouldn't exactly endear them to the local population, or bring them closer to their strategic objectives.

In less than two hours, the president would address the nation, and the world. But what should he say? What did the U.S. want to achieve? What *could* it achieve?

16
★ ★
★

GALISHNIKOV AND SA'ID were emotionally and physically drained.

They'd each seen men and women die before. But this was different. There was a savagery to the killings that neither of them had experienced before. Both men knew the history of the region and the risks of living there. But neither had ever personally witnessed a suicide bombing. They'd never seen people vaporized. Nor had they ever expected to see Americans attacked like this.

It had never dawned on them that they or anyone in this delegation might be in real physical danger. Like many people around the world, they sometimes had mixed feelings about American foreign policy and the role of the United States in trying to advance—some would say *impose*—her brand of democratic capitalism around the globe. But also like so many non-Americans, they still subconsciously thought of the U.S. as somehow invulnerable to attack.

Obviously they were wrong. And now they knew it firsthand. From their "gilded cage"—Tariq's private quarters—neither man was being allowed to call home or send and receive e-mails. Not yet, anyway. They could, if they wanted, watch satellite television and monitor the Internet off two notebook computers, one for each of them. But neither wanted to think about how many people were wounded and dying above them. They'd had enough of bloodshed and suffering. They'd had enough of wars and rumors of wars. So, alone and unsure of what Bennett and McCoy were doing or how long they might be here, they kept the TV and computers turned off. Each man mostly kept to himself. One showered and shaved. The other drank tea and read a new John Grisham novel. Eventually, Sa'id fell asleep on one of the bunk beds while Galishnikov dozed off in one of the overstuffed chairs.

* * *

It was 6:23 a.m. Washington time, 1:23 in the afternoon in Gaza.

More information and analysis weren't going to help. The president needed to get back to the Oval Office. He needed time to think and make some decisions. He thanked everyone for his and her counsel and asked each principal to continue coordinating throughout the morning through Marsha Kirkpatrick. He'd let them know what he finally decided through her. Agent Sanchez opened the door of the Situation Room and prepared to wheel the president out. Chuck Murray was waiting for them. He had to brief the press at 6:45 and had no idea what he was supposed to say.

"Jon," the president suddenly said, looking back at the monitor. "You still there?"

Bennett was just beginning to unhook his microphone. "Yes, sir, Mr. President. I'm still here."

"One more thing, young man."

"What's that?" Bennett asked, hoping to find out what the president was going to decide.

"Don't forget to call your mother."

And with that, the transmission went dead.

* * *

The two men couldn't have been more different.

Both Galishnikov and Sa'id were born into poverty. Both were the first in their families to graduate from college and the first to become professionals, a petroleum engineer and an investment banker, respectively. Each of them was forced to leave his homeland in his early twenties, Galishnikov because he emigrated from Russia to Israel, and Sa'id because he couldn't make a living under the Arafat regime and had moved to the Persian Gulf, where he became one of the world's wealthiest Palestinians. But that's where the similarities came to an end.

Sa'id was a fatalist. He had seen his share of hardship. For all their tough talk and lofty pro-Palestinian rhetoric, most Egyptians, Jordanians, and Saudis—most Arabs, actually—despised Palestinians and treated them, at best, as second-class citizens. For some, this planted the seeds of victimhood. But not for Sa'id. Over the years he'd become more optimistic about life. He'd seen challenges turn into opportunities. He'd seen his small investments pay big dividends and his start-up companies become behemoths. He was convinced that his fate was not in his own hands. Deep in his soul he believed unseen forces were guiding him, keeping him from harm, giving him a measure of success of which he'd never dreamed, and somehow protecting him from developing a hatred for the Jews that infected so many of his fellow Palestinians, and certainly each of his three brothers.

Galishnikov, on the other hand, was a pessimist of the first order. He was absolutely convinced that utter disaster was always just around the corner. Sometimes—like today—it was hard to argue that he was wrong. Even before the attacks of the last few hours, Galishnikov had been convinced that everything the two men had worked for was falling apart. He worried particularly about the new dynamics in Iraq. Yes, he was glad Saddam was gone. But suddenly he faced a fearsome new competitor.

How much oil did the Iraqis really have? How many wells had been blown up and set on fire by Saddam's forces? How badly had Iraq's drilling, production, and refining facilities been damaged during the war? How badly had they atrophied during decades of neglect by dismal managers, poorly trained workers, shoddy workmanship, pathetic maintenance regimes, and the lack of readily available spare parts and supplies? And more to the point: how quickly could the Iraqi oil industry be revamped and brought on line, how much would it cost, who would pay for it, and how would it all affect Medexco, the joint Israeli-Palestinian petroleum company of which Galishnikov and Sa'id were cofounders?

Iraq posed an enormous threat to Medexco, Galishnikov believed. The business plan he and Sa'id had created for their joint venture hadn't envisioned—much less factored in—Saddam Hussein and his regime being gone, the Americans and Brits being in control of Baghdad, and millions of barrels of Iraqi oil flooding the market within the next few months. How exactly were they supposed to deal with those new prospects? Even if through some miracle the Palestinian civil war now under way could somehow be brought under control—and even if Medexco's initial drilling, pumping, refining, and shipping centers could be completed and brought on line in the next eighteen to twenty-four months—how could they compete against a revitalized Iraqi oil industry?

After the Saudis and the Canadians—now with 180 billion barrels of proven reserves, thanks to advanced drilling and refining equipment just coming onto the market—the Iraqis had the third-largest oil reserves in the world, with more than 112 billion barrels of proven crude oil reserves. At one point—before the Iran-Iraq war—the Iraqis had been producing as many as 3.5 million barrels of oil a day. More recently, they were producing only two-thirds that amount, and of course production had been shut down completely when the latest war with the U.S. and its coalition allies began.

But new reports coming out of CENTCOM suggested that the country's southern oil fields could be back on line soon. They could begin producing more than a million barrels a day sometime within the next seven to eight weeks. The Rumeila South oil field alone could be producing half a million barrels of oil a day within a month or two, and production in the northern oil-rich cities like Mosul and Kirkuk could be even higher.

Iraq could be pumping 2.5 to 3 million barrels of oil a day by the end of the next year. Export sales could bring Iraq somewhere between $20 billion and $25 billion a year. Possibly more—possibly much more, especially since U.S. officials were saying that significant investments in repairs and new technology could double oil output over the next few years. Did that mean Iraq could really be in a position to sell upward of 7 million barrels a day?

Setting aside for a moment whether OPEC would allow the new Iraqi government to flood the market, neither Galishnikov nor Sa'id had factored any of that into their plans. Nor had Bennett and McCoy. And now Iraq would soon be getting not only U.S. and British help but U.N. and E.U. assistance as well.

Ibrahim Sa'id had been trying for weeks to convince his Russian partner that he was missing the big picture. First of all, Sa'id argued, it would require a massive investment of foreign capital—a minimum of $3 to $5 billion over the next couple of years—simply to get Iraqi oil production back up to pre–Gulf War levels from 1990 and 1991.

Second, while it was true that Iraqi oil production could eventually be doubled, that would likely take at least five years, and more likely ten to fifteen years.

Third, a new, pro-Western, pro-American oil-producing regime in Baghdad could mean a dramatic shake-up of the internal politics and practices of OPEC. As the biggest player on the block, it was the Saudis who effectively controlled OPEC. But tensions were again rising between the U.S. and the royal family. They were demanding that all U.S. military forces leave the kingdom forever, and just last weekend President MacPherson had sent Defense Secretary Burt Trainor to Riyadh to agree to an American withdrawal. What did that mean? Sa'id argued it meant the cozy ties between the United States and Saudi Arabia could very well be coming to an end. The U.S. could be looking for new, non-OPEC oil partners. It could eventually begin shifting its massive oil purchases from Saudi Arabia to Iraq, and then—*inshallah*, if God was willing—to Medexco. Yes, that might take time, but Sa'id was convinced it was possible, and anything that made the oil cartel weaker would make it easier for Medexco to operate internationally.

Fourth and finally, no Iraqi oil—or, to be more precise, precious little Iraqi oil—could or would be sold on the world markets until the U.N. sanctions were lifted and the oil-for-food program was scrapped entirely. There was no question, Sa'id agreed, that the sanctions would eventually be lifted and those oil sales would begin. But exactly when was an open question. There were serious disagreements among key Security Council members and within the secretary-general's office itself on how to proceed. It could take months to work itself out, and every delay could help Medexco move closer toward achieving its own objective: being fully operational and ready to sell Israeli and Palestinian oil and natural gas on the world markets.

Galishnikov wasn't sure what to make of it all. Sa'id's argument had merit. But Galishnikov was an anxious man, a cautious man, perhaps even somewhat paranoid. He found it hard to trust, and harder still to relax. But he came by his neuroses honestly. His were traits conceived in persecution, born in suffering, and refined in the gulag. He'd been a Jewish petroleum engineer at the height of the Soviet empire, arrested by the KGB and sentenced to eight years' hard labor in Siberia, only to be brought back to Moscow and sentenced to three years in Lefortovo, the KGB interrogation prison.

The fact that he, an atheist Russian Jew, was alive at all was its own miracle. The fact that he was now a multimillionaire CEO of an Israeli petroleum company in a historic joint venture with Ibrahim Sa'id and Jon

Bennett, now an advisor to the president of the United States, was even more remarkable. Maybe he should have faith that this deal really would work out. Maybe he should have faith that they'd all get rich beyond their wildest imaginations.

He'd come this far, hadn't he? Maybe the end wasn't so near.

★ ★ ★

"Pretty impressive in there," McCoy whispered in Bennett's ear.

Bennett wasn't ready to claim victory. "What do you think he's going to do?"

"I think he's going to follow your advice."

"Really? Why?"

"Two reasons. First, it's the right thing to do, and you made the case well. Second, if he has to, the president can always change his mind and tell the Israelis to go in after all. But it's better to hold them back as long as possible."

Bennett again winced in pain.

"You look awful," McCoy said, feeling his forehead.

"My stomach is killing me. My head's killing me."

"Lie down for a while. There's nothing we can do until the president decides."

"I don't know. Maybe you're right."

The two got up and headed back toward Ziegler's quarters.

"You need me for anything right now?" McCoy asked when they got there. She was finally about to get a hot shower and some desperately needed rest.

"No, take it easy for a little while. You deserve it."

"What about you?"

Bennett promised to lie down soon. First he needed to connect with Galishnikov and Sa'id and get them working the phones, per the president's directive. He made sure McCoy got into the room, then figured out which hallway led to their two friends.

"Hey, don't you have a phone call to make?" McCoy called after him.

Bennett turned around.

"President's orders." She smiled.

"Don't worry." He smiled back. "I won't forget."

17
★ ★
★

BENNETT ARRIVED at the "holding room."

It was actually Tariq's private quarters, and Bennett entered the
seven-digit access code Tariq had given him earlier. The door unlocked
electronically. Galishnikov stood up immediately as Bennett entered their
room. Sa'id remained seated. He said nothing, but his eyes spoke volumes. The storm raging over Gaza was also raging within him.

"Jonathan, how are you, my friend?" Galishnikov asked, shaking his
hand.

"Hanging in there, thanks—please, have a seat. You guys all right in
here?"

"Couldn't be better," the Russian lied.

"You guys aren't watching the coverage?"

"Ibrahim has . . . well, we've both had enough sadness," Galishnikov
answered.

"Look, I'm really sorry about this—you guys don't deserve to—"

"*Nyet, nyet*, please, Jonathan, you don't have to explain. We're safe.
We're well fed—well, Ibrahim refuses to eat, but I'm well fed—and we're
all washed up."

Despite the gloomy mood, Bennett couldn't help but laugh. "You've
had showers then?"

"That too," said Galishnikov, a thin smile on his face.

He sat down on the couch beside Sa'id. Bennett sat down next to them
in an armchair. There was so much he needed to tell them, and even more
he needed them to do. But it was also apparent to him that he needed to

respect the trauma both men were experiencing. Each handled it differently, and there was an awkward restlessness in the room.

Finally, Sa'id broke the silence. "Arafat was like a father to us. He was like our Moses. He wandered around with us through the wilderness for many years. He talked tough to the pharoahs—to Bibi and Sharon and Doron—all of them. He put our cause on the world's map, and that was no small thing. But there is more to leadership than making noise. You must make progress. You must achieve something.

"And where are we now? Arafat lived by the sword, and now he has died by the sword. For decades, he has been playing a dangerous game—talking peace in English and encouraging an armed revolution in Arabic. I could not swallow it and so I left to make my fortune elsewhere. Because if you play a game like that you are going to lose. I do not care how clever you think you are; you cannot live a lie for so long without being found out. I knew one day Arafat's game would catch up with him, and now it has. And who is suffering? Is he? Is Arafat? No. Perhaps he is in the arms of seventy virgins. I don't know. I am not a devout Muslim, and for all his talk I am not sure if Arafat even believed in Allah. I don't know where he is right now. But I know where I am. I know where my people are."

Sa'id stared into the screen of a television that wasn't on. "He should have followed Oslo. He should have taken Barak's deal at Camp David. He should have accepted Bush's Road Map. Anything. But he did not. And now we have nothing."

Bennett was silent. He'd never heard Sa'id talk this way.

"Just like Moses," Sa'id continued, "Yasser Arafat had his day, but he never took us into the Promised Land."

Galishnikov was hardly religious, but he snorted at the irony.

"Well, okay, we're already in the Promised Land," Sa'id conceded.

"The *over*-Promised Land," his Russian friend added.

"Yes, the Palestinian people are here geographically. But have we arrived emotionally? diplomatically? financially? Look at us. We are lost. We are a proud people, Jonathan, rich in culture and heritage and intellectual capital. And we have a serious case to make to the world. We have suffered much, first under the Egyptians and the Jordanians who did nothing to give us a state, and now for all these years under the Israelis who treat us like rabid dogs in a kennel, present company excepted."

Galishnikov waved him off, unoffended.

"After all these years," Sa'id continued, his anger controlled but rising, "after all this suffering, after so many wars and intifadas, what do we have to show for ourselves? Our people live in squalor. Around the world, *Palestinian* means terrorist, criminal, suicide bomber. And what did Arafat do? Did he lift a finger to stop the violence? Recently, yes, a bit. But for years—while we lived under curfew, and the tourists dried up, and incomes went into the toilet—did he rein in the violence? Did he throw the gangsters into prison? Did he claim the moral high ground and lead us to a new era of peace and prosperity, much less freedom and democracy?"

No one said a word.

"No. Arafat said nothing—*did* nothing—when Saddam Hussein sent money to Palestinian families to turn them into suicide bombers. How did that help us? The E.U. and you Americans send millions of dollars in aid to help build a Palestinian economy and society. So where is it? Who has gotten wealthy here in Palestine? No one. I made my money in the Gulf, not here. Why? Why can't Palestinians grow and prosper here? The Israeli occupation? Of course. But that is not the only reason. It was because of Arafat and his corrupt regime. Everybody knew it. Let me put it to you this way, Jonathan. Are you on the *Forbes* four hundred list yet?"

Bennett shook his head.

"No, not yet. But I am sure you will be someday. That is a dream of yours, I know. And I am sure you are going to achieve it. But Yasser Arafat? He is already on that list. *Forbes* says he has—had—more than 1.3 billion stashed away, probably in Swiss banks. How? How did Arafat make that money? Was he a Wall Street strategist like you? Did he produce and refine and ship oil like me? How did he make all that money? That is my point. Yasser Arafat got rich stealing people's money, stealing people's dreams, while the Palestinian people kept sinking further and further.

"Jonathan, I am not about to say these things in public, in Ramallah or Jenin or Gaza City. Certainly not now. I would be shot by Rajoub or Dahlan or one of Arafat's other thugs. But someone has to say these things. Someone has to stop this madness. It is insanity. I mean, just look at what has happened. Arafat spent the last twenty years turning up his nose at various peace plans and funding an entire generation of suicide bombers. Now the whole country is committing suicide."

"Do you see *any* chance for peace, Ibrahim?" Bennett asked, wondering why he'd done so the moment the words left his lips.

The businessman leaned back and sighed. "You know, the strange thing, Jonathan, is that I do. People want this madness to end. It was true when I woke up this morning. I think it is even more true now. They want the freedom of which your president speaks—freedom from hatred, freedom from fear. They want democracy. They are worn down—worn out. Not everyone. There are still radicals out there, obviously. But with your war against Iraq, something happened. People watch Al-Jazeera. They listen to the BBC. They see most Iraqis rejoicing that Saddam and his evil regime are dead. They see Iraqis free even to curse the very Americans who set them free. And Palestinians want that too. They are hungry for freedom after being starved half to death. And they are beginning to believe that a half a loaf of something might be better than nothing at all."

✯ ✯ ✯

European and Asian financial markets were already reacting.

Investors around the world could see the handwriting on the wall and were rushing to short sell American companies. Most foreign stock exchanges were down 5 to 6 percent already. MacPherson expected the New York Stock Exchange to lose between 6 and 8 percent at the opening bell. Tech stocks would probably do worse. The NASDAQ could easily lose upward of 8 or 9 percent. Trillions of dollars in corporate value were going up in smoke, or were about to. It would only get worse.

He needed to get the economy back on track. Not just consumer confidence. He needed to muscle his flat-tax plan through Congress, and he'd lay out all the details during the State of the Union, just a few weeks away.

At least the prospect of imminent, cheap, abundant Gulf oil was calming inflation fears. Iraq, after all, had the second-largest proven oil reserves in the world, behind Saudi Arabia. Once Iraqi wells got back on line, the price of sweet crude would begin to drop from the wartime high of over $43 a barrel back to around $25 a barrel. Once Iraq's oil industry was modernized, prices could very well drop below $20 a barrel. And if the Medexco oil and natural gas fields off the coasts of Israel and Gaza ever got going . . . well, perhaps that was too much to think of, dream of, or imagine.

But the president couldn't help it. He knew the moment was right. The Middle East *was* poised for a new era of peace and prosperity. Bennett's plan was solid. Saddam Hussein was gone. Rank-and-file Palestinians were exhausted from years of fighting. So were most Israelis. There was a deal to be had—and somehow he couldn't let go.

* * *

It was quiet for a moment.

Bennett desperately needed something for his pain, but he was riveted by what Sa'id was saying. He'd just made a similar case to the president. Still, it was better hearing it from a Palestinian of Sa'id's intellect and reputation.

"Where do we go from here, Jonathan?" asked Galishnikov.

"Well, first of all, Dmitri, the president would like you to get on the phone with our old friend Dr. Mordechai."

"What has Eli got to do with any of this? He has not run the Mossad for years."

"The president wants to know what he makes of all this, and so do I. What's he hearing from his friends in the Mossad? What's he hearing from the top brass of the IDF? You know, the inside stuff, the stuff they're not telling Langley."

"*Da*, I can do that," Galishnikov agreed, "so long as they give me an open line."

"Already done. The lines have been up in here since I walked in."

"Good. What specifically are you looking for?"

Bennett thought about that for a moment, then looked Galishnikov in the eye. "Just tell Eli to follow the money, Dmitri—he'll know what I mean."

* * *

"I want the AG to cut a deal with Iverson."

There was silence at the other end of the line.

"You sure?" Corsetti finally said.

"I'm sure," said the president. "There's too much at stake. We need to know what he knows as fast as we can. Get on the phone with Neil. Have him make the deal within the hour. I want a full progress report by close of business today. Got it?"

"I got it," said Corsetti, "I'm just not sure I like it."

* * *

"What about me?" Sa'id asked. "What can I do?"

Bennett could see in his eyes the fire of determination.

"Well, that gets complicated. Israel's offering to send in ground forces."

"Good God, no," Sa'id blurted out. "Jonathan, you cannot let him—"

"Why not?" Galishnikov broke in. "Of course Doron should send in forces. It's your people that are getting slaughtered up there, Ibrahim."

"You think I don't know that? Of course I know that," Sa'id snapped back with such force he took both Bennett and Galishnikov off guard. "But you cannot let the Israelis attack. You will be playing right into their hands."

"Whose hands?" Galishnikov asked.

"Whoever set this in motion. I don't know who it was. But there is absolutely no way it was Dahlan or Rajoub or one of the other Arafat minions."

"Why? How do you know?"

Now it was Bennett asking.

"I know because I know. Because they are dogs, not men. When Arafat told them to sit, they sat. Lie down, they lay down. Roll over, they rolled over. They are incapable of original thought. They were terrified of Arafat. They could not function without him. He gave them their power, their money. He gave them their orders. There is no way one of them turned on him. Besides, he was an old, sick man. Sure, they were all plotting how to succeed him when he died, but I would bet my life that none of them would dare lay a finger on him. Absolutely not."

"Then I need to know who did, Ibrahim."

"How? How can I . . . ?"

"Get on the phones. See if anyone you know in the legislature is still alive. Call them at home. Get them on their cell phones. Pump them for information. We need to know who was behind this, first of all, and we need to know what the legislature wants to do next."

"What about Doron?"

"You've got to tell your people that Doron is about to unleash."

"Jonathan . . ."

"I know—believe me, I know—but whatever's left of the Palestinian government has got to step up to the plate and make its case to the president and to the world."

"Did you tell the president—?"

"I did—exactly the case you're making—that an Israeli invasion is a death blow to the peace process, pure and simple."

"And what did he say?"

"He's thinking about it. I don't know what he's going to do. But, Ibrahim, listen to me. People are getting butchered up there. You guys aren't watching it. But every network in the world is broadcasting live images of a Palestinian civil war, and the political pressure for somebody—anybody—to do something is going to become unbearable. You don't want the Israelis in here. The Israelis don't want the E.U. in here. We don't want the U.N. in here."

"So where does that leave us?"

"Nowhere good," Galishnikov muttered. He was up now. He was pacing and lighting a cigarette.

"No, no, no—listen to me, Ibrahim," Bennett insisted, looking the man square in the eye. "Listen to me. You get on the phone to every member of the Palestinian Legislative Council you possibly can. Find out what they know. Take their temperature. Get their reaction. Find out what they want to do next. Find out who *they* want to lead the Palestinian people now that Arafat is gone."

* * *

McCoy was grateful to be alone.

She locked the door to Ziegler's quarters, locked herself in the bathroom, turned on the shower, and cranked up the steam. She thanked God for protecting her, for keeping her and Bennett and Galishnikov and Sa'id alive. She asked Him to have mercy on the agents who might still be out there, and to comfort the families of those who'd fallen in the line of duty. She tried to push away the faces of all her friends who'd died over the last few hours. But she couldn't. The emotions overpowered her, and she began to cry, quietly at first, and then in sobs she couldn't control.

* * *

Bennett left Galishnikov and Sa'id and headed back down the hall.

He needed a shower and something to eat. But first he needed to call his mom.

Now sixty-nine and alone, Ruth Bennett was still an early riser, usually up by six, rarely later than six-thirty. She had her routine, and it didn't include radio or television or reading the *New York Times*. Not anymore, at least. After her husband's death, she'd said no, finally, to the steady assault of information that for so long defined her life.

He could still hear his mother's shaky voice over a scratchy satellite phone connection to his hospital room in Germany, breaking the news to him that he'd missed his own father's funeral. It wasn't really his fault, of course. But the hesitancy in her voice made it clear to him that forgiveness was coming slowly.

When they'd finally reconnected, she described to him the quiet, private ceremony, held in Queens, not far from where Solomon Jonathan Bennett was born on December 6, 1941. The hearse had moved quietly down simple tree-lined streets where Sol once played stickball. They had driven by the row houses to which he once had delivered the *New York Times*, the great "Gray Lady" to which he would go on to devote his life, from New York to Moscow to Washington, until a frustrated, bitter retirement exiled him to a condo village outside of Orlando. They arrived at a small cemetery, where she and the casket were greeted by a small group of crusty old men, former colleagues from the *Times*, and by an angel she had never met.

Erin McCoy had arrived from Washington unannounced. She brought with her an American flag as a gift from the White House and a handwritten note of condolence from the president of the United States. It was a warm and thoughtful gesture, Mrs. Bennett told her son, unexpected and in such contrast with the rest of the day.

She described the flat, emotionless words of the hastily chosen minister they had never met before, from a church they had never attended before, about a "better place" they had never believed in before. She described how she and Erin had shared a quiet, lingering lunch together and a pot of tea after the service. And, with the permission of the president, Erin had begun to explain where Jon was, what he was doing, and why. It was a story his mother found hard to digest. Though she occasionally asked for more details, she was not the reporter her late husband had been. But in Erin's soft smile she said she'd found a small measure of hope that everything would be okay after all.

They spent a long afternoon together. Then Erin had driven her back into Manhattan and gotten her settled for a few days in a room at the Waldorf. The room was compliments of the president, until she was finished with the estate lawyers and paperwork and was ready to go back to Florida. Mrs. Bennett had a key to her son's place in Greenwich Village, and Jon had insisted she stay there. But she said she didn't want to be a bother, didn't want to be in the way. "In the way?" Bennett had argued. "Mom, I'm in the hospital on the other side of the world. Whose way are you going to be in?" But Ruth Bennett was in no mood to argue. She simply didn't want to be an imposition.

McCoy had handled it all graciously, Bennett recalled. She gave his mom a private cell-phone number to call if she needed anything. A car and driver. A shoulder to cry on. Erin would be in town for a few days on business, and she'd make herself available for whatever Mrs. Bennett needed. That night, a bellhop arrived at the widow's hotel room door with a dozen white roses, and a note that read simply, "Don't worry, Mrs. Bennett. Jon will be home soon. I'm praying for you, and for him. God bless you, Erin." It was another thoughtful touch, and it had won her a friend for life.

Bennett turned the corner and arrived back at Ziegler's room. He entered the security code, stepped inside, and closed the door behind him. A moment later, he slumped down into one of the couches and stared at the phone.

The shower suddenly shut off and McCoy called out from the bathroom. "Jon, that you?"

"Yeah, I'm about to call my mom—*president's orders.*"

"Say hi to her for me, okay?"

"All right," he said, his voice heavy with fatigue.

Bennett began dialing, then glanced at his watch.

The president would be speaking in less than ten minutes. Bennett felt nauseous. The back of his neck was perspiring. He needed sleep. He needed a drink.

The phone began ringing. He dreaded this call. The poor woman had been through so much already. He didn't want to worry her further. The phone kept ringing. He wondered if McCoy would be willing to talk with her for a few minutes, as soon as she was done with her shower. His mother had obviously fallen in love with Erin McCoy. Maybe he should too.

No one was answering. He cursed himself. Why hadn't he insisted she get an answering machine after his dad died? Why hadn't he simply bought one for her?

☆   ☆   ☆

The bathroom door clicked open.

McCoy didn't want to interrupt Bennett's conversation. But she did want to catch the president's address. She poked her head in and looked around the room. The television was on. Tim Russert was just finishing his analysis from NBC's Washington bureau and the image now switched to the Oval Office.

The president began to explain the events of the last few hours, adding that he was asking the Israelis not to get involved.

But Ziegler's room was quiet. Where was Bennett? Had he gone to the main control room to watch the speech? Had he gone back to Sa'id and Galishnikov's room? He couldn't be missing this, could he? The president had just taken *his* advice, against the counsel of his own national security advisor and CIA director.

In sweats and a T-shirt, a towel wrapped around her head, McCoy turned off the light and fan in the bathroom and tiptoed through the walk-in closet, around the bunk beds, to the couch by the TV. She found Bennett there sleeping like a baby, still holding the satellite phone in his right hand. He looked so quiet, so peaceful. She didn't have the heart to wake him, even for this. She pulled a wool blanket over him, sat down beside him, and watched the rest of the president's remarks. Then she gently brushed some strands of hair from Bennett's eyes, leaned down, and gave him a little kiss on the cheek.

"Good night, Point Man," she whispered. "Sleep well."

18
⋆⋆
⋆

NO ONE in the White House had ever heard of Akiva Ben David.

Born in Brooklyn in 1958, he'd been a straight-A student, graduated with honors from Yeshiva University, and spent summers studying the Torah in Jerusalem from the time he was fifteen. He'd never served in the U.S. military. He'd only briefly held an American driver's license.

The CIA had no file on him. Neither did the FBI or the Department of Homeland Security. He had never popped up on any American or international terrorist watch list. He had no outstanding warrants in the United States or on the Interpol system. To the analysts at Langley who prepared the daily "threat matrix" for the director of Central Intelligence and the president of the United States, he would hardly be classified as a low-level risk. He simply didn't exist.

Nor did he seem to exist in his adopted country of Israel. He'd emigrated there in June of 1980 and obtained dual citizenship at the tender age of twenty-two. But for most of his adult life, he'd largely kept to himself, politically speaking. The Mossad had no file on him. His name popped up in a Shin Bet report or two for joining the mailing lists of several far-right, ultra-Orthodox organizations of some concern. But he'd never done anything more than subscribe to their literature.

He hadn't shown up at, much less organized or led, any political demonstrations, so far as the authorities could tell. He wasn't particularly vocal. He hadn't signed any provocative petitions or staged sit-ins at the Knesset or sent angry or threatening letters to the prime minister or any of his cabinet officials. Thus, he simply wasn't perceived as a threat of any kind, which is exactly the way he wanted it. He was a nonentity, free to fly under the radar, as it were, where it was quiet and comfortable and safe. And up until now, that had suited him just fine. But soon, all that would change.

Akiva Ben David was no longer a young man. But he was in excellent physical condition, especially for a graying, middle-aged rabbi from Bed-Stuy. For the past six years he'd been working with a physical trainer, burning fat and bulking up. He was a disciplined man; of that there could be no doubt. Not to his wife, at least. He was up every morning at four, and headed straight to the gym on the settlement where he and his family now lived, nestled along the Jordan River. By six-thirty every morning, he was home, showered, dressed, and hidden away in his private study, reading the Torah and saying his morning prayers. By eight, he was having breakfast with his wife and four children, one son and three daughters, all under the ages of thirteen. By nine he was in his home office, where he served as the founder and executive director of an obscure little nonprofit group known as the Temple Mount Battalion. Except that it wasn't so little anymore.

Officially, the Temple Mount Battalion existed to promote a better understanding of the importance of building the Third Temple on the ancient, holy site of the first two, in the heart of Jerusalem. Ben David and his group of volunteers (no employees, just his wife, Dalia, who did the bookkeeping) had no land, no schools, no factories or fancy offices. They had no logo, no letterhead, no whiff of creativity or originality at all. They simply ran a nondescript little Web site explaining the importance of the Temple in Jewish history and religious teachings, its history and origins, its dimensions and specifications as laid out in the Hebrew Scriptures, and its role in the End Times.

It wasn't a flashy Web site—no music, no pictures, no graphics of any kind. The site didn't take much time or effort to maintain, which was good because Ben David had absolutely no training, formal or otherwise, in Web site design, construction, or maintenance. Nor did the site require much money to run, which was also good because when he'd launched the site it averaged only a few dozen hits a week.

By contrast, the Web site run by the Temple Institute in the Jewish

Quarter of Jerusalem's Old City was far better funded and more impressive. In large measure, this was because the Temple Institute was not simply an educational organization. It was more like an architectural firm, general contractor, and interior decorating shop all rolled into one. Its leaders weren't just talking about a future Temple. They were already in the process of building it.

Since 1987, they'd been actually re-creating authentic sacred vessels and musical instruments and priestly garments for use in the coming Temple, using the precise materials and following the precise specifications laid out in the Bible. When Exodus chapter 27 said that one type of Temple altar should be made of "acacia wood . . . five cubits long, and five cubits wide," that it should be "square, and its height should be three cubits," and that "you shall overlay it with bronze," that's exactly how these modern-day artisans were building it. When Exodus chapter 30 said another type of Temple altar—the Altar of Incense—should be made of acacia wood but "you shall overlay it with pure gold," and "you shall make a gold molding all around for it," that is precisely how it was being done.

These Temple implements weren't models. They were the real thing, and they were being handcrafted by the hundreds. When the time was right, the Jews would be ready to erect and furnish a rudimentary version of the Third Temple with less than twenty-four hours' notice. And that, a Yiddish Martha Stewart might say, was a good thing.

But to Akiva Ben David, it wasn't good enough. Something had been stirring inside him for nearly a decade. He wanted to go beyond just *educating* Jews about the Temple, or merely *preparing* the vessels and implements for a future Temple, as noble and useful as those roles were. The Temple Institute was doing an excellent job at that, as was another well-funded Jerusalem-based organization known as the Temple Mount Faithful. This group had already crafted a four-ton cornerstone for the Third Temple that was ready to be laid in place on a moment's notice. In the quarries in the Negev Desert and elsewhere, kindred spirits like these were patiently, steadfastly carving and stockpiling tens of thousands of stones to be used to reconstruct the Temple. Plans were already completed to build massive parking lots in Jerusalem for all the pilgrims and tourists who would come to see the Holy Temple.

Detailed, painstaking preparations were being made day after day, year after year. Nothing was being left to chance. Nothing was being over-looked. This too was a group entirely committed to rebuilding the Temple, and they were preparing for that moment. They too believed that the Hebrew prophets like Daniel and Ezekiel foretold of an even more dazzling Holy Temple to be built in the last days. And this too was good.

But in his heart, Akiva Ben David refused to accept that simply educating and preparing were good enough. They weren't good enough for him. He wanted more. He wanted to *force* the hand of God.

It was time to rebuild the Temple *now*, not a hundred or a thousand years from now. So under the radar—unseen by the Israeli authorities—he'd begun secretly recruiting a political movement who agreed. As time passed, his patience grew thinner and his convictions grew stronger. Somewhere, somehow, the dream of seeing ancient prophecies fulfilled became an obsession. He would take matters into his own hands, and he began scanning the horizon for anyone who might be willing to help.

Through his own modest Web site, Ben David gathered names of people who signed up to receive a free weekly e-mail newsletter. It was an e-mail he personally researched, wrote, and edited. They were short, punchy. They were provocative and chock-full of the latest news and information from the Promised Land regarding war, peace, religion, and the preparations for building the Third Temple.

But what made these e-mails different from his religious competitors was their nuance, their sense of urgency and edge of militancy. They didn't quite call on Jews to storm the Temple Mount and seize it by force—not overtly. But over time, people who read them got the message. Muslims were desecrating Judaism's holiest site, he argued. They were destroying the religious and archeological artifacts on the site. They were weakening its physical base, threatening to cause the Temple Mount to collapse under the weight of a quarter million Muslims praying each week at the Al-Aksa Mosque. They were also preventing Jews from even entering the site. But their time was running out.

Originally, Ben David had hoped he could sign up a few hundred interested souls. He'd hoped to find some kindred spirits who might, in time, be willing to help him with the funding necessary to go on an international speaking tour to spread the word about the Temple's importance in human history, and the need to reclaim the Temple's rightful place on earth.

And then something happened.

A fellow rabbi back in Akiva Ben David's native Brooklyn became one of the first subscribers. He loved the weekly reports, and began a little e-mail correspondence. He affectionately dubbed Ben David's electronic missives "the kosher equivalent of Chinese water torture," slowly persuading the world—"week by week, drip by drip"—of the need to rebuild the Temple.

Soon, the rabbi began forwarding Ben David's e-mails to members of his congregation. They hit a nerve. They tapped into a deeply held but seldom articulated sense that modern Orthodox Judaism was so focused on other issues that they were indeed neglecting the centrality of the Temple in Jewish life.

Without the Temple, there was no Holy of Holies. There was no place for the Almighty to reside on earth. Nor was there a gathering point for Jews to worship and pray the way they had in the days of King Solomon or even the Roman occupation.

Sure, there was the Western Wall, also known as the Wailing Wall, for all the tears that had been shed there after the destruction of Herod's Temple by the Romans. But whatever you called it, wasn't it still just a wall? Wasn't it just a remnant of something greater and far more profound? How could modern Judaism have gotten so distracted that it sent millions of people to pray at a mere wall, as though this was the pinnacle of the Jewish experience? Didn't the Prophets speak of something more important than a *wall*? Hadn't Jewish heroes fought and died for something more eternal than a *wall*? Didn't the Jewish people deserve something better? Of course they did.

But even more important, the readers of Ben David's e-mails began to consider another fundamental premise. Without the Temple, there was no place for animal sacrifices. The Torah—the Hebrew Scriptures—was emphatic on that point. No sacrifices could be done anywhere but in the Holy Temple, and without such sacrifices, there could be no ritual shedding of blood. Without the shedding of blood, there could be no forgiveness of sin. Without the forgiveness of sin, how could one truly become holy? How could one truly be spiritually pure enough to enter the presence of a pure and perfect and holy God? How could one enter heaven at all without the Temple? How could one truly be saved from the fires of hell? These were no trifling little theological questions. They were matters of eternal security or damnation. Why were so few people wrestling with them? So much was at stake.

Ben David had never thought of himself as a particularly persuasive speaker or writer. Nevertheless, the passion of his heart came through loud and clear. People began forwarding his e-mails to family and friends and business associates throughout the United States, and then in the U.K., across the European continent, to Australia, New Zealand, and South Africa. Soon people were getting the e-mails forwarded back to themselves from people they'd never heard of. And in just a few months, the little Temple Mount Battalion list grew to more than fifteen thousand names.

Speaking invitations came in by the hundreds. Then financial donations began pouring in through a secure, online credit card program he had installed on the Web site. The average monthly tax-deductible gift per person was a mere thirty-nine U.S. dollars. But multiplied by fifteen thousand people over the course of an entire year, Akiva Ben David was raking in serious cash. Something was happening, something he needed to figure out and get ahead of, and fast. So much money was going to attract government attention soon, if it hadn't already. He needed a plan, something to invest the funds in, or spend it on.

And then a plan was conceived. Over the past few months it had quickly grown and taken shape. It was a plan about to be baptized by fire.

★　★　★

Bennett tossed and turned.

It was hard to believe that only seventy-two hours earlier he'd been driving his forest green Jaguar XJR through the streets of Georgetown on Christmas Eve, actually feeling relaxed for the first time in a long time.

Traffic had been light. He pulled under the portico of the Four Seasons Hotel and stopped in front of the main doors. A bellhop agreed to watch his car for a moment, and he went into the lobby, picked up a phone, and dialed. There was no answer. Perhaps she was already on her way down. Normally, he'd be anxious. Typically, he'd be pacing. He hated to be late, almost as much as the president did. But tonight, for some reason, he wasn't worried at all. He was going to the White House staff Christmas party, and he was going with the prettiest girl in Washington.

It wasn't a date. Not exactly. He hadn't described it that way when he'd asked if they could go together. Each of them was going anyway. It was a command performance, of sorts. And though Bennett wasn't much for staff parties of any kind, this one might actually be fun, all the more if the two of them were going together. And now they were. He poked around the gift shop, flipped through some newsmagazines, bought some Rolaids and popped two in his mouth. An elevator bell rang. He turned as the doors opened, and saw her coming around the corner.

Bennett had never seen Erin McCoy look as beautiful as she did that night—a simple yet elegant black dress, black shoulder wrap, and black pumps, accented by pearl earrings and a gorgeous string of pearls around her neck. A few minutes later, they were flashing their new White House badges to the uniformed Secret Service officer manning the bulletproof guard booth at the northwest gate and pulling into Bennett's exclusive new parking spot on West Executive Avenue.

"Follow me," she'd insisted, and led them around to the center of the North Lawn.

For a few minutes, neither of them said a word. They simply stood there, looking up at the White House that somehow seemed to glow in the cold night air. Every window was adorned by a Christmas wreath and white candles, and a huge pine wreath hung over the door. And from somewhere deep inside the White House, Bennett could hear singing.

★ ★ ★

In time, the movement would grow.

So too would Akiva Ben David's resolve. People were reading his e-mails. They were being stirred by the case he was making, however obliquely. They were responding with passion and determination. They were offering their time, talent, and treasure to help force the hand of history. Was this not a sign that he should stop cogitating, stop agitating, and start activating a team that would help him accomplish their movement's unstated but clearly understood mission?

Eight months earlier, during their family's private Passover meal, Ben David concluded the seder with these words: "Next year, in the Temple."

Why? He hadn't meant to say it. It had simply come from his heart, and suddenly he and his wife, Dalia, were electrified.

Something cosmic had just happened. Something supernatural.

They put the kids to bed, quickly finished the dishes, then retreated to his study to begin plotting their strategy. Money was something of which they suddenly had more than enough. They still couldn't believe it. But they were grateful and took it as a confirmation that they were on the right track. What they needed were allies, or, perhaps more precisely, coconspirators. That wasn't going to be easy.

They certainly couldn't send out an e-mail asking for volunteers to risk a holy war with the Muslims for the sake of recapturing the initiative of Jewish history. Nor was it something for which they could simply put a full-page ad in the *New York Times* or *Jerusalem Post*: "Help Wanted— Carpe Diem—Come Rebuild the Temple." Identifying help would be tough. There were no two ways about it. Establishing contact with volunteers would be difficult too. Where would they meet? Where would they train? How could they keep a low enough profile not to be noticed by Israeli intelligence or by the Palestinians?

Even now, eight months later, Ben David and his Dalia could remember how they felt. With their hearts racing, they sifted through thousands of e-mails they'd received, looking for people willing and able to help them. Secrecy, they'd decided right there and then, would have to be their highest priority. What they were considering could get them imprisoned for life, if not shot and killed. But they felt compelled to move forward, as if unseen forces were pushing them over the edge. They had no doubt they could find kindred spirits. Nor did they have any doubt they could accomplish the dream taking shape in their hearts. And now, here they were. Somehow, it had all gone so much faster than they'd ever expected. They were ready. The zero hour was almost here.

Let history begin.

19
★ ★
★

OUTSIDE IT HAD BEEN growing dark and windy.

Inside the Oval Office it was crackling with Christmas spirit and flowing with a few alcoholic spirits as well. There was a roaring fire in the fireplace. A statuesque, nine-foot, and beautifully decorated blue spruce twinkled with lights and White House Christmas ornaments from each of the past fifty years or so. The sounds of old carols and hymns wafted gently through the West Wing. But there was no more time to listen. It was time to depart for their traditional trek to the National Cathedral for a candlelight and communion Christmas Eve service, and the president didn't want to be late.

Bennett felt a twinge of guilt for not having invited his mom up to Washington for the weekend. She would have loved an evening like this, and loved seeing him off at Andrews Air Force Base on Sunday. She needed to get out of the house. She was still struggling with almost debilitating bouts of depression. She refused to take any antidepressant medication or even talk much about her grief. She'd always been a quiet person, but now she was withdrawing even further.

He felt guilty for being too busy for her right now. He felt guilty for always being too busy for her. But there was nothing he could do until he got back. Perhaps he could get her something for Christmas from Jerusalem. She'd always wanted to go to the Holy Land, but despite all her husband's world travels, she'd never been. Maybe later that spring he should take her with him on a private tour of the land of milk and honey. It might do her some good.

"Ladies and gentlemen, please," said the president, clicking a champagne glass with a fork. "Our rides are ready and we need to depart posthaste. But I just want to say a quick word to all of you. It's been an extraordinary month, an extraordinary two years, in fact. But we've tried to keep faith with the American people, and I think the new polls Bob laid out for us earlier today are a wonderful early present, a sign that somebody out there thinks we're doing something right."

A round of applause arose from the little assembly.

"Each of us knows how much more work lies ahead. But my hope and prayer is that a few years from tonight, two states will be living side by side. Investment capital will be pouring *in*. Oil and gas will be flowing *out*. And a new Marriott or a Hilton will be open for business in Bethlehem, so that no young couple will ever again have to worry about finding room at an inn."

Everyone laughed and applauded and enjoyed the moment. No one more so than Bennett. It was his dream too, and seventy-two hours ago it had actually seemed possible.

★ ★ ★

Now what?

The president had no idea. He and Corsetti sat alone in the Oval Office and said nothing for a few minutes. All was quiet, but for the occasional rumble of thunder and the steady sound of sleet hitting the tinted, bulletproof windows. The technicians were all gone now, as were their television lights and cameras and sound equipment. White House staffers were busy carrying out a blizzard of presidential directives issued over the course of the past hour. The press was analyzing every nuance of the president's remarks. And the First Lady was in an armor-plated sedan, surrounded by Secret Service agents, heading to the home of the grieving widow of the late secretary of state.

Corsetti broke the silence. He said the speech had been a solid "double." It was brief and to the point. It kept the game moving forward and bought them time while they figured out their next moves.

The president had forcefully condemned the attacks and appropriately mourned the dead. He'd put all of the various Palestinian factions on notice that they must cease the violence immediately and strongly hinted that severe international repercussions could result if the civil war did not end quickly. He'd praised the Israelis for showing restraint. And he'd vowed that the United States would bring the terror masters to justice and continue working for peace no matter how long it took or how much it cost. He'd done just what he'd needed to do. At least for now.

MacPherson took a sip of coffee and stared out the window at the relentless storm battering the nation's capital. "Bob?"

"Yes, Mr. President?"

"Was Bennett actually suggesting that I send forces in?"

"Into where? The West Bank and Gaza?"

"Of course."

Corsetti was puzzled. "He didn't say that, did he?"

"No, not in so many words . . ." The thought trailed off.

Again the room was silent for a few moments.

"What are you getting at, sir?" Corsetti finally asked, watching the president's thoughts churning.

"I don't know exactly," MacPherson responded. "I'm just sitting here replaying that NSC meeting over and over again and I just can't . . . "

"You can't what?"

"Jon was adamant that we keep the Israelis out, right?"

"Right."

"Jack, on the other hand, was equally adamant. He and his team at CIA feel strongly that somebody has to go in and stop all the killing, that we can't just sit by and watch Palestinians slaughter themselves on CNN."

"Right."

"And what was the question Jack taunted Bennett with?"

Corsetti thought about that for a few seconds, but couldn't recall precisely.

Fortunately, the president proceeded to answer his own question. "Jack asked, 'Then who's going to go in, the U.N.?' Right?"

"Okay, I remember that. And Jon was about to answer but the vice president cut him off and took his side, said the Israelis shouldn't go in."

"Exactly."

"So what's your point?"

"What was Jon's answer?"

"I don't know."

"I don't know either."

"But you suspect he wasn't going to back a U.N. peacekeeping force?" Corsetti pressed.

"How could he? He knows my concerns about the U.N. An international force would take forever to authorize, much less deploy."

"Maybe he didn't have an answer one way or the other. Maybe Jack was about to stump him."

"Not likely. Jon's a strategist, and a pretty good one too. He's wired to think five or six moves ahead. I trained him myself."

"God help us all." Corsetti laughed.

"Nevertheless"—the president smiled—"he might actually be right."

Corsetti considered that, then shifted gears. "You're not really thinking about sending in troops, are you?"

"I don't know."

"Sir, Jon's a sharp guy with great Wall Street instincts. There's nobody in the White House or on the NSC who disputes that. But let's not kid ourselves. Jon is not a diplomat. He's not a trained negotiator. He's got no military or CIA training. And with all due respect, I don't think we—*you*—should be turning to him on military matters. I mean, sir . . ."

"I'm not turning to him on military matters, I'm—"

"Of course you are. *Invading the West Bank and Gaza? Sending in U.S. troops when we're already occupying Iraq?* No one is advising you to do this, sir. No one. Not on your NSC team. Not at Defense. No one at State. No one at the CIA. For that matter, Bennett himself hasn't actually even come out and said it—not in so many words."

"So what's your point?" demanded the president.

"My point, sir, is that I'm concerned that your desire to nail down a peace deal is clouding your judgment. The peace process is over. It died a grisly death this morning, in Gaza. Period. End of sentence. Our job now is to contain the damage, not create more. I mean, how exactly does going to war in the West Bank and Gaza help us put points on the board here at home? in the Arab world? within NATO? within the E.U.? How does it help us build international support for a new regime in Iraq? For crying out loud, Mr. President, wouldn't you say we've got enough problems without changing the definition of *occupied* territories from *Israeli*-occupied to *U.S.*-occupied?"

"No, no, no, Bob—you're missing the point."

"Am I? Because—"

"Bob, think about it. Are we serious about winning the war on terrorism or aren't we? Do we really let this mafia war in Palestine run its course? You want to wake up one morning and find yourself facing a Palestinian Michael Corleone—someone smarter, tougher, more ruthless than the Godfather, more dangerous than Arafat himself?"

Corsetti said nothing.

"Bob, I'm not saying we *should* go in. I'm saying we shouldn't rule it out. Get the guys at the Pentagon and CIA war-gaming something—fast—and let's think it through. That's all I'm saying."

Corsetti took a sip of coffee. It was cold. "Mr. President, it's your call, obviously. I'm just saying that you pay me to give you political advice. And, sir, I'm telling you that what you're considering—even the act of considering it—is politically very, very risky."

"And the alternative is what, exactly? A couple of U.N. resolutions? Sending Jimmy Carter over there? What do you want me to do?"

"I don't know, sir. Not yet."

"Neither do I," MacPherson admitted. "I just want to know what my options are. So get me some options—fast."

Corsetti reluctantly nodded, excused himself, and stepped out of the Oval Office.

It was then that the president began to realize just how alone he really was.

* * *

The press conference began promptly at 9:00 p.m., Iraqi time.

It was, after all, designed primarily for domestic Iraqi consumption. But given its import, it was also carried live by most major television networks around the world, including in the United States, where it broke into the afternoon soaps at 1:00 p.m. Eastern Standard Time.

"Good evening," said a well-coiffed older American gentleman in a navy pin-striped suit, a crisp white cotton shirt, and a red power tie.

A blinding of flashbulbs and 35 mm autoadvancers quickly confirmed to everyone watching that the ornate hall they were seeing on their screens was in fact packed wall to wall with scores of international journalists.

"My name is Troy Moreaux. As all of you are aware, the president has sent me here to oversee the Office of Reconstruction and Humanitarian Assistance and to assist the Iraqi people in establishing an interim government, and that is what I intend to do."

More flashbulbs. More autoadvancers.

"Four weeks ago, the United States and our allies faced a catastrophic threat—indeed, an existential threat—from the regime of Saddam Hussein. Therefore, acting in self-defense, we used the force necessary to defeat those threats and end Saddam Hussein's murderous regime. It wasn't easy. But it was worth it. And now the United States and our friends and allies throughout the free world stand ready to help the Iraqi people exit the long, cold night of your suffering into the warm sunshine of peace and prosperity. We will be here as long as it takes, but not one minute more. The United States is here to liberate, not dominate."

The hall erupted with applause.

"Tonight, then, I announce the formation of an Iraqi interim government."

Another burst of applause went up from the gathered Iraqi dignitaries standing behind Ambassador Moreaux, as well as from several dozen other Iraqi officials filling the hall.

"Allow me, then, to introduce the six senior members of the new interim government, which will be known as the Coalition Provisional Authority, or CPA. There are two dozen members total, and my staff is handing out to each of you a press release with the complete list of names and bios. But let me just quickly mention these gentlemen, beginning with Ayad Allawi of the Iraqi National Accord."

This brought a smattering of applause.

"Jalal Talabani of the Patriotic Union of Kurdistan."

Another smattering of applause.

"Masoud Barzani of the Kurdistan Democratic party."

Still more light applause.

"Abdel-Aziz al-Hakim of the Supreme Council for Islamic Revolution in Iraq."

Now the applause was intensifying.

"And, of course, Achmed Chalabi of the Iraqi National Congress, and Mustafa Al-Hassani of the Iraqi National Alliance."

At the mention of Chalabi's and Al-Hassani's names, the crowd erupted in sustained shouts and fervent clapping. The two were clearly the most respected and powerful of the various factional leaders in the room, and arguably throughout all of Iraq, Chalabi because of his role in building and unifying the Iraqi opposition in exile, and Al-Hassani because of his role in inspiring the Iraqi people as a dissident who somehow had survived nearly eleven years in one of Saddam Hussein's most notorious prisons.

Now, with Chalabi back on liberated Iraqi soil and working so closely with the coalition forces to prepare for a civilian government, and Al-Hassani out of prison and addressing the people daily on the radio station formerly controlled by the Ministry of Information (read: *Propaganda*), the world was looking to these two men for a credible plan to rebuild Iraq's shattered infrastructure and psyche.

When the applause began to quiet down, Ambassador Moreaux turned the podium over to Al-Hassani, the graying, bearded, seventy-one-year-old intellectual grandfather of the Iraqi freedom forces. The photo op quickly shifted gears.

"Thank you, Mr. Ambassador. It is an honor to be with you all today, and especially to be here in one of Saddam Hussein's palaces—a far cry from where I have been over the past long, dark decade. Each one of us knows firsthand the bitter bloody legacy of Saddam Hussein and his reign of terror. And each of us knows that however much we personally have suffered, we are among the lucky ones. We are the ones who survived. Just this week, coalition forces uncovered the bodies of fifteen thousand Iraqi men, women, and children in a mass grave south of Baghdad. This is just the latest evidence of the war crimes against humanity perpetrated by the Saddam regime. The blood of our brothers and sisters and children cries out from the sands and the streets and the prisons. It cries out for justice. It cries out for a fresh page, a new chapter in the long, proud, enduring history of the Iraqi people."

The hall again erupted with cheers. For the next ten minutes, the retiring, soft-spoken Al-Hassani outlined the new interim government's mandate and structure. Then he took questions.

"This question is for Mr. Chalabi," began an Al-Jazeera reporter. "Sir, will you now denounce the United States before the entire international community for committing war crimes in Iraq?"

A hush came over the crowd. It was the question on everyone's mind, and now it had been asked of Achmed Chalabi, arguably the most pro-Western and pro-American Iraqi leader in the room, an exile long backed by American money and political support, now seeking to build a power base in a country he hadn't lived in for decades. With a senior representative of the U.S. government in the room. With the president of the United States and every member of Congress no doubt watching on television. With the U.N. secretary-general watching the press conference in Paris with members of the French parliament. With vast segments of the Arab and Islamic worlds watching in prime time.

Chalabi cleared his throat, looked the reporter in the eye, and spoke softly. "If there is one thing I have learned in my lifetime of struggle, it is this: freedom is not free. Many have died in this war of liberation, and they are heroes. Heroes, I tell you—martyrs of the freedom revolution. We will forever remember their sacrifice. We will forever remember that they died so that we might live, that we might breathe and speak our minds and control our destinies. We will celebrate their lives. We will honor their deaths. We will build great monuments in Baghdad and Tikrit and tell their stories to our children and our grandchildren. But we will not blame foreigners for our suffering. It was Saddam Hussein who did this to us, and it is Saddam Hussein who we and our children and our children's children must denounce every day of our lives."

The room unexpectedly erupted in sustained cheering, with Mustafa Al-Hassani leading the way. Chalabi lowered his eyes and stepped back as Al-Hassani stepped up to the podium and the bank of microphones, called for quiet, and then caught everyone off guard, including his own colleagues.

"What is past is past," Al-Hassani said. "It is time to move forward, and tonight, as my first act in this interim government, I make a proposal."

Flashbulbs began popping again.

"After we meet the needs of the suffering people of Baghdad—after we get them the medical and humanitarian assistance they need and deserve—I propose we move the capital of Iraq."

A collective gasp could be heard, even from the gathered dignitaries.

"Baghdad represents the old Iraq, does it not?" the small, slightly stooped man continued. "Does not Baghdad represent Saddam Hussein's Iraq, not our own? Now it is ruined and suffering because of evil ways and bloodthirsty leaders. Why should we rebuild Saddam's capital as it once was? What says we must? Why accept the narrative that Saddam Hussein wrote for us? This is a new day. This is a new chapter. And a new Iraq deserves a new capital, a capital worthy of the rich and proud and glorious history that has long been ours. . . ."

You could hear a pin drop at that moment.

"Tonight, I call upon the great Iraqi nation to build a great new capital city, with the trillions of dollars of new oil money that will soon begin to flow. Like the great economic and political capitals of our sister states all around the Gulf—capitals like Riyadh and Kuwait City and Abu Dhabi—let us believe that out of the barren desert sands can rise towers of steel and glass, practically overnight. Let us build homes and schools and factories and stock exchanges. Let us build museums and theaters and stadiums and gardens. Let us together build a great economic center that rapidly becomes the envy of the world. More precisely, let us rebuild a great political and economic power of global importance where none has existed for thousands of years. . . ."

It was as though a billion viewers leaned in to hear the news for themselves.

"My friends, it is time to rebuild the city of Babylon, the city of our dreams."

20

★ ★
★

MIDNIGHT DESCENDED on the Iraqi desert.

The air was cold and black. Storm clouds obscured a full moon. No lights could be seen for miles in any direction. Bitter winds howled through the wadis and canyons, and Daoud Juma wondered how much longer it would take.

They were still headed for the town of Al Qa'im and the Syrian border village of Abu Kamal, but both remained quite a ways off. A junior feda-yeen officer drove the Renault while Daoud reclined in the backseat and tried unsuccessfully to get some sleep. Ahead of them was the Range Rover packed with commandos and their weapons. Bringing up the rear was the minivan with still more men and supplies.

He checked his watch. It was just before midnight back in Baghdad, not yet four in the afternoon in New York and Washington. He tried to picture what he and his men would be doing twenty-four hours later. Would they have been able to reach Canada yet? Would they have already slipped across the border into the United States? Would the cars be ready? What about the weapons?

If everything went according to plan, each man would regroup in an old cabin tucked away in the high peaks region of the Adirondack Mountains, not far from Lake Placid. Everyone had been briefed already, and all of them had been trained on the new GPS equipment. The cabin shouldn't be hard to find. He just hoped they were all as ready for the snow and ice and cold as they insisted they were.

None of these Al-Nakbah shock troops had ever been outside of their home countries of Iran, Saudi Arabia, or Palestine, other than the last eighteen months they'd spent in Iraq, training night and day at Salman Pak, just outside of Baghdad. All of them were from small towns or desert villages. None of them had any experience in the United States, much less the extreme weather of the Adirondacks or the American northeast. But in every other way they were ready, and he'd have to trust them.

Each had been chosen by commanders he'd personally recruited and trained. Each was in top physical condition. Each was trained as either a sniper or a suicide bomber. And each was ready to give his very life to wage jihad in the belly of the Great Satan. These were men without the slightest trace of fear, and soon enough, they'd have the chance to prove their mettle.

Once safely across the Canadian border into the United States, and once convinced they weren't being tracked, they'd rendezvous at the cabin, set up their shortwave radios, and gather any last-minute intelligence they could about homeland security preparations under way in their target cities. Finally, when all systems were go—when Daoud Juma said the time had come—they would fan out in four teams of three men each.

The first two teams would head to Manhattan. The third team would head to Boston. Daoud himself would lead the fourth team to Chicago. There were, of course, a hundred ways their mission could fail. He knew that better than any of these men, and he was sure his plan had taken all of those ways into account.

Backup teams—men he'd never seen before, never wanted to see or know—would move in through Seattle, others through Tijuana, others through Miami. Some were traveling in groups. Others were traveling alone. Some would head to Las Vegas, some to Phoenix. Some would descend upon Chicago, others on Des Moines. He had a team headed for Montgomery, Alabama. Another was tasked for Jacksonville, Florida, while another was headed for Palm Beach.

What made his plan so brilliant, thought Daoud, was its inherent flexibility. Each individual was responsible for his or her own targets—malls, restaurants, movie theaters, supermarkets, and the like. They weren't required to tell him, or even their fellow cell members, exactly where they were headed, unless they wanted to work together to maximize their destructive impact. They weren't even required to make a final decision on their target package until they got into their assigned city and got the lay of the land.

It wouldn't be difficult to find a highly populated and highly vulnerable strike point. Beyond obvious points of entry, U.S. homeland security was a joke. Thousands of miles of borders were Swiss cheese, and once inside the country most sites that attracted crowds—aside from government buildings and major sporting events—had minimal if any security. Why would they?

Before September 11, 2001, commercial airport security throughout the United States had been lax, because Americans had never experienced an Islamic kamikaze. They couldn't envision the magnitude of destruction inflicted upon them by Osama bin Laden and Al-Qaeda.

Before November 24, 2010—just last month—*private* aviation security in the United States had been effectively nonexistent. No one getting on a private plane was subject to metal detectors or photo ID checks or bomb-sniffing dogs or security procedures of any kind. Why? Because Americans had never really taken seriously the prospects of a private business jet being hijacked and used on a kamikaze mission. Then Saddam Hussein commenced Operation Last Jihad and sent fedayeen trained by Daoud Juma to attack the presidential motorcade outside of Denver International Airport using a Gulfstream IV, and the world had changed forever.

Now it would change again.

Americans had never experienced a wave of suicide bombings and sniper attacks on the order Daoud's Palestinian brethren were inflicting upon the Israelis. Because they'd never seen it happen, they never really believed that it could happen. But they would soon learn. Now Daoud would teach the Great Satan a lesson it would never forget. His men had full authority to switch cities if necessary to maintain operational security. No one but he knew precisely how many fedayeen members were deployed to the United States, and even he would have no idea how many actually got into the country and avoided detection and arrest. The only thing each cell member was encouraged to do, if at all possible, was strike on the same day, or more precisely, the same night.

New Year's Eve.
Just four nights away.

* * *

Yuri Gogolov didn't like what he was seeing.

Not all of it.

True, the gun battles in the West Bank and Gaza were going better than he could have expected. Every television network in the world—except perhaps state television in North Korea and Cuba—was showing the carnage nonstop, and there was no question the attacks had caught Washington completely by surprise. Moreover, a new scrap of intelligence had just come in from one of Al-Nakbah's informants in Gaza. The source hadn't ever given them anything of particular value in the past, but the initial reports, though sketchy and unconfirmed, were tantalizing, to say the least.

The question was, were the reports true? Could they actually have stumbled onto the safe house where this Bennett and his team were hiding? It seemed unlikely, but Jibril had convinced him that it wasn't a possibility they could afford to ignore. Not with the stakes so high and the game so hot. Who knew? Maybe they'd get lucky.

That said, however, President MacPherson's speech had been a serious surprise. Gogolov could only admit that to himself, of course. But it was true, and part of being a great chess player meant accepting the state of play as it actually was, not wishing for something that wasn't. The truth was the grand master had been caught off guard. The Israelis were *not* on the move. IDF forces were *not* battling Palestinian forces. Palestinian casualties at the hands of the Jews were *not* occurring at all, much less mounting rapidly.

Instead, the American's speech was winning high marks in every European capital, including Paris and Moscow. The feckless, spineless Mubarak—the faux pharaoh of Cairo—was actually claiming credit on Radio Monte Carlo and the BBC. It was disgusting, thought Gogolov. Mubarak was telling the world he had personally intervened, demanding that President MacPherson take a hard line toward Doron and keep the Israelis out of the Palestinian territories. And Mubarak was getting away with it.

All that would have been bad enough. But the problem went deeper than that. Something was rumbling on the "Arab Street."

A new *Jerusalem Post* story quoted Amin Makboul, a senior Fatah official in the West Bank, as saying, "The Arab regimes have no credibility. In order to face external challenges, the Arab leaders should give their people freedom and democracy." Another top Fatah activist, Taisir Nasrallah, told the *Post*, "The entire Arab order is in urgent need of reconstruction. What happened in Baghdad proves that the Arab order is dying." Muawiyah al-Masri, a Palestinian legislator, added, "What is needed now is the democratization of the Arab world according to the wishes and aspirations of the Arab masses, and not as a result of American pressure."

Such thinking was heresy, but it was bubbling up everywhere.

"It is not Saddam Hussein who fell. What collapsed are the big lies that accompanied him, praised him, and glorified him," declared an editorial in the London-based Saudi daily *Alsharq Alawsat*. "In this war against the Americans, the Arabs were divided into two groups. One claimed that this is a war of survival, a war for honor, a war against the American conspiracy. The other group—silent either because they are in exile abroad or oppressed within Iraq—knew that this was a war of liberation, a war to rid them of a corrupt, murderous regime that should go out as it came in. It is a historical event for the regime, for which there is no precedent. All the past wars were wars with Israel or wars of regimes. But this one is the first of its kind. It is a war against the evil Arab situation."

Not that Yuri Gogolov cared about the "Arab situation," evil or otherwise. He wasn't an Arab. He was a pure-blooded Russian—an ultranationalist, to be more precise, though some called him a Fascist. He was proud of who he was and what he believed. He had no love for Saddam Hussein or his regime. It was, after all, he and Mohammed Jibril who had sold Saddam the tactical nuclear weapons they'd stolen from Russian stockpiles. It was he and Jibril who had persuaded Saddam to launch Operation Last Jihad against NATO and the Israelis. It was he and Jibril who, at the last moment—through Stuart Iverson and several other intermediaries—had tipped off the Americans and the Israelis, triggering a war that left Iraq smoldering. And their plan had worked flawlessly.

But Gogolov's mission wasn't to set in motion a wave of democratic capitalism throughout the Arab and Islamic world. Far from it. Gogolov's vision was to restore the glory of Mother Russia, to cleanse her of the capitalist pigs who let mafia bosses and prostitutes run rampant in the streets of Moscow and St. Petersburg, to make her a force the world not just feared but worshiped.

To succeed—to reemerge as the world's only superpower and leave the Americans gasping for oxygen—Russia would need to be purified of President Grigoriy Vadim, the whelp who ran the country now. He was driving the country's economy into the sewer. He was allowing the army to disintegrate for a lack of funding and expansionist missions. He was allowing Russia's nuclear arsenal to be systematically dismantled. And he was too cozy with the West—with Washington in particular—and also with the Jews.

Russia was no longer a superpower. It could barely be considered a world power at all. Indeed, it was in danger of imploding in a thousand ancient ethnic feuds. The festering rebellion in Chechnya was symptomatic of just how feckless the New Russia really was under Vadim's limp hand. It was time to reverse the decline before it was too late, before Russia was an international laughingstock of breadlines and beggars.

Reviving the Great Russian Empire would not happen overnight. It would take time, leadership, and luck. It would require assassinating President Vadim, no small venture. It would require mounting a *putsch*—a coup—against Vadim's government and the spineless thieves in the Duma. And once Vadim was gone, then things would really get difficult.

Russia would need hard currency. Massive amounts of hard currency. For that she would need to control the oil supplies of the Persian Gulf. She would need to combine this with her own oil and natural gas reserves. She'd need to control warm-water ports in the south and the shipping lines used to move the oil to all points east and west. That, in turn, would require an alliance with the Islamic Republic of Iran.

It was no small undertaking. But it was a goal worthy of their sacrifice. A Russian-Persian axis—a nuclear alliance that was virtually immune from challenge by the United States, NATO, or a newly defanged Iraq—this was precisely the goal for which Gogolov and Jibril were plotting their strategy and making their moves.

They weren't in a hurry. They understood full well that there were pieces on the chessboard that needed to be moved around before they put the king in checkmate. But they also knew they weren't simply playing chess against Grigoriy Vadim. They were playing against James "Mac" MacPherson. And now against Jonathan Meyers Bennett. They were up against two idealists, two men infecting the Arab world with Western visions of "free men, free minds, and free markets."

And it was clear. They must be stopped.

Gogolov picked up the telephone and dialed Mohammed Jibril's private digital cell phone number. It was the wee hours of the morning, too early for either of them. But this could not wait. It was time to counter MacPherson's move. It was time to get back on the offensive. It was time to force the Israelis to invade the West Bank and Gaza, douse all this talk of freedom and democracy, and reignite the fires of jihad.

☆ ☆ ☆

Bennett never heard it.

The black phone on the desk in Ziegler's private quarters rang twelve annoying times. But Bennett was still sound asleep on the couch. A disoriented Erin McCoy, startled out of her own nap in the chair beside him, finally managed to grab the receiver on the thirteenth ring. It was Jake Ziegler, calling from the main control room.

Yes, he was well aware of the fact that it was only 2:19 Tuesday morning. But back in Washington it was only 7:19 Monday evening. The president was about to begin another secure videoconference with his National Security Council, and he wanted Bennett and McCoy to join them immediately.

☆ ☆ ☆

By this point, everyone on the NSC knew what the president was thinking.

They knew he was considering sending forces in not just to rescue Bennett's team and any DSS agents out there that might still be alive but also end the Palestinian civil war and bring some semblance of order to the disputed territories. Their staffs were feverishly working on a range of tactical military options, target packages, intelligence needs, and subsequent diplomatic scenarios. But the president knew none of them were ready to talk details yet. This meeting, therefore, was to talk about strategy, not tactics.

Specifically, if the United States went in, what geopolitical objectives would they want to achieve? What *could* they achieve? More to the point, should the United States back any one of the factional leaders now battling it out in the streets of Palestine? Could one of them reasonably be able to become a U.S. partner for peace?

For this the president turned to Erin McCoy. The president had known McCoy all her life and he trusted her judgment. Over the past thirty-one years, he'd not only watched her grow up, he'd seen her emerge as one of the Central Intelligence Agency's most effective operatives, following in her late father's footsteps.

When Erin had graduated as an Arabic specialist from the Defense Language Institute, the MacPhersons flew out to Monterrey, California, to celebrate with her. When she'd completed the CIA's Arab-language undercover training program in Casablanca, they met her in Paris to celebrate at her favorite Moroccan restaurant. When she'd been chosen for the "Bennett assignment," MacPherson had personally grilled her for hours until he was satisfied beyond the shadow of a doubt that she could handle the job. And now she was all grown up, and he wanted her assessment of the situation.

"Erin, there aren't too many people who have a better idea of what I'm hoping to accomplish and the facts on the ground than you do," MacPherson began. "So here's what I need. Give me your take on who could end up replacing Arafat, and if there's anyone in particular we should get behind. Now, I'm operating under the assumption—based on all of our meetings prior to the trip—that we're not inclined to trust one of Arafat's longtime political cronies, be it Saeb Erekat or Hanan Ashrawi, or one of the major Fatah leaders. But I don't really know much about these factional leaders waging the war right now—Dahlan or Rajoub or that other guy."

"Barghouti?"

"Exactly. I mean, who are these guys? Is any of them actually capable of making peace when the dust settles?"

21

McCOY wasn't quite sure where to begin.

She knew the dossiers on these guys inside and out. Ever since the CIA had assigned her to work on Bennett's team and the Medexco deal had begun gaining steam, she'd made it her mission to become an expert on all things Palestinian. But the president wasn't asking for factoids. He was asking for her assessment of their character and their potential for leadership.

McCoy asked Ziegler for a glass of water, and then began her narrative with the leading candidate to succeed Arafat, and perhaps the most powerful man in Palestine at the moment—Mohammed Dahlan.

Dahlan, she explained, served as head of the Palestinian Preventative Security Forces in Gaza from 1995 through 2002, resigned to go into business and make money for a few years, and then came back into government under Abu Mazen as head of all Palestinian security forces and effectively the "interior minister," though he didn't officially hold that title. Tall, dark, and dashing, with a dazzling smile and closely cropped black hair, Dahlan was married with three children. He was fluent in Hebrew, passable in English, had a huge power base in Gaza and the West Bank, and long fancied himself the rightful heir to Arafat, though he'd made a tactical decision to back Mazen when Arafat appointed Mazen as prime minister back in 2003.

Born in 1961, in a refugee camp in Gaza, Dahlan began life under the control of the Egyptian government. He was six in June of 1967 when the

Israelis won the Six Days' War. From that point on, he lived under Israeli occupation and thus began a deep and passionate hatred of the Israelis. As a teenager, he joined Arafat's Fatah, the armed political base of the PLO, began launching terrorist attacks against the Israeli Defense Forces, and eventually rose to become a commander of operations for Fatah. Between his twentieth and twenty-fifth birthdays, Dahlan was arrested ten times by the Israelis. That's where he learned fluent Hebrew—in Israeli prisons.

The Israelis' mistake, McCoy said, was ever letting him go. In 1987, almost as soon as Dahlan got out of an Israeli prison, he became one of the young leaders of the first intifada uprising against Israel. He recruited young people to become terrorist cell leaders. He trained them. He supplied them. Again he was arrested. Again he was released. This time he was deported to Jordan, where he fled to Egypt, then fled to Iraq, then eventually slipped back into the West Bank.

His rap sheet of terrorist acts went on page after page, and he had an unfathomable network of other terrorist factions with which he worked. At times he would sidle up to the Islamic radicals and encourage their actions. At other times, when he had power and was worried the Islamists were gaining too much power at his expense, he'd clamp down on them, imprisoning hundreds of Hamas and Islamic Jihad radicals and even tipping off the Israelis and Americans about the whereabouts of wanted terrorists.

At best, Dahlan's record was schizophrenic, McCoy observed. A few years before, he had been the alleged mastermind behind the bombing of an Israeli bus in Gush Katif and then another bloody series of attacks against Israelis in Gush Katif and Netzarim a month later. A few months later, Dahlan and his deputy, Rashid Abu Shabak, were believed to be behind a series of mortar attacks against Israelis. Then it was rocket attacks against Israeli buses. In one, an American citizen and three kids had their legs blown off.

"Back at CIA headquarters, we've actually got tapes of intercepted telephone calls in which Dahlan is ordering rocket and other terrorist attacks. The Israelis have their own tapes. Eventually, the Israelis had enough," McCoy explained. "They realized they'd made a mistake to keep jailing Dahlan and then letting him go. So they turned up the heat. Israel tried to take him out, but they missed."

✳ ✳ ✳

"Okay, tell me about Rajoub," the president continued.

McCoy proceeded to give a brief profile of the longtime chief of Palestinian security forces in the West Bank. Essentially, she began, Colonel Jibril Rajoub was Dahlan's counterpart, but he was responsible for a much larger swath of territory and thus potentially more powerful. Paunchy, dark skinned, balding, and with a small mustache, Rajoub hardly looked like a mafia boss. But he was not to be underestimated.

Vulgar, crude, and blunt, he had a ferocious temper—frequently on display—and he instilled fear in the hearts of those who lived under his rule. He brazenly took on Palestinian rivals. He was known for organizing bloody attacks on Israeli civilians. He was even known to torture journalists who wrote stories criticizing him. Some on the West Bank actually privately referred to him as the "Palestinian Saddam."

Rajoub was born in 1953 on the West Bank, in a little town near Hebron. At age seventeen, Rajoub—a rising young commando and recruiter in Arafat's Fatah—was captured by the IDF, tried in an Israeli military court, and sentenced to life in prison for throwing grenades at Israeli soldiers. Like Dahlan, Rajoub learned Hebrew in prison and English from television. Released in May of 1985 during a prisoner exchange between Israel and the PLO, Rajoub again became active in terrorist operations against the Israelis, becoming a key commander during the first intifada, which erupted in December of 1987. Like Dahlan, Rajoub was also eventually expelled by the Israelis, in his case to Lebanon in 1988. And also like Dahlan, Rajoub slipped back into the West Bank and eventually was targeted by the IDF for assassination. Three Israeli mortars landed on Rajoub's home one night, but he narrowly escaped, unharmed.

Rajoub's relationship with Arafat was also complicated, McCoy explained. He'd once been fired by Arafat, and they'd had numerous behind-the-scenes run-ins. The difference with Dahlan was that Rajoub wasn't so open in public about his interest in succeeding Arafat. But his relationship with the Islamic radical groups was probably just as tenuous as Dahlan's, because at times he'd fought against them to keep them from gaining too much power, while at other times he'd made common cause with Hamas and Islamic Jihad to strengthen his political base.

On May 27, 1998, for example, Rajoub told an Al-Jazeera television reporter, "We view Hamas as part of the national and Islamic liberation movement. . . . At the top of my list to defeat is the occupation and not Hamas. We are not interested in arrests."

Time after time, Rajoub had been quoted supporting an armed campaign of terror against the Israelis. Once, during a lecture at Bethlehem University, Rajoub told a crowd of students, "We sanctify the weapons found in the possession of the national factions which are directed against the occupation. . . . If there are those who oppose the agreement with Israel, the gates are open to them to intensify the armed struggle." Another time, he told a reporter that the only way for Palestinian terrorism to go away was for the Israeli prime minister "to remove all the settlers from the West Bank and Gaza and transfer them to hell," and then warned that he and his forces would "distribute weapons to the Palestinian residents and return to the armed struggle."

"If someone contacted this guy and asked him to stand down his forces for the sake of peace, would he listen?" the president asked. "Would he do it?"

"Not likely," McCoy said bluntly. "He's got too much invested to go down without a fight. And there's no way he's going to let Mohammed Dahlan climb to the top of the greasy pole and rule in Arafat's place. He thinks Dahlan is a playboy, not a serious player. There's no way he's going to bow down to and kiss Dahlan's ring—and there's no way he's going to kiss yours either, Mr. President."

*　*　*

The president bombarded McCoy with questions.

Bennett was impressed with her command of information. So were Ziegler and the rest of the NSC. As far as Bennett could tell, neither Mohammed Dahlan nor Jibril Rajoub sounded like a man with whom the U.S. could work. Neither sounded like a man inclined to establish the kind of peace treaty he'd been sent to achieve. But if there was any hope of salvaging the peace process at all, they had to find somebody they could work with. And then what? Would the U.S. really be in a position to take sides? to influence who seized control and who didn't? to choose the next Palestinian leader in the midst of a civil war? The whole thing seemed

preposterous. But something inside the president drove him to keep looking, and for this Bennett was grateful.

✳   ✳   ✳

McCoy moved to the next name on the list.

Marwan Bin Khatib Barghouti was another "son" of Arafat fighting
viciously for control, another Fatah member long imprisoned by the Israelis, and then, almost inexplicably, released to cause more death and destruction. Born in 1959, Barghouti grew up initially under Jordanian
occupation and was only eight years old when the Israelis won the Six
Days' War and seized control of the West Bank and Gaza.

Barghouti was a natural leader at an early age. At Birzeit University, a
hotbed of Palestinian radicalism, he quickly emerged as student council
president, became active in Arafat's youth militia, and helped organize
terrorist attacks against Israel during the first intifada, from 1987 through
1992. Then he too was arrested, tried, and convicted, and spent seven
years behind bars in an Israeli prison before being deported. There he also
learned Hebrew and developed the reputation among young Palestinian
militants as the leader of a new and rising generation.

In 1989, McCoy noted, though he wasn't even in the West Bank or
Gaza, Barghouti became the youngest member ever elected to the Fatah
Revolutionary Council. He came back to the West Bank in 1994, and
went on to be elected from Ramallah as a representative to the Palestinian
Legislature Council in 1996.

Along the way, Barghouti emerged as the secretary-general of Fatah,
rejected the Oslo peace accords between Israel and Yasser Arafat, and became the head of the Tanzim, an armed youth faction of Arafat's political
party. In that capacity, he began stockpiling German MP5 submachine
guns via Jordan and Egypt, building a network of commandos, and accru-
ing a budget of more than $2 million. He also helped create and lead the
Al-Aksa Martyrs Brigades, one of the most dangerous and radical of the
Fatah factions, responsible for many of the suicide bombings that killed
Israeli and American civilians from 2000 onward.

McCoy whispered something to Ziegler, who then opened a file cabinet, pulled out a flash drive, and loaded it into the computer on his desk. A
moment later, McCoy was directing the president and the NSC principals

to a series of PowerPoint slides on a large-screen monitor in the Situation Room.

McCoy began at the top, reading a quote by Abdel Bari Atwan, editor of the Arab-language *Al* newspaper: "'Marwan Barghouti has always identified with the grass roots rather than the Arafat leadership. . . . His star really came into it its ascendancy after he spoke out against the Palestinian Authority leadership.'

"That, Mr. President, is what makes Barghouti a potential successor to Arafat," said McCoy. "He's got a very strong grassroots network of fighters. He's willing to do anything to keep and maintain power. And he's fearless—he and his followers absolutely don't care if they live or die. They're not quite as committed as the devoutly religious Islamic fighters. But they're close. They're very well organized, and from what my guys can tell, they're moving into the streets and into the battle against Dahlan's and Rajoub's forces with a vengeance."

McCoy flashed more PowerPoint images on the screen, all excerpts from Barghouti's thick CIA dossier. Much of the material was obtained from the Mossad and Shin Bet, and it was a chilling read.

Slide 37: "On April 14, 2002, an IDF force in Ramallah arrested Marwan Barghouti, head of the Fatah supreme committee in the West Bank and leader of the military wing of the Al-Aksa Martyrs Brigades, which between September 2000 and April 2002 carried out thousands of terror attacks against Israel, including suicide bombings."

McCoy nodded to Ziegler. He pushed a button and the image changed.

Slide 38: "Marwan Barghouti served as secretary-general of Fatah in Judea, Samaria, and Gaza; a member of the Palestinian legislature; head of the Tanzim; and the founder of the Al-Aksa Martyrs Brigades, which has carried out a large number of deadly terrorist attacks, killing scores of Israelis and wounding hundreds. In the framework of his activities, he has received large amounts of funds from different sources both inside and outside Israel. Among these sources is the Palestinian Authority. The specific allocations of these funds were authorized by the actual signature of Yasser Arafat. These funds were used by Marwan Barghouti to finance many activities carried out by terror cells in the West Bank."

McCoy had Ziegler advance the image to the next slide, but this time she stayed quiet. Everyone read the material silently. The evidence, a partial list of the "more heinous terror attacks" for which the Israelis believed Marwan Barghouti was implicated, spoke for itself.

January 17, 2002—the shooting attack during a bat mitzvah celebration at a banquet hall in Hadera. Six Israelis were killed in this attack; twenty-six were injured.

January 22, 2002—the shooting spree on Jaffa Street in Jerusalem. Two Israelis were killed, thirty-seven wounded.

February 25, 2002—the shooting attack in the Jerusalem residential neighborhood of Neve Ya'acov. One Israeli policewoman was killed; nine Israelis were wounded.

February 27, 2002—the murder of an Israeli at a coffee factory in the Atarot industrial zone of Jerusalem.

February 27, 2002—the suicide attack perpetrated by Daryan Abu Aysha at the Maccabim checkpoint in which two policeman were injured.

March 5, 2002—the shooting spree at the Tel Aviv Seafood Restaurant. Three Israelis were killed, thirty-one wounded.

March 8, 2002—a suicide terrorist was killed in Daheat el Barid as he was on his way to carry out an attack in Jerusalem.

March 27, 2002—the interception of an ambulance and the confiscation of an explosive belt that was being smuggled from Samaria into Barghouti's terrorist infrastructure in Ramallah.

The president closed his eyes. The list of horrors went on for pages. But he couldn't take any more. What if one of these thugs actually ended up in power? What if he let it happen?

He called an end to the meeting. They'd been going for more than an hour. Now he needed time to think, and Bennett and McCoy needed time to rest. He ordered both of them, and Ziegler, to call it a night. They'd all regroup at 9:00 a.m. Wednesday, Washington time.

Ten minutes later, Bennett was out cold.

22
★ ★
★

IT CAME without warning.

One minute the Hotel Baghdad was standing. The next minute, it was not.

The attack came at precisely 4:49 a.m. local time. Without warning, the five-story structure above Gaza Station began to implode, rocked by three massive explosions and an eighteen-hundred-degree firestorm.

The east face came down first, followed by the south portico. Then, just a few seconds later, the rest of the building came down in a deafening roar of shattering glass and disintegrating concrete. The street filled with smoke. Flames shot out from every crevice, and thick clouds of smoke and ash began rising into the night sky.

Bennett was thrown to the floor. Covering his head with his arms, he desperately tried to shield himself from chunks of ceiling crashing down all around him. Everything in the room was shaking violently. He could hear the pipes in the bathroom being ripped through the tiles and erupting into a ceaseless spray of water. The lights flickered, sparked, and shorted out, and then several more explosions rocked the so-called safe house.

Disoriented and half asleep, Bennett was overtaken by an almost paralyzing sense of fear. His thoughts were racing. He tried to make sense of what was happening around him—on his stomach now, coughing, gagging, struggling to fill his lungs with anything but the hot, toxic gases rapidly filling the room. There'd been three successive detonations, followed by two or three more. It was a devastating surprise attack. But by whom? Was it a car bomb? Could that be causing so much destruction so quickly? That might explain the first explosion, but what about the others? Missile attacks? Mortar rounds? RPGs? From where? Who was firing at them? Who knew they were here?

He knew the questions had to wait, but more kept pouring in. Where was McCoy? Was she safe? What about Galishnikov and Sa'id? Had they told anyone where they were? How could they have? They didn't know. Not precisely. He needed to get his team out of here alive. But how? And where would they go? The minute they surfaced outside—assuming they could find a way out of the rubble, through the raging fires and the suffocating smoke—weren't they likely to get cut down in a hail of machine-gun fire?

The explosions stopped. Debris stopped falling. The temperatures were spiking quickly, and it was getting more and more difficult to breathe.

Bennett crawled his way through the broken glass of the television and shattered mirror and picture frames over to the door. He put the back of his hand against the door, just like his father had taught him when they'd stayed in hotels. It was hot—too hot—and he winced in pain, quickly pulled his hand back, and blew on it. He could see an orange glow through the cracks in the door frame. The fires had to be close. But he didn't really have any choice. If he stayed in Ziegler's room, he was a dead man. That much was certain. He decided right there—he might not make it out of this place, but at least he was going to die trying.

Bennett took off his right shoe, pulled off his sock, and put it over his left hand. Then, using that hand, he turned the handle and pulled the door opened. A blast of superheated air hit him in the face and he drew back, using the door as a shield. He put his sock and shoe back on and looked around the room. The fires in the hallway provided more than enough visibility to see the destruction that had been wrought all around him. He'd been lucky to survive the initial blasts. It was an oddly comforting thought, but it didn't last long.

Suddenly he heard the crackle of automatic gunfire. It was muffled and distant. For a moment he couldn't tell if it was aboveground or from the other side of the sprawling Gaza Station complex. Either way, a shot of adrenaline coursed through his veins. He had no way of knowing who was shooting at whom. But how was he supposed to defend himself if he had to—*when* he had to? McCoy always had that 9 mm Beretta with her, usually in her bag. His eyes darted around the room. He didn't see it. Maybe she had it with her now. He hoped she did. Maybe she was working her way back to him from wherever she was. Then again, maybe she was dead.

The thought terrified him. She couldn't be dead. He was falling in love with her. He couldn't even explain why. Not exactly. She had something he didn't have, and he had everything. She knew something he didn't. She *was* something he wasn't, and it drew him to her like a magnet. Better yet, she loved him. She'd never said it. But she'd never had to. He just knew it. It was instinct, and he had great instincts. That was his job—finding buried treasure—and he'd found it in McCoy.

Another explosion ripped through the building. Bennett wiped his face. It was soaked in sweat, as was his entire body. The temperature in this room had to be heading past a hundred degrees. Out in the hallway, it had to be fifteen to twenty degrees worse. He was out of time. He couldn't stay here. He needed to make his way down the hall, to the main control room, to Galishnikov and Sa'id's room. He needed to find McCoy, to make sure she was safe, to get them all out of here, come what may.

First, though, he moved to Ziegler's desk. The heat was unbearable. The floor was rapidly filling with water from the shattered pipes in the bathroom. He tore open the desk drawers and began ripping out everything he could find. But it wasn't until the bottom file drawer on the right-hand side that he found what he was looking for—two .357 Magnums, locked and loaded. Bennett clicked off both safeties, used his shoulder to wipe the sweat off his face again, then moved toward the hallway, holding both guns out in front of him. His heart was racing. His mouth was dry. His head was pounding with question after question. *What if he didn't shoot fast enough? Or worse, what if he shot one of his own?*

★　★　★

He worked his way to the door of the main control room.

He was on his stomach, on the floor—the only place he could breathe—covered in at least a foot of water. The water was ice-cold now and pouring out of a dozen other shattered pipes. But in forty-five minutes to an hour, it would be heating toward a boil. He didn't have any choice. He had to keep moving.

Bennett could hear men shouting in Arabic—he assumed it was Arabic, anyway—but he hadn't seen anyone, dead or alive. Where were they? All he could see were flames and smoke and the water he was crawling through. He was oddly, slightly grateful for the flames—at least they provided some light in this subterranean labyrinth. But the raging electrical fires in the walls and ceilings also worried him. It would take only one wire or cable falling into all this water and he'd be electrocuted instantly. An involuntary shudder rippled through his body.

His eyes—bloodshot and stinging from all the smoke—searched wildly for escape routes. But his options, limited from the beginning, were narrowing fast. The fires blocked his path to Galishnikov and Sa'id's room. Now they also blocked the way back to Ziegler's room. He wasn't completely trapped, but it was only a matter of time. He couldn't move laterally. He couldn't go back. The only way out was forward. There was only one door through which he could be saved. The question was, who or what was on the other side?

A gun battle had been under way in the control room for the last few minutes. But now things were quiet. Should he take a chance, or wait and keep listening? What was worse: the prospect of being electrocuted or boiled to death by staying put, or being shot in the head the minute he went through this door? It wasn't much of a choice, and only the thought of finding McCoy tipped the scales. The smoke was too thick to let him stand up. He'd suffocate for sure. All he could do was yank on the door handle and roll into the control room like he'd seen on TV. A moving target in a smoke-filled room with no light but exploding computer consoles and a back draft in the walls and ceilings couldn't be that easy to hit, right? He made up his mind. He'd move fast and take his chances.

Bennett took a deep breath. Then he lunged for the handle, tugged the door open, and rolled into the room.

The sound of the door swinging open and the sloshing water was a near-lethal combination. The place exploded with automatic gunfire. Bennett could hear the rounds smashing into the concrete walls and ricocheting into the water all around him. In the noise and confusion, he dove under a desk. He pressed himself flat against the floor, his eyes and nose just barely above the waterline. Then he held his breath and tried to be completely silent, completely still.

A few seconds later, the gunfire stopped. All was quiet again.

★　★　★

Bennett squinted through the smoke.

His eyes burned. His lungs burned. He glanced to the left, then back to the right, scanning the room for movement. His vantage point was actually pretty good. He was under Tariq's desk and next to one of the mainframe computer consoles. He had decent cover and could see most of the open spaces in the room from here.

He couldn't see into the various conference rooms and hallways jutting off this main control room. He had to assume that's where the gunfire was coming from. But at least he knew there was no one behind him, and he'd be able to see anyone who tried to approach him from the front or sides.

But now what? Was he supposed to just lie here, pinned down forever? The hatch to the Hotel Baghdad was only five or six yards ahead. But how could he make it without getting shot in the back? Even if he did make it up the ladder, he wouldn't be able to get out, would he? That lobby no longer existed. It was buried in five stories of concrete. If there was another way out, he had no idea what or where it was.

Suddenly he heard the slosh of water behind him. Someone was yanking the door open. Bennett rolled onto his back and pointed both guns at the door. Sprinting through the door wasn't a face he recognized. It wasn't a face he'd ever seen before. It wasn't a face at all. It was a man shrouded in a mask—a black hood, actually—like the ones he'd seen on the streets of Gaza City as they'd tried to escape the ambush at the PLC headquarters. He held a machine gun. He was moving fast, moving toward him.

Bennett didn't think twice. Both weapons fired. Both guns exploded. The man in the black hood snapped back, slammed against the wall, and slowly slumped to the floor into the water rapidly turning red. He was dead. Bennett had killed him. But now everyone knew where he was. The room again erupted in automatic-weapons fire.

Bennett rolled right—away from the dead man, toward the hatch. He didn't know why. He was operating purely on adrenaline and instinct and fear. Bullets were crashing into computers and files and walls. He saw a figure in the shadows, on the other side of the room, moving to take up a better position, also masked in black, his eyes red in the fierce glow of the flickering flames.

Bennett rolled into the small conference room where he and McCoy had spoken with the president and NSC just a few hours before. Inside, he pressed his back against the wall, then pivoted hard and thrust both arms—both guns—out the doorway. He fired two shots from each into the firestorm, then pulled back. The figure scrambled left and let loose another burst of gunfire. Bennett waited, pivoted again, fired again, but the rounds hit a television console that exploded on impact. He pulled back as more gunfire erupted into the conference room.

Bennett waited, then popped his head out the doorway to see where this guy was hiding. The roar of the fire was deafening. Bennett pulled back again. He was shaking uncontrollably. The smoke was so acrid, so pungent, that he could barely suck in enough air to fill his lungs. The heat was so intense that his raw, exposed skin was beginning to blister and boil. In a few minutes, the entire control room would be completely engulfed by fire, and there was no way out. He couldn't leave this room without being blown away, and even if he could, he had nowhere to go.

He didn't dare shut his eyes, though they were burning with pain, but he tried to picture Erin McCoy. He had no idea where she was. He had no idea if she was dead or wounded. But he tried desperately to imagine what she'd be doing right now if she was still alive in this inferno. She'd be fighting and she'd be praying; that much he knew. With her last breaths, she'd be firing back, defending this place and these people with her life. And she'd be asking God to protect them all from this hell, and the one to follow.

He knew it. He knew it because she'd done it before. When he'd been shot by the Iraqi at Dr. Mordechai's house in Jerusalem, he'd been slipping in and out of consciousness, but he'd heard her praying. She was literally begging God to save his life and his soul. She talked to God like she knew Him, like He could hear her, like she expected to see the supernatural. It was completely out of the realm of his understanding and experience. Yet it gave him the strangest sense of peace he couldn't explain away.

But that was *her* God, not his. It was *she* who had no fear of evil, not him.

Bennett could feel the evil in this room, and it terrified him. Something was stalking him. Something was hunting him. With the fires raging all around him, the temperature had been shooting past a hundred degrees, but Bennett's entire body felt chilled, as though an unseen presence, cold and dark, was moving through the room. It encircled him, surrounded him. It was poised to crush the life out of him. His body was trembling. He wanted to scream, but no sound would come. He wanted to run, but his legs would not move. He wanted to cry out to God to help him, to save him—but it was too late.

Bennett heard the burst of gunfire. He saw the grenade slam against the back wall of the conference room and drop into the water on the floor. Then the room erupted. All of the oxygen was sucked out. Flames tore into his eyes and consumed his flesh, and in an instant, it was over.

23

***

BEEP, BEEP, beep, beep.

The senior controller snapped to attention.

He hadn't been drifting off. But after nine hours on patrol on an E-3 AWACS some thirty-three thousand feet above the barren deserts of Iraq in the middle of the night, he wasn't exactly in top form. His eyes were heavy, his breathing slow. He was on his umpteenth cup of bad coffee and starving for something decent to eat.

But all that suddenly changed. He had an unknown contact—it had to be hostile—and he snapped back to life. The controller held the headphones tight against his ears and scanned his instruments. He called over to his commander. He had a vehicle of some kind—no, two—wait, make that three—and they were moving west-northwest.

"Can't be up to any good, can they?"

"Not likely, sir."

It was a convoy all right, racing for cover at eighty, maybe ninety miles an hour.

"Breaking for the Syrian border, are they? I guess we'd better stop them."

He punched a few buttons and opened up a secure channel with a pair of Apache helicopter gunships on patrol to the north. "Mongoose One Five, Mongoose One Six, this is Sky Ranch. Do you copy? Over."

"Sky Ranch, this is Mongoose One Five, copy you five by five."

"Ditto that, Sky Ranch. This is Mongoose One Six. Tell me you've got some action, sir. Ain't nobody out there but the Eighty-second, the Third ID, and a whole lot of sand."

"If you hustle a little, this just may be your lucky night."

"Every night is lucky with you, sir."

The E-3 commander filled in the Apache pilots on what little he knew so far. "Nobody gets across that border. That understood, boys? Nobody."

"You got it, sir. Mongoose One Five, inbound hot."

"Mongoose One Six, I'm right on his tail."

The Apaches broke out of their patrol pattern and raced south. Their rules of engagement didn't allow them to cross into Syrian airspace. That meant they didn't have much time. At most, they had three or four minutes to intercept whoever was in such a hurry to get out of the frying pan and into the fire. Who knew? This could be fun.

✳   ✳   ✳

The large red-and-white bus pulled away from Dizengoff Center.

It was a miserable night to be out, still pouring rain. The storm hadn't let up a bit. The driver made a few stops along the way, then began making his way north toward the Tel Aviv University campus. It was the last run of the night, which made it the last run of his career. He'd been with the Israeli transit authority for exactly twenty-five years and one month, and he was retiring to spend more time with his wife, his four grown children, and his six grandchildren. His two daughters still lived in Israel. One had just gotten married. His two sons and their families lived in the United States—one in Los Angeles, the other in Seattle.

They were good kids, and smart. For that he and his wife were blessed. They'd worried themselves sick with how to pay for each of them to go to college. It wasn't easy to raise a family on a bus driver's wages, even if his wife worked part-time as a dental hygienist. But they needn't have worried at all. In the end, each of their kids had won full scholarships to MIT, Caltech, Cornell, and Princeton. They met good Jewish kids along the way, got married, and started having children of their own. Now, finally, it was time to enjoy them—all of them—and as soon as they were finished taking some vacation time of their own down in Eilat, they'd start their "world grandkids tour."

The bus was noisy and chaotic. It was packed with foreign students, mostly Americans from TAU's Overseas Student Program, all of whom had stumbled out of a row of bars just now closing. Everyone was on break for a few weeks, celebrating Hanukkah and Christmas. How could they all be so drunk during the holidays? Didn't any of these kids have a religious bone in their body? Of course, thought the driver, his didn't either. Nor did he, for that matter. At least he wouldn't have to drive on New Year's Eve. Maybe he'd get drunk himself. One more stop and they'd be at the TAU campus. He could let all these kids off, and he'd be free at last.

He pulled over to the curb and opened the door. A young woman got on—the only person dumb enough to be out in the rain this late at night, the driver noted. She couldn't have been more than twenty or twenty-one, maybe younger, and she wore the green fatigues of the Israeli Defense Forces and a thick, padded army jacket. She was carrying an armful of packages and struggled up the steps. But she paid her fare quickly and nervously looked from side to side, presumably for a seat. There weren't many, the driver told her in Hebrew, maybe one or two in the back.

She seemed confused, even intimidated by so many kids, not much younger than her, yelling and laughing and carrying on. She slowly began making her way down the aisle. The driver closed the door, checked his mirrors, and pulled away from the curb. Two more miles, and he'd have peace and quiet all the way back to the bus compound.

★　★　★

"You hear that, Colonel?"

Daoud Juma was finally asleep. After two days and hundreds of miles on the run, he was bone tired and desperate for rest. But someone was calling him. Someone was asking him a question. Why? Couldn't they see he wanted to be left alone?

"Colonel? Colonel Juma? Sir, can you hear that? Something's approaching."

It was Arabic. Daoud could hear the words. He knew someone was talking. But he struggled to understand the words. He was fighting his way out of REM sleep, and he wasn't happy. He tried to open his eyes. They were covered over in film. The infection was coming back. He angrily wiped his eyes with a handkerchief and cursed the driver he now could see and hear all too well, even in the darkness.

"Sir—Colonel—I'm sorry to wake you . . ."

Sure you are, thought Daoud.

". . . but I think that's the sound of a chopper echoing through the canyon."

The night was as black as he'd ever seen it. But for their headlights and the internal lights of the dashboard, there'd be no light at all. He looked out the side windows, but all he could see was his own reflection. He'd have to take this kid's word for it. They were in a canyon of some kind, probably still winding along the Euphrates River. They couldn't be far from the border now. Or had they crossed over already and he hadn't been told. No, that was impossible. They wouldn't dare fail to keep him apprised. Even if he was sleeping. And there'd be border guards. Passport checks. Officials to confer with. Money to change hands.

A chopper? Was that what he'd just said? No one had helicopters out here—not coming from behind them. The Iraqis certainly didn't. Not anymore. That would have to be American. Daoud's eyes widened.

The junior officer's radio crackled to life. The men in the minivan behind him were also reporting what sounded like a helicopter several miles behind them. For a few moments, there was a lot of cross-chatter. Then came the question from one of the fedayeen commanders: what did Colonel Juma want to do?

"Any of you geniuses have a Stinger missile?" he barked over the walkie-talkie sitting on the backseat beside him. He was fully awake now.

"Yes, sir. We've got one left."

"Then in the name of Allah, use it," he shouted.

Surely he'd trained these men better than this. The convoy sped up, hugging the dirt road through hairpin turns. On straightaways, they were pushing at least ninety miles an hour. The problem was none of them knew the road well and were having trouble anticipating upcoming twists and turns. On top of that, the dust and sand they were kicking up was cutting visibility—already minimal—to just a few dozen yards, at least for the second and third drivers in the convoy.

Someone from the Range Rover came over the radio, asking if they should all cut their lights. Daoud put an end to such nonsense. If this was really an American helicopter, it was an Apache or a Cobra gunship, perhaps a Blackhawk. Either way, all of the Americans had night-vision systems and state-of-the-art FLIR technology—forward-looking infrared thermal-imaging systems that could pick up the heat signatures of their bodies and engines. Shutting off their headlights wouldn't trick the infidels, he stormed. It would only cause the three of them to crash into the canyon walls or into the river. Just floor it, he told them, and get that Stinger ready to fly.

The minivan driver was on the radio. His eyes were glued on the road ahead, but several of his men could see the lights of the chopper behind them. It was coming in fast and low. It couldn't be flying more than thirty or forty feet above the ground and was coming in at upward of 180 knots.

The Stinger operator raced through his procedures. He hadn't even had the thing out of the box until a few seconds ago. He was having trouble getting everything together in the dark, in the back of a packed minivan. But he'd have to do it fast. The chopper was bearing down on them, and he was running out of time.

Okay, he was almost ready. He needed to power up the battery and establish the range to target. Just a few more seconds—that's all he needed.

☆ ☆ ☆

"What the—we're getting painted."

"Mongoose One Six, this is Sky Ranch, say again—I repeat, say again."

"Sky Ranch, I said we're getting painted. Probably a Stinger."

"One Six, do you have a visual on the convoy?"

"Roger that, sir. We can see the convoy. Three cars. The last one just shot out their windows and they're painting us up. Do we have permission to fire, sir?"

"How many people in the last vehicle, One Six?"

"Looks like five or six, sir—they're on the run."

"Roger that, Mongoose One Six, you have authorization to fire."

The canyon narrowed. The convoy was moving at nearly a hundred miles an hour. It was a wonder the Renault could keep pace. But it wasn't the Renault they were after.

"I've got lock."

The Apache was closing in, but the pilot could also see the mountain walls narrowing still further. He might have time for one clean shot. After that, he'd have to pull up and reacquire the convoy on the other side of the pass.

"I've got tone."

The Apache pilot could see someone leaning out of the back of the minivan. The Stinger was ready to fire. He flipped a switch and took his weapons system off safety.

"Fox one, fox one."

The Hellfire missile exploded from the side of the chopper. It sizzled through the cold night air and devoured its prey. The fireball filled the canyon. The Apache pilot pulled up immediately and narrowly cleared the mountain pass ahead of him.

The Renault lost control. It skidded from side to side, then careened off the right side of the road, down toward the banks of the Euphrates, and barely came to a stop before plunging into the fast-moving river.

The Range Rover kept moving. Its driver and crew didn't have time to worry about the fate of the men behind them, even Colonel Juma. They blew through the narrow mountain pass and figured they had the Americans beat. Until they came around the next bend. That's when they saw Mongoose One Five. The other Apache. It was a half mile down the road, hovering no more than twenty feet off the road, and exploding from its side was a Hellfire missile with their names on it. Every man's eyes went wide with fear. And for good reason. It was the last image they'd ever see.

* * *

The driver glanced back at some of the rowdies.

They were throwing paper airplanes and singing "Ninety-nine Bottles of Beer on the Wall" in English and Hebrew. These kids were in college? It was pathetic. They were like a bunch of five-year-olds. The Americans should put all their high school graduates into the military for a few years, he decided. All of them. Put them through basic training. Make the guys serve at least three or four years. Make the women serve at least two. Just like in Israel. Teach them some discipline. Teach them some manners, if nothing else. It had worked for his kids—zapped the childish arrogance right out of them.

It had worked for him, too. He'd loved the army—and his annual reserve duty. It had forced him to get in shape and stay in shape. And driving a Merkava tank sure beat driving a bus. He wished he were mobilizing right now. He'd love to bulldoze his way into Gaza. He'd love to blow Mohammed Dahlan's headquarters to kingdom come. Too bad he was too old.

The driver noticed the young woman in the IDF garb sitting toward the back of the bus. She said nothing. She didn't look anyone in the eye. She was soaking wet but didn't seem to care. He looked back at the road and stopped at the approaching red light. It was odd, he thought. She didn't have a weapon with her. No sidearm. No M16. Wasn't it dangerous enough to be out alone on a night like this? And come to think of it, she wasn't wearing boots, was she? Those were tennis shoes. Not even nice ones. They weren't just soaked from the storm. They were filthy. And cheap. As the father of four and the grandfather of six, the man knew sneakers. He knew each brand and he knew how much they cost. After all, he'd been footing the bill for them for almost thirty years.

He glanced in the mirror again. They weren't American sneakers, or anything from Europe. They weren't made in Israel either. Those shoes were from . . . where were they from? The light turned green and he pressed down on the gas and began turning right. Hebron. They were from Hebron, the kind you could buy for a few shekels in East Jerusalem if you were too poor to buy anything else. After his brother was gunned down by a Palestinian sniper in Bethlehem when he was a kid, he'd vowed never to buy any product made by the Arabs. And he didn't care if he was just a lousy bus driver. He wasn't buying his kids sneakers made in Hebron. He'd rather take out a loan from the bank and . . .

He cursed and slammed on the brakes. Everyone lurched forward. He glanced back. The woman had fallen face-first on the floor. He reached under his seat and grabbed for his pistol. She was getting back up. Everyone was screaming. Her coat was off. She was wearing a suicide bomber's belt.

The driver found his gun. He flicked off the safety and wheeled around in the aisle.

"*Allahu Akbar!*" the woman screamed.

"*No!*" he screamed back.

She pulled a long red electrical cord from her pocket and reached for the ignition switch. He fired his weapon again and again and again—but it was too late.

The force of the explosion actually lifted the bus off the ground and flipped it over like a child's toy. The thin metal roof was ripped off like the top of a can of tuna. The windows were blown out and the seats inside the bus simply melted away.

Everyone on board was incinerated in a blinding flash of orange fire. Then glass and shrapnel and body parts began raining down in a 360-degree radius, just outside the Tel Aviv University dormitories. Dorm windows facing the street were shattered, and students not thrown from their beds were jolted awake by the enormous force of the explosion.

It took emergency vehicles and first responders less than four minutes to reach the blast site. Police cars, ambulances, and fire trucks came screaming from all directions. Shin Bet counterterrorism agents also raced to the scene, as did reporters from dozens of different news organizations and an FBI investigative team from the American Embassy.

They all descended upon a scene from a horror movie. Pieces of the bus and shoes and other, unspeakable things that used to be attached to human bodies were found in the trees and on parked cars and on apartment balconies hundreds of yards away. Emergency personnel, now numbering in the dozens, struggled to keep back local residents coming out of their homes to see what was going on and to offer whatever assistance they could.

In New York and Atlanta and Fort Lee, New Jersey, American cable television networks cut into prime-time programming with live coverage from the grisly scene of breaking news. The images were almost too horrific to broadcast in family rooms all over the world, and hard facts and actual, confirmed details in those early minutes were sketchy. The only thing certain was that the scene was absolute chaos.

But the worst was not yet over. In the darkness and rain and chaos no one noticed—or bothered to pay attention to—the dark young man approaching from the south on the sidewalk closest to the dorms. He looked like any other Israeli grad student trying to look more Western than Middle Eastern.

If any of the dozens of local police officers on the scene had bothered to check his papers, they would have discovered that the twenty-six-year-old Mohammed Saleh was not Israeli but a native of Jericho. If anyone had bothered to check his duffle bag, they would have discovered it wasn't filled with clothes or books but five pounds of nails and broken glass and fifteen pounds of military-grade TNT, scraped out of Egyptian mines littered throughout the sands of the Sinai Desert. If anyone had bothered to check his Walkman, they would have discovered that it contained no cassette tape or CD but a sophisticated ignition device built in Iran and smuggled six months earlier through Saudi Arabia and Jordan and then into the West Bank. But no one bothered to check the young man at all. There was too much to do, too many to console.

So Mohammed Saleh moved almost invisibly through the crowd, maneuvering for the best view of the crime scene, on the opposite side of the street from the pack of hungry media wolves, in full view of the lights, cameras, and boom microphones. He worked his way to the center of the crowd, numbering at least fifty or sixty at this point. He closed his eyes, bowed his head, and said a silent prayer to Allah. Then he pressed Play.

The second explosion was not as powerful as the first, but it was far more diabolical. The force of the blast melted torsos and decapitated victims closest to the flash point, as flying nails and broken glass, hurling through the air at the speed of sound, shredded bodies in the next perimeter, all in full view of a worldwide television audience. And little did anyone know that so much more was coming.

★   ★   ★

Yuri Gogolov watched the coverage without emotion.

He did not grieve for the victims or their families. But he could already imagine their reaction, and the visceral reaction of Israel's top leaders. Their rage was palpable, even from Tehran. So was their hunger for vengeance. Reciprocity.

They would force Doron to act. They would insist that he unleash the full fury of the Israeli Defense Forces on the Palestinian population centers, and Doron would oblige them. Because that's the way the game was played.

24

⋆ ⋆
⋆

BENNETT SAT bolt upright.

He was trembling, soaked with sweat. He felt clammy and disoriented. He gulped in oxygen and tried not to hyperventilate, not to succumb to the panic rising within him. The air was cool, even chilly. He couldn't smell any smoke. There were no flames, no trace of fire or burst pipes, no hint of any kind that Gaza Station was under attack or that the Hotel Baghdad had collapsed above them. So where was he? What had just happened? Where was McCoy?

The narrow, windowless room was pitch-black but for the luminescence of his wristwatch and the digital clock on the DVD player a few feet away. Bennett ran his hands through his wet hair and tried to get his bearings.

Had all that just been a nightmare?

It seemed hard to believe. It was too vivid, too real. But nothing else made sense. He was still alive. That much seemed certain. If it had been real, if he'd just been killed in a massive underground explosion, then . . . then what?

The question terrified him. He wasn't sure if he believed in a higher power or a life hereafter. But what if he was wrong? How many times had he cheated death in the last few hours, the last few weeks? More than he cared to count. But he was gambling, and he knew it. One of these days—perhaps sooner than he realized—his luck was going to run out. One of these days he was going to know for certain the truth of what was on the other side, because he'd be there, and that's what scared him.

"It's not that I'm afraid to die. I just don't want to be there when it happens."

It was an old Woody Allen line. Bennett couldn't even remember where he'd heard it. But it suddenly resonated. So did another Allen quip: "If only God would give me some clear sign! Like making a large deposit in my name at a Swiss bank."

Bennett had spent his whole life avoiding any serious thought of death. Now it was catching up to him. In a sense, God *had* made a large deposit in Bennett's account, hadn't He? Nine-point-six-million dollars, to be exact. He'd been feverishly stashing away cash for years. But what good would it do him if he died tonight in Gaza?

Bennett stared into the darkness. His heart rate was slowing, but his mind wrestled with unsettling thoughts. In a way, God and the afterlife were kind of like gravity, weren't they? It didn't matter if he believed in gravity or not. Gravity was a fact, a simple physical law, a force of nature. A person could stand on the top of the Empire State Building shouting, *"I don't believe in gravity. I can't see it. I can't taste it. I can't touch it. It doesn't exist."* And then jump. But what then? Would his lack of belief in gravity cushion his fall? Of course not. He'd smash on the pavement and die.

Gravity couldn't be seen. But that didn't mean it wasn't true. The truth about gravity could be discovered. And wasn't it smarter to discover gravity before it was too late? Maybe the same was true about God. Maybe it was smarter to find Him before jumping blindly into eternity like a fool without a parachute.

Bennett looked at the clock on Ziegler's DVD player. The numbers read 4:53, but that didn't compute—a.m. or p.m.? Bennett's eyes struggled to adjust. It was a.m.

Had he really slept so long? What day was it? He squeezed his eyes shut, trying desperately to focus. It was Monday—no, it was Tuesday—December 28. His body wasn't rested. The impending sense of danger was so acute that it was almost physically painful. He reconciled himself to the fact that he'd just experienced a nightmare—not reality—but somehow it didn't make the anxiety any less real.

Something told him evil was coming. He couldn't see it. He couldn't prove it. But he had no doubt Gaza Station faced a new threat. But what should he do about it? What exactly was he supposed to say to Ziegler and McCoy when he found them—*if* he found them? *He'd had a little nightmare so they should all abandon ship?*

It sounded ridiculous. He was a strategist, not a fortune-teller. His job was to trade in facts, not premonitions. Why then did he feel so certain? He often acted on less than complete information. He often went with his gut instincts. It's what kept him ahead of his competitors. It's what got him so far at GSX. He'd trusted his instincts, advised others to put their faith in them, and made a lot of people, including himself, very rich in the process. That's what finding buried treasure was all about.

But this was different. The decisions he made in the next few hours, the decision the United States made, had enormous consequences. He needed to do more than simply find a way to save his own life and the lives of his friends from the evil that was coming. He needed to find a way to get the peace process back on track and to stop the evil already unleashed. But how? He'd never prayed before. He felt like a hypocrite for even thinking about it. But maybe McCoy was right. Maybe he'd get an answer. Every fiber of his being doubted it. But what could it really hurt?

"God, if you're there, if you really exist, please help me. Get us out of here alive. I'm scared of dying, scared of what's coming. I admit it. But I'm asking you to please protect Erin, wherever she is. And my mom—she's suffered enough already. Amen."

Bennett finished his prayer and waited. He'd done it the best he knew how. The room was dark and quiet. He wiped sweat away from his eyes and neck. He wasn't sure if he should expect an answer—a voice, a light, something.

The longer he waited, the more stupid he felt. He had a job to do. He reached over to the desk, picked up the phone, and dialed Orlando again. He needed to talk with the president. But first he needed to talk with his mom.

No luck. The phone kept ringing. No one was answering. He looked at his watch again, then put the phone down. He called his own voice mail in New York, at home and the office. He called his voice mail at the White House. He rechecked the front desk at the Willard InterContinental Hotel in Washington, where he was staying until he found a place to rent.

Lots of messages—colleagues worried for him, Marcus Jackson from the *Times* trying desperately to track him down. But none were from his mom. How long should he wait before worry turned to action? And what then?

* * *

The radio receiver crackled to life.

"Shlomo Six to Shlomo One, do you read me? Shlomo Six to Shlomo One, do you read me? Over."

The Hebrew coming into his tiny earpiece was but a whisper. But even amid the driving rains and rumbling thunder, the voice was still clear and audible. The ferocity of the storm did seem to be lessening somewhat. They'd been able to get the small prop plane up in the air, after all, and their overpaid pilot hadn't been shot down by the Israeli Air Force. Now he and his team were descending rapidly, almost at the strike point.

All systems were go. They were about to actually do what for years they could only dream about. They were witnessing one miracle after another. This was history in the making, and he was in the driver's seat.

"Shlomo Six, this is Shlomo One, I read you loud and clear. Go ahead."

Akiva Ben David glanced at his wrist. With his gloved left hand, he wiped the rain off his goggles, then off his altimeter. They were passing down through three thousand feet, he told his colleague, who quickly passed the information to his fellow commandos in position not far from the Western Wall. As expected, the crosswinds were intense, but all six of them were handling their chutes well. He expected they would all be hitting the Temple Mount—*Har Habayit* in Hebrew, *Haram esh-Sharif* in Arabic—any moment.

"Shlomo One, give me a status check—what's your ETA?"

Altogether, there were only twelve of them—six coming in from the air, six more on the ground. It was not a large force, and he would have liked more. But most of his followers were ultra-Orthodox and very few of them had any military training at all. He had more than fifteen thousand dues-paying members worldwide. Some were sabras, native-born Israelis. Others lived in Australia, New Zealand, or Central or South America. Most lived in the U.S., predominantly from New York, New Jersey, and New England. But very few of them had ever held a gun, much less fired one, or done so on a daring assault on the most holy site in all of monotheism. And jumping out of airplanes at eleven thousand feet in the middle of the night in the middle of a raging electrical storm? As his friends back in Brooklyn might say, *Fugghedaboudit*.

"We're in position. We think we can get to you in less than six minutes."

"What about the others?" Ben David asked, the tension in his voice rising.

"Everyone's in position. We're ready to move. Over"

"*Tov*. Stand by one."

His team thought he was crazy for moving tonight of all nights. But Ben David was adamant. The civil war in Judea, Samaria, and Gaza was a godsend. It meant the Palestinians' attention was elsewhere. By the time they organized a counterattack, it would be too late. Doron was moving Israeli forces to the borders, sealing them off from the rest of Israel, and Jerusalem in particular. No Palestinian would be able to get to the Temple Mount tonight. Not from the territories.

Besides, the Temple Mount Battalion would have already succeeded. They'd have destroyed the Dome of the Rock and the mosque. With any luck, they'd begin to erect the new Jewish Temple. The raging storm was just more divine icing on the cake. IDF patrols weren't flying. Security personnel on the Mount were staying inside, their feet up on their desks, watching TV, playing cards, drinking coffee, doing everything possible to stay out of the whipping winds and bone-chilling rains. Ben David and his men would have the critical element of surprise, and that should make all the difference.

Ben David made visual contact with his fellow paratroopers. They'd be on the ground inside soon, and it was time for a weapons check. He double-checked his own M4 carbine 5.56 mm machine gun with laser scope and his 9 mm Glock sidearm. He clicked the safeties off both and adjusted his night-vision goggles. The others followed suit. Then he checked his altimeter again and strained to see something—anything—through the heavy rain and fog. A moment later, there it was.

"I can see it," he shouted into his headset. "I can see the dome straight ahead."

Even Akiva Ben David had to admit it, at least to himself. He'd certainly never admit it out loud. But it was an empirical fact. Qubbat al-Sakhra—known in English as the Dome of the Rock—was an awe-inspiring sight, even to the founder and leader of the Temple Mount Battalion. With its hand-painted cobalt blue tiles and stunning twenty-four-carat golden roof—all lit up by powerful spotlights—the splendor of the dome simply wasn't in dispute. Islam's third-holiest site, together with the Al-Aksa Mosque, was breathtaking, even when seen through the greenish haze of night-vision goggles.

But that was hardly the point. It didn't matter to Ben David that the site claimed by a billion Muslims worldwide was supposed to be the exact place where Mohammed was taken up to heaven to meet with Allah. They were simply wrong.

The Muslims could believe whatever they wanted. But theirs was a false religion. Theirs was a false god. And they were occupying sacred ground, Jewish ground. That didn't mean their architecture wasn't sublime. It was, especially from this angle.

What the Muslims thought or believed or preached didn't matter to Ben David. What mattered was liberating the Temple Mount and ending its desecration at the hands of Islamic invaders. What mattered was ushering in the triumphant arrival of the coming Jewish Messiah. What mattered was forcing the hand of God.

Soon his feet would touch down on the site where King David's son Solomon built the First Temple, nearly three thousand years ago. The Babylonians, of course, had destroyed the Temple in 586 BCE. But that hadn't stopped the Jews from rebuilding it in the exact same location. Construction of the Second Jewish Temple began in 520 BCE and came to completion around 20 BCE, during the reign of King Herod. The Romans, of course, had destroyed it in the year AD 70—and the city of Jerusalem as well—burning the Temple to the ground and not leaving one stone standing upon another. For two thousand years, the Jews had been scattered around the globe, without a home and without a Temple. But no more. Now they were home. And it was time to rebuild.

This, he told himself, was Jewish ground. This was holy ground—the most coveted thirty-five acres on the face of the earth. And the most dangerous.

Every few years, ever since the Israelis seized control of the Temple

Mount during the Six Days' War of 1967, teams of Jewish zealots, worried that the Israeli government might be persuaded to give away part or all of the Old City of Jerusalem in the name of peace, had tried to seize the Temple Mount and blow up the Al-Aksa Mosque and the Dome of the Rock. On March 10, 1983, twenty-nine Jewish terrorists armed with machine guns, grenades, and dynamite scaled the walls of the Temple Mount, stormed the grounds, and were stopped by security forces only at the very last minute. One of the most dramatic attempts occurred in January of 1984, when a team armed with hundreds of pounds of dynamite, grenades, and mortars again scaled the walls, sprinted for the dome, and very nearly accomplished their mission.

Much to the disappointment of Akiva Ben David and his followers, however, the zealots were spotted by Arab guards and an alert unit of the Israeli Border Patrol. They were captured, arrested, and eventually convicted in an Israeli court of law. The government tried to make an example of them, hoping to send the message that any attacks on Muslim holy sites would be dealt with severely. It was a pretty simple calculation, after all. Someday, some militant Jewish sect might actually succeed in blowing up the Dome of the Rock in the name of building the Third Jewish Temple. But in so doing, they would unleash the wrath of a billion Muslims and two dozen heavily armed Islamic nations, not to mention the entire world.

It was a volatile situation, to say the least. The head of the Shin Bet, Israel's domestic intelligence service, had once sent a confidential letter to Israeli prime minister Ehud Barak warning that an extremist strike on the Temple Mount would likely lead to an "all-out war" and "unleash destructive forces that would imperil Israel's existence." It was a letter passed along to every Israeli prime minister since.

Nothing held the power to trigger an apocalyptic holy war so quickly as failing to protect those thirty-five sacred acres. It was no wonder, therefore, that the Israeli police forces vowed to protect the Temple Mount at all costs.

But tonight, Akiva Ben David had found a weak link in the armor.

★　　★　　★

One of the phones on Ziegler's desk rang.

Startled, Bennett grabbed the phone. Maybe it was his mother. It wasn't.

"Jonathan, it is me, Dmitri," whispered an exhausted Galishnikov.

"What's going on?" He could hear Sa'id in the background, talking heatedly on another phone.

"You need to hear it straight from Ibrahim. Only him. How fast can you be here?"

"I don't know. I just woke up—I need a shower, a shave—"

"No, no, you don't understand—we need you here in five minutes—no more."

The line went dead. Bennett wasn't used to taking orders from Dmitri Galishnikov. But this time he didn't seem to have a choice.

25

THE FIRST BULLET sliced past his head.

It missed by inches. A second shot ripped through his parachute—then a third, and a fourth. The ground was coming up fast. He had to concentrate. He had to choose.

"Shlomo Six under fire—we're under fire. Move, now—*go, go, go.*"

Akiva Ben David was shouting as he twisted his head from side to side, trying to see who was firing at him through sheets of rain. He only had a few seconds before he smashed down on the stones below. If he wasn't dead by the time he hit the ground, he'd soon be a sitting duck for sure—covered with a parachute, tangled up in cords, exposed and out in the open, a good thirty or forty yards from his target.

He cursed his ground units for not being in position already. He cursed himself for having trained them so poorly. *Fools. How badly did they want this to happen? They knew what was at stake. Weren't they ready to make history? Where the heck were they?*

Then he saw the shooter. Out of the corner of his eye, he could see a guard sprinting from the northeast corner. Ben David lifted his M4 carbine, aimed the laser scope, centered the red dot, and squeezed off two rounds, one after the other. The guard dropped instantly, landing in a pool of his own blood.

Now the entire Temple Mount erupted in a ferocious gun battle. Everyone was shooting. Tracer bullets whizzed back and forth through the cold night air. Security horns began blasting. Sirens could be heard approaching from every direction. The entire operation was a matter of split-second timing. Ben David figured they had less than fifteen minutes, and that was his best-case scenario. In that time they had to take out the guards already stationed on the Mount, hold off the reinforcements, and rig the two buildings for detonation.

He'd played the scene over and over again in his mind's eye for years, and vivid images now flashed before him. He could see the stunning Byzantine architecture of the dome, built by Umayyad Caliph Abd al-Malik in the year 692. He could see the somber black dome of Al-Aksa, started by Abdul al-Malik ibn Marwan, completed by his son al-Walid in the year 705, reconstructed in the year 1035, then refurbished during the Second World War. He could see the backpacks stuffed with C4 explosives positioned strategically in and around the structures.

He could see, too, the massive, simultaneous explosions—the cataclysmic fireballs—the raging flames and towers of smoke that would be seen for miles, all of which would be captured by at least a dozen security cameras, possibly more.

They would catch the world off guard. No one was expecting this. No one had predicted this. The attacks would dominate international headlines for weeks. The world would be talking about them. Who were they? Why had they chosen to strike? And why now? Was the attack related to the war in the territories? Was it payback for the suicide bombings? Would the Temple really be rebuilt? Was it a sign of the last days, the fulfillment of ancient prophecies?

Soon enough, the Israelis would have to release the videotapes made by all those security cameras. The international media would demand it. And the Israeli Supreme Court would eventually require it. Then, finally, the world would see exactly how Ben David and the Temple Mount Battalion had done it—the first airborne attack on the Temple Mount in history—all to right a wrong and unleash a movement of religious Jews ready to seize their destiny.

Three police officers burst out of a guardhouse. Ben David saw them immediately. He raised his weapon, fired two bursts, and saw two of the men drop instantly to the ground. The third dove into a grove of trees and began returning fire. Three of his fellow commandos were about to touch down. One, if he was lucky, might even land dead center on the golden dome. Perhaps he'd be able to attach explosives far above where anyone on the ground could easily get at them. They'd thought about that. They'd trained for it. But Shlomo Five might actually get to do it.

More machine-gun fire. Two more teammates were already on the ground, about forty yards away. They were unhooking their parachutes and about to sprint to the octagonal base of the dome, spectacularly adorned with brilliant blue hand-painted tiles. But again Ben David cursed to himself. *Where were the ground units? Why weren't they providing cover fire?*

A scream suddenly exploded through his earpiece.

"I'm hit. I'm hit."

In all the gunfire and noise, Ben David couldn't make out the voice. He didn't have time to figure it out either. For a moment, he let go of the M4 strapped to him, pulled down on the cords dangling close by to slow his landing, bent his knees, and touched down perfectly, just as he'd mastered it in months of training in the western deserts of the United States. He dove to the ground for cover and began rolling right.

Bullets were slicing the night sky above him. He needed to get the chute off quickly and get moving. He was now exposed on the southeastern corner of the massive plateau. The Mount of Olives was behind him. The Al-Aksa Mosque loomed dead ahead. Over his headset he could hear more screams. The crackle of gunfire was almost deafening. But somehow the cries of a dying man—a friend and comrade-in-arms—cut through it all.

* * *

Bennett showered and threw on jeans, a white T-shirt, and a black sweater.

They were Ziegler's. He'd give them back later. Seven minutes later, he was punching in Tariq's code number and opening the door. Galishnikov and Sa'id were sitting on the couches near the TV, huddled around the coffee table with McCoy and deep in discussion. All three looked up to greet him, but it was McCoy who immediately noticed how pale Bennett was.

"You okay?" she asked. "You don't look so good."

"It's nothing; I'll be fine," Bennett lied, not sure where to begin.

"Jon, obviously you're not fine. What's the—"

"I said I'm fine," Bennett shot back, more abruptly than he'd meant to. He didn't mean to be harsh, certainly not with her, and he was surprised by the edge in his voice. But he didn't have time to process all the thoughts and emotions roiling under the surface. He felt lazy for sleeping so long and guilty for being out of the loop. He wanted time to talk to Erin alone. But for now his top priority was to get back up to speed as fast as possible.

"Erin, I'm sorry. I really am. It's just—I'm sorry."

They were all punchy. They were all under a lot of stress. Certainly McCoy was, and she hadn't gotten anywhere near the sleep Bennett just had. She could feel herself ready to fire back. But she held her tongue. Now was not the time to get into a fight. Too much was at stake. She nodded, accepted his apology, then looked over at Ibrahim Sa'id, the man whose news was about to change everything.

★ ★ ★

Marsha Kirkpatrick was suffering from sleep deprivation.

So was the rest of her team. Now they were tracking a series of suicide-bomber attacks throughout Israel. The carnage began with the bus bomber and then the Walkman bomber at Tel Aviv University. But those weren't isolated incidents. Another bombing had ripped through a nightclub along the beach in Tel Aviv. Ten minutes later, another incinerated a bus stop in the French Hill section of Jerusalem. Eight minutes later, a bomber had attacked the bus terminal in Haifa.

Prime Minister Doron and his Security Cabinet were meeting behind closed doors to discuss their options. They knew full well the risks of launching an all-out invasion of the West Bank and Gaza, and they knew the American president had asked them to stand down just the previous day. But if a Palestinian civil war was going to mean a new wave of attacks against innocent Israelis, the prime minister and his government could not afford to sit on their hands, no matter what the international repercussions might be. That was the message Doron had delivered to Kirkpatrick by phone ten minutes earlier, just before going back into the emergency session with his top advisors. It was a message he needed to have passed on to President MacPherson, immediately.

Kirkpatrick promised to get back to him quickly, but asked that Israel do nothing until the two leaders could speak. Doron agreed, but he made it clear—they were running out of time.

"Mr. President, I'm so sorry to wake you. It's Marsha in the Situation Room."

"What . . . what's going on?" MacPherson stammered, barely conscious.

"We need to meet. All of us."

He tried to focus on the small digital clock beside him. "Right now? The whole team?"

It was just after eleven at night. He'd been asleep less than two hours.

"I'm afraid so, sir." Kirkpatrick knew the president was still recovering from his own life-threatening injuries sustained during the terrorist attacks against him in Denver just before Thanksgiving. She knew the immense pressures he faced and how badly he needed some rest. And she knew that the White House doctor had insisted that MacPherson break away from the almost nonstop NSC meetings just a few hours ago to get some sleep and try to regain his strength. But the president also knew that his national security advisor wouldn't call—wouldn't insist on a meeting—if it wasn't absolutely critical.

"Okay, gather the team. I'll be right down."

★ ★ ★

Ben David pressed himself to the ground.

He flipped on his night-vision goggles and scanned the courtyard. Two of his men were sprinting for the Dome. He could see they had bags of C4. They were firing off bursts of machine-gun fire on the run. An Israeli opened fire from behind a stone. Ben David could clearly see the muzzle flashes. He took aim and squeezed off six rounds. The flashes stopped, but not for long. By his calculations, they now had less than three minutes before Israeli commandos would swarm in from every direction.

"Shlomo One, this is Shlomo Six—where are you guys?"

It was chaos on the radios. Gunfire, men screaming—he'd never heard it this bad. His men were rattled. The Arab guards and Israeli first responders were putting up a far tougher fight than they'd expected.

"I'm at Mughrabi Gate—we're under heavy fire. We've got two KIA.

Repeat, two KIA. Taking sniper fire from one of the minarets. Shlomo Nine and Eleven are badly wounded. Don't think they're going to make it. Shlomo Ten and Twelve are pinned down in a gun battle on the North Portico."

Ben David's mind reeled. They were on the cusp of victory, the cutting edge of history. They were so close. They couldn't fail now. His people had trained so long and so hard for this operation. They knew the stakes, and he wanted desperately to believe they were uniquely chosen for this moment in history, in Jewish history.

They all knew that in the "last days" the State of Israel would be reborn after two thousand years of desolation and exile, and that Jerusalem would—someday, somehow—once again become the eternal, undivided capital of the Jewish people. They knew beyond the shadow of a doubt that the Holy One of Israel would supernaturally draw the Jewish people back to the land of Abraham, Isaac, and Jacob. And they knew, too, that the day of Israel's eternal redemption was drawing near.

They knew because he'd taught them day after day, verse after verse. The "Day of the Lord" was almost here. Events were already in motion. The divine clock was already ticking. Akiva Ben David could still hear the scratchy, crackling voice of Israeli general Mordechai Gur on his parents' transistor radio in June of 1967, announcing for all the world to hear, "The Temple Mount is in our hands." It was a moment he would never forget, a moment of electrification, a moment of instant identification with five thousand years of Jewish history. It was as though in a split second, something inside of Ben David—something deep inside millions of Jews worldwide—clicked on, a palpable sense that he was part of something larger than himself, something transcendent and real.

Ben David's family was not religious at the time. They were all agnostic, secular Jews. Living on the Upper East Side of Manhattan in a world of wealth and sophistication, they barely even thought of themselves as Jews. They were Americans. They were modern, hip, cosmopolitan, not a bunch of knuckle-dragging Neanderthals trying to find the source of fire and the meaning of life. But something happened. Israeli forces were standing on Mount Moriah.

For the first time in thousands of years, Jews were standing where Abraham once stood, where he nearly sacrificed his only son, Isaac, until

God intervened and provided a ram as a substitute. Moreover, these Jews weren't simply standing at the epicenter of monotheistic faith. They now controlled it forever—the Temple Mount, the site of two great Temples, and a third yet to be built.

Ben David's stomach tightened. A wave of nausea swept over him. But he couldn't stay where he was. He began racing for the mosque.

Crack, crack, crack.

Bullets smashed into walls and pavement all around him. He was twenty feet from the side door. The stones were slick from the rains. Ben David worried he'd—

Suddenly, two tremendous explosions went off, one to his right, one on his left. The concussion of the blasts—one right after the other— knocked him off his feet and sent his machine gun and night-vision goggles flying. He skidded along the ground, drenched to the bone and freezing cold. Then came another shower of gunfire.

Momentarily unable to see or hear, Ben David scrambled forward until he reached the eastern porch of the mosque, desperately trying to get out of the line of fire. Only then did he realize his head and face were raked by shrapnel and shards of glass. He could feel himself shaking, about to slip into shock. He feverishly wiped smoke and blood out of his eyes.

That's when he saw a guard charging toward him.

Through the blood gushing from his forehead down across his face, he could see that the man was at least sixty, white hair, white beard. Even through the rains he could see the two pistols the man brandished, one in each hand. They were firing again and again and again as the man raced toward him. He could see the flashes. He could hear the explosions. And then he felt the fiery rounds smash into his chest and arms and face, and it was all over. The battle was done. The Temple Mount Battalion had failed.

26

⋆ ⋆
⋆

IT WAS 11:17 P.M. in D.C., 6:17 a.m. in Israel and the territories.

All the key principals were present and accounted for. Joining from Gaza Station were Jake Ziegler, Erin McCoy, and Jon Bennett.

"Okay, let's go. What have we got?" the president began, taking a sip of fresh coffee and anxious to get moving.

"Mr. President," Kirkpatrick began, "over the last few hours, we have seen the crisis in the Middle East take a serious turn for the worse."

She walked the president through an executive summary of each suicide bombing, the fact that no Palestinian group had yet taken credit, and an overall casualty count.

"How many Americans?" the president demanded.

"At last count, we're looking at forty-one Americans dead."

MacPherson couldn't speak.

"All of them were students at Tel Aviv University, Mr. President—part of the Overseas Student Program, some for one semester, some for two."

The room was silent.

"So far, fifty-two Israelis are dead, and three Canadians," Kirkpatrick continued. "Israelis wounded at this point—let's see, it looks like two hundred and thirteen. An American family of six was also wounded at the bus station in Haifa."

It was the first Bennett had heard of the attacks. He hadn't had time to be briefed by McCoy or Ziegler, and he suddenly felt sick to his stomach.

A gasp rippled through the NSC team as well. They were all professionals. They'd all seen civilian carnage before. But the images on the screens were unreal, as were their political implications. The dynamic was changing, rapidly.

"Sir, unfortunately, that's not all. In the last few minutes, an obscure Jewish extremist group—"

"Terrorist group," interjected the CIA director.

"—terrorist group known as the Temple Mount Battalion launched a series of attacks against the Dome of the Rock and the Al-Aksa Mosque, armed with over a hundred pounds of C4 plastic explosives, about thirty or forty grenades, light arms and several thousand rounds of ammunition."

"Oh no," said the president. "Please don't tell me they succeeded."

Kirkpatrick dialed up a live video image from a billion-dollar, American-made Keyhole spy satellite orbiting over Jerusalem, cross-linked from the National Reconnaissance Office in Chantilly, Virginia.

"Almost, sir—but not quite."

"How many were there?"

"We're monitoring all Israeli police and border patrol radio traffic. Best we can tell so far is that there were somewhere between ten to fifteen terrorists. Most are dead. It seems as though the Israelis have at least two of the attackers in custody, wounded but likely to survive."

"Jack, what do you think the Israelis will do?" the president asked.

The president considered Jack Mitchell a close friend and a first-rate spy, a man whose judgment he could trust, a rare commodity in a town like Washington.

"I know for a fact Doron is meeting with his Security Cabinet right now," said Jack Mitchell. "My sense is that in the next fifteen or twenty minutes, they're going to come out of there ready to unleash everything they've got against the Palestinians."

"Should they?" asked the president.

"If they don't, they're inviting more Jewish terrorists to take matters into their own hands. I'd recommend, sir, that you call Doron and give him the green light immediately."

The president looked around the room. Mitchell had a good point. But none of them yet knew what Bennett knew.

* * *

"Forget the Americans, Avi—we need to get on the offense."

Yossi Ben Ramon, the fifty-eight-year-old, take-no-prisoners, chain-smoking head of Israel's internal security forces known as the Shin Bet, was furious. He hadn't slept all night. He and his team had suffered one disastrous failure after another, hour after hour. Scores of Israelis were dead and critically wounded as a result. And then came the crisis on the Temple Mount. Ben Ramon wanted Palestinian heads to roll, not his own. He was pushing for a crushing invasion of the West Bank and Gaza within the hour.

Mossad chief Avi Zadok wasn't so sure. Somehow they'd been spared the worst-case scenario on the Temple Mount. The dome and the mosque were intact, effectively untouched and unharmed. It had been a bloody affair. It exposed serious deficiencies in Shin Bet's domestic intelligence gathering and analysis. And it had given them all a terrifying reminder of just how serious an unthwarted Jewish terrorist attack against such revered Islamic religious sites would be. Israel again, somehow, had dodged a bullet. They should be grateful, not foolish. Now was not the time to send fifteen or twenty thousand troops into Palestinian strongholds—certainly not to distract attention from Yossi Ben Ramon's incompetence. Now was the time to sit tight and ride out the storm.

Prime Minister David Doron sat behind the large conference table and listened to his senior aides battle it out. At this point, the room was split. On the pro-invasion side were Ben Ramon and General Uri "the Wolf" Ze'ev, chief of staff of the Israeli Defense Forces. On the anti-invasion side were Defense Minister Chaim Modine and Brigadier General Yoni Barak, head of Aman, Israeli military intelligence. The foreign minister and deputy prime minister were both out of the country, in London and Moscow, respectively. The rest of the Security Cabinet members were still on their way.

Doron knew he didn't have much time. Israelis were calling for blood, and understandably so. The past few hours had seen the worst terrorist attacks inside of the Green Line in nearly five years, not counting the four horsemen attack on Jon Bennett's team inside Jerusalem the month before.

★　★　★

"Mr. President, I'm afraid we've got something else."

"Can it wait? We need to make a decision and get to the Israelis ASAP."

"I realize that, Mr. President," Kirkpatrick concurred. "But this is an extremely serious development, and it may have bearing on what you decide."

"All right, just make it fast."

Kirkpatrick gave the floor to Defense Secretary Burt Trainor.

"Mr. President, last night one of our patrols operating in western Iraq intercepted a convoy of three vehicles headed for the Syrian border. The convoy was preparing to fire a surface-to-air missile at one of our Apache helicopters. That vehicle and its occupants were destroyed. The lead vehicle attempted to evade capture. It opened fire on a second Apache. It too was neutralized."

"And?" MacPherson pressed, eager to get to the point.

"Sir, the middle vehicle was stopped. Its two occupants were captured and taken into custody. For the past twenty-four hours or so, we've been interrogating the prisoners and trying to confirm their identities. Turns out, we hit the jackpot."

"Who'd you get?" asked the vice president.

"Both are senior members of the fedayeen forces. What's interesting about these two—particularly the one named Daoud Juma—is that they're both Palestinian. They're both responsible for training Palestinian suicide bombers."

"That's about right." Jack Mitchell nodded.

"Go on," said the president.

"We believe Juma is the head of the fedayeen forces, responsible for engineering the deaths of more than four hundred people worldwide, mostly Jews and Christians. One of the reasons he's been so effective and stealthy over the years is that he does much of his terrorist training outside the borders of Iraq, mostly in the Bekaa Valley, along the border of Lebanon and Syria."

"Okay, I'm with you, Mr. Secretary," said the president with genuine appreciation. "But connect the dots here. What's the immediate threat?"

"Mr. President, we've been interrogating Daoud Juma pretty intensely over the past day, as well as the other guy we captured with him, a guy who appears to be Juma's senior deputy. A few hours ago, the deputy began to break."

"What'd he say?"

"He says a massive new terrorist operation is being planned against the U.S."

The mood throughout the Situation Room and Gaza Station instantly darkened.

"Over the next few days, we're looking at two dozen Palestinian suicide bombers attempting to infiltrate the homeland to attack civilian population centers."

"Oh no," gasped the president.

"What kind of targets are we talking about?" asked DHS Secretary James.

"Mr. Secretary, the targets we've identified so far include New York, Washington, Chicago, Seattle, Los Angeles, Dallas, Atlanta, Miami, and Orlando. But we must add that there may be targets we don't know about."

"Orlando?" Bennett interrupted.

"Disney World would be our guess," the defense secretary responded. "But I can't confirm that. Not yet."

McCoy's stomach tightened. She quickly looked over at Bennett and could read the anxiety on his face. They'd both been trying to call Bennett's mom every few hours to let her know Jon was safe. But neither had gotten through. Perhaps Ruth Bennett was staying with friends. Perhaps she'd gone to see her sister in Buffalo. There were any number of reasons why she wasn't home, or wasn't answering, and none of them were necessarily bad. But sharp pains again began shooting through Bennett's stomach.

"Go on, Burt," said the president, his anger rising at the thought of a wave of suicide bombers coming to unleash *their* evil on *his* country.

"Well, sir, as of this moment we can't confirm many of the operational details. We can confirm the basic outline of the original—and I stress, *original*—plan. As we understand it, the original plan called for teams to begin slipping out of Iraq and into Syria. We don't know if any operatives have already left. We're working on several angles, and the interrogations continue."

"When are we talking about?" asked FBI Director Scott Harris.

"It's sketchy, but I think we're probably looking at New Year's Eve. But again, we must be clear that the attacks may not be linked to any specific day or event at all."

"Mr. President?"

It was Bennett.

"Yes, Jon?"

"Sir, I hate to bother you with this, especially right now, but—"

"What is it, Jon? You don't look so good."

"Mr. President, it's just that . . . well, sir, my mother lives in Orlando."

"I know. Did you call her like I—?"

MacPherson stopped in midsentence. The moment seemed to freeze in time. The president suddenly registered what Bennett was saying. "Tell me you've been in touch with her, Jon. Tell me you called her."

"I've been calling every few hours. So has Erin. There's been no answer, sir. I'm trying to tell myself there's a reasonable explanation, but now . . ."

The president turned to Scott Harris and ordered the FBI to work with Orlando PD to figure out what was going on. Maybe there was a simple explanation. But everyone now feared the worst. They had a serious crisis brewing, and Orlando might just be the tip of the iceberg.

★ ★ ★

MacPherson forced himself to stay focused.

"How will they get to the U.S.?" he asked.

The chairman of the Joint Chiefs took that one. "The evidence our teams have pieced together from Daoud Juma's vehicle, laptop, and cell phone—together with the interviews with Juma and the driver—suggest the teams will make their way to Canada and Mexico, infiltrate our borders, and prepare to strike," said General Mutschler. "What's not clear is whether they'll link up with sleeper agents here, or operate on their own."

"Either way, they'll be tough to track," noted the FBI director.

"And tough to stop," added the homeland security secretary. "We can deploy more forces to the borders. But who are we looking for? We've got an extensive database of Middle East terrorists, suspected terrorists, and people with ties to terrorist individuals, groups, or states. But everyone we know about is already on our watch lists. What I worry about is the threat from people we don't know about."

"How will they get explosives into the country?" asked Deputy Secretary of State Cavanaugh.

"It wouldn't be hard, I'm afraid," said Scott Harris. "It's a two-thousand-mile border. We've got a quarter of a million people coming into the U.S. from Canada every single day. And those are the legal ones, the ones we know about. Heck, we've got five thousand trucks coming southbound through Detroit alone every single day. Along the Mexican border, down in Laredo, for example, we've got more than four thousand trucks coming northbound into the U.S. We've done an awful lot to toughen our border defenses. You guys know all that. You authorized the money. But look, no matter how much we've done to tighten things up, getting weapons or explosives into the country by truck or container ship is a whole lot easier than trying to get a bomb or a box cutter onto a plane at JFK or O'Hare or LAX."

The Israelis were intercepting between forty and fifty Palestinian suicide bombers a month. They were keeping the toll of casualties quite low, given the constant threats they were facing. But they had decades of experience and a country smaller than New Jersey. How would the U.S. do, thought Bennett, trying to protect a continent?

"Why now?" the president asked Jack Mitchell.

"Retaliation after Iraq, the peace process, an attempt to finish their attack on you—there could be any number of reasons why they'd try to strike now."

"Marsha, what do you make of all this?"

"Well, sir, assuming the story we're piecing together here is accurate, my first instinct is that it's unlikely the attacks will be against major Washington or political targets. It would likely be more random. That would certainly follow the history of the attacks in Israel—random, devastating violence designed to terrify the population and paralyze the economy."

"McDonald's, Pizza Huts—that kind of thing?" the president asked.

"Exactly—and grocery stores, Wal-Marts, schools, hospitals, malls, churches, synagogues—you name it," the national security advisor continued. "It's hard to say precisely where they'll hit. There's no real pattern in Israel, except that it's not airplanes or military installations. Nothing secure. Nothing that's hardened."

"In other words, it's open season?" asked the president.

"It may be," said Kirkpatrick. "We're an open society, and a big target."

* * *

Nadir Sarukhi Hashemi was late.

It was almost nine o'clock at night, Pacific time. He was supposed to have crossed the Mexican border into the United States nine hours earlier. Instead, he'd gotten drunk on piña coladas and tequilas at the hotel the night before. If he wanted to enjoy his last days on earth, why shouldn't he? But now he cursed himself. He was Muslim. He was committed to jihad. He had to stay focused. He couldn't succumb to temptation. It wouldn't happen again. At least he was now in his Ford Taurus, heading north.

Nadir inched his way forward through the Tijuana, Mexico, border crossing, perhaps the world's busiest. His destination: San Ysidro, California, then twenty more miles or so to San Diego. He would switch cars, stock up on food and bottled water, and race cross-country, eastward, for Atlanta and Savannah. There he'd get his weapons and more instructions.

The trip was almost 2,400 miles. It'd take forty hours of driving, not counting refueling stops, food, and rest. And that was if he took the most direct route, but that didn't seem safe. It would keep him too close to the border with Mexico, and right through El Paso, swarming with federal agents—border guards, INS, customs, DEA, ATF, the FBI, and on and on and on. It was far too risky when instead he could simply work his way through the interior of the country and cross the Midwest. It would take a little longer. But he was pretty sure he could still make it in time.

* * *

The president again turned to his national security advisor.

"Where do we start first?"

"Step one is to take the entire country to Threat Level Red. Step two, we seal the borders. Nobody comes in. Nobody goes out. No international flights in or out of the country for at least the next seventy-two to ninety-six hours, though we can take it day by day. I'd recommend we mobilize the National Guard—a massive call-up—get them on the front lines. We put the guard positioned at every border crossing. Every international airport. Train stations. Bus stations. At the same time, we mobilize the coast guard immediately. Cancel all leaves. Move coast guard patrol vessels into the major harbors, and coordinate closely with the air force and navy. That'll take some time, Mr. President, and it will cost a lot. But I don't see that we've got a choice."

"Lee, would you concur on all that?" the president asked his homeland security secretary, Lee James.

"I do, Mr. President. I'd further recommend that we split functions here. My team can coordinate defensive homeland-security operations through my office. We've got the war room set up at the NAC," the secretary said, referring to the Nebraska Area Complex, a former navy administrative headquarters in Washington, D.C., where the Department of Homeland Security was centralized. "That's defense, trying to keep the bad guys out, or off balance. The FBI should handle the offense—proactively going after the bad guys. Rounding up potential suspects. Shaking down sources. Coordinating a massive manhunt as new details come in of who we're looking for. Director Harris can speak to that in specifics. But that's what we've been war-gaming in recent weeks, trying to make sure that what happened to you, Mr. President, doesn't happen again."

The president turned to his FBI director. "That work for you, Scott?"

"It does, Mr. President. We've vacuumed up an enormous amount of information just in the last few weeks. I can put my team into motion the minute you say go."

Corsetti now took the floor. "Mr. President, we still need a decision on what you'll say to the Israelis."

"Yes, I'm getting to that," the president responded. "But let's nail this thing down first. We are now at Threat Level Red. Lee, Scott, I'd suggest you get moving on this stuff right now. Get your teams into crisis mode. Send out bulletins to all state and local law enforcement. Chuck, page the White House press corps. Get them back in here. Have your team alert the networks and the newspapers. I want you to do a briefing in the next half hour, once we figure out what and how much we can and should say. But I want to make sure lots of information gets in the East Coast papers and that's going to be tough. Many of them are on or past deadline, right?"

"That's right, sir," the press secretary confirmed.

"Scott, Lee, I want you two to do live briefings here at the White House within the next forty-five minutes. Coordinate with Bob and Chuck, okay?"

"Yes, Mr. President."

"Okay, go to it. The rest of us will shift our attention back to the situation in Israel. Let me know what else you need from me."

★　★　★

Nadir Sarukhi Hashemi tried to stay calm.

A U.S. federal agent approached and asked for his passport, asked a few questions, then went back to her guard station to run a computer check. Nadir thought about his five and a half months at the training camp, the brothers he'd met—Syrians, lots of Saudis, some Jordanians, a few Chechens, but mostly Palestinians.

They'd all been trained in light arms, how to hijack airplanes, and how to use explosives—C4 and TNT—to attack a country's infrastructure. Military bases, nuclear plants, electric plants, gas-storage facilities, airports, railroads, large corporations, public buses, and trains. They'd been taught how to carry out operations in cities, how to block roads, how to assault buildings and elementary schools, and various strategies for evasion and escape. What they hadn't been taught—or taught well, Nadir suddenly realized—was how to fight the urge to bolt the minute it looked like their cover might be blown.

A moment later, the border officer returned. She stared Nadir in the eye. Her face bore no smile, nor makeup. She was almost at the end of her shift, and exhausted.

"And why again are you visiting the United States?" she asked.

"I am here on business," Nadir said, only partially lying.

"Why aren't you flying in directly from Rome?"

"I had some business in Mexico City. I'd never been to Mexico before. I thought it might be nice to drive a bit and see some scenery."

"Where are you staying in San Diego?"

"At the Del Coronado—let's see, I've got my reservation number."

Nadir frantically fished through his briefcase, trying to find the paper, cursing himself for not having it out already, yet trying not to betray how nervous he really felt. A few seconds later, he found the paper.

The customs agent read it over and gave it back to him. "Have a nice stay in the United States." She smiled and waved him through.

It couldn't be that easy. First stop: San Diego to exchange rental cars and get one with American plates. Then he'd race cross-country. He had to be in position in less than seventy-two hours and he still had to pick up the "package" along the way. He reached into his coat pocket and pulled out a bottle of Tylenol. It was actually full of amphetamines. He popped two into his mouth, washed them down with bottled water, thanked Allah, and gunned the engine.

He still couldn't believe it. He was in.

27
★ ★
★

IT WAS decision time.

He'd heard all the arguments, sifted through all the intelligence, asked all the questions. Now it was his decision to make, and his alone. Again.

David Doron stood up and thanked his Security Cabinet. He asked them to reassemble in fifteen minutes, then walked out of the conference room, back to his personal office, trailed by his four ubiquitous bodyguards. He needed a few minutes alone—time to think, time to process.

At seventy-one, he was getting too old for this, he told himself as he strode down the hall—too old, too tired, and worst of all, too cynical. Growing up in Jerusalem in the 1940s and 1950s, he'd never imagined that one day he'd be the prime minister of Israel. Sometimes it was hard for him to believe there still was a State of Israel. How could the Jewish people, much less the Jewish state, still be around after the horrors of the twentieth century? What drove so many to try to exterminate the Jews? Why couldn't he and his family and his people just live a quiet, peaceful, uneventful life?

As a combat veteran of four Arab-Israeli hot wars—the Six Days' War of 1967, the Yom Kippur War of 1973, the invasion of Lebanon in 1982 to destroy the PLO, and the launch of the first Palestinian intifada in December of 1987 (he'd been too young for the War of Independence in 1948 and the Suez Crisis in 1956)—he'd seen with his own eyes the worst human beings could do to one another. He had seen his closest friends blown to pieces right beside him.

There'd been those three months as a prisoner of war in Iraq, the terrors of which he still refused to talk about with his wife of forty-one years. Why should he burden her more? She and her father were Holocaust survivors. Somehow they'd made it out of Auschwitz alive. Her mother and three sisters had not. She still bore emotional scars so deep that they rarely talked about her past. How could he, then, talk about his? Instead, they talked constantly about the future, but their future always seemed to hold in store another war that threatened to annihilate everyone and everything they'd ever held dear.

The more pain they experienced, the more cynical he'd become, determined to protect Israel's security at all costs, yet increasingly exhausted by the conflict with the Arab world in general and with the Palestinians in particular. He didn't believe peace would ever come, not now, perhaps not ever, but frankly he was sick of being such a passionate ideologue.

In public, he was careful to preach his party's line—no Palestinian state, no compromise on the Golan Heights, no dismantling of the Jewish settlements, no relinquishing Jewish access to the Temple Mount, and not one single solitary inch of Jerusalem would ever be given away. *Ever*. That's what he said in public. And he was turning out to be a rather eloquent speaker, despite his wife's constant teasing that his Hebrew was almost as bad as his English.

But in private he was slowly coming to the point that he just wanted the whole mess to be over with. He didn't know how. He didn't know when. He didn't have the energy or the political self-interest to try to figure out a way forward. He just knew he was tired. So was his country.

If he could, he'd give away Gaza in a heartbeat. Only as a demilitarized zone, of course. But of course he'd give it back to the Palestinians. Who wanted to occupy such a wasteland? Even Likud's patriarch, Menachem Begin, had tried to give Gaza back to the Egyptians during the Camp David peace talks in the late 1970s. The Egyptians said no.

As for Judea and Samaria—what the world insisted on calling the West Bank of the Jordan River—yes, Doron believed that the God of the Bible had given that land to the Jews for time immemorial. Bethlehem, for example, was on the so-called West Bank. But it wasn't a Palestinian town. It was Jewish. It was the birthplace of David, King of Israel—David the Jew—David whose son Solomon built the First Temple in Jerusalem—

David who *defeated* Goliath the Philistine—that's right, *Philistine*, from which the modern-day word *Falastine* or *Palestine* was derived.

Jericho was on the so-called West Bank, but it wasn't Palestinian, Doron had long argued. It was conquered fair and square a couple thousand years ago by Joshua, the Jewish right-hand man to Moses, the leader of the Jews, not the Arabs. And what of Hebron? It too was on the so-called West Bank of the Jordan. But it was the home of Abraham, Isaac, and Jacob, the great Jewish patriarchs who first established the Jewish presence in the land of milk and honey.

So yes, Doron believed all these things. But somehow, such arguments were beginning to wear thin, at least to him. Not because they weren't true. They most certainly were. But they weren't the only truths on the ground.

The West Bank was now home to nearly 3 million Arabs. They were angry at the appalling living conditions in which they found themselves. They were bitter and resentful, and rightfully so. They lived in hopelessness, and something had to give.

He'd never give away Jerusalem, of course. But he hated everything about the current situation. He hated the idea of the Jewish people being an occupying power. He hated sending young Israeli soldiers into the "disputed territories" to kill and get killed. He did it only because he had to. He had a job to do, to protect his people, and he took his job seriously. But in his heart, Doron knew the current situation was unsustainable.

Occupation—was there honestly any other word for it?—was steadily eroding the character of the Jewish people and the Jewish state. It was turning them into a hard, bitter people. The generous, hospitable spirit of the Israeli people was slowly fading in the intense heat, and it grieved Doron.

Yet here he was. The prime minister of Israel. It didn't seem real. Somehow, he'd become a successful cynic. Somehow, after Doron had gotten out of the army, he'd been fortunate enough to get a bachelor's degree from Tel Aviv University, and then a master's and doctorate in economics from the University of Chicago. He'd eventually been tapped as a young economic advisor to Prime Minister Yitzhak Shamir, then deputy finance minister for Bibi Netanyahu. Somehow—he still looked back in amazement—the Likud party had insisted that he run for a seat in the Knesset, Israel's parliament, and he'd won handily. Eventually he'd been asked by Prime Minister Ariel Sharon to serve as deputy foreign minister, then as minister of industry and trade, then as a deputy prime minister. Then he'd run, albeit reluctantly, for the top slot—and won.

Now he had to choose. At his command, Israel had held back during the Americans' recent war with Iraq, even when her very existence hung in the balance. It was an enormous risk, a gamble that could have cost millions of lives. That time it worked out. The question was whether he was prepared to acquiesce to American pressure again.

This White House and State Department's insistence upon Israeli "restraint" in the face of relentless, barbaric terror was absolutely preposterous. It was downright hypocritical, not to mention incredibly dangerous.

Why was it that every time Palestinian homicide bombers—that is what they were, after all, cold-blooded murderers, committing *homicides*, not suicides—why was it that every time the Palestinians killed Israeli women and children, the Americans demanded that the *Israelis* exercise *restraint?* And not just the Americans, of course. The Europeans all demanded that Israel show *restraint.* So did the Russians and, of course, the Arab League.

Restraint? What in the world did that mean?

Had the Americans shown *restraint* against Al-Qaeda or the Taliban in Afghanistan? Absolutely not. Had Washington shown *restraint* against Saddam Hussein? Of course not, and thank God. Had the British shown *restraint* against IRA terrorists? Had the Russians shown *restraint* against Chechen terrorists?

The whole notion was as foolish as it was infuriating. How dare President MacPherson demand on worldwide television that in the wake of Palestinian terrorists blowing up Yasser Arafat, Abu Mazen, the U.S. secretary of state, and dozens upon dozens of Americans and Palestinians, that somehow Israel should "exercise restraint" and not "inflame the situation"? Doron could feel his blood pressure rising, not a good thing for a man approaching his seventy-second year.

The temptation to strike hard and fast and wipe out every last vestige of these lethal Palestinian mafia factions was almost overpowering. Everything in him wanted the violence to be over once and for all. Perhaps this was the only way. The world would no doubt condemn him. The question was, would his conscience?

* * *

It was decision time at the White House, as well.

The president turned to his senior team, cognizant of the fact that they were out of time, and resigned to the fact that it was probably time to unleash the Israelis after all.

"All right," he began, shaking his head, "back to the territories. I think we all know what needs to happen. I asked you all to work up military options in case there was some reason for us to go in unilaterally instead of the Israelis, or in case we needed to lead an international peacemaking or peacekeeping force. But it doesn't look like that's going to be necessary. If everyone's in agreement, I'll give Doron the go-ahead to commence operations, while we concentrate on a massive global manhunt to hunt down these suicide teams. Does that sound about right to everyone?"

Bennett struggled to keep his mind focused on the conversation. He worried about his mom, berated himself for not having done something sooner. She was practically all alone in the world now. She needed him, and he was half a world away, so consumed in a crisis that he might in fact have fatally neglected her. Still, as guilty as he felt about it, thinking about her safety and security was actually a luxury he couldn't afford right now.

He could see that MacPherson was battling mental and physical fatigue, not to mention an overwhelming consensus among his top political, military, and diplomatic advisors that the peace process was over. A new Palestinian-Israeli war was about to begin. It was a war whose ferocity, duration, and death toll could very well be unlike anything the Holy Land had experienced for decades, and Bennett could feel his window of opportunity slipping away.

"Mr. President?" he broke in, knowing he was about to go up against some tremendous resistance. "I realize events are moving very rapidly. But there are some new developments here I think you should know about before you make a final decision."

Before MacPherson could respond, his CIA director cut in.

"Jon, I appreciate what you're trying to do here, son; I really do," Mitchell said with an edge of condescension. "But we've crossed the Rubicon. The Israelis are going in, and that's that."

Bennett was instantly defensive. "Mr. President, I understand that, but—"

"Jon, really, I'm afraid Jack's right," MacPherson said, cutting him off. "You've done a great job mapping out this peace plan, and maybe when this war is over, after the two sides cool down—I don't know when—maybe we'll have another shot down the road a few years. But not right now. I'm afraid it's just too late."

"No, Mr. President, please—I need two minutes of your time. Just two minutes."

"Jon, really, I don't see how—"

"Two minutes, Mr. President. That's all I'm asking for."

Both rooms were dead silent. The tension was palpable. Bennett worried he'd overplayed his hand, but he didn't see how he had a choice. He had to take a shot, and he was prepared to face the consequences, regardless of what happened next.

The president stared at him through the video camera in the Situation Room, then glanced around the room at Kirkpatrick, Corsetti, Mitchell, and the vice president. Bennett was tempted to seize the moment and just start talking, to get out the facts as quickly as he could and see what happened. But he hesitated. The stakes were too high. He couldn't come off looking emotionally involved. It wasn't his call, after all. It was the president's. His job was to give the man the facts and his best judgment, not to blast his way through an NSC meeting and expect to ever be invited back. Yet wasn't this precisely why he'd been hired? To be the "point man for peace"? McCoy jokingly drilled it into his head day after day. But maybe she was right. What kind of point man was he if he didn't do everything in his power to force the president to seek peace, not war? So many lives hung in the balance. How could silence be an option? How dare he hesitate?

Bennett shifted in his seat and leaned forward. He began opening his mouth to speak. But before he could—before anyone noticed he was about to—he suddenly heard the voice of the vice president.

"Mr. President," the VP said calmly, "I don't think two minutes can hurt."

All eyes were on the president. MacPherson looked at the VP, then down at his hands, still scarred from the attacks just a few weeks before. He took a deep breath, leaned back, and nodded. He'd put Bennett through an awful lot. Hadn't he earned the right to be heard, even for a few minutes? Perhaps Checkmate was right.

"All right, Jon, you've got two minutes—but I don't want a speech. If you've got something new, fine. Otherwise we move on."

McCoy exhaled with relief. Bennett did too.

"Absolutely. Thank you, Mr. President. Yesterday you asked me to talk to Galishnikov and Sa'id and get them pressing their sources to find out what was going on. I got the answer just before we started this videoconference."

MacPherson looked over at Kirkpatrick and Mitchell. Did they know where Bennett was going with this? The blank looks on their faces made it clear they didn't.

"Two hours ago," Bennett continued, "Sa'id was on a conference call with the seventeen highest ranking members of the Palestinian Legislative Council who are still alive after the attacks. There are a total of fifty-three PLC members still alive. Thirty-five were killed in the initial attacks, or in assassinations over the past twenty-four hours. The seventeen that Sa'id talked to are the inner circle—all top-ranking, experienced, and, as it turns out, fairly moderate PLC legislators. Ironically, it appears that most of the hard-line, anti-Israel, anti-peace members of the PLC were in the court-yard Monday morning. They were trying to signal Arafat and particularly Abu Mazen not to do something they'd regret. Most of them ended up dying in the blast."

"Where are these seventeen?" asked the president.

"They're holed up in the communications center under the PLC building. It's a bunker of some kind. They've basically barricaded themselves in—they're terrified for their lives and they're furious at the Islamic radicals who they say have set all this into motion to sabotage the peace process. But they've been in touch with all the other surviving members, scattered throughout the West Bank and Gaza."

"What do they want?"

"Sir, I don't think you're going to believe me. I have to admit, I didn't believe Sa'id, at first."

"You've got a minute and forty-five seconds," said the president. "Try me."

28

ALL EYES were now on Bennett.

"Mr. President," he began, "the PLC asked Ibrahim Sa'id to get a message to you. They've got four points. Sa'id asked me to pass along this message and get an answer back to him and the PLC within the next half hour."

The president was in no mood for ultimatums, if that's what this was. But he was listening—for another minute and forty-five seconds, anyway. "Proceed."

"Thank you, Mr. President. Okay, first point: the PLC says they have evidence that the initial attacks—the suicide bombing and the initial gunfire and RPG attacks—were ordered by someone in Iran, though they're not sure exactly who."

"How do they know that?"

"The PLC sent a team to raid the home of the suicide bomber—"

"Khalid al-Rashid?" asked Kirkpatrick.

"Right, Rashid—they raided his home and offices about an hour after the attacks. They grabbed his computer, phones, Palm Pilot, whatever they could, and they've begun to piece together the trail. It's early, and they've got a lot more work to do. But they say the trail without a doubt leads back to Tehran. I can't confirm it. Neither can Sa'id. We're just passing on what they're saying. But according to Sa'id, the PLC is absolutely livid."

"Yeah, right," snapped Mitchell. "The PLC's never been too *livid* about Iranian operations in the territories. They weren't *livid* when Arafat bought fifty million bucks' worth of weapons from Tehran and tried to smuggle them into Gaza a few years back on that ship, the *Karine A*. Why should we suddenly believe they're so hot and bothered now?"

Bennett was expecting that one. "The difference, Mr. Director, is that the Iranians never tried to assassinate Yasser Arafat before."

"Maybe they should have," said Mitchell.

"All I know is that Sa'id says these PLC guys couldn't stand Arafat. They hated his corruption. They were furious that he was lining his pockets with billions of dollars in foreign aid money from us and the E.U. They despised his constant double-dealings over the years with Iran and the Islamic radicals. These aren't Arafat fans. But they deeply resent Tehran ordering his assassination. They're terrified that with Tehran freed up from the worry of a hostile Saddam Hussein to their west, they're now stepping up their war against Israel and using the Palestinians as pawns. And they're devastated by the death of Abu Mazen. They were hoping Arafat would eventually give him full authority and Mazen could start steering a more moderate path. Anyway, that's the first thing they want you to know. It looks like an outside job, and all roads seem to lead to Iran."

MacPherson and his team considered this for a moment. It wasn't like the Palestinian Legislative Council to point fingers at the Islamic Republic of Iran. It had the air of plausibility.

"All right, give me the other three, quickly."

"Okay, second, the PLC says they *want* the Oil for Peace deal to go forward as quickly as possible."

"They do?"

"I know. That's what I thought. They've been cool to the whole idea from the beginning, at least until now. But Sa'id talked to all fifty-three surviving members over the phone—forty-eight want the oil-and-gas project to move forward. Only one voted against pursuing some kind of deal, and four want more information before they decide. They all know they're sitting on a gold mine. They're worried the radicals are going to destroy everything. It seems like they're coming to the conclusion they'd better make a deal fast or lose everything."

"Unbelievable," sniffed Mitchell. "Who are these people? Abba Eban was right. The Palestinians never miss an opportunity to miss an opportunity. How do they think there can be an Oil for Peace deal now? The whole country is going up in flames."

"Mr. President, if I may continue . . ."

Mitchell shook his head in disgust and impatience. But MacPherson allowed Bennett to continue. No one but Mitchell was watching the clock anymore.

"Thank you, sir. Point three: the PLC has unanimously voted to appoint Ibrahim Sa'id as acting prime minister of Palestine."

A buzz went through the Situation Room.

"It will be an eighteen-month provisional appointment," Bennett continued, "subject to recall by a supermajority vote of the PLC. The key is that after eighteen months, there will be democratic parliamentary elections, followed by a legislative vote for prime minister, all monitored by international observers, supervised by the U.S. and United Nations."

It was a jarring development, but there was more.

"And what's Ibrahim say about all this?" asked the president. "Is he even remotely interested? I thought he hated politics and politicians."

"Well, that actually brings me to point number four, sir. Sa'id was stunned at first, and resistant, as we might imagine. You're right, sir. He's always told me he hates politics and politicians, present company excepted. But after the initial shock of the PLC's offer, he told them and me that he'll accept on one condition."

"Which is?"

"He wants you to send Special Forces into Gaza and the West Bank to stop the fighting, round up the terrorists, and restore order."

"What?" asked MacPherson. "Are you kidding?"

"Sa'id is absolutely insistent that the Israelis not move in. If the Israelis invade, he says all deals are off. No oil deal. He won't serve as prime minister. Nothing. He wants us—not the Israelis—to come in immediately."

"And do what exactly?" Kirkpatrick pressed.

"He says the mission should have three objectives. First, to take out the various rogue militia commanders and their forces, all of whom they say are operating in direct defiance of PLC orders to cease and desist. Second, to hunt down and arrest or destroy any outside forces operating on the ground in the West Bank or Gaza. Sa'id says he absolutely does not want a Palestinian state to be dogged from day one by Islamic insurgents, especially not ones funded and trained directly by the mullahs in Tehran. He's completely inflexible on this point."

"And the third objective?"

"The third objective would be to establish order, calm things down, and then help the PLC recruit, train, and deploy an entirely new security force, one untainted and completely unaffiliated with the corruption of the current factions. He'd also want physical protection for himself and his family, like what we've given Hamid Kharzai in Afghanistan and the new interim government in Iraq."

"And if we do all that?" asked the president.

"Sa'id will call the PLC back, say yes, and he'll be the new prime minister of Palestine. We could have the deal done in less than fifteen minutes."

"What then?"

"As soon as the deal is set, the PLC officials in the communications center will set up a satellite connection with Al-Jazeera and Abu Dhabi Television. They'll go on the air to explain the current situation, denounce the rogue militias, reassert their legitimate authority over Palestine, announce the appointment of Sa'id, and request American assistance. Then, they'd like us to provide Sa'id with a satellite hookup as well. They want him to make a short speech accepting the position and explaining what's at stake."

"Whoa, whoa, wait a minute," Kirkpatrick interrupted. "Sa'id won't last five minutes in the territories. All kinds of people will be gunning for him, and neither the PLC nor a U.S. security force could guarantee him security, not during several weeks of intense fighting, at least."

"I agree. So does Sa'id. So does the PLC. When the weather clears, they'd like you to send in an extraction team to take Sa'id and the rest of my team to a secure location—outside of the region—where he'd like to open up immediate peace talks with Prime Minister Doron."

"Peace talks—those are his words?"

"They are, Mr. President."

"And the PLC is okay with all this?"

"The PLC just voted fifty to three in favor of Sa'id's requests. They're faxing over the paperwork to make it official even as we speak. But the offer expires in twelve—no, make that eleven minutes."

"Why such a fast deadline?" Mitchell demanded to know. "Who do they think they are, trying to dictate terms to us?"

"No, no, they're not trying to dictate any terms," Bennett shot back. "They know we're meeting in emergency session. They know the Israelis are about to invade, and they're saying that if that happens, all deals are off. Once the Israelis cross the Green Line, the PLC believes all chances for persuading their own people that a peace deal is possible will be out the window. If they can persuade us to persuade Doron to hold back—no small feat, given what's going on right now—then they think they've got a shot. That's all. But now we've got ten minutes. That's it."

It was a stunning turn of events. No one was quite sure what to make of it.

"I don't like it," Mitchell finally said. "I don't like being backed into a corner. We don't know who we're dealing with. For all we know, this is a gambit by the Islamic radicals themselves, or by Iran, to stop the Israelis from invading."

"Oh, come on, Jack, that doesn't make sense and you know it," the vice president suddenly countered. "Think about it. Assume for a minute that this offer and the intelligence the PLC is offering us are all legit. If Iran is really behind the assassinations of Arafat, Abu Mazen, and the secretary of state, then it's Iran that *wants* Israel to invade. That makes sense, doesn't it? They know full well that an Israeli invasion would doom the peace process. And in our hearts, everyone in this room knows it too. Look, I've been as big a supporter of a tough, strong Israel as anyone in this town for going on four decades. No one can accuse me of trying to undermine Israel's security, and certainly not right now. I'm saying it's in our interest, and in Israel's, that Doron not go on offense right now, as much as he'd like to. But somebody has to, and it is my assessment, Mr. President, that such a task has now fallen to us."

The room was quiet. Vice President William Oaks commanded tremendous respect inside the MacPherson administration, and inside the leadership of both political parties. Everyone knew Checkmate was a man who carefully weighed every option, every action and reaction, and weighed his words carefully as well. If he was now squarely siding with

Bennett in advocating a U.S. military response, everyone knew he was likely to persuade the president.

"Besides," the vice president added, "think about it. Are we ever going to get a better deal than a man like Ibrahim Sa'id as the prime minister of Palestine? Mr. President, you've watched this guy pretty closely over the years. Jon and Erin know him personally. They've dealt with him for years. He's been totally honest, aboveboard, critical of Arafat but no pie-in-the-sky idealist. Jack, your own team totally vetted Sa'id, declared him clean of all terrorist connections, for crying out loud. Mr. President, I know things are moving pretty fast. But I've got to tell you, my gut says this is a good deal and we'd better take it fast."

"And if it's too good to be true?" asked Mitchell.

"It's not," the VP replied. "But it will be in about seven minutes."

✶ ✶ ✶

Marcus Jackson desperately wanted the story.

It would make an incredible follow up to the "Point Man for Peace" profile he'd written about Jon Bennett a few days earlier, the one that ran in Sunday's *New York Times*, front page, top of the fold. Jackson already had the headline: "Point Man Pinned Down as Gaza Erupts in Civil War." But a headline alone wasn't enough. He needed the whole story, the inside story. He needed the ticktock, the play-by-play of the most riveting story in the world at the moment. The only way to get that was to make contact with Bennett, and thus far that was going nowhere.

Bennett refused to cooperate. Jackson had been sending him pages and e-mails on the hour for the past twenty-four hours. Yet Bennett wasn't calling back. Jackson knew Bennett's pager was new and top-of-the-line. And he'd always been able to get him by e-mail, even at the military hospital in Germany two weeks before. Bennett hadn't really cooperated with him for the "point man" profile. He'd insisted that he was merely "a behind-the-scenes kinda guy and liked it that way." He refused to say anything else, wouldn't even let his picture be taken by a *Times* photographer. But at least he'd had the decency to return Jackson's calls and explain, albeit briefly, why he was flattered but unwilling to play ball. Now he was obviously stiff-arming Jackson, and Jackson was getting angry. Even repeated calls to Bennett's mom had struck out. No answer. No answering machine.

Was Jon Bennett dead? Had he been killed in the initial attacks, or during a cross fire later that day? It was possible, of course, but it didn't seem likely. The White House would confirm that, wouldn't they? What reason would there be to hold back such information? It would come out eventually. Was Bennett severely injured? That too was possible. But again, White House Press Secretary Chuck Murray was being pretty forthcoming about U.S. casualty figures in the territories thus far. It didn't make sense that he'd refuse to confirm or deny the whereabouts of Bennett and his team, unless . . . unless what? It didn't make sense, and that made Jackson wonder all the more.

There was a story here. He knew it. He could feel it. He just had to get it. A former *Army Times* correspondent who'd covered the Gulf War, then moved back to his hometown to work for the *Denver Post*, Jackson had joined the *New York Times* less than ten days before James "Mac" MacPherson—aka Gambit—announced his campaign for the GOP nomination. From that point forward, Jackson practically lived with the MacPherson family for months on end during the primaries and the general campaign. He got to know the entire team, including Jon Bennett, with whom he got along reasonably well, in part because both of them were closet Democrats. Now Bennett was a senior advisor to the president of the United States. Jackson was the chief White House correspondent for the country's newspaper of record. And one way or another, the latter was going to find the former.

★   ★   ★

The president turned to Defense Secretary Burt Trainor.

"Okay, let's say the vice president is right. Let's say we should take this deal and send in U.S. forces. Bottom line, Burt—can we do this?"

"Send a strike force into the West Bank and Gaza to accomplish the PLC's objectives—establish order and extract Sa'id, Bennett, and Bennett's team?"

"Exactly."

"We can, Mr. President, but it'll be messy."

"How messy?"

"Overnight, the Joint Chiefs did a crash update of a scenario we'd wargamed out a few years ago—before you got here, sir—when Secretary

Powell was headed to Ramallah, and Hamas was threatening to blow up the peace process. Cheney, Rumsfeld, and Wolfowitz were concerned that Hamas might lash out at the Powell delegation, that an attack could unleash a civil war, and how could the U.S. respond if our people were pinned down inside the territories. It was a scenario not dissimilar to what we've got right now, but at that time it was solely an extraction mission—an NEO, we call them, a noncombatant evacuation operation—not orders to simultaneously hunt down terrorists and secure the peace. The Powell extraction scenario was Op Plan 109D. This is Op Plan 109E and 109F. We've code-named the first part, the rescue of Bennett and Sa'id and their team, Operation Briar Patch. The overall seizure and liberation plan and the name we would release to the media, with your approval, Mr. President, would be Operation Palestinian Freedom."

"Walk me through it, Burt—quickly," urged the president.

"Yes, sir. Basically, what we'd do is ask the Israelis to step up their operations along the Green Line, stir up a lot of radio traffic—lots of chatter in the media and elsewhere—all to appear as if the Israelis are about to invade. But this would simply be a diversion. While the rogue Palestinian forces begin redeploying their forces to stop fighting each other and prepare to stop an Israeli invasion, we'd send teams of Army Rangers and Delta Force operators who are currently on the ground in the western desert of Iraq and send them eastward, over Jordan and Saudi Arabia, into the West Bank. We've got pretty good intel at this point on what's happening on the ground, and the Israelis could secretly give us whatever else we need, if they'll agree to hold back in the first place and let us go in. Delta and the Rangers would be backed up the 160th SOAR, the Special Operations Aviation Regiment also in the Iraqi theater at the moment, and several Air Force Special Ops Spectre Gunship Teams."

MacPherson held up his hand and stopped him there. "Marsha."

"Yes, Mr. President."

"Get over to the op center across the hall. Get on the line with Doron immediately. Tell him it's urgent. Get him out of whatever meeting he's in. Walk him through this as fast as you possibly can—tell him we're under a deadline—and get his reaction, *ASAP*. Tell him I'll get on the line with him in just a few moments."

"Yes, sir, Mr. President."

"Good, thanks—and, Erin, can you hear me?"

"Yes, Mr. President."

"Go talk to Mr. Sa'id. Tell him to open up a direct line with the PLC and ask for more time. Tell him we're intrigued with their proposal and are starting talks with the Israelis. But we need more time."

"Yes, sir."

"Okay, Burt," said the president, "continue."

"Sir, the bottom line is that I'm not so worried about moving our forces into the West Bank. Weather's breaking a bit, and we could have our forces airborne and on their way to the West Bank within six hours if you give us the order. But Gaza's more trouble."

"Why?"

"Well, sir, the plan calls for sending in an MEU—a Marine Expeditionary Unit—from the *Roosevelt* and *Reagan* to establish a perimeter around Gaza Station. Then SEAL Team Eight would come in on choppers, fast rope onto the roof of the Hotel Baghdad, and extract Sa'id, Bennett, and his team. Once the extraction was successful, we'd send in Rangers and Delta operators. The problem, Mr. President, is that Gaza is densely populated. Islamic strongholds. Lots of RPGs. It's arguably the most dangerous urban-warfare environment in the world. The risk of casualties is very high."

"Worst-case scenario?" asked MacPherson, quickly running out of time.

"It could be Mogadishu all over again, Mr. President."

29

★ ★
★

THE PHONE RANG at exactly midnight Washington time.

It was 7:00 a.m. in Gaza.

Ibrahim Sa'id glanced over, then looked away and kept pacing. He couldn't sit down. He couldn't stay still. He was on his fourth cup of coffee in less than an hour and his nerves were raw.

On the surface, leaning back on the couch with his feet propped up on the coffee table, Dmitri Galishnikov tried not to look worried in the slightest about who or what might be on the other end of that call. But it was just an act. He'd already worked through one pack of cigarettes since waking up, and he was about to begin his second.

McCoy was closest to the phone. She was dying to answer it herself, but she knew who was calling, and it wasn't for her.

Bennett picked up the receiver on the third ring. "Yes, sir . . . I did. . . . Just waiting for your word. . . . Yes, Mr. President, he's right here. . . . One moment."

Sa'id stopped pacing.

Bennett held out the phone. "It's the president."

Sa'id looked over at Galishnikov. The Russian suddenly looked pale, even numb. He set down his new cigarette and lighter, straightened up, and pulled his feet off the coffee table. Then he motioned to his Palestinian friend to hurry up and take the call.

"Thank you, Jonathan," Ibrahim said quietly, then accepted the phone and cleared his throat. "Good morning, Mr. President. . . . No, no, please, the honor is all mine, sir. . . . Well, thank you, that is most kind. . . . It is a very difficult time for all of us. . . . Please allow me to express our deepest sorrow for the barbaric attacks on the American delegation and our condolences for the loss of innocent American lives, beginning with the secretary of state—Mr. President I simply can't begin to express the anger and shame we are all feeling right now. . . . Well, perhaps . . . I'm grateful for the opportunity to talk with you directly, to let you know that this civil war has changed everything, and we need your help. . . . I'm not sure; let me ask Jonathan. . . ."

Sa'id put his hand over the receiver and whispered to Bennett, "Are you and Erin able to join in on the call?"

"I guess so," said Bennett, glancing at McCoy. "Why?"

"I don't know. The president wants you both on the line."

Bennett nodded at McCoy and checked to see if the receiver Sa'id was holding had a speakerphone. It didn't, nor did the other two phones in the room. No one in the CIA had ever expected to map out an American invasion of the Palestinian territories—or strategize the birth of a Palestinian state—from a safe house in Gaza, much less from the bedroom of the station's number-two man. It was another bizarre twist to an increasingly bizarre chain of events, thought Bennett.

Both Bennett and McCoy picked up extensions and stood, listening, looking at each other from across the room.

"Mr. President, it's Jon."

"Good, I think it's better if you're on with us," MacPherson said. "It'll save us some time, and I want you in on all these decisions since you're going to have to be my eyes and ears on the ground there for a while longer. Is Erin there also?"

"Yes, sir, I'm here," McCoy added quickly.

"You okay?"

"I am, sir, thank you for asking."

"Very well. I wanted to talk to you both and the new prime minister."

There it was. Confirmation. MacPherson was going with Bennett's plan.

"First of all," MacPherson continued, "may I call you prime minister?"

"I suppose. It's going to be a hard thing to get used to."

"I know how you feel."

"I know that you do, Mr. President, and I appreciate your help. I want you to know that I have no political ambitions. I will do everything in my power to bring about the day someone far more qualified than I am is elected by a popular vote of the people. The Palestinian people have been cheated of many things over the years, but chief among them is a right to determine our own leaders and our own destiny. I see this unexpected turn of events as a way to remedy that, and I would very much value your help toward that end, Mr. President."

"You have it, and not just my support for the creation of a Palestinian democracy. Once we finish this discussion, I'll begin briefing the congressional leadership, and I know they'll want to pass on to you their full support."

"That is very kind. Please say a special thank-you to the Speaker of the House, who was kind enough to meet with Dmitri and myself when we were in the States last summer. Once this operation is successful and order is reestablished, I can assure you that one of my first acts as prime minister will be to ask the PLC to reestablish a completely new relationship with the United States, one based on openness, mutual trust, and shared interests, not the suspicion and hostilities of my predecessors."

"And likewise, you and your wife are invited to the White House at your soonest possible convenience. In fact, we'd be happy to facilitate your discussions with Prime Minister Doron at Camp David, if you'd like."

"You are most kind, Mr. President, and I am most grateful. And, with your permission, perhaps that is a good transition into the substance of the talks we need to have right now."

"Please, go right ahead."

"I have to confess that I am very concerned about how this will all play out. In addition to the physical danger facing the Palestinian people, and your forces, there are enormous political and perceptual dangers we both face, and if you will forgive me, I believe it is best that I am candid with you about my concerns, and then we can figure out how best to address those concerns, if at all."

"By all means. You and I and our nations may not always see eye to eye, Mr. Prime Minister, but I want you to know I have the utmost respect for you, your people, and the challenges you face. I think history will show that the Palestinian people have no greater friend in the world than the American people, and I hope that you will find that you and your team have no greater friend than this administration."

* * *

With formalities out of the way, Sa'id got down to business.

"Mr. President, I need to know if the U.S. is prepared to send in military forces to help us establish control."

"We are."

"How soon can you begin?"

"Will the PLC help us with intelligence and target packages?"

"We are preparing them now."

"My commanders advise me they could commence operations in six hours."

"Very well, then. Here is how I would like the scenario to play out. As soon as we finish this call, I would ask that you call Prime Minister Doron and relay to him the substance of our call. I would like to go on television at one o'clock local time and publicly declare that he is readying Israeli forces to invade the West Bank and Gaza."

Bennett and McCoy looked at each other, unsure where this was going.

The president's voice suggested similar hesitation. "Why?"

"It is essential, Mr. President, that my people see the PLC—and me—defending them from Israeli aggression. To have any legitimacy at all, the PLC and I must be perceived as military victors of some kind, powerful enough to stand up to Doron and stop him in his tracks. That means Doron needs to declare war on us, and continue to mass his forces on the Green Line, fly his jet planes and helicopters over the territories."

"Okay, I'm with you."

"The speaker of the PLC will then go on radio and TV to announce that the Islamic radicals have not only killed our leaders but now they are about to kill any hope of a Palestinian state whatsoever. He will announce that the PLC is in negotiations with me to appoint me interim prime minister, but that I am demanding a U.S. security force come in to rout out the radicals and defend us against an imminent Israeli invasion."

"Keep going."

"I will come on the air soon thereafter to explain for myself why we must band together against the Israelis. I will explain that I have already opened up an initial dialogue with the White House. But I will say that President MacPherson is resistant to the idea of the U.S. sending in forces. I will say that the United States has absolutely no interest in becoming an occupying power, and that never in its history has the United States taken military action to directly oppose the Israelis."

Bennett could see where this was headed. He'd always been impressed with Ibrahim Sa'id, one of the wealthiest and most successful entrepreneurs in the Arab world. Now he was impressed even more.

"Now, it is absolutely critical," Sa'id continued, "that the PLC's move and my speech be seen as a *reaction* to Doron, a *reaction* to an imminent invasion by the Israelis. People have to see my appointment—and the possibility of U.S. military action—not as a sellout of the Palestinian revolution for independence but as a *defense* of it. This is vital. Doron has to let himself be seen in the eyes of the Palestinian rank and file, and in the eyes of the world, as the aggressor, as someone who is about to swallow and reoccupy—perhaps forever—the West Bank and Gaza. Only that will give me the political justification for asking for U.S. intervention, and you the justification for agreeing to intervene. Otherwise, U.S. military action will be seen as a *provocation* against the Palestinians, not a *protection* of the Palestinians, something that would do irreparable harm to both of our interests. Mr. President, I cannot stress enough the importance of this distinction."

"Don't worry, I hear you," said MacPherson, also fascinated by where Sa'id was going. "You need Doron to look like the big bad wolf. And you need to look like the Palestinian savior, demanding the U.S. come to the rescue of the Palestinian cause."

"Not just demanding," Sa'id stressed. "My people and the world have to see me not just demanding U.S. action but somehow persuading you against your better judgment. There can be no hint that the U.S. is eager to do this. In fact, anything you can do over the next six hours to leak the word that many senior White House and State Department advisors are opposed to U.S. intervention would be very helpful."

"I must remind you, Mr. Prime Minister, it's midnight here in Washington, and 9 p.m. on the West Coast. Most Americans aren't going to be tracking the nuances of this argument as carefully as you might think."

"Maybe not, but my immediate concern is the Arab press. Believe me, Mr. President, everyone in this part of the world is huddled with their families, listening to hour-by-hour coverage of the civil war. They will be tracking every nuance of the next six hours more closely than you can possibly imagine. And this is my point. U.S. military force cannot just happen. We have a drama we must play out today. And every actor must do his or her part. The Israelis have to play the bad guys. Every Arab will expect this and it will certainly ring true. The PLC taking decisive action to forestall an Israeli invasion will be a surprise to many. We have not been as decisive in the past as we should have been. Many will be skeptical, and few will know who I am at all. Yes, they know I am very wealthy, very successful. But through my speech and the interviews I do and the information the PLC and our other sources give out, we must build—in just a matter of hours—an impression of an Arab leader who commands international respect and can simultaneously stand up to Israel, and the Americans, and the terrorists in our midst. Does that all make sense?"

"It does," said MacPherson. "At what point do you want me to agree to send in forces?"

"At the last possible moment," Sa'id insisted. "The drama has to play over the course of many hours—back and forth, like a tennis match or the World Cup. Doron has to dismiss the PLC at first. Then dismiss me. Hour by hour, he needs to torque up the rhetoric until it is white-hot, until every Palestinian believes Israeli tanks are going to mow them all down, scoop us all up, and deport us to Jordan or the Sudan or Uganda somewhere. Likewise, all signs out of Washington have to be skeptical of my request—at best—or downright hostile to the notion of engaging in more warfare in the Middle East. Public perception in the territories—indeed, throughout the Arab world—has to get to the point that there is no hope, that all is lost, that the Palestinians have defeated themselves and the Israelis are about to conquer us once and for all. At that point, I will come on television and radio and virtually denounce you. I will say that all the talk of American evenhandedness over the years was all lies, that if President MacPherson does not come and help us then it is just proof positive that he is a tool of the Zionist entity."

MacPherson couldn't help but laugh. "I bet you'll enjoy that."

＊　＊　＊

MacPherson asked a few practical questions.

Sa'id answered them as best he could. But MacPherson could tell there was something else Sa'id wanted to tell him, something that apparently wasn't easy for Sa'id to bring up. Time was running out. He needed to get back to Doron immediately. This was going to take a lot of explaining, and a whole lot more convincing, and MacPherson wasn't sure the Israelis were going to buy it. But he couldn't simply cut off the call now.

"Mr. Prime Minister? I'm getting the sense there's something else you want to say, something else you want me to know. Is that the case?"

There was a long pause.

"Well, yes. . . . It is just that you must all understand—and Prime Minister Doron must understand, as well—something that is difficult for me. . . . I . . ."

"You're among friends here, Ibrahim," assured the president. "Please."

"Very well. It is just that—you must understand how central the concept of honor is in Arab society. So few American presidents have truly understood this. The Arab people have felt abused for so many centuries by foreign occupiers, by our own bloodthirsty dictators, by radicals of all kinds. We have repeatedly been stripped of our honor, and this has had a devastating psychological impact. We look at our military weakness compared to the West, compared to Israel. We look at our poverty compared to the West, compared to Israel. We look at how few great works of art or music we have produced or how few literary or scientific discoveries we can point to in the modern age. We look at how poorly educated our children are, how many of our women are illiterate, how many of our men are illiterate, how the West and the world and even our worst enemies in Israel are just surging past us in so many areas of life—we see it on our satellite dishes and we know it to be true—and we are deeply ashamed."

As Sa'id spoke, his back was turned to Bennett, McCoy, and Galishnikov. He looked as though he carried the full weight of the Arabs' painful history, and was almost desperate to explain it all to his American friends that they might have even the slightest glimpse of the psychological minefield through which he was about to walk.

"We feel like we have failed as a society," Sa'id continued, "that we have so little to show for centuries of bloodshed and hardships. Especially when we can look back and see that the Arab civilization and Islamic civilization were once the greatest the world had ever known. We once dominated in every area of life. And now we have fallen so far behind the Christians and the Jews, and it stabs at our hearts. Honor and shame are sacred values we have in the Arab world, and what do we have that is honorable in the eyes of the world? These are the questions we are wrestling with today. What went wrong? How did we sink so low? And what do we do about it?"

The room was quiet. The man was baring his soul, and the soul of his people, and none of them dared interrupt him. There were many questions that would have to wait.

"Some say we have forgotten our roots, that we are living under sin and Allah's judgment," Sa'id went on. "They say that we must get back to a more fundamental, more militant form of Islam to become great again. And those who believe this—the mullahs in Iran, the wahabbis in Saudi Arabia, the remnants of Al-Qaeda—these are the ones who are waging a jihad, a holy war, against the West. These are the ones who believe the Arab world can rise again only when every Christian and Jew is wiped off the face of the earth. These are the ones who sent jet planes into the World Trade Center and the Pentagon. These are the ones who blow themselves up in Israeli buses and cafés. These are the ones who set into motion the civil war being waged up above us. And these are the ones we must fight to the bitter end. There can be no compromise with such people. They are extremists, and they pose the worst kind of danger."

He paused for a moment, to take a breath, to order his thoughts.

"But, Mr. President, these extremists represent a small fraction of the Arab world, and a small fraction of the Palestinian people. Most of us yearn for freedom. We want to raise our children in safety and security, with the freedom to choose our own leaders, and start our own businesses, and travel around the region and the world without being treated as terrorists and criminals. We *are* the silent majority. And when we have had no leadership, and our prospects for a future and hope have grown dimmer and dimmer, we have—in our weaker moments—cheered on the militants. Because though they are wrong, they are dying with honor. They are dying as heroes. And we want heroes. We are *desperate* for some heroes. We want men of honor to show us that we are not second-class citizens, that we can take on the Israelis and win, that we can stand up to the Americans and get Washington to do what *we* want, not bow down to their every demand."

Bennett stopped taking notes. He set his pen down and just listened, as Sa'id tried to break through to three Americans who saw the world from the top of the heap, and had no idea how it looked or felt from the bottom.

"In the historic pantheon of Arab heroes, Mr. President, there are no businessmen. Only generals, and commandos, and fedayeen. Because people believe it's on the battlefield—not in the boardroom—where a man can prove he has honor. Now, I was raised differently. I see the world differently than many of my countrymen, at least those who currently hold guns and thus power. I am willing to give my life, if that is what it takes, to try to take the Palestinian people to a new place. I will do everything I can to take us into a new era of peace and prosperity. But I cannot ignore our culture or traditions. And that is why I am asking you to follow this admittedly bizarre script. Not because I can guarantee you it will work. But because it offers the thinnest reed of a possibility that people will follow me, and right now I may be the only thing that stands between a slim prospect of peace and a thousand years of darkness."

30

★ ★
★

BENNETT NOW took the lead.

Dozens of decisions needed to be made immediately. Bennett had started scribbling down a checklist of issues and questions during the conference call, and with MacPherson's permission, he began working his way through them one by one.

"Mr. President," Bennett began, "are you comfortable with the scenario so far?"

It was a huge gamble, no question about it. Sa'id might be right. There might not be any other way, and they had almost no time to come up with a plan B. But the risks were enormous. In a sense, Sa'id was asking MacPherson and Doron and their top advisors to deceive their own countries, the world, and the Palestinians. Well, *deceive* might be too strong. It felt like deception, but it wasn't really a lie, was it?

Doron *was* about to order an invasion of the West Bank and Gaza. The prospect of massive Palestinian casualties at the hands of Israeli forces *was* high and growing higher by the hour. The White House *was* deeply reluctant to launch another series of U.S. military strikes in the region, and particularly in the West Bank and Gaza, a place where U.S. forces had never been before. The PLC *was* appointing Ibrahim Sa'id to be acting prime minister, and it was doing so *precisely* because of the connections Sa'id had to the MacPherson administration. And Sa'id *was*, in fact, a reluctant participant. He *was* demanding the introduction of U.S. forces in Palestine as his price of admission. And he *was* doing so—in part, at least—to keep Israeli forces at bay. He was also doing so, in part, to strike a lethal blow at Islamic radicals operating in the West Bank and Gaza, and to dismantle or destroy all twelve separate and competing Arafat-era Palestinian security organizations, whose mafialike reign of terror had to come to an end once and for all.

All this was true. But how many people outside Gaza Station, the PLC, and the White House knew, understood, or were focused on these truths? Not many. Not at the moment. Hardly anyone understood their significance, or how they might be interrelated. So Sa'id had a point. If Palestinians and the world were really going to follow his lead, they would have to see the situation as he saw it, and draw the same conclusions he was drawing. And perhaps the only way for that to happen in such a compressed time frame was for the White House to participate in the Kabuki dance Sa'id was now choreographing.

"I'm getting there," the president confided. "Erin, what's your sense of it?"

"It's a solid plan, Mr. President," she said without hesitation. "And I think the prime minister is right. It's really our best option at this point."

"How about you, Mr. President?" Bennett asked.

"I need to confer again with Prime Minister Doron. But yes, I'm on board."

Bennett looked over at Sa'id and saw something in his face. It wasn't quite a smile. There was a long way to go before any of them would be ready for smiles. But there was something in the crinkles around the eyes of his Palestinian friend that suggested an ever-so-slight glimmer of hope.

* * *

Certainly no one in Albuquerque knew the Viper.

He'd never been there before. He'd never be there again. He just needed a cheap motel, four or five hours of sleep, a shower, and some breakfast. Then he'd be back on the road, racing eastward. The road sign said thirty-five more miles. He'd already driven nearly eight hundred over the past fourteen hours. At least he'd be there in less than a half hour. He'd be in bed in less than an hour, and that would suit him just fine.

Hour upon hour of country music were all that kept Nadir Sarukhi Hashemi company. He'd much rather listen to music of his youth, of course, or the Koran on tape or CD. But his training had been explicit. In the pursuit of jihad, do nothing to draw attention to one's self or one's religion.

He could still hear the voices of his instructors and his classmates as they chanted the Code morning after morning. First, "have a general appearance that does not indicate Islamic orientation (beard, toothpick, book, long shirt, small Koran)." Second, "be careful not to mention the brother's common expressions or show their behaviors (special praying appearance, 'may Allah reward you,' 'peace be on you' while arriving and departing, etc.)." Third, "avoid visiting Islamic places (mosques, libraries, Islamic fairs, etc.)." Fourth, "avoid outward signs of Islamic or Arabic belief or behavior or traditions in public (speaking in Arabic, singing in Arabic, praying five times a day, reading the Koran or anything in Arabic or about the Middle East or Islam, listening to the Koran or Islamic/Arabic music, etc.)." And fifth, "blend into the local culture as much as possible to deceive the enemy and appear as one of them (wear modern Western clothing, cut your hair short, be clean shaven, frequent bars and nightclubs, wear a crucifix or Star of David or hang one on the wall of your home, have a Bible among your possessions, etc.)—these are not violations of the Koran, they are not forbidden if you are in faithful pursuit of jihad against the infidels."

The Code followed the hourly recitation of the holy *fatwah*, the orders they had received from the Al-Nakbah high command: "In compliance with Allah's order, we issue the following *fatwah* to all Muslims: The ruling to kill the Americans and their allies—civilians and military—is an individual duty for every Muslim who can do it in any country in which it is possible to do it, in order to liberate the Al-Aksa Mosque and the holy mosque in Mecca from their grip, and in order for their armies to move out of all the lands of Islam, defeated and unable to threaten any Muslim. This is in accordance with the words of Almighty Allah—'and fight the pagans all together as they fight you all together,' and 'fight them until there is no more tumult or oppression, and there prevail justice and faith in Allah.' We—with Allah's help—call on every Muslim who believes in Allah and wishes to be rewarded to comply with Allah's order to kill the Americans and plunder their money wherever and whenever they find it."

It felt good to say those words again. They were soothing and familiar.

But there were times he missed those drill sessions, their sense of mission and comradery, the feelings of brotherhood with fellow warriors, each willing to sacrifice his very life for such a high calling. But human contact wasn't something that he missed tonight more than usual. He'd spent most of his thirty-nine years alone or on the run, looking over his shoulder and listening for the sounds of footsteps coming up fast.

The son of Palestinian refugees who fled to Iraq from Jericho on the West Bank during the Six Days' War of 1967—Al-Nakbah, "the Disaster"—Nadir grew up in Saddam City, a Ba'ath Party stronghold inside greater Baghdad. He'd not grown up in poverty or squalor. His parents were actually quite well-off. His father had been a banker for a Jordanian branch office until the war, and he'd looted close to thirty-seven thousand dollars before taking his family and fleeing into the night, bound for the Persian Gulf.

But neither he nor his mother nor his four older brothers had known that his father had stolen the money until many years later. After he had gotten a job as a teller in the National Bank of Iraq, main branch. After he'd worked his way up to branch manager. After Nadir's brothers had all grown up, served in the army, gone to college, and were now serving in various respected capacities throughout the country. After Nadir had served fifteen years in a Republican Guard Special Forces unit as a demolitions expert and twice-decorated instructor in the use of explosives for terrorist and tactical battlefield operations. After his mother had passed away four years ago from a brain hemorrhage.

One night, three weeks after his mother's funeral, Nadir and his father were alone in their top-floor apartment overlooking Baghdad. It was one of those August nights when the daytime temperatures have topped 120 degrees, and still haven't dropped below 100, and the humidity is near 85 to 90 percent, and the air is still and there is simply no wind or breeze at all.

The two men just sat completely still in the shadowy living room, lights off, the ceiling fan set on high. Both men were stripped down to their boxer shorts and covered with sweat. Both held towels soaked in ice-cold water with which they wiped their faces and necks as they sipped bottled water stuffed with ice chips and tried not to talk. Nadir's father was not a man who liked to talk. No one in Saddam Hussein's Iraq was much of a conversationalist. Especially not if he worked for the government, not if he handled the government's money, as all money in Iraq ultimately was.

But on this sweltering, oppressive night, Nadir's father began to talk. For the first time in Nadir's life, his father began telling him stories about growing up in Jericho, about life on the West Bank, about summers hiking through the Judean Hills with his friends, picking olives and begging for scraps of pita bread from owners of Arab cafés dotted along the Jordan River. He told stories of sneaking past Jordanian soldiers, into the Old City of Jerusalem, as a teenager without his parents, and winding his way through the aromatic alleyways of the Muslim Quarter. He could still remember breathing in the colorful spices, most of which he'd never heard of, and the smell of lamb roasting on spits in every restaurant and on every corner. And he remembered meeting a beautiful teenage girl named Rania who would soon become his wife, and bear him five beautiful sons, and make a life with him far away from the city she grew up in, the city she loved.

"Your mother was from Jerusalem," Nadir's father told him, "when it was controlled by the Arabs, when it was the home of good Muslims, not the Jews."

Then he reached over and took Nadir's hands and held them in his own, and made his youngest son promise him that he would exact vengeance on the Zionist infidels who had broken his mother's heart and driven her into a long and bitter exile.

"Your mother, on her deathbed, made me promise her," his father told him in a whisper, his voice barely audible. "She made me promise that when she was gone, when it was safe, I would tell you she had one final request of you."

"What is it, Father?" Nadir had asked, taken by surprise by the tremor in the man's voice and the moisture in his eyes.

"You need to leave Iraq. You need to use all the military skills that Allah has given you, and use them no longer to advance Saddam's kingdom but to regain Palestine and Al Quds—Jerusalem—the city of your mother's birth."

"But how, my father? If you ask me to, I will do it. But how could I possibly do such a thing? I have no passport. No money. No contacts, except those in my military units, none of whom I could turn to or trust."

For the next hour Nadir's father spoke in hushed tones, as though Saddam's secret police—the Mukhabbarat—were listening in and about to burst through the door and take them down in a blaze of machine-gun fire. He told Nadir of the men he'd met through the bank, the men who ostensibly worked for Saddam, but were actually building a secret army to liberate Palestine from the river to the sea. He told Nadir how he'd earned the trust of such men, how the men had chosen to begin banking with him almost a decade earlier precisely because they had heard that he and his wife were Palestinians, a fact Nadir's family did nothing to broadcast and everything to keep to themselves. His father told him how these men had secretly been stashing money in small accounts through the Iraqi national banking system, and always allowing their favorite teller—and later branch manager— to skim off a little for himself, as a sign of their goodwill.

Over the years, and combined with the thirty-seven thousand dollars his father now explained he had stolen from the Jordanians on June 7, 1967—a night he would never forget—he had amassed nearly $150,000 in various international currencies, none of which were Iraqi dinars. And he was giving it to Nadir. To run. To flee the country. To join Al-Nakbah. To train suicide bombers. And then to become one himself.

This was his mother's dying wish, and thus his father's in his old age. The man was almost eighty-five now. He was old, and without his precious wife of almost seventy years, he would soon die too. He would die penniless and alone, but with the hope that his son would redeem all his wasted years in exile by inflicting vengeance upon the Jews and freeing Palestine from the grip of the infidels.

Nadir could feel his eyes getting heavy. He was catnapping for a few hours at a time, feverishly racing for the East Coast. Time was short. He had no way of knowing how many others had or were about to make it across the borders and into the United States. There was no way to know how many were en route, even now, to complete their mission and strike terror in the heart of the Great Satan. But he was here. He had made it through. His mother's dying prayers to Allah were guiding him—propelling him—forward. He would succeed. He would make his mother and father proud.

Perhaps his father would be able to turn on the radio in that stifling little banker's apartment in a few days and hear of a heroic attack in a major East Coast city, and fall asleep with the pride of knowing his youngest son had done his duty. But for now, Nadir needed to sleep. He would be no good to the revolution if he dozed off at the wheel and veered into the path of an oncoming eighteen-wheeler.

As Nadir saw another sign for Albuquerque go by, he began to wonder why his mother and father had chosen him for this honor. He'd always been the least successful son in the family. Of his four brothers, one was a professor of mathematics. Another was an engineer, designing and building bridges in the southern tier of Iraq. The third was a police constable. The fourth was a tank commander. He had no idea where any of them were now, since the American rape of Iraq. But they were all men of distinction. All were married. All had borne their parents grandsons. All were highly respected by their families and their peers.

How, then, had he turned out so poorly? He was not married. He had no lover. He had no close friends to speak of, no home or material possessions or much of anything holding him back. For years this had weighed heavily upon him, made him feel lonely and rejected and a failure.

But perhaps Allah had prevented him from settling down and getting comfortable. Perhaps it was his will that he be restless and free and ready to carry out his parents' wishes. Of all five sons, only he was truly qualified and willing to give his life for the cause. Perhaps his mother had understood this all along. Perhaps she was waiting for him in paradise, waiting to see if he would fulfill his destiny, waiting to tell him, "Good job, my son. I am proud of you. You have honored your father and me. Enter into the joy of Allah." Of all this he was not certain. But he knew one thing. He was ready to die in a blaze of glory, and that day was coming up fast. So was his exit, and Nadir clicked on his turn signal, checked his mirrors, slowed to thirty-five, and carefully made the exit.

★　★　★

"Should we hold the peace talks at Camp David?" asked MacPherson.

Sa'id and the PLC wanted to start talking with Doron immediately. But something in Sa'id's gut was warning him away from the historic presidential retreat site. "It's a very kind offer," he began.

"But . . ."

"I think we need to avoid the big, media-driven peace talks of the past—the one in Madrid in '93, the one Clinton tried to engineer between Barak and Arafat at Camp David in 2000. It's my sense that those typically end in failure."

"Why do you say that?" asked the president.

"Because they are *media*-driven events. They are designed to posture, not produce."

"What do you have in mind?"

"To be honest, I am not sure exactly."

"Jon, how about you?"

"You know, I have to agree with the prime minister, Mr. President. I'm thinking the best-case scenario would be for Sa'id and Doron to meet somewhere in the region, not on U.S. soil, for secret talks—without the glare of the media, and without dozens of aides and advisors whispering a million reasons in their ears why making peace isn't such a good idea after all. If they can strike a deal, great. If they simply begin a relationship and lay the groundwork for a deal down the road, that's fine too. But it should happen fast, and it should happen under the radar."

"But don't we need to send a public signal that the peace process is under way?"

"Eventually," Sa'id explained. "But right now, people are totally focused on the war, as they should be. I don't want to confuse people by being in peace talks—at least publicly—while there is a fight for survival going on in our homeland."

"Mr. President," Bennett now added, "perhaps we should think of it like the major mergers or acquisitions we used to do on Wall Street. A leak to CNBC that a new deal might be in the works could sometimes be useful, to stir the pot a bit, get people interested, and gauge reaction. But only when the talks were well under way, or essentially done, right? We never wanted to conduct negotiations amid the glare of the media, and for good reason. It totally changed the dynamics when everyone knew exactly what was going on."

"True," MacPherson conceded. "Are you okay with that, Mr. Prime Minister?"

Sa'id thought for a moment, then answered. "If you can persuade Prime Minister Doron to come to the talks to negotiate in good faith, then yes—I don't see why not. He just needs to know one thing."

"What's that?" asked MacPherson.

"I have negotiated multibillion-dollar deals with the slimiest sheikhs and charlatans in the bloody Middle East. I don't plan to take any nonsense from him."

31

SIERRA VISTA was no Palm Beach.

Built on the outskirts of Orlando by a development mogul from Philadelphia a dozen years ago, it was a retirement community for the middle class, not the rich. But it was safe and affordable for northeastern professionals ready to cash in their equity, collect their pensions and their Social Security checks, and settle down for some sun, some golf, a pool and recreation center, and two full-time activity directors.

Most events were over by nine. The pool closed at nine-thirty. By ten o'clock at night, most of the residents were sound asleep. That was certainly true tonight as two Orlando Police Department squad cars pulled through the front gates.

The officers wound their way down Sunset Courtyard and stopped in front of the last condo on the left. They knocked loudly and repeatedly on the front door. There was no answer. They dialed the phone number again. There was no answer. They walked around the house. The back door was locked, but there was some paint and chips of wood missing near the lock. Had someone tried to pry it open?

A moment later, they jimmied the lock on the front door. Both officers entered carefully, not sure what they might be walking into. Each held a flashlight with one hand and his weapon with the other. They called out, but there was no answer. They moved room by room, starting on the main floor. Nothing. They went down to the basement. Nothing. Then the second floor, and the attic. That's when they really started getting worried. Not only was Ruth Jean Bennett nowhere to be found, there was no sign that she'd even been there for days.

★ ★ ★

A half hour later, the call came from Operations.

FBI director Scott Harris listened carefully and asked a few questions. But the more he learned, the more his sense of foreboding intensified.

On the surface, nothing in Ruth Bennett's home suggested a break-in or a struggle. It was not immediately apparent that the television or VCR or stereo system were missing. All components appeared to be in their proper places. It was possible that cash or jewelry was missing, since neither of the patrolmen had any sort of an inventory from Jon Bennett, who'd rarely been there over the past few years and could remember very few salient details. Several jewelry boxes had been found on Mrs. Bennett's dresser, and they were all full and appeared untouched. A safe was found in an upstairs closet. It was still closed and locked and showed no signs of having been tampered with. Both cars registered in the names of Solomon and Ruth Bennett were still in the driveway. But none of this seemed to ease Harris's fears.

The house contained no home security system. Electrical power to the home was still working, as were the phones. The Bennetts' LUDs— line-usage details—showed no calls in the past seventy-two hours, and just a handful of outgoing calls in the week prior. A few to some neighbors. A few to some local takeout restaurants. Two to the 716 area code just outside of Buffalo.

That number belonged to Dave and Dorothy Richards. An agent had just woken them up. Dorothy Richards, it turned out, was Ruth Bennett's sister. Yes, they had spoken twice. Once on Christmas Eve, and again for nearly two hours on Christmas Day. They were scheduled to talk again sometime New Year's weekend. Had Mrs. Richards heard of the events transpiring in the Middle East? No, she and her husband were retired and lived on an old farm about thirty miles south of Buffalo. A huge snowstorm had knocked out their power and frozen up their satellite TV system. They were operating on a generator, and not bothering to listen to the radio. They knew more lake-effect snow was expected, and more after that. It was Buffalo, after all. They were just enjoying their fireplace, lots of wool blankets, and a stack of murder-mystery novels they'd given each other for Christmas.

"How did Mrs. Richards react when you told her about Jon Bennett's situation?" Harris asked the Op Center watch officer.

"She couldn't believe it, and now she's terrified for her sister, and her nephew. She said some of her sister's friends may have heard the news about Jon and taken Mrs. Bennett in for a few days so she wouldn't be alone. She gave us a few names and phone numbers. We're in the process of calling all of them right now. Wait, hold on."

Harris could hear several agents briefing the watch officer on their canvassing of the neighborhood and their calls to Mrs. Bennett's friends. She was still nowhere to be found. Several of them had, in fact, been calling her repeatedly, upon hearing the news of the crisis in Gaza. They were worried about her, especially with everything happening so soon after the death of her husband and the attack that nearly killed her son in Jerusalem. A few had dropped by, knocked on the door, peered inside the windows, but none knew where she was. They just assumed she was with someone else. They all had their own children and grandchildren in town for the holidays, so they'd been too busy to worry about it much. But they were all worried now. What had happened to her? And why?

Harris wasn't inclined to assume the worst, but the most obvious and benign answers weren't panning out. The president was expecting an update. Harris decided to call Homeland Security Secretary James first. Together, they'd brief the press at the top of the hour. What should they say? Should they even mention this at all? What did they really know at this point?

The FBI, of course, would put out an APB on the disappearance—complete with photos and a detailed description of Mrs. Bennett. It was impossible to think the news media wouldn't pick it up immediately. After all, in a few hours, the country would wake up to headlines telling them a wave of suicide bombers were heading for the United States, and that some might have already arrived. It wouldn't take much to add one and one together and assume the worst—that the mother of the president's "point man for peace" was missing and presumed kidnapped by radical Islamic extremists. So what was worse: going public and fueling a national panic, or holding back and being accused of not enlisting the public's help in finding this woman?

* * *

Dr. Eliezer Mordechai checked his watch.

They were right on time. The white Chevy Suburban from the U.S. Embassy in Tel Aviv arrived at exactly four, snaked up the narrow, winding road to his home, built into the hills overlooking the Old City of Jerusalem, came to a stop in his muddy driveway, and honked the horn three times. That was the signal. He picked up his garment bag and punched his personal code into his home security system, arming it until his return. He had no idea when that might be. A few days? A few weeks? Once again, he was about to enter unknown territory, his natural habitat.

Three agents were waiting for him. One remained in the driver's seat. One stood watch, an Uzi in his grip. The third came up the steps to greet him. He too carried an Uzi, but more importantly an umbrella.

The winds were dying down. The lightning and thunder seemed to have disappeared. There was no question the weather was improving at the margins. But this was still no weather to be flying in, and even in good weather Dr. Mordechai hated to fly.

Soon they were back on Highway 1, bound for the FedEx processing center at Ben Gurion International Airport. At this hour, and with this weather, it could take up to two hours, instead of the usual one. But Dr. Mordechai wasn't worried. He had full confidence in the men around him, and the men he was going to see.

Less than two hours before, he'd received a startling call from his old friend, Dmitri Galishnikov. Events were unfolding rapidly. Galishnikov wasn't authorized to say much, only that the president and Jonathan Bennett were requesting his immediate assistance for a project of the highest international priority. He'd be gone indefinitely. He could bring nothing with him but clothing and some toiletries. And he could tell no one. For a legendary, retired chief of the Israeli Mossad, there was no other way to go.

* * *

Yuri Gogolov awoke to someone pounding on his door.

With one hand, he reached for his gold-rimmed spectacles sitting on the end table next to him. With the other he clicked off the safety of the semiautomatic pistol he held on his lap. The pounding continued, and it was getting louder.

Gogolov moved quietly through the dark living room, adrenaline pumping into his system. Wearing no shoes, his feet made no sound on the Persian rugs. He was ready for whoever was stupid enough to be trifling with him now. His hand slowly reached out for the dead bolt above the doorknob.

"Who is it?" he whispered in Farsi.

"Mr. Gogolov, sir, it is Mahmoud," a voice yelled back. "It is urgent."

Gogolov cursed under his breath. It was Jibril's driver, a burly idiot of a man better suited to be a bouncer at a nightclub than a personal bodyguard for the most deadly terrorist on the face of the planet. He unlocked the door, let him in, closed the door behind him, and told the man to shut up.

"Is this how the mullahs trained you?" Gogolov growled through clenched teeth. "Did they teach you to alert an entire building of families that have absolutely no idea I'm here—that would sell my location to the Americans or the Israelis or the Russians in a heartbeat if they knew how much I was worth captured, dead or alive? Is that how your father once protected the ayatollah in Paris? By pounding on the door of his flat for all the world to hear? You moron. You disgust me. Show me your weapon."

The driver just stood there stammering. He'd been calling on the phone for nearly an hour, but there'd been no answer. Gogolov had apparently turned the phone off for a while to get some badly needed sleep. But the message was urgent. Mohammed Jibril insisted that it be delivered in person. What else was he supposed to do?

Mahmoud Hameed reached into his coat, soaked with the winter rains still plaguing Tehran, and pulled out a pistol. It was fitted with a new silencer, custom built by Al-Nakbah's "friends" in the Iranian Secret Service. He passed it over to his master for inspection. Such inspections were not uncommon. But they were never pleasant. They were often accompanied by Gogolov's increasingly common fits of rage, and with a barrage of questions Mahmoud never knew quite how to answer.

Gogolov, a former Russian *Spetznatz* commando and senior officer, took the weapon in his hands. He examined it carefully, checked the chamber to see if there was a round in it, and checked the safety to see that it was on. It was. And now it wasn't.

Now it was pointed at Mahmoud Hameed's face. The man's eyes went wide with terror. Two muffled snaps. Two puffs of smoke. A single shot through each eye, and it was over. Hameed's body lurched backward, then crumpled to the floor, his legs still writhing in spasms as the brain's last signals reached their intended destinations.

Gogolov had no use for weak men. He could not build a global terrorist force with such incompetence. He wanted only the best, and he needed to send a message to those already under the command of Mohammed Jibril, and thus under his own. Just as Mahmoud Hameed's blood was seeping out into the carpets around him, so too the story of his death would seep out into the fabric of Al-Nakbah's entire network. It would strike fear into the hearts of every officer, every operative, every informant, every financier. Mistakes would not be tolerated. Even your own weapons could be used against you.

Gogolov reached into his pocket, pulled out his cell phone, and turned it back on. He speed-dialed Jibril and told him he needed a new driver.

Jibril didn't know what to say. He had no time to mourn such a death, let alone clean it up. But it bothered him. It was a waste. They had a war to run. They couldn't be eating their own. They shouldn't always have to move to new safe houses, leaving a trail of blood and questions behind them. But Gogolov couldn't seem to help himself. It wasn't simply that the man needed to kill someone occasionally. That was expected in their business. It was that he *wanted* to kill. He enjoyed it. He relaxed when it was over, until the pressure built up again and his bloodlust resurfaced without warning.

Jibril tried to shake such thoughts from his mind and refocus. The newest package Gogolov had ordered was wrapped, stamped, and ready for the post office.

"Very well," Gogolov whispered, taking a deep breath and smiling for the first time in days. "Deliver it now."

★ ★ ★

Bennett and McCoy sat alone in Ziegler's room.

Sipping piping-hot Turkish coffee, they fielded a slew of incoming phone calls from Langley and the White House. They monitored satellite news channels, Kol Israel Radio, the BBC, and a variety of regional and international news sites on the Internet, simultaneously tracking developments on four different continents. Over the course of the last four and a half hours, they had watched the carefully scripted drama play itself out. Now they were in a holding pattern. There wasn't much more either of them could do except wait, and hope for the best.

★　★　★

"Sir, we've got a problem."

It was 5:33 p.m. local time in Gaza. Ziegler was on a secure call with Langley, DIA, and CENTCOM, finalizing target packages in the West Bank and Gaza, when Tariq stuck his head in the door of the adjacent conference room and summoned him back into the main control room.

"Can it wait a few minutes, Tariq?" Ziegler asked his second-in-command.

"No, sir. I need you right now."

Ziegler could see a flash of panic in Tariq's eyes. He excused himself from the call, promising to get back with the senior commanders in a few minutes, then stepped back into the control room. What he saw on the first black-and-white security monitor he looked at terrified him. Six men—their faces shrouded by black-and-white-checked kaffiyehs—were setting the VW van on fire.

Scanning from one monitor to the next, Ziegler could see at least a hundred men, possibly more, all covered by kaffiyehs, gathering on the narrow streets in front and behind the Hotel Baghdad. Some were throwing rocks at the windows. Some were firing machine guns into the air. One was burning an American flag. All of them looked violent, and Ziegler couldn't process the images fast enough.

How could anyone know where they were? Had someone seen them enter the hotel? Hadn't the van been stolen? Hadn't it been untraceable? Of course, that was all history, water under the bridge. What kind of threat did this mob pose? That was the real question. How secure was Gaza Station? They were about to find out.

Beep, beep, beep, beep, beep, beep.

Lights and buzzers on the internal security panels began going off. Sensors indicated intrusions in the center east quadrant of the hotel foyer.

Beep, beep, beep, beep, beep, beep.

Now sensors in the southwest quadrant began going crazy. The mob was trying to break through the back doors as well.

Suddenly, a powerful explosion hit the northeast corner of the building. Even three stories down, Ziegler and Tariq could feel the impact as everything around them began to shake. The lights flickered. Then came a second massive explosion, and a third.

Ziegler's eyes darted from screen to screen. The unthinkable was happening. The Hotel Baghdad was beginning to teeter. It appeared ready to implode. Again the lights in the main control room flickered.

Ziegler grabbed the headset on the desk in front of him, and flicked on the microphone, activating a direct line to the Global Operations Center at CIA headquarters in Langley, Virginia. "GOC, this is Gaza Station. We are under attack. I repeat, we are under attack. Communications may soon be compromised. We need air support and extraction immediately. I repeat, we are under a Level Five attack and need immediate assistance."

No sooner were the words out of his mouth than the entire bank of video screens in front of him went dead. Then the lights went out. Gaza Station was shaking furiously. All power was gone. They were standing in complete darkness.

32

★ ★
★

THOSE LIVING UNDER the Hotel Baghdad never knew what hit them.

But all of them could feel the five-story structure above them disintegrating, succumbing to the three massive explosions and an eighteen-hundred-degree firestorm. The east face came down first, followed by the south portico. Then, just a few seconds later, the rest of the building's core collapsed as the crushing weight of the top floors became too much for the lower floors to bear. A noxious cloud of smoke filled the air. Flames shot out from every crevice.

Bennett smashed to the floor. Instinctively covering his head with his arms, he tried desperately to shield himself and McCoy from the chunks of ceiling crashing down all around him. Everything in the room shook violently. He could hear the pipes in the bathroom being ripped through the tiles and erupting into a ceaseless spray of water. The lights flickered and sparked, then all shorted out. Several more explosions rocked the safe house.

And then, the explosions stopped. Debris stopped falling. The temperature in the room began spiking quickly. It was getting more and more difficult to breathe. Bennett was numb. Hadn't he been through this already? Hadn't it all been a dream, a nightmare? Yes, he told himself, yes—both. But this was no premonition. This was no vision of an evil yet to come. This was real.

"Erin, you okay?" he whispered in the darkness, a rising anxiety thick in his voice.

"I don't know. I'm bleeding from some glass, I think. But nothing seems to be broken. How 'bout you?"

"Same, I think. I'm okay. Can you walk?"

"I think so."

"Where's your Beretta?"

"It's here, somewhere—what just happened?"

Bennett didn't answer. He crawled his way through the broken glass of the television and shattered mirror and picture frames over to Ziegler's desk. He felt around in the pitch-blackness for the file drawers, then pulled open the bottom one on the right. Sure enough, it was unlocked. And sure enough, they were there—two loaded .357 Magnums and boxes of spare rounds of ammunition, just like in the dream.

"What are you doing?" asked McCoy, feeling around for her purse and the handgun and spare clips inside it.

"The other night, I had a nightmare. I saw this exact situation, except you weren't with me."

"What?" She suddenly found her purse under the shattered coffee table.

"The Hotel Baghdad just collapsed. Three huge explosions. I think one of them was a car bomb. Maybe a truck bomb. I don't know for sure."

"What are you talking about?"

"I told you. The dream I had last night—there was a huge explosion. I was in this room. All the lights went out. But I could see Gaza Station filling up with fire and smoke—burst pipes, men firing AK-47s, coming in through gaps in the ceilings. Look, we don't have much time. We need to get Sa'id and Galshnikov and find Ziegler and Tariq and anyone on their team still alive."

McCoy didn't know what to say. She didn't know what he was talking about, or what to believe. No one knew Jon Bennett better than she did, but she'd never heard him talk like this. Dreams? Premonitions? It wasn't like him. It didn't make sense. But he was right about one thing—they didn't have much time to get out alive. Worse, they had no idea how to get out. There was no way they could go back up the silo by which they had entered. They had to find Ziegler or his deputies.

She chastised herself for not getting briefed earlier on all the possible escape options. It was standard operating procedure for every operative at every CIA safe house—planning for every contingency, always preparing for the worst. She hadn't done any of it. She'd let her guard down, and now it might cost them.

McCoy felt around in the darkness for the phones on Ziegler's desk. Finding one, she grabbed one of the receivers and began to dial the control room. "Jon, the lines are dead."

There was a long silence.

"Jon, in your dream, did you see how to get out?"

He hadn't. He didn't know. Not for sure. All he'd seen was a shootout in the main control room, the one that ended with him getting killed. But he couldn't tell her that. She'd already done so much for him. She'd saved his life countless times. He owed her as much, and he was determined to protect her at all costs.

"Just follow me and stay close," he said, then scrambled over to the door, holding the two .357s out in front of him.

As he'd done in the dream, Bennett put the back of his hand against the door, just as his father had taught him when they'd stayed in hotels. It was hot—too hot—and he winced in pain and quickly pulled his hand back and blew on it. He silently cursed himself. He should have seen that coming. He could see an orange glow through the cracks in the door frame. The fires had to be close. But they didn't really have any choice. If they stayed in Ziegler's room, they were as good as dead. That much was certain. He decided right there. They might not make it out of this place, but at least he was going to die trying.

Bennett set the pistols down on the floor, took off his right shoe, pulled off his sock, and put it over his left hand. Then using that hand, he quickly turned the handle and pulled the door open. A blast of superheated air hit him in the face and he drew back, using the door as a shield. He quickly put his sock and shoe back on, looked around the room, and scooped up the guns. The fires in the hallway provided more than enough visibility to see the destruction that had been wrought all around him. Bennett just stared at it all, then looked back at McCoy. Her face was sweaty and glowing amid the raging flames, but her eyes sparkled with an inner life that he found so magnetic.

"You ready?" he whispered, his mouth close to hers.

"I guess."

His face moved still closer to hers. He wanted to kiss her before he died. Now seemed as good a time as any. But suddenly, another explosion rocked the building. They could hear the crackle of automatic gunfire. It was definitely inside the Gaza Station complex, but it wasn't close. It had to be on the other side, closer to the main control room. But a shot of fear and adrenaline coursed through his veins. He had no way of knowing who was shooting at whom. How was he supposed to defend them if he had to—*when* he had to?

They worked their way to the junction of two hallways, staying low to avoid suffocating on the smoke snaking along the ceilings. One of the hallways led to the main control room. Ziegler, Tariq, and their team were probably in there, and the urge to keep going in that direction was almost overpowering. They had to find them. They had to find out how to get out of this place before it was too late.

The other hallway led to Sa'id and Galishnikov's room. They had to find them, too, especially Sa'id. The man was now the prime minister of Palestine. They were all under direct orders from the president of the United States to protect him at all costs. Still, what good would it do to find them if they had no idea where to take them? Couldn't they come back for those two later, after they hooked up with Ziegler and his men?

Bennett froze for a moment. His eyes scanned both hallways, looking for any sign of friends or enemies, as he processed both options. Finding Ziegler first made more sense. It seemed logical, and it was closer, faster. But it was a seduction, a temptation. He knew it. He could feel it. Something was luring him in. Something was warning him off. He agonized as the flames and heat grew more intense. They couldn't stay still. They had to keep moving.

Dressed in blue jeans and a black T-shirt, Bennett was on his stomach, on the floor—the only place he could breathe—covered in at least a foot of water. McCoy, in navy blue sweatpants and a thick gray fleece, was right behind him, shivering in the ice-cold water pouring out of at least a dozen shattered pipes. But in less than an hour, she figured, that water would be heating toward a boil. She was coming to the same conclusion. They had no choice. They had to keep moving. They could hear men shouting in Arabic, but hadn't seen anyone, dead or alive. Not yet. Not a soul. Where were they? Had all of the Gaza Station team been killed either in the initial explosions or the gun battles that followed?

Not seeing a single living soul besides themselves was an eerie feeling. All they could see were flames and smoke and the water they were sloshing through. Still, Bennett was actually grateful for the flames—at least they provided some light in this subterranean labyrinth. But the raging electrical fires in the walls and ceilings worried him. It would take only one wire or cable falling into all this water and they'd be electrocuted instantly.

His eyes—bloodshot and stinging something fierce from all the smoke—searched wildly for escape routes. But their options, limited from the beginning, were narrowing fast. Small but rapidly growing fires seemed to block their path to Galishnikov and Sa'id's room. Now more fires blocked the way back to Ziegler's room as well. They weren't completely trapped, but it was only a matter of time. The only way out seemed to be forward. But something in Bennett's gut whispered that it was a trap, told him to go to the right, through the flames, to Sa'id and Galishnikov, before it was too late.

Flashbacks from his nightmare came like a strobe light. He remembered the gun battle in the control room. He remembered the overwhelming presence of evil he felt, and being trapped in the conference room, where he'd almost died. It was as though sirens were calling him to that control room, luring him forward. Maybe he'd been wrong. Maybe he'd woken up to soon. Maybe it wasn't a death trap but a road map he could follow better this time.

Fresh bursts of automatic gunfire—closer, louder, and coming from the main control room in longer bursts—snapped Bennett back to reality. He looked over his shoulder, made sure McCoy was okay, then silently motioned her to follow him down the hallway—now almost completely engulfed in fire—to Tariq's quarters, to Galishnikov and Sa'id. Maybe it was suicide. But there was only one way to find out.

☆　☆　☆

Both phones and his pager went off all at once.

It was well past midnight, but such was the life of a *New York Times* White House correspondent. Forever electronically tethered to a world that never stopped moving. Marcus Jackson clicked on the light beside his bed and tried to get his bearings. He raced into the bathroom to grab one of the cell phones out of its charger, and just in time.

"You wanted to know about Bennett?" said the voice at the other end.

"Talk to me."

✦ ✦ ✦

Danny Tracker raced downstairs.

The hastily scribbled note passed to the CIA's deputy director of Operations during a crisis meeting in his office bore only a few words—"GS down . . . L5 . . . request immediate extract." But the message was devastating. Everything was suddenly at risk. If it was true—if Gaza Station had really been compromised, or worse, was going down in flames—the implications were unthinkable. Losing a $25 million intelligence-gathering facility would be bad enough. Losing Bennett and McCoy, plus Ziegler and his team, would be a nightmare. But losing Ibrahim Sa'id, the newly appointed prime minister of Palestine, would be catastrophic. Everything now hinged on him. He needed to be protected and extracted at all costs.

Mitchell wasn't at Langley. He was in an armor-plated SUV, en route from the White House, and his phone was busy. Tracker raced down the stairwell to the Global Operations Center. He tried Mitchell again—still busy. Then he tried Ed Mutschler, chairman of the Joint Chiefs.

"Mutschler—go."

"General, it's Danny," shouted Tracker as a guard opened the door to the Global Ops Center and waved him through. "You see what I'm seeing?"

"Gaza Station?"

"We've got to go in now, General," said Tracker. "Are your guys ready?"

"My guys are always ready. The real question is, are they even still alive?"

33

* * *

"ALL SET?" Bennett whispered.

McCoy looked down the long hallway at the flames shooting from the electrical wiring in the ceiling. They'd have to get down on the floor on their stomachs in the rapidly rising water, hold their breath, and make a dash for it. It was the only way they knew of to get to Sa'id and Galishnikov, and such as it was, the window was closing fast. Soon the entire hallway would be engulfed in flames.

"You sure about this?" she whispered back, not really expecting an answer.

"No," he conceded. "Not really."

"How do we get back?"

Bennett thought about that for a second. "I have no idea," he admitted again.

Well, at least he was being honest. "All right," said McCoy. "After you."

Bennett nodded, then got down in the water and began to inch his way forward. It was hard to see, and harder to breathe. The smoke was getting thicker. The flames were growing longer, threatening to reach down and lap up the water at any moment. McCoy was right behind him, her hand on his back so they wouldn't get separated.

"Ready. Set. Go."

Bennett sucked in a lungful of oxygen, then plunged down into the water and tried to hug the floor, pressing against the walls to keep himself from rising in the water up to the flames just inches above him. Six seconds later, he was through. He came up gasping for air and wiping the sooty water out of his eyes. A few seconds later, McCoy came through as well. She came up like a swimmer, head arched back, wet hair streaming down her back, her Beretta ice-cold but still glued to her right hand.

The two were soaked to the bone, shivering and short of breath. But they were together, and they were safe, at least for—

A massive explosion shook the hallway. A huge, gaping hole suddenly opened up at the far end of the hallway, about thirty yards ahead of them. Concrete and Sheetrock came pouring down into the water. A cloud of dust and smoke began moving toward them. Then three, maybe four men dropped down into the hallway. It was hard to see them clearly. But they were shouting in Arabic and both Bennett and McCoy knew instantly.

"Jon, get down, get down," shouted McCoy, pushing Bennett's body back into the water as automatic-weapons fire erupted all around them. She took aim through the smoke and dust and began firing.

The screams were instantaneous, but they came with return fire. Bennett refused to stay down. Flames now completely engulfed the hallway behind him and McCoy. There was no way out.

Hugging the wall and staying as low to the floor as he could, Bennett raised his head, lifted both .357s, and began firing into the haze and flames and smoke ahead of him. He couldn't see faces. Neither could McCoy—only shadows and movement. Bullets were smashing all around him. McCoy ducked to reload. Bennett kept firing—first one trigger, then the other, in rapid succession. Before he realized it, he'd unleashed every round from both clips. He was pulling triggers and hearing nothing but metallic clicks.

McCoy popped back up out of the water, her Beretta reloaded. But suddenly, the gunfire fell silent. No return fire. No shadows. No movement of any kind ahead of them. All was quiet, besides the sloshing of the water around them and more water falling from burst pipes a few dozen yards behind them. Had they killed them all? How many were there? Were there more? Bennett looked over at McCoy, who nodded her agreement. The flames behind them were just a foot or two away. They had to press forward.

As McCoy covered him, Bennett reached into his pocket to get the other clips. Then he signaled McCoy and the two forced themselves down again into the ice-cold water. With Bennett leading, they began to creep forward. When they got ahead about fifteen or twenty yards, to the corner of two adjoining hallways, they could see what they'd done. Near a pile of rock and concrete and dirt—the remains of the explosion by which the terrorists had breached the station—the riddled bodies of five men they'd just gunned down floated in water as bloodred as the kaffiyehs that covered their faces. Bennett shuddered. He could feel his hands trembling and the back of his throat began to burn, as though he were about to throw up.

McCoy carefully checked the pulse of each man, her pistol ready to strike if any of them were still alive. But they were gone. Each man held an AK-47 in a death grip. None of them carried any ID. McCoy and Bennett quickly stripped the men of their ammunition and backed away. As quickly as they could, the two worked their way down the next hallway and reached the door to Tariq's room. Neither said it. Neither dared to. But the same question worried them both.

Who would they find on the other side?

★ ★ ★

The five SH-60F Seahawks were powered up and ready to go.

The rugged sixty-four-foot all-weather choppers were originally built for antisubmarine warfare. But these five—the navy's version of the famed army Blackhawk—were uniquely outfitted for special operations and assigned to the newest nuclear-powered supercarrier in the American arsenal, the USS *Ronald Reagan*.

The first Seahawk—code-named Storm One—was the command-and-control helo, carrying SEAL Team Eight commander Eduardo Ramirez, code-named Br'er Rabbit; a senior intel officer; and two radio operators, one to coordinate combat operations in the air, the other to coordinate operations on the ground.

In the second Seahawk—Storm Two—eleven members of Gold Cell or Gold Team, ST-8's premier counterterrorist assault force, checked their gear and prepared for liftoff. On board Storm Three, Red Cell ran through their final checklists, while on board Storm Four, Blue Cell did the same. Joining these four and bringing up the rear would be a fifth Seahawk, Storm Five, the transport helo and responsible for the safety of the "package"—Bennett, Sa'id, and their team. Some carried M16s equipped with laser sights and fifty-five-watt halogen spotlights for close-quarters combat at night or inside buildings. Others preferred the M4A1 carbine, similarly equipped. Those responsible for initial perimeter security tended to go with the SASR .50-caliber sniper rifle. All were loaded up with as much ammunition as they could carry.

SEAL Team Eight would be the first in—on the ground in less than fifteen minutes. They'd be backed up by the Sixth Fleet and the STRIKFORSOUTH command out of southern Europe. On the ground, they'd be joined by two hundred crack fighters from the 26th Marine Expeditionary Unit from the USS *Kearsarge*. Deemed special operations capable—SOC—the 26th MEU excelled at rapid-response, high-risk, high-threat missions into hostile territory. In June of 1995, they'd rescued Air Force Captain Scott O'Grady, shot down over Bosnia and trapped behind enemy lines. In May of 1997, they'd rescued two hundred Americans out of Sierra Leone. "A certain force in an uncertain world" was their motto, and over the years they'd more than lived up to their billing. The men and women of the 26th MEU lived for this stuff, and once again they were about to step up to the plate in service of their country.

If the plan held and weather cleared a bit more, another two thousand Marines and their mechanized equipment would hit the beaches in the next twenty-four to forty-eight hours. And they'd soon be reinforced by a detachment of Rangers and as many Delta commandos as U.S. commanders on the ground in Iraq could spare.

This was it, the tip of the spear.

It was the riskiest gambit yet in James MacPherson's already high-risk presidency, and everyone involved knew there were no guarantees.

★ ★ ★

They were at Tariq's door.

Bennett rechecked his .357s and tried to steady his shaking hands. He glanced at McCoy. She was double-checking her Beretta as well and trying to slow her breathing. They were as ready as they were going to be. They just hoped these guys were still alive, and that no one else was in there.

Bennett took the left side of the door. McCoy took the right. They looked each other in the eye and nodded. As rapidly as she could, McCoy punched in Tariq's passcode. Bennett then kicked open the door, careful to stay out of the line of fire. The room was pitch-black. Only the flickering flames from in the hallway ceiling provided any light at all. Bennett glanced in, the .357 in his right hand out in front of him, then pulled back. He couldn't see a thing. Neither could McCoy. No eyes. No movement. Nothing.

"Ibrahim? Dmitri?" Bennett whispered. "You guys okay?"

For a moment, it was silent. Bennett whispered again, his palms sweating against the handle of both weapons. "Ibrahim? Dmitri? You guys in there?"

"Jonathan? Is that you?"

It was Galishnikov's distinctive Russian baritone.

"Dmitri?"

"*Da.*"

"Dmitri, it's me. Erin's with me. You guys all right?"

"*Da, da,* my friend, we are good—never better—and look, we've got company."

Suddenly, the bedroom filled with light. Startled, Bennett and McCoy cautiously peeked in, only to find Tariq and two of his operatives—Nazir and Hamid—kneeling behind the couch in flak jackets and helmets, with fully locked and loaded M4 submachine guns in their hands and two portable lanterns sitting on the desk and the coffee table behind them. Sa'id was huddled in the corner next to Galishnikov, who was also holding an M4. They were safe after all, and it couldn't have been a more welcome sight. Both Bennett and McCoy breathed a huge sigh of relief. A fast round of handshakes and hugs ensued, and then the group quickly got back down to business.

Tariq went first, laying out their escape plan. "The hotel is gone. Gaza Station's breached in at least two places we know of."

"Three," McCoy interrupted. "Jon and I saw an explosion down the hallway just a few moments ago. We took out five guys coming in that way. But there have to be more coming in any second."

Tariq rubbed his eyes. He'd already been up all night. His nerves were raw. "Well, look, all the more, then, we need to get Mr. Sa'id and the rest of you out of here. Mr. Ziegler just talked to Langley. Here's the plan.

SEAL Team Eight is inbound from the *Reagan*, along with an assault force of Marines. ETA is about nine minutes. Maroq and Mr. Ziegler are back in the main control room, destroying papers and equipment and trying to hold off the infiltrators. It's my job, along with Nazir and Hamid here, to provide security for Mr. Sa'id. Erin, you need to provide security for Mr. Bennett and Mr. Galishnikov. All right?"

Everyone nodded.

"The original NEO plan was for us to be airlifted off the top of the hotel," Tariq continued. "But obviously that's not going to work anymore. So we're going with plan B. I just got off the satcom link with Commander Ramirez with the SEALs. We've got to make our way about five blocks through a sewage tunnel that runs under the main street. It's not going to be the most pleasant experience, but it's all we've got. It'll take us to a burned-out café we're code-naming Alpha Zone. Once we get there, we'll reestablish contact with Ramirez and the SEALs will scoop us up and get us out of here. In the meantime, I'll take the lead. Hamid brings up the rear. Any questions?"

"What about Ziegler and Maroq?" asked McCoy.

"Don't worry about them. We've got a squad of Marines coming for them. They'll be fine. Anyone else? All right, let's move out."

Fires were raging throughout all the main hallways now, but fortunately they didn't have to go far. About halfway down the hallway they were in, Tariq stopped; instructed Nazir, Hamid, and McCoy to set up a perimeter; and pressed a passcode into what looked like an ordinary utility closet.

A second later, the door electronically clicked open, but inside were no brooms, mops, or buckets. There was another submarine hatch, similar to the one they'd all used to get down into Gaza Station. This one would take them down again, into Gaza's sewage system, but God willing, it would also take them all out of this hellhole once and for all.

Tariq punched in another passcode, opened the hatch, then stuck his M4 with its small halogen search lamp into the silo, scanning it for any signs of life. The good news was there was no one down there. The bad news was the stench was horrendous, and they were going in anyway.

Tariq reached onto a shelf in the closet, far above the steel hatch. Finding a large box, he pulled it down and began distributing a gas mask to each person. He put his own on and then helped Sa'id and Galishnikov get theirs on and adjusted. He looked over the group, got the thumbs-up from everyone, nodded, and proceeded down the silo. Three minutes later, they were all together again, slogging through a putrifying combination of waste and slime, illuminated only by the lights on their M4s and a small flashlight Tariq had given to Sa'id.

"I've been meaning to ask you something, Tariq, ever since we got here," said Bennett, as the group pressed forward. His voice echoed through the huge steel pipe.

"What's that, Mr. Bennett?" Tariq replied.

"How did you guys ever build Gaza Station, anyway? I mean, you know, without the whole world knowing about it."

Bennett instantly recoiled. He'd just betrayed the name of a CIA safe house. True, these men were friends. They knew most of one another's secrets. But not all of them. Nor could they. The world had just changed. He had to be more careful.

Tariq's stomach tightened too. He knew the station's entire history. How the Hotel Baghdad had once been the headquarters for Egyptian intelligence in Gaza since first being built in 1962. How the facilities—including the underground bunkers and tunnels—were secretly offered to the CIA by President Sadat in the spring of 1980, after the Camp David peace accords were concluded; how senior State Department officials, seething with bitterness at the CIA for its failure to anticipate the Islamic revolution in Iran and prevent the takeover of the American Embassy in Tehran in November of '79 persuaded Carter to turn down the deal. And how the Reagan administration, soon after the release of the hostages from Tehran, secretly reopened talks with Sadat and nailed down a deal that neither the Israelis nor the Palestinians ever knew about.

Galishnikov's ears perked up. He'd also wondered about the history of this "Gaza Station."

So had Sa'id, and the wheels began to turn. Sa'id had always suspected the CIA was operating in Gaza, but he'd never known it for sure. Now he did. He'd been inside. He'd seen some of its layout. He knew its name. He knew who worked there, and some of their capabilities. That could prove to be valuable, could it not?

Yes, these men had saved his life. And yes, he still needed them to lead him out to safety. But the world had just changed. He wasn't simply a businessman caught in a cross fire. He was a prime minister. He was going to have to build strong ties not just with the Americans but with his own legislators, with other Arab leaders, with their generals and intelligence officials. It was a dangerous neighborhood he lived in, and would now have to govern. He had to work with the Americans, but he couldn't be their puppet. He needed them to take care of the Islamic militants, and to force—perhaps *persuade* was a better word—Doron to cut a deal. But there would come a day, no doubt sooner than he'd prefer, when he'd have to stand up to the Americans. Declare his independence. Show his people and the Arab world that Washington was doing *his* bidding, not the other way around. Kicking the CIA out of Palestine wouldn't be a bad first step.

Tariq knew that a significant portion of the $2 billion a year Washington gave to Egypt in foreign aid was to buy Cairo's continued silence about the facility's location and purpose. And he knew nearly every sordid detail of the bureaucratic tug of war inside the CIA that had prevented Gaza Station from coming on line for year after frustrating year. Besides the president, Jack Mitchell, Danny Tracker, and a handful of others on the National Security Council, only Jake Ziegler knew as much as he did about the origins and history of Gaza Station. But he didn't dare utter a word. Not with their lives in grave danger. Not with the new prime minister of Palestine just a few yards behind him.

Didn't Bennett get it? This was a world where every mistake could be your last.

"I'm sorry, sir," Tariq finally said. "I'd tell you. But then I'd have to kill you."

34

THE STRIKE FORCE shot hard and fast into Gaza.

Twenty choppers. Almost 250 special ops forces. Orders to rescue the new Palestinian prime minister and the American "point man for peace." Operation Briar Patch was under way.

"Br'er Rabbit, this is Br'er Fox," said the pilot of the lead Super Cobra.

Commander Ramirez in the command-and-control helo, Storm One, adjusted his headset and opened his microphone. "Go ahead, Br'er Fox. I read you five by five."

"Roger that, Br'er Rabbit. I've got the Tar Baby in my sights and it's swarming with bandits. Please advise. Over."

"Are the bandits armed?"

The lead pilot scanned the situation on the ground. The rains were still torrential, and visibility was minimal. Still, through night-vision goggles and the chopper's onboard thermal imaging, the pilot was learning all he needed to know to make an assessment.

"Armed and firing, Br'er Rabbit. I say again, armed and firing. There are several large flashes under way. They appear to be using explosives to penetrate the Tar Baby."

"Roger that, Br'er Fox. Commence firing. I repeat, commence firing."

The lead Super Cobra took one pass at less than five hundred feet, with two others right behind him. They cleared the target, banked right, then came back around and began unleashing their guns. Tracer bullets lit up the sky and the insurgents on the ground began dropping like flies.

Five blocks away, Storm Three now swooped in.

It took up a hovering position just a few feet over a six-story tenement building, the tallest in the squalid, crumbling neighborhood. Out of both sides of the chopper, ST-8's Red Team jumped out and moved like lightning. Each man knew his job. Each worked in rhythm with his teammates.

"*Go, go, go,*" shouted their team leader, a thirty-one-year-old lieutenant from the Bronx, a graduate of Annapolis and the son of two career naval officers.

Three American snipers took up positions on the roof. Others cut power lines. They shot up the transformer box on the roof, shutting down all the power in the building. At the same time, a breacher smashed through the door to the stairwell, using a sledgehammer and just two swings. Six shooters and their leader—each clicking on their night-vision goggles—now raced inside, weapons up, safeties off.

The top floor was abandoned, as was the fifth floor below. Only the rats—their eyes glowing red in the flashlight beams of the commandos—counted the dark places home. The SEALs proceeded cautiously through the shadowy stairwells, littered with shards of broken glass, giving away their position with every step. Each man wished they'd had more time to prepare, to send in a recon team to find out just what they were up against, to get precise floor plans and map out every step. They were moving blind, and even the Rangers and Deltas in Somalia were better prepared than they were.

Crunch, crunch.

Red Four and Red Five were on point, both just shy of their twenty-third birthdays. Their breathing was steady but their hands inside the Nomex gloves were damp with sweat. Moving in tandem—in radio silence, using only hand signals between them and to the men half a flight above them—they worked their way down the central stairwell inch by inch, shrouded in complete darkness. All the lightbulbs were smashed or nonexistent. There were no exit signs. No emergency power boxes. Just the eerie green imagery from their night-vision goggles.

As they slowly turned the corner, they could see the door to the fourth floor. It was closed. Just a thin slice of light seeped from the hallway. But from what? The building's power was out. The hallway had no windows. Where was the light coming from? The light moved. Just a little, but both men saw it and tensed.

Suddenly, two men kicked open the door and began shooting. Two more men popped up from the stairwell below and opened fire as well. Bursts of automatic machine-gun fire exploded around them. Concrete shrapnel was flying everywhere. The SEALs hit the deck and returned fire. Nonstop flashes erupted from the muzzles of their weapons as both sides fought viciously for control.

Red Six pulled pins on two grenades and tossed them both—one at the door, one down the stairwell at the attackers below. "Grenade," he shouted, and the Americans stopped firing and took cover.

The explosions were nearly instantaneous, one after the other, and they achieved their intended effect. One of the Palestinian gunmen was killed instantly. Three of the four were screaming uncontrollably. Red Five lifted his head and peered through the smoke and dust. He could see one gunman engulfed in flames. He fired off two rounds at the man's head and one at his chest. All three hit their mark and the man collapsed down the stairs onto the lifeless body of his comrade-in-arms.

"Let's go, let's go," he yelled, grabbing Red Four and helping him to his feet.

They raced for the smoking hole in the wall where the fourth-floor door had been and dove through, guns blazing. Red Six and Seven moved past them, down the stairs and burst onto the third floor. More gunfire erupted. Both floors were engaged now.

"Red Four, Red Four, talk to me—what've you got?" the team leader shouted over his radio.

"Heavy resistance on the fourth floor. Shots coming from the corner apartments."

"Red Four, can you take them on your own?"

A response came back, but it was almost impossible to hear with all the shooting in such tight quarters.

"Say again, Red Four, say again—can you take them on your own?"

A hiss of static. The words were garbled.

". . . support, we ca—"

The whole building seemed to be exploding around them.

"Say again, Red Four—I can't hear you."

". . . we can't move, can't get a better position—need close air support into the corner apartments immediately."

"Roger that, Red Four, and stand by one."

"Red Leader, this is Red Six. We've got the same situation on the third floor. Request CAS into all four corner rooms. Over."

"Got it, Red Six—stand by."

The team leader turned to his radio operator, as both men remained hunkered down in the stairwell. "Get me Storm One, now."

Ten seconds later, he was on the radio with Commander Ramirez. "Br'er Rabbit, this is Red Leader, do you copy?"

"Roger that, Red Leader. This is Br'er Rabbit. Go."

"Sir, we've got heavy resistance on the third and fourth floors here, from each of the corner apartments. Request immediate CAS, over."

"Roger that, Red Leader. Close air support on the way."

"Thank you, Br'er Rabbit," the lieutenant acknowledged, then radioed the rest of his team. "Okay, guys, hang in there—hold your ground—air support's on the way."

Less than a minute later, four jet-black Little Bird assault choppers took up positions off the four corners of the tenement. Using enhanced thermal imaging, they could see the shooters in each room, on each floor. They confirmed their targets and their orders with the C-2 bird, and got the clearance they wanted. Seconds later, all four began simultaneously unleashing their .50-caliber heavy machine guns through the windows and walls into all four rooms. The snipers never knew what was coming, and a moment later it was over. All was quiet in the smoky, shattered hallway.

Red Team was back on the move.

* * *

Across the street, Blue Team also fought its way down room by room.

Three Blue Team snipers hunkered down on the roof, picking off anyone stupid enough to fire a round at U.S. forces or aircraft descending into the neighborhood. Inside, resistance was heavier than expected, and Blue Leader worried the intense gun battle might be catching women and children in the cross fire. It was impossible to tell for sure. Most of the shooting was coming from small cracks in apartment doors, and his men had no choice but to punch back with overwhelming firepower, including grenades and the heavy machine guns on the Little Birds buzzing outside the windows.

It was a slow, nasty process. But it was critical. They were keeping the Islamic militants who'd taken over the building occupied, keeping their attention off the main event at the café across the street.

Storm Five circled off the coastline, waiting for their signal, while commandos of the 26th MEU fast roped onto roofs and into streets in concentric circles around Alpha Zone, the extraction point chosen by Ziegler and Tariq less than half an hour before. They too were encountering heavy resistance from random snipers and bands of militants moving about in jeeps and small trucks, just now getting word of the U.S. action and eager to hunt the Great Satan.

Flashes of grenades and mortar rounds lit up the sky. Tracer rounds streaked back and forth, and everyone's ears were filled with the roar of multiple explosions and staccato bursts of machine-gun fire. But the Americans' flood-the-zone strategy seemed to be working. One by one, enemy guns were falling silent, and hastily erected U.S. roadblocks at the major intersections were cutting off any hope of the radicals getting desperately needed reinforcements.

Twelve minutes later, Alpha Zone was secure. Storm Two—flanked by three Super Cobras on hair-trigger alert for any further signs of trouble—swooped in and hovered thirty feet over the street facing the café. The pilots scanned the surroundings, then gave the thumbs-up.

"All right, that's it—let's go, let's go!" shouted Gold Leader.

One by one, his team fast roped to the street, taking up positions on each corner and surrounding the scorched timbers of the once quaint little watering hole.

A moment later, Gold Team was in place. All his men were in position, and Gold Leader slapped his pilots on the back as Storm Two ascended rapidly, out of sniper range, and waited to be called back in.

★　★　★

Ziegler and Maroq were finished.

And they knew it. Together, they'd destroyed nearly all of their most sensitive equipment and papers. But there wasn't enough time to finish the job. They were being overrun. They'd picked off at least two dozen militants trying to enter the main control room. But they could hear more amassing in the hallways. It was only a matter of time.

Any moment, killers would storm through those doors. Both Americans shuddered at what their fates would be. They wouldn't simply be shot. They'd be drilled for information about U.S. intelligence operations in Gaza and the West Bank. No form of torture would be off-limits.

Each man knew all too well the stories of Israeli operatives and informants who'd fallen into the hands of Islamic terrorist cells over the years. They could expect their fingers to be cut off—or shot off—one by one. They could expect electric cattle prods to be used on them for mock colonoscopies. If they didn't talk—or didn't tell their interrogators what they wanted to hear—their tongues would be cut out of their mouths while they writhed in unfathomable agony.

But agreeing to talk wouldn't save them. Eventually, one way or the other, their genitalia would be cut off and mailed to their relatives in sealed plastic bags.

It wasn't speculation. It was fact. If they were caught, they'd be shown no mercy. They were going to die one way or another. Better it be fast, and for a purpose.

"Br'er Rabbit, this is Tar Baby," Ziegler radioed from inside Gaza Station, as Maroq fired another burst at both doors, hoping to buy a few more minutes. "I repeat, Br'er Rabbit, this is Tar Baby. Come in. Over."

"Tar Baby, this is Br'er Rabbit. You guys ready for us?"

"It's too late. We're being overrun, sir. Equipment and papers at risk. Requesting immediate Samson strike on our location, sir."

It was a chilling request.

Commander Ramirez was stunned. All the men in Storm One stopped what they were doing, though a dozen different requests were coming in from all sectors. Overall, the battle was going well. Operation Briar Patch would be over in less than fifteen minutes. What Ziegler was asking for seemed unthinkable.

Ramirez looked at his men, then clicked his microphone back on. "You sure you know what you're asking, son?"

But Ramirez could hear the gunfire and screams over the radio. He could hear the fear in Ziegler's voice. And then he heard the voice of resignation.

"Melt us down, sir. It's the only way."

Ramirez closed his eyes. He wasn't required to send this one up the chain of command. He had the authority to approve all tactical operations, and he'd been given written orders, personally signed by General Mutschler himself, that Gaza Station not fall into enemy hands under any circumstances. He'd love to pass the buck on this one. But there wasn't time.

He knew what Ziegler was asking, and he knew why. He couldn't imagine being captured by these people. It was a fate worse than death, and that alone settled it for Ramirez. He couldn't let these brave Americans fall into such hands, not when they clearly knew the stakes and knew precisely what they were asking.

A Samson strike didn't just mean Ziegler's and Maroq's deaths. It meant the deaths of all those coming after them, and the complete and utter destruction of Gaza Station as well. It was the worst-case scenario for any American in a hot combat zone. And, ironically, it had been invented right here in Gaza.

"Very well. Samson strike approved. May God be with you guys."

"Thank you, sir," Ziegler replied, his voice flat and unemotional. "And may God bless the United States of America."

With that, all radios fell silent as every man—those engaged in the firefight on the ground and those flying overhead—contemplated the fate of the two Central Intelligence operatives about to meet their Maker.

Sixty seconds later, two AV-8B Harrier fighter jets streaked across the sky. They locked on their target—the flaming rubble of the Hotel Baghdad, swarming yet again with more Palestinian militants trying to break in—and unleashed a salvo of air-to-ground missiles. Massive plumes of fire and smoke filled the skies of Gaza.

Barely four minutes later, a B-2 bomber on strip alert at an Israeli air base in the Negev—just in case—arrived on target. The flight crew double-checked the coordinates and received strike confirmation from Br'er Rabbit, circling and down the coast on Storm One. Then, with all systems go, the B-2 released its cargo and bolted for home.

The two-thousand-pound "bunker buster" hit the remains of the Hotel Baghdad dead center. In the blink of an eye, everyone and everything inside Gaza Station and a one-block radius was incinerated in a hellish inferno that would burn for weeks.

Word spread rapidly as radio and television networks led with the

story. Within minutes, everyone in Gaza knew what had happened—
everyone, that is, but Bennett and his team, underground in the sewers.

* * *

At first they thought it was an earthquake.

There'd already been four in the past twenty-four hours—in Turkey,
in India, another in Japan, and a monster in Tangshan, China. All measured over 6.8 on the Richter scale, and the combined death toll was already in the tens of thousands.

The ground shook violently, more violently than anything Bennett,
McCoy, or their team had ever experienced. The intensity of the shock
wave and the roar of the explosion surging through the sewage tunnel
shook them to their core. It knocked all of them off their feet, just as the
last of them were climbing up another silo, into the basement of Alpha
Zone.

And then it got worse. A wave of superheated air began howling
through the underground tunnel system. McCoy suddenly realized the
danger they were in. *"Get up—keep moving—go, go, let's go,"* she shouted,
sensing what was coming.

Tariq was already up the thirty-foot silo. So were Nazir, Sa'id, and
Galishnikov. All were soaked and filthy and trying to catch their breath for
a moment in the cold damp basement of the café. Bennett was halfway up.
McCoy was just starting up the lowest rung, as Hamid awaited his turn.

Bennett turned back to see what was going on. McCoy shouted at him
to move faster. She was scrambling up the metal ladder—freezing cold
and covered in all kinds of unimaginable filth—and closing in on him.

All of them could feel the temperature spiking. Hamid struggled to stay
on his feet as the fiery winds raged through the tunnel. As Bennett reached
the top, he grabbed Tariq's hand, pulled himself up the last few inches, and
turned back to help McCoy. The silo was shaking. The entire basement was
shaking and the ceiling of the half-century-old structure seemed about to
collapse. Bennett was terrified McCoy might slip off the slick metal rungs,
but she was holding on for dear life. She was three-quarters of the way up
and moving fast. A few more feet and she'd be safe.

"Come on, come on, Erin—I've got you!" yelled Bennett, his arms and
hands straining for her.

Suddenly, McCoy's left hand lost its grip. Her right hand began slipping as well. She screamed. So did Bennett. Her eyes went wide. She was dangling over an abyss with only seconds before a firestorm consumed them.

"Tariq, grab my feet!" Bennett shouted as he moved headfirst farther into the silo, desperate to grab hold of her.

An instant later, he could feel not just Tariq but Nazir holding his legs and belt. He carefully inched himself lower. His hands shook as he strained farther to reach her. Sweat was pouring off his face. Noxious fumes came rushing up at him. He could see the fear in McCoy's eyes. He could see Hamid coughing violently. Her fingers were slipping—a little farther, a little farther.

"No, no!" Bennett screamed.

He could see her first finger peel off the rung, then another, then . . .

His hand made contact. He grabbed her right wrist, just as her entire hand slipped free. McCoy screamed, her body twisting and jerking in the surging winds.

"I got her, I got her—pull me up!" he screamed as his fingers and nails dug into her wrist, desperate not to let her slip away.

Tariq and Nazir braced themselves and yanked hard. Bennett now grabbed hold of McCoy's other wrist and squeezed.

"Again, pull up, pull up!"

The two men yanked again and again, and with one final tug, pulled Bennett and McCoy to the point where she could get her feet back on the metal ladder. With Bennett's help—his hands still locked like a vise around her wrists—she scrambled out of the silo and into his arms. He pulled her to himself and rolled out of the way. She was safe, but there was no time to take comfort.

Bennett and Tariq turned back to help Hamid. He was struggling to hold on to the lowest rung. The look of terror and helplessness in his eyes was haunting, but there was nothing they could do. Bennett wanted to look away, but he couldn't. He began moving back into the silo, to help Hamid as he'd helped McCoy. But it was too late.

Just as Bennett and Tariq peered down into the silo, the firestorm reached Hamid. With their eyes locked on his, they saw him disintegrate in a wall of flame. His flesh and muscles literally melted away from his bones right as the flames shot up the silo, threatening to incinerate them all. Tariq pulled Bennett away. He pivoted fast, cleared the silo, and slammed the metal hatch down, just in time.

A damp basement—glowing orange and red just seconds before—was now pitch-black. The floor was shaking uncontrollably. The demons below raced forward, hunting new victims. But Bennett and his team were safe. Trembling, terrified, but safe.

Four Gold Team commandos burst through the basement door, weapons at the ready, lasers and flashlights shining into the darkness.

"Gold Leader, this is Gold Six. I have the package. I say again—I have the package. They are secure. Repeat—they are secure. Requesting immediate extraction. Have medical personnel standing by when we arrive."

"Roger that, Gold Six. Storm Five is inbound. Stand by for extraction."

* * *

Three minutes later, "the package" was gift wrapped.

Bennett and his team were onboard Storm Five, skimming over the treacherous waters of the Mediterranean, surrounded by a team of Navy SEALs and four Super Cobras ready to blow away anyone who got in their path.

Sa'id and Galishnikov were lying down in the back of Storm Five. They were attended by a team of medics who hooked each man up to IVs and began treating them for shock. Tariq and Nazir were huddled in the back, each under a thick wool blanket, sipping hot coffee and keeping to themselves.

Bennett and McCoy were also wrapped in blankets. From their seats just over the shoulders of the pilots, they could see the horizontal rains pelting the front windshield as the wipers swooshed back and forth at high speed. They could feel the intense winds buffeting the chopper, and after a few minutes, the faint outline of the USS *Ronald Reagan* appeared a few miles ahead. The deck looked hardly bigger than a postage stamp, and the sharp, shooting pains in Bennett's abdomen grew worse.

Neither of them had ever landed on the deck of an aircraft carrier before. The last time Bennett had been extracted by a SEAL team—out of Dr. Mordechai's house in Jerusalem—he'd been taken to Ben Gurion In-

ternational Airport, put on a navy medical transport plane, and flown to
Germany, via Incirlik in Turkey. But he'd been unconscious the whole
time. Now he could see the pitching, heaving carrier all too well, tossed
about like a toy boat in a bathtub.

"Don't worry," said Captain Lance "Buzz" Howard, a nineteen-year
navy veteran. *"We'll be fine."*

Bennett wasn't so sure. But he didn't have the strength to ask questions. These guys had just saved his life. He'd just have to trust they
wouldn't let him crash into the Atlantic. The deck of the *Reagan* was coming in fast now, and the Seahawk began its slow, careful descent from just
over fifteen hundred feet. A few seconds later, they could feel steel
crunching steel. The Seahawk's motors shut down immediately, and all of
them breathed a huge sigh of relief.

Minutes later, a flash traffic message reached Washington:

1907L DEC 28 2010

FLASH TRAFFIC

FROM: USS Ronald Reagan

TO: NMCC, Pentagon OPS

White House Situation Room OPS

NSC, Washington DC DIR

DCI, CIA-Langley, Washington DC DIR

CLAS—EYES ONLY—PRIORITY ALPHA

SUBJECT: Operation Briar Patch

Package arrived . . . principals safe . . . one (1) KIA,
Hamid Al-Shahib.

Transfer to "Mount of Olives" by 1800 local time tomorrow.
Professor en route, as requested. . . . Sunday arrival.

end

35

★ ★

AN AMERICAN NOOSE tightened around the neck of the radicals.

The Defense Intelligence Agency issued an eyes-only report to the president and the Pentagon listing the most dangerous extremists in the Palestinian arsenal—names, photographs, dossiers. This was augmented by a top-secret report by the CIA listing all suspected Al-Nakbah insurgents, as well as hard new intel from the Palestinian Legislative Council. There were well over two hundred names on the combined most-wanted list. Each name had a bullet next to it, and it was open season.

One by one, U.S. Special Forces—led by Delta operators, SEALs, Army Rangers, and a handful of Green Berets—were hunting down the men who had long terrorized the civilian Palestinian population and were now eating their own. Hour by hour, air-to-ground missiles fired by U.S. Air Force and Navy jets slammed into police stations and municipal buildings in Gaza City, Ramallah, Hebron, Jericho, and points in between.

Most of the targets were headquarters or field offices of the twelve different Palestinian security organizations operating during the Age of Arafat. Some were freshly verified headquarters of the various Palestinian rogue forces controlled by Mohammed Dahlan, Jibril Rajoub, and Marwan Barghouti. Each was a command-and-control center for the prosecution of the bloodiest war in the history of the West Bank and Gaza, a Palestinian war against itself.

Top officials of the Palestinian Legislative Council—many of them barricaded inside the communications center underneath the PLC's bombed-out headquarters in downtown Gaza—were now in direct and hourly contact with Jack Mitchell and Danny Tracker at CIA and General Mutschler, operating out of the NMCC at the Pentagon. Their cooperation and inside information were proving absolutely invaluable, as were tidbits coming in from Egyptian and Jordanian intelligence and, of course, critical though completely confidential Israeli intelligence assistance from Shin Bet and Mossad agents still on the ground inside the territories.

A number of Israeli intelligence operatives disguised as Arabs—some as older Arab women, covered in traditional robes and scarves—were assisting U.S. air and ground forces, weaving in and out of heavy population centers, helping mark targets and identify radical safe houses. Others eavesdropped on Palestinian military radio frequencies, intercepted cell and landline telephone calls and e-mails, and monitored all long-distance lines. They provided rapid translations, summaries, and even full transcripts when needed to their American counterparts—directly to Langley, at times, or to CENTCOM headquarters in Tampa, if the information was of imminent military value.

None of this was publicly acknowledged, of course. Nor would it ever be. The Israelis didn't want credit for ripping up the last vestiges of a mafia empire. Washington didn't want to give it.

Armed with such real-time, actionable intel and surprisingly solid though no doubt temporary international support for defending Palestine from the Israelis without and the extremists within, Washington held nothing back. The president's rationale wasn't complicated. The faster the operation could be completed, the better the chances for peace, and the better the chances of staving off universal condemnation by the Arab world and the United Nations as a whole if the operation bogged down and civilian casualties began mounting. And the only way to get done quickly was to strike with overwhelming force.

This was not a Pentagon photo op. There were no reporters, American or otherwise, embedded into the operation. This was an unprecedented opportunity to smash the Palestinian terror network once and for all, and to see if peace had any chance whatsoever of taking root in the rocky, barren soil of the territories, long poisoned by bitterness and blood. Thus, within forty-eight hours of the first American boots on the ground, a total of two thousand U.S. troops and Special Forces were air-lifted into the theater. Dozens of U.S.-owned and -operated M1 Abrams tanks, Humvees, and Bradley fighting vehicles were moved in as well, and were now choking off every major artery into the West Bank and Gaza.

Ostensibly, the heavy mechanized forces were there to keep the Israe-lis out. At least, that's what the press and public were told. More to the point, such hardware and the troops that operated them were tasked with keeping suicide bombers from infiltrating Israel. Any new Israeli deaths by Muslim extremists could force Doron's hand, making it politically impos-sible for him not to order punitive strikes into Palestinian nerve centers.

MacPherson was taking a huge risk, and he knew it. But once commit-ted, he pulled out all the stops. If the United States was going to "own" Palestine for the next few weeks, it was going to stop at nothing to make sure every known and suspected terrorist was taken off the streets.

"I want Israel blocked from any possible incursion into Palestinian areas, and I want Palestinian terrorists hunted down and rounded up until they're gone, all of them—no exceptions, no regrets."

That was the blunt message he'd delivered to the troops through armed-forces radio, and that was the sound bite that led the evening news Wednesday night in the United States and throughout the world. Accord-ing to the White House, it was a MacPherson original—unscripted and unrehearsed. Or so went the spin from the press office and their surro-gates. Either way, it was having its intended effect. International and con-gressional support was holding, for the moment at least.

Also as much under the heading of international public relations as operational necessity, U.S. forces were taking special care to secure Chris-tian, Jewish, and Muslim holy sites, and had done so from the opening hours of Operation Palestinian Freedom.

Just three hours after Bennett and his team were extracted from Gaza, U.S. Ranger teams fast roped into Bethlehem to surround the Church of the Nativity, the traditional memorial site of Jesus' birth. Is-raeli intelligence had started picking up reports that suicide bombers were planning to attack the church and destroy it in a lightning-quick raid. Doron ordered those reports sent immediately to the Pentagon and CIA, where officials—to their credit—moved quickly and decisively to avoid a religious and archeological catastrophe of the first order.

The president ordered in the Rangers. Within hours, sites like Rachel's Tomb and Abraham's Tomb were being secured by U.S. forces, as were two dozen other sites on a list personally drawn up by Prime Minister Doron and faxed to the president. Every few hours, Press Secretary Chuck Murray stepped back to the podium to announce an updated list of holy sites that were now secure in American hands. At Marsha Kirkpatrick's suggestion—and the president's approval—Murray also did his first live broadcast interviews with Al-Jazeera and Abu Dhabi Television, as well as an informal press gaggle with reporters from Arab and other Muslim countries.

It was a full-court press, and this White House was working all the angles.

✮ ✮ ✮

Nadir Hashemi was glued to CNN.

Holed up in a $49-a-night motel room by a truck stop in rural Arkansas, just outside of Little Rock, he was taking no chances. Not anymore, at least.

Less than an hour after he'd crossed the border, the United States had gone to Threat Level Red, triggering an immediate closure of all borders and the most sweeping security lockdown in U.S. history. But for nearly twenty-four hours, the Viper had been oblivious to any of it.

He hadn't been listening to the radio. He'd pulled into rest stops only long enough to fill his tank and empty his bladder, never long enough to watch television or listen to the frantic talk of fellow diners, worrying about what this new war in and for the Holy Land might mean to them. It might have been a fatal mistake. What he didn't know *could* kill him, Nadir told himself. He had to be more careful, and that meant tracking the news on the hour.

The FBI, he quickly learned, was conducting a massive manhunt in the United States, Canada, and Mexico for a Mrs. Ruth Bennett, the sixty-nine-year-old mother of Jonathan Meyers Bennett, the senior White House advisor and chief architect of the administration's Arab-Israeli peace plan apparently now scuttled by the violence spreading throughout the territories and the introduction of U.S. peacemaking and peacekeeping forces. In light of the nation's threat level, officials were listing the woman as missing and presumed kidnapped, and the FBI and DHS—Department of Homeland Security—were offering a reward of $5 million for any information leading to the safe retrieval of Mrs. Bennett and the indictment and conviction of the perpetrators.

At the same time, a massive federal and international manhunt was under way in search of anyone who could even remotely be a possible suicide bomber, inside or headed for the United States. Palestinians and those of Arab origin were prime suspects, of course, and all sorts of organizations in Washington and Detroit were crying foul and raising red flags about the prospect of mass numbers of civil-liberties violations.

But a report a few hours ago on MSNBC had quoted an unnamed senior Homeland Security Department source saying officials had reason to believe a small handful of non-Arabs might also have been recruited to carry out the attacks. Speculation seemed to be centering on young to middle-aged American and European women who were currently dating or married to men of Middle East descent, or had been within the last three to five years.

Meanwhile, the airtight security federal officials initially imposed only on Washington for the president's return from the NATO summit in Madrid was now being replicated in major cities throughout the country, particularly those up and down the eastern seaboard. This posed a serious problem.

Nadir was hoping to pick up his supply of plastic explosives from a sleeper agent in Atlanta, and several firearms from another contact in Savannah. From there, the plan was to try to slip into Washington or New York for New Year's Eve. But he was still a good ten to twelve hours away from Atlanta, and it was almost midnight Thursday, the thirtieth of December. At this point, there was almost no way he could reach his intended target on schedule. With all the roadblocks, checkpoints, and other security measures up across the country, it would be hard enough to connect with his suppliers on time.

Nadir let out a string of curses in Arabic. The world had gone mad. Palestine was burning. Gaza was on fire. And American infidels were desecrating the land of his mother and her family. He seethed with a rage he'd for so long controlled. He wanted to bolt. He wanted to jump back in the car, pop down more amphetamines, and tromp on the accelerator. He could make it to Atlanta in less than a day. He had to. But how?

It wasn't a matter of mileage and ground speed. He had to be careful. He had to watch his back and his steps. He couldn't afford to be caught speeding, or under the influence of narcotics. He couldn't afford to be caught at all. His father and brothers were counting on him. So was his mother, wherever she was in a paradise that awaited them all. His rage would find its outlet. The Great Satan would feel his fury.

Patience, Nadir, he could hear his mother whisper.

Patience, young man, and you will go far.

★　★　★

The morning sun was not yet visible on the Mount of Olives, the site chosen for the Israeli and newly appointed Palestinian prime ministers for the beginning of their peace talks.

Nor would it be this Friday. Storms still blackened the skies, though the forecast called for a break in the wind and rain over the next few days. Not that it mattered to Jon Bennett, his team or the two prime ministers in his care. They weren't anywhere near the real Mount of Olives. They were now half a world away from Jerusalem, in a labyrinth of caves and secret military bunkers, deep inside a mountain of Jurassic limestone, drilled at great cost by British forces trying to defend Europe from the Nazis' gathering storm.

The "Mount of Olives" was a code name handpicked by President MacPherson, and it was a name known to only a few dozen U.S. military and intelligence officers, a handful of senior White House and State Department officials, and the British prime minister and his top staff. It referred to the secure, undisclosed location of the peace talks about to begin, and every measure was being taken to prevent that location from leaking out. There were, after all, lives at stake, and there were men who would stop at nothing to destroy the lives of those now gathered in this mountain. Thus, of the few people entrusted to know the term "Mount of Olives," fewer still knew precisely to what it referred. Even Bennett and McCoy didn't know, not until they'd arrived under the cover of darkness at a place most simply called the Rock.

Towering over the entrance to the Mediterranean, the Rock of Gibraltar was three miles long and fourteen hundred feet high. The ancient world considered it one of the two Pillars of Hercules—the other being the North African Mount Hacho on the other side of the Strait of Gibraltar—not to mention the very "ends of the earth." The tiny peninsula below the Rock was only six and a half square miles in size and home to fewer than thirty thousand people. But however one measured it physically, Gibraltar was of incalculable strategic value—the choke point between Europe and North Africa, the gateway to the Mediterranean.

Churchill's forces had survived massive aerial bombardments inside the Rock's 140 caves and underground bunkers. Eisenhower had successfully directed the rescue of North Africa from these very same installations. Now the Brits and Americans maintained highly sophisticated electronic intelligence-gathering facilities on the Rock, including a state-of-the-art Echelon listening station, linked by secure satellite ground stations and digitally encrypted fiber-optic pipelines run by the National Security Agency.

Gibraltar remained a source of contention between Britain and Spain, as it had been for nearly three centuries. The Spanish yielded control to London in the Treaty of Utrecht in July 1713 and had been moaning and complaining about the deal ever since. The dispute was a thorn in the flesh of both sides. But for the past three hundred years it had been largely political, not military in nature, so Gibraltar was now the peaceful, prosperous home to Muslims, Jews, and Christians, the homes and shops and houses of worship, not to mention Pizza Hut and Burger King franchises, increasingly ubiquitous among free and modern people the world over.

A disputed territory free from terrorism and war? What better place, thought Bennett, to seek a new peace and prosperity for the people of the Book. All they had to do now was keep it a secret.

* * *

Bennett finally got up at 5:00 a.m. local time.

Another restless, fitful night was over. He'd been up three times since going to bed at midnight, checking his e-mails and scouring the Internet for updates about his mother, the hunt for the suicide bombers on their way to the U.S., and the latest developments in the West Bank and Gaza.

The news of the reward should have encouraged him. Five million dollars? Maybe he should double it, or match it himself. He had the money. McCoy would give everything she had to have her mother or father back. He should too.

Bennett tried not to think about where his mother could be at the moment. He tried not to let himself think about what she could be going through. But it wasn't easy. He'd seen some horrible things in the past month, and been briefed about even worse. Bennett knew what these people were capable of, and they made Al Capone look like Mother Teresa.

The thought of his own flesh and blood in the hands of these monsters almost made him sick. But what else could he do? He couldn't let it paralyze him. Somehow he had to stay focused. His responsibilities would consume his time over the next few days and weeks and demand his full attention. The full resources of the American government were doing everything humanly possible to track her down and bring her home safely. It would do no good to micromanage every move the FBI and the DHS made. He would have to trust them. He had no other choice.

That, of course, was easier said than done. Ever since they'd been airlifted out of Alpha Zone by SEAL Team Eight, he'd been a wreck. Unable to sleep. Unable to keep food down. Running a slight fever. Nightmares. Flashbacks. And early signs of dehydration. The chief physician on the *Reagan* put him on an IV the minute he arrived, and for the next twenty-four hours he had been on forced bed rest. So had Sa'id and Galishnikov, it turned out. Bennett was almost relieved to hear it—not because he wanted them to be suffering, only because it made him feel slightly less guilty at not being strong enough to have sailed through Gaza unscathed.

Physically, McCoy, Tariq, and Nazir had weathered it best. But emotionally, the loss of Ziegler, Maroq, and Hamid was almost too much. Bennett's team wasn't on bed rest, per se. But they were being encouraged to rest and read and spend some time with the chaplains onboard. What they all needed was some serious R & R, a chance to get away for a few weeks—maybe longer—and take their time recovering. But such rest was not in the cards. Not for some time to come.

Bennett looked over at the half-empty bottle of sedatives he'd been prescribed to bring down his blood pressure and help him get some badly needed rest. They weren't helping much. But he certainly couldn't take any more. He had work to do, and time was of the essence.

He couldn't believe it was already the last day of the year. In many ways it was the day for which he'd been preparing for nearly an entire decade. He finally got out of bed for the last time and went over to the large desk in the guest suite to which he'd been assigned. The room, the very one used by Eisenhower, had no windows, as it was deep inside the Rock. But it was comfortable enough, with a spacious work area, multiline phone, cable television, broadband Internet connection, and a small, round conference table and four maroon leather chairs.

Sitting down before his notebook computer again, he clicked onto the Internet and scanned the headlines, where he found a little good news. Operation Palestinian Freedom was proceeding apace and racking up tangible victories, bit by bit. The Pentagon was reporting that Bethlehem, Jericho, and their surrounding towns and villages were now securely in U.S. hands. So was the Jordan River valley, a two-mile security perimeter around the outskirts of East Jerusalem, and the main thoroughfare between Jerusalem and Jericho.

A sudden chill ran through him. It was strange, in a way. Bennett had never been to Sunday school. He'd never read the Old Testament all the way through, and had barely skimmed the New Testament during a college class on comparative religions. Yet somehow, just reading the names of these ancient biblical towns stirred something inside him. These were not just names of modern-day battlegrounds. They were keys to a lost world, metaphysically linked across space and time to the icons of Western civilization, men such as Abraham and Moses, Caleb and Joshua, Jesus and the disciples. These were ancient battlegrounds, where apocalyptic wars were once fought with Persia (now Iran), Babylon (now Iraq), the Assyrians (now modern-day Syria), the Egyptians, and the Philistines of Gaza on the coastal plains of the Mediterranean. Now such cities were again front-page news.

It was surreal, and unsettling, though he couldn't precisely put his finger on why. It felt at once ominous and inevitable. Babylon was back in the news after three hundred centuries buried under the desert sands. Men were trying to blow up the Temple Mount and rebuild a Temple laid waste nearly twenty centuries ago. Philistines and Israelites were at war again, forty centuries after David and Goliath.

Why? What was happening? What did it mean? Bennett didn't know.

All he knew for certain was that something was taking him where he did not mean to go. He was being drawn, against his will, into the epicenter of the world's darkest, cruelest conflict. Men and women were dying all around him. The destruction he'd seen just in the last few days was beyond his deepest fears.

But it seemed there was nothing he could do to resist or slow his journey. Unseen forces were forcing him further and further away from the safe and familiar. He was being driven out into dark waters, out into the shadow lands. No longer was he in control of his own destiny. He wondered if he ever had been. He was suddenly a branch being swept along by a raging river, a river that had carried prophets and priests and poets before him, a river whose increasingly swift currents now threatened to consume him without mercy, without warning.

36

★ ★
★

NO OTHER PART of the world cast the same spell.

The more Bennett stared at the headlines on his computer, and the more he thought about the past few weeks, the more it seemed the world was hypnotized by the Middle East—obsessed with its oil, intoxicated by its mysteries, seduced by its tales of the supernatural. And so was he.

Even at the peak of the bipolar world—the East-West cold-war clash between free people and the Evil Empire—the Middle East was the main event. The central battleground. The '48 war. The Suez Crisis of '56. The Six Days' War of '67. The war of attrition. The Yom Kippur War of '73. The Arab oil embargo. The explosion of OPEC and petrodollars. The civil war in Lebanon in '75. The Israeli invasion of '82. The atheists armed the Muslims. The Christians armed the Jews. Thousands died. Millions more were maimed and orphaned. There were other skirmishes, other hot zones. But again and again the world's attention was drawn back to the Middle East, as it was being drawn now. Why?

McCoy didn't think the term *Middle East* quite fit. Nor did *Near East Asia*. Nor did *the Arab world*. Not precisely. She called it NAMESTAN—North Africa, the Middle East, and the stans—Afghani*stan*, Paki*stan*, and the Muslim former Soviet Central Asian republics such as Kazakh*stan*, Uzbeki*stan*, Tajiki*stan*, and the others. But by any name it smelled just as foul.

Without question, the region comprised the most fought-over real estate in the history of mankind. And it wasn't just over oil. That might partially explain recent times, but not the long arc of history. The Romans hadn't conquered the region for oil. Nor had the Ottomans. The Assyrians, Babylonians, Egyptians, and Persians slaughtered each other for control of NAMESTAN for thousands of years before anyone knew of the black gold buried under its sands.

Why then did all roads lead to it, and to the jewel at its navel, the city of Jerusalem, the City of Peace? What were the mystical sirens that drew the kings and conquerors of history? Why were a few hundred reporters assigned to Beijing, but more than two thousand to Jerusalem? What was the narcotic that transformed rational men in this part of the world into bloodthirsty killers, willing to annihilate women and children and entire towns and villages to possess it? What was drawing him?

It was a question he couldn't shake. Bennett hadn't sought this journey. But something or someone was forcing him to proceed. Regardless of what he did, it refused to let go. And it scared him. It wasn't simply his fear of death that now kept him awake at nights. It was the certain knowledge that his fate was not his own.

Bennett logged in to his AOL account to check his personal e-mails. He'd lost his BlackBerry PDA somewhere between Jerusalem and Germany, and there hadn't exactly been any spare time to buy a new one. He guessed the White House communications office would probably issue him one. But that, too, took time he didn't have.

"You've got mail."

Too much, as it turned out. He scrolled through 138 messages. A handful were from former colleagues at GSX worried about him and his mom. Most of the rest were spam—ads for weight-loss programs, hair-transplant treatments, laser eye surgery, special offers for Viagra, Russian mail-order brides. It was ridiculous, and infuriating. No wonder AOL was in trouble. He deleted everything in sight, except two new messages that caught his eye.

The first was from Mordechai. He'd be arriving at the "Mount of Olives" on Sunday, just after noon. It was about time, Bennett thought. The good doctor was absolutely, positively supposed to have been here overnight. Now he was going to be a full four days late. Bennett read further. First came an apology, followed by an explanation. It was cryptic, to say the least. But reading between the lines, and knowing the old man as he did, he basically figured out what was going on. Storms had grounded all flights out of Ben Gurion for nearly forty-eight hours. The FedEx jet he was using for cover had apparently then taken him to Istanbul, then to Rome, then on to London. It was the best he could do without taking the risk of flying on standard commercial aviation.

Every intelligence service in the world, after all, knew who Dr. Eliezer Mordechai was. They knew he'd been the director of the Mossad's Arab Desk from '76 to '84. The director of the Mossad's Nuclear Desk from '85 to '87. Full director of the Mossad from 1988 to 1996. They knew he'd helped plan the rescue of Israeli hostages in Entebbe, Uganda, in 1976. They assumed he'd helped plan the bombing of the Iraqi nuclear reactor at Osirik in 1981. And they suspected he'd personally ordered the assassination of Khalil al-Wazir, the PLO terror master, in Tunis on April 16, 1988.

Thus, even if he used a false passport, facial-recognition software recently installed at every major airport in Europe was sure to pick him up and identify him. He'd be tagged. He'd be followed. And he'd lead them to Doron and Sa'id. It was a risk none of them could afford taking. So McCoy had suggested flying him on a series of FedEx planes. It was a technique the CIA used from time to time to move NOCs—nonofficial cover operatives—around the globe with the least chance of them getting picked up by Interpol or foreign spooks. Jack Mitchell loved the idea, as did Mordechai.

It was the last line of the e-mail that intrigued Bennett the most: *Looking forward to seeing you. I bear gifts from afar.* He read it again, then a third time. "Gifts from afar"? What in the world was that supposed to mean? Bennett had had enough surprises for one lifetime. He didn't need any more. He hit the reply button, typed three lines—*Skip the gifts. I just have one question. Did you follow the money?*—then hit *Send*.

The second e-mail was from Marcus Jackson at the *New York Times*. The guy was relentless. He refused to give up. He said he felt bad about Bennett's mom and hoped the FBI found her safe and sound. But he was hunting Bennett down. He was determined to do another story, the inside story of the firefight in Gaza. He knew some of the details already, and his information was eerily precise. Jackson knew what absolutely no one else had reported yet—the code name, Operation Briar Patch. He knew Bennett was no longer in Palestine. He knew McCoy was with him, and he suspected Sa'id and Galishnikov were too.

Bennett felt another twinge of pain shoot through his stomach.

Where was Jackson getting all of this? And if he'd gotten this much, how soon would it be before he got the rest? After all, this wasn't even Bennett's official White House e-mail account. Jackson had that address, and they wrote back and forth from time to time. But this was Bennett's personal e-mail account. How had Jackson gotten that?

Bennett clicked off his computer. He shut his eyes and tried to breathe deeply. Then he headed to the private bathroom, just off the large master bedroom. He needed to clear his head and get focused. He shaved quickly and jumped in the shower.

Twenty minutes later, he was ready to go, dressed in fresh blue jeans, a white T-shirt, a black cotton sweater, and brown leather loafers. All of his clothes had arrived safely from the King David Hotel in Jerusalem. There were power suits and power ties he could wear if he wanted. But despite the imminent commencement of "formal" peace talks between the Israeli and Palestinian prime ministers, Bennett wanted the atmosphere to seem anything but formal.

★ ★ ★

At precisely 7:00 a.m., there was a knock at the door.

It was McCoy, and she looked incredible. Nothing glamorous or overtly showy, just light makeup, blue jeans, a brown wool sweater, and brown leather boots, with her hair pulled back.

"Hey, Point Man, how'd you sleep?" She smiled, her eyes dancing with life.

"Don't ask," groaned Bennett. "How 'bout you?"

"Slept like a baby."

"Woke up and cried every few hours?"

She laughed. "No, actually, I feel pretty good, considering. You ready?"

"I don't know." He sighed. "I guess."

They sat down at the round conference table in Bennett's suite and went over the plan. In less than thirty minutes, they'd meet Doron and Sa'id for breakfast. No aides or advisors were with them. None had been allowed to come.

It would just be the two prime ministers, McCoy, and himself, and a small cadre of Israeli and American security agents outside the doors.

President MacPherson had been insistent on the basic framework of the negotiations, and Bennett and McCoy had readily agreed. This had to be the work of two men who truly wanted to make peace, and who personally understood the high price of failure.

Both men could and should consult with their governments back home, of course, and the U.S. had secure communications facilities that would be made available to both sides. But naysayers and meddlers—particularly those from the U.N., the E.U., and the rest of the Arab world—need not apply. Indeed, they wouldn't even be told of the existence of such negotiations unless the talks began to bear fruit.

What was needed now was privacy, secrecy, and the time to get to know each other. This would begin with a casual, friendly breakfast. It would be their first meeting ever. It would be time for two men to shake hands, break bread, and get comfortable. Bennett would brief them on the progress of Operation Palestinian Freedom, and both men would have an opportunity to compare notes and offer feedback, concerns, and suggestions. If necessary, they could hook up a videoconference with the president and the National Security Council, though the chance of such a move leaking was high enough that Bennett wanted to avoid that if possible.

McCoy would then brief the two leaders on the progress of the international effort to track down the terrorists on their way to the United States. Countries throughout Europe, Asia, and Latin America provided tremendous assistance over the past twenty-four hours, and the president wanted Doron and Sa'id—particularly Sa'id—to see themselves as part of an international antiterrorist coalition, not simply as two warring parties trying to reconcile their seemingly irreconcilable differences.

The key was keeping expectations low. They needed to baby step their way from areas of wide agreement to areas of serious contention. They would begin, therefore, by focusing on something to which both sides were now firmly committed—waging a war on terror. They'd finish by 9:30 a.m. local time, 10:00 at the latest. Both leaders would then have a few hours to consult with their governments. Then they'd reconvene for a working lunch and begin the long pilgrimage to peace.

It was Friday, the Muslim holy day, but Sa'id insisted they not wait. Too much was at stake. Too many Palestinians were dying. Doron quickly agreed, and offered to continue the meetings on Saturday, despite the fact that it was the Jewish Sabbath.

"The Psalmist urged us to never stop praying for the peace of Jerusalem," said Doron, not much of a religious man himself. "If we can pray for peace on the Sabbath, I think in this instance we can work for it as well."

It was a good sign and, Bennett hoped, a good omen for what lay ahead. And thus, at MacPherson's directive, Bennett would begin to lay out the administration's Oil for Peace proposal. Friday he'd focus on oil. Saturday he'd focus on peace. No real negotiations of any kind. Not at first. He'd simply make the president's case and answer any initial questions the two leaders had. Day one and two weren't about haggling over the price, just about viewing the merchandise.

✲ ✲ ✲

It was a somewhat awkward beginning.

But perhaps that was to be expected. Bennett made proper introductions, and the two prime ministers shook hands and made some chitchat. Doron seemed comfortable enough, but it was Sa'id who struck Bennett as unusually reserved. It could have been the lack of sleep, or the traumatic events of their stay in Gaza and narrow escape. It might also be the fact that Sa'id was just beginning to get used to the role of being the Palestinian prime minister and careful not to give his Israeli counterpart the impression this was going to be easy. They had some very tough days ahead of them. Perhaps Sa'id was just lowering expectations.

Either way, it wasn't exactly warm and cozy in the opening minutes, but soon enough they were seated for fruit salad, bagels, and Turkish coffee. It was a round table, purposefully chosen for the occasion, with place cards written in black calligraphy for each principal. In the center of the table were three small flags—American, Israeli, and Palestinian. Sitting in front of each prime minister was also a small wrapped gift, framed illuminations of Psalm 122:6, "Pray for the peace of Jerusalem"—the very verse Doron had quoted earlier—hand-painted by Nancy Warren, the White House artist-in-residence.

The four gathered in the private, paneled dining room of Marty Kunes, the tall, lanky, fifty-six-year-old commander of Echelon Station and a twenty-eight-year veteran of the U.S. National Security Agency.

Kunes was a legend in the American intelligence community, nicknamed Magic Marty. He and his team routinely scored some of the most valuable electronic intercepts of any U.S. or British station, and were known for their quick turnaround and accurate translations. They weren't showboats, never sought attention within the NSA, just kept their heads down and turned out consistently impressive work.

But none of the four were likely to meet Kunes or his team on this trip. On direct orders from his superiors in Ft. Meade, Maryland, Kunes had completely cleared out of his living quarters, as had his senior officers. They'd basically cleared three entire floors for their VIPs, though only Kunes himself knew who their visitors actually were.

Doron and Sa'id had each arrived separately under the cover of darkness, surrounded by small security details. Fifteen Shin Bet Secret Service agents were protecting Doron, while Tariq, Nazir, and thirteen Gold members of SEAL Team Eight were tasked with protecting Sa'id. Bennett, McCoy, and Galishnikov had entered the Rock the same way, guarded by fifteen members of ST-8's Red Team.

Rounding out the team were two dozen male and female "house staff," all agents from the CIA's Directorate of Operations, sent by Danny Tracker to Gibraltar to cook, clean, do errands, provide communications and administrative support, and act as a backup security detail. Nine were on duty from 6:00 a.m. to 2:00 p.m. Nine more from 2:00 p.m. until 10:00 at night. Six took the night shift. All were experienced field operatives. All spoke fluent Arabic, Farsi, or Hebrew, and were all handpicked by Tracker and approved first by Jack Mitchell, then by the president and vice president themselves.

At 8:00 a.m., Galishnikov was still in his room, sound asleep. The house staff finished serving the four principals, then cleared the room and locked the doors behind them. Meanwhile, the American security details maintained their protective vigilance, even inside a mountain protected by a detachment of Royal Marines and three infantry rifle companies of the Royal Gibraltar Regiment, British army commandos.

Bennett took a sip of water, cleared his throat, and smiled at his two friends. This was really it. Even though his presentation was merely a briefing—perhaps even of information these two men already knew, at least in part, from their own governments—he still had butterflies. He wasn't simply beginning a conversation with two friends. They were leaders of two nations—nations at war.

"First of all, again," Bennett began, still seated, "on behalf of President MacPherson and his senior team, and Erin and myself, let me welcome you to the 'Mount of Olives.' "

Both men nodded graciously.

"And let me say thank you to both of you for the courage you've displayed already by agreeing to these talks, and by waging a very difficult war against the extremists who have spilled so much blood to keep these talks, and others before them, either from happening at all or from bearing any fruit."

Again, both men nodded.

"These aren't exactly the most scenic accommodations," he continued, getting a small laugh, "but we'll do everything we can to make your stay as comfortable as possible, and to make sure you both have secure communications with your home governments and plenty of time to confer with your advisors by telephone or by videoconference. Again, our only request is that everyone maintain strict operational security, that none of your teams refer to our actual location during any of their communications, simply to the Mount of Olives. My security team, as I'm sure you know, has already briefed your teams about a wide range of contingency operations, should anything go wrong. But so long as the world doesn't know where we are, we don't foresee any problems."

Bennett took another sip of water, then shifted gears. "If you'll indulge me for a moment, I'd like to begin this morning with a story. One of Aesop's fables, to be precise—the story of the North Wind and the Sun."

He hadn't told McCoy about this. He hadn't been entirely sure he'd go through with it. Now he was trying to ignore the intense curiosity in her eyes.

"The North Wind boasted of great strength," Bennett began. "The Sun argued that there was great power in gentleness. 'We shall have a contest,' said the Sun. Far below, a man traveled a winding road. He was wearing a warm winter coat. 'As a test of strength,' said the Sun, 'let us see which of us can take the coat off of that man.' 'It will be quite simple for me to force him to remove his coat,' bragged the Wind. The Wind blew so hard that the birds clung to the trees. The world was filled with dust and leaves. But the harder the Wind blew down the road, the tighter the shivering man clung to his coat. Then, the Sun came out from behind a cloud. Sun warmed the air and the frosty ground. The man on the road unbuttoned his coat. The Sun grew slowly brighter and brighter. Soon the man felt so hot, he took off his coat and sat down in a shady spot. 'How did you do that?' said the Wind. 'It was easy,' said the Sun, 'I lit the day, and through gentleness I got my way.' "

Bennett's tone was not accusatory. But he was firm, and direct, and to the point. "We all want something from each other. You both want something from each other. Your people want something each of you is unsure he can deliver. Those who've gone before us have failed. I'm not here to assign blame. I'm not here to point fingers. But let's be honest with one another. Maybe one side wasn't ready. Maybe neither was ready. Perhaps the U.S. wasn't perceived as being an honest broker. Perhaps we weren't. But for whatever reason—and I suspect there were many—our predecessors failed to make peace, and many more from all sides lie dead. I hope we can all agree that the North Wind's approach hasn't worked."

Bennett was trying to be evenhanded. It was hard to read the thoughts behind each man's stony exterior. But he continued.

"The bluster. The rhetoric. The ultimatums. The violence on both sides. None of it has worked—not in and of itself—unless we accept that all of it has brought us to this point, to this place, to you two men as leaders of two great nations. And now we have a shot at accomplishing something extraordinary: a real peace, a lasting peace. Let's not kid ourselves. The road to peace is narrow. It won't be easy. 'Broad is the road that leads to destruction.' The way to peace is hard to find. But all I ask, all my government asks of you both, is that we not miss that narrow path in the heat of the moment. Let us not miss it for our lack of gentleness."

37

BREAKFAST WENT well enough.

Both leaders seemed satisfied that Operation Palestinian Freedom was proceeding according to plan, and accomplishing real results. Both were also impressed by McCoy's briefing and her breaking news.

Overnight, federal agents had intercepted six suicide bombers trying to cross into the U.S.—three in Maine, two at the Niagara Falls border, and one in a dramatic shoot-out in Washington State that left the suspected terrorist dead and two U.S. border guards in the hospital. With the exception of the Washington incident, none of the others had been reported by the media yet. The five Syrians, Saudis, and Palestinians in federal custody were being interrogated, and no official announcements would be made until it was determined whether these men were willing to talk.

At one o'clock in the afternoon local time, the four principals reassembled for a working lunch. They munched on pita, hummus, various salads, light sandwiches, and soft drinks, and sipped endless cups of Turkish coffee. Kosher provisions for Doron were brought in from a local restaurant, as was fresh baklava for Sa'id, and after an hour or so, they moved to a living-room area with four large, comfortable leather chairs surrounding a large glass table, upon which were bowls of fresh fruit, pitchers of cold water, a supply of napkins, and plenty of coasters for their drinks.

The mood was casual. Both sides were slowly beginning to warm up to each other. And once everyone had finished eating, Bennett began his second presentation of the day. It was aimed primarily at Doron, who was hearing the details of Bennett's Oil for Peace proposal for the first time. He'd been briefed by his Foreign Ministry officials, of course, and he'd read various tidbits about the plan in the papers. But Doron was looking forward to finally getting the full presentation directly from its chief architect.

"Gentlemen," Bennett began, "as you know, there's long been a common misperception that the Holy Land is the only place in the Middle East that isn't blessed with petroleum. Most people don't realize that since 1948, more than four hundred wells have been drilled in Israel, the West Bank, and Gaza. To be sure, many have come up dry, or haven't proven to possess commercial quantities of oil and natural gas. Some, on the other hand, have proven to be quite valuable. But until recently, most people have had absolutely no idea exactly how much black gold is actually there."

Bennett reached for his glass, took another sip of water, and continued. "In part, of course, this was because the political and military climate made venture-capital resources scarce, and thus serious exploration difficult, to say the least. In part, it was because until very recently the technology simply wasn't available to do sophisticated exploration from space and using smaller, more advanced drilling equipment. And in part, there simply wasn't the entrepreneurial spirit to hunt for buried treasure. Most of the Israeli gas-and-oil industry was owned by the government and run by bureaucrats without any imagination and without any incentive to hunt for such treasure because they had no stake in the cause. They weren't going to make a single extra shekel if the Israeli government struck oil, so why bother?

"But all that began to change in 1988. As you of course know, Mr. Prime Minister, your government began privatizing the exploration, drilling, and production companies at the time, a process that continued throughout much of the 1990s. At the same time, the Gulf War seemed to neutralize—at least for a while—the Iraqi threat. The Israeli-Palestinian peace process picked up speed. Israel signed a peace treaty with Jordan. The world economy was growing. An explosion of new technology came onto the market, making petroleum exploration easier and cheaper. A confluence of many different events meant suddenly everything was changing. And one man who saw these changes and decided to take advantage of them became a friend of mine.

"Now, that said, I must tell you, Prime Minister Doron, that one of the few men in the world who knows what treasures lie beneath is right here at this table. Ibrahim Sa'id has shown tremendous foresight and true entrepreneurial moxie to get where he is today. And one of the central questions we've gathered here to answer is whether or not his unexpected rise to leadership of the Palestinian people offers a window of opportunity for both sides to find a measure of peace and prosperity never before imagined."

Bennett paused to let his rhetorical flourish sink in. "It is Ibrahim Sa'id and his company—the Palestinian Petroleum Group, known more commonly as PPG—who have partnered with the Israeli company Medexco, run by Dmitri Galishnikov. They've formed an extraordinary joint venture that crosses racial, religious, and national bounds, a joint venture my government believes could literally change the course of history. As you know, Mr. Prime Minister, Erin and I, in our previous nongovernment lives as senior executives at Global Strategix, Inc.—GSX—and the Joshua Fund, one of the world's largest and most successful global growth mutual funds, got to know Mr. Sa'id and Mr. Galishnikov. We learned their remarkable stories. We vetted them. And we chose to invest one billion dollars into their joint venture to turn a dream into a reality. We've crunched the numbers a thousand times from a thousand different angles, and I daresay every fact and figure is now part of our very souls."

McCoy caught Bennett's eye. She could see he was finally in his element, and enjoying every minute of it, no matter how anxious he'd been leading into the luncheon.

"Prime Minister Doron, some of this, I suspect, will be new for you. All of it is in the briefing book Erin just handed to you. But let me just say, sir, that the figures are almost unimaginable. Let me take some time to walk you through them."

★　★　★

Something was wrong.

It was just after 2:00 p.m. Gibraltar time, just after 8:00 a.m. in D.C. FBI director Scott Harris stepped back into his office after briefing the president at the White House with Homeland Security Secretary Lee James. Harris's chief of staff, Larry Kirstoff, was waiting for him.

"What is it now?" Harris asked, seeing the anxiety in his colleague's face.

"We just got a hit."

"On what?"

"Ruth Bennett's ATM card," said Kirstoff.

Harris swallowed hard. "Where? Just now?"

"Eighteen minutes ago. At a bank near Radio City Music Hall."

"New York? You're sure?"

"I just got the call from the ELINT unit a few seconds ago. They're sure."

"You think it was her?"

"We've got no idea. Not yet. But the cops aren't taking any chances, especially if we're dealing with suicide bombers."

"Eighteen minutes—why'd it take so long?"

"Some glitch in the system. Can't say for sure yet. We're checking on that. But for now NYPD is flooding the area—uniformed officers, SWAT teams, helicopters—the works. They're shutting down a twenty-square-block radius and all points in and out of the city. We've got our own units on the way. We'd like to put the Hostage Rescue Team on standby in New York, just in case."

"Do it—whatever you need. And get me the president—*now*."

* * *

Bennett had no idea what was unfolding back home.

The entire country was glued to breaking television news coverage of the manhunt in Manhattan. It wasn't just cable. All four major broadcast networks broke into regular programming with a story in their own back-yard.

The images were riveting. Every car, every taxicab, every truck and bus was being stopped at gunpoint. Local and federal agents dressed in black and armed with automatic weapons were taking people out of vehicles and searching them one by one. But who or what were they looking for? Ruth Bennett? Was she still alive? Had someone forced her PIN number out of her before . . .

Before what? No one wanted to say out loud the worst-case scenario. Especially not network anchors. But the thought was on everyone's mind.

If Ruth Bennett was dead—or held hostage somewhere in New York, or anywhere on the eastern seaboard, for that matter—how exactly were they going to find her? And who else might they be looking for? Faces on the federal terrorist watch list, to be sure. Anyone of Arab or Middle East descent or looks? Anyone some law enforcement official deemed "suspicious"? It had the potential to be a civil-liberties nightmare. But in the adrenaline of the moment, that wasn't the first worry on most people's minds.

Additional security was rushed to protect the New York Stock Exchange and NASDAQ. The Empire State Building was shut down. Heavily armed police officers stood watch outside city hall; One Police Plaza; and all local, state, and federal government buildings. Every tunnel was sealed by the Port Authority. All bridges were being shut down. Scott Harris briefed the mayor while Lee James briefed the president. On top of everything else, there was another question to decide. It was New Year's Eve. A quarter of a million people were expected to descend upon Times Square as night fell. It would be the perfect target for a suicide bomber— high profile, high security, but almost impossible to fully defend. Should everything be canceled?

★   ★   ★

Bennett turned on a PowerPoint projector and continued.

"When they first secured exploration licenses from the Israeli government and the Palestinian Authority and began doing some preliminary test wells off the coast of Gaza, Ashdod, and Ashkelon, Medexco and PPG thought they were getting themselves into a natural-gas deal. So did we, to be honest. And, as our friend Dmitri might say, *dayenu*—that alone would have been enough. But that, it turned out, was just the beginning."

Bennett clicked to the first slide, revealing a satellite photograph of the coast of Israel and Gaza. "Tracts of natural gas were actually discovered back in 1999, by accident. A marine geologist working for *National Geographic*—the same one who'd actually located the sunken *Titanic* in the North Atlantic—was trolling the floor of the Mediterranean with high-tech sonar equipment near Ashdod, just north of Gaza. He was looking for the shipwrecks of ancient Phoenician vessels, and he'd found them— two of them—dating back to seven hundred and fifty years before the time of Christ."

The next slide showed underwater images of both vessels.

"But this geologist hadn't just found sunken ships. He'd found buried treasure. He'd unknowingly found the most spectacular energy discovery in the history of modern Israel and Palestine—hidden underwater reserves capable of producing millions of cubic feet of natural gas *per day*, every day, for decades, perhaps centuries."

Bennett now had Doron's full attention, and he could see Sa'id warming as well, excited to see his counterpart becoming engaged.

"But it turned out there was more," Bennett added, carefully building the drama. "Last year, a team of Medexco and PPG geologists—paid for by GSX—discovered oil as well. Unbelievable amounts of oil. Perhaps enough oil to make Israel and Palestine—if they were to work together to drill it, pump it, and refine it—the second-largest oil producer in the world, behind Saudi Arabia."

A new slide showed the top ten oil-producing and exporting countries in order of their annual production. The next slide showed the top-ten list in order of annual sales. The next showed Israel and Palestine in the number-two position.

"Now, the Saudis have about a quarter of the world's known petroleum reserves, and they pump about eight and a half million barrels a day. When the price of oil is between twenty-five and thirty dollars a barrel, they gross somewhere north of two hundred million dollars a day—nearly eighty to ninety *billion* dollars a year. Iraq also has tremendous potential, and we believe they are going to become a very aggressive new player in the international oil markets. By aggressive, I mean in the competitive business sense, not the military, nuclear sense, of course."

That got a laugh from all of them and bought Bennett more goodwill.

"Now, Prime Minister Doron, I'd be happy to get into Iraq's potential if you'd like. But the details aren't particularly important. What's essential to understand is that they've got a huge head start on you both. Their equipment is substandard. It's old. It's poorly maintained. It needs to be replaced, and that's going to take time and a lot of money. But they've got the whole world hoping the U.S. will secure order, the new provisional government will get the country functioning again, and the U.N. will lift the sanctions and allow Iraqi oil to be sold on the open market.

"Once that happens—and I believe it will happen relatively soon—

Iraq's oil industry is poised for explosive growth. If they accept foreign direct investment, they will have the opportunity to begin dealing with their technology problems fairly quickly. And, of course, they have quite a bit of infrastructure already in place, regardless of its quality. You don't. All this oil and gas is sitting off your coastlines. But no one can start getting it out of the ground and into refineries and into the world markets until there's some kind of political agreement, some real assurances that there's going to be peace between Israel and the Palestinians—and that there will be enforceable property rights and legal mechanisms necessary for the proper functioning of a free market."

★　★　★

"Sir, we've got a body."

FBI Director Scott Harris heard the words but couldn't believe them.

He was in one of the bureau's black-and-gold jet helicopters heading to New York from Washington on orders from the president. He and Chief of Staff Larry Kirstoff and three bodyguards were three thousand feet above the coast of New Jersey. They were inbound for a press conference with the mayor and police commissioner at city hall. Thus far, the manhunt hadn't turned up anything. Now he feared the worst.

"This is Harris. Talk to me—what have you got?" he asked the bureau's lead investigator on the ground.

"Sir, one of the NYPD's search-and-rescue units just found a floater in the East River. Probably been there twenty-four to thirty-six hours, best they can tell."

"And?" pressed Harris, hesitant to ask the obvious question on a frequency that was probably being monitored by the media.

"Hard to say, sir. The body's badly disfigured. The ME is on the way—but my guys tell me it's definitely a woman, somewhere between the ages of forty and sixty."

Harris didn't know what to make of that. The age range was a bit young. But in the fog of war, first reports were often wrong.

Investigators had also just confirmed that it was indeed Ruth Bennett's ATM card used to withdraw $300 at a Chase Manhattan branch near Radio City Music Hall. But the ATM's security camera apparently had malfunctioned. There was no video of the transaction. Fingerprints were useless. At least eight other people had used the same ATM before the police could secure the scene.

No one remembered anyone matching Ruth Bennett's photograph being seen in the area. But no one could positively say they hadn't seen her either. It was too early in the morning. Too much was going on.

★ ★
★

38

PRIME MINISTER DORON had questions.

"Assuming Prime Minister Sa'id and I and our respective governments and countries can come to some agreement—that's a big assumption, I understand, but let's just make it for the purpose of this portion of our discussions—"

"Fair enough," said Bennett.

"—how long would it take for the oil and gas to start flowing? And, more to the point, how long would it take for the *money* to start flowing?"

"It's a good question, and, of course, there are all kinds of variables. The first and foremost being that the Medexco joint venture currently has exploration licenses, but not drilling and production licenses. Before the oil, gas, and money start flowing, Medexco needs to be granted such licenses.

"This could take several forms. One way would be to grant a concession to Medexco, whereby the company essentially leases the drilling rights, does all the work, and pays the Israeli and Palestinian governments a certain dollar amount each year, or a certain agreed-upon percentage of gross revenues. The government could then put these revenues in public trust and distribute them annually by way of royalty checks.

"The state of Alaska does this. It leases petroleum and mineral rights to private companies. It collects about twenty-five billion dollars a year in fees, aside from corporate taxes. It puts all that money into what it calls the Permanent Fund, which it made part of its constitution back in the seventies when they struck black gold on the North Slope. At the end of the year, every official resident of Alaska gets a royalty check of more than fifteen hundred American dollars. It's not the only route, of course. But it's a relatively clean and simple process, and it would put hard, cold cash directly in the hands of every Israeli and Palestinian adult every single year of their lives."

"And the other routes?"

"Well, there are lots of them, actually. But the most attractive would be some form of direct ownership."

"Meaning?"

"Meaning Israel and Palestine would basically grant Medexco drilling and production rights for a nominal fee, and the right to tax its profits at a low, flat rate. In exchange, Medexco would hold an initial public offering—an IPO—and become a publicly traded company. It would distribute shares of its common stock to every adult Israeli and Palestinian, as well as to its employees, venture-capital partners, et cetera. Rather than receive an annual royalty check, Israelis and Palestinians would simultaneously be creating wealth in two different ways. First, each shareholder would, of course, receive dividend checks. The size of those checks would depend on how many shares a person held and the profits generated by Medexco that quarter or year. Second, each person would in all probability see the value of their stock rise—perhaps exponentially—overnight and then over the long haul. There would be a holding period, of course, during which you couldn't sell the stock."

"How long?" asked Doron.

"Depends. It's really up to you two, whatever you negotiate. But I'd say anywhere from eighteen months to three years would be a reasonable time frame. The idea is to prevent people from flooding the markets with their stock instantly. Create some stability. Give people a chance to see the company growing, maturing. Give people a stake in its security, and the security of the region. And, quite frankly, give people the chance to see the value of their stock increase dramatically in a relatively short period of time. The longer people hold on to their stock, the more wealth they'll have, the more they'll see the value of this joint venture and peace between these two peoples."

"Okay," said Doron, "so, again, assuming for a moment that all these details—and all the political details—could be worked out. Licenses. Concessions or IPOs, or whatever. How much time would it take to get drilling platforms and pipes and refineries and all that in place?"

"Well, again, there's lots of variables. But I think it's fair to say—and, Erin, please correct me if I'm wrong—that the first oil and gas could begin coming out of the ground within one year of the signing of a peace agreement."

McCoy nodded. "That's about right. The drilling platforms will be the quickest items to get into place, and we can begin building pumping and storage facilities simultaneously. What you won't have at first is much refining capacity. There's some in Israel by private companies. The rest would have to be outsourced. And of course, you don't have a deepwater port in Gaza, so there'd be some challenges there, as well. But all of these are manageable."

"The key here is the dynamic that is set into motion," Bennett interjected. "Arab and Israeli gas and oil companies—as well as all of the majors—are going to see what's going on and want a piece of the action. They'll raise capital and start building whatever they need to get into the game. Assuming there's peace, investors will be throwing billions of dollars into the mix. And the more they put in, the faster everything gets done. Everything that's needed can be built within a few years."

And then, once he knew he had Doron's attention, Bennett sweetened the pot. "The president has also authorized me to tell both of you that if both sides sign a fair and just agreement along the lines of what we'll be talking about over the next few days . . ."

He paused for effect. Both men were listening intently.

". . . my government is prepared to underwrite the work and provide substantial loan guarantees to both sides."

" 'Substantial'?" asked Doron. "What does that mean exactly?"

"Well, that all depends on the two of you," said Bennett. "I'm not prepared to give you a precise answer right now. We want to see what kind of deal you two make together. But let me just say this: The president is ready to get behind this project in a big way. I think he's already shown the lengths to which he is willing to go to get this peace process on track, and we are ready to see it through to the end. We see its potential. Heck, we may be the only people who really see the full potential. Most Israelis and

Palestinians have no idea how big this could be. And we believe that once all the proper equipment and facilities are built and in place and everything is running at full speed—several years to be sure, but far sooner than most people would think—the joint Israeli-Palestinian venture known as Medexco could rapidly become one of the largest petroleum companies in the world."

"Meaning what?" Doron pressed.

"We project it could eventually pump between five and six million barrels a day, grossing—conservatively—about fifty to sixty *billion* dollars a year, just from raw oil-and-gas sales alone, to say nothing of all the other refined products and retail sales they could produce down the road."

It was the first time Doron had heard the figures, and he was visibly taken aback.

"When one factors in all the other potential products and sources of revenue that Medexco, GSX, and the Joshua Fund have outlined in their business plan—that's included in your briefing book—Medexco could before too long, I believe, do gross annual sales somewhere on the order of a hundred eighty billion dollars to two hundred twenty billion dollars a year."

Now Doron sat back in his chair and stared Bennett in the eye. "Our *entire* GDP is only one hundred twenty billion a year."

"Indeed," said Bennett. "Almost overnight, Medexco would become one of the largest oil companies in the world, on the order of ExxonMobil, which typically rings up about a quarter of a trillion dollars a year in gross sales."

Bennett put up slides laying out the numbers vis-à-vis other major oil companies. "Of course," he continued, "all of these figures were based on low-intensity violence in the region before the war with Iraq, and, of course, before the current military operations began in the West Bank and Gaza.

"Medexco's oil-and-gas drilling platforms and refinery facilities—if actually built—would be vulnerable to attack. But the Iraqi threat is now neutralized. And if some kind of real peace between the Israelis and Palestinians could actually be found—and particularly if together we can eliminate or severely minimize the threat of radical Islamic extremism in the Palestinian areas—then the calculations made by our team may be moot, or conservative at best. The real value of the company could be in the trillions of dollars, virtually overnight."

* * *

Bennett now upped the ante.

The presentation was almost over. But he had one more point to make, and it was central to his Oil for Peace concept.

"We'll talk about the details of our peace proposal tomorrow, but for now I want to talk about how to make the benefits of peace tangible for everyone. Recognizing that there are a number of ways to go about it, nevertheless, we would recommend that your two governments leverage the Medexco proposal into an initial public offering, and that this IPO take place on the New York Stock Exchange to ensure the greatest access to international capital markets. We further recommend that every Israeli and Palestinian man and woman over the age of eighteen be given shares in the new company. In essence, we're recommending that you make everyone an owner of this new company, and thus give everyone a tangible, financial stake both in its success and in its safety."

Sa'id sat motionless, Bennett noticed. It was as though he was afraid of doing anything that might distract Doron, who was clearly intrigued with the concept.

"We believe the IPO would raise hundreds of billions of dollars," Bennett continued. "That would accomplish two objectives simultaneously. First, even low- and middle-income Israelis and Palestinians could become wealthy overnight. And second, Medexco could raise enough capital to complete all the necessary facilities as quickly as possible. While the president has no interest in micromanaging such an undertaking, as a former Wall Street CEO and chairman of the Joshua Fund and GSX, he understands the opportunities and nuances of this project, and he has some suggestions."

Doron nodded, as did Sa'id.

"In no particular order, the president would like to see a deepwater shipping port built in Gaza, capable of receiving supertankers and other oceangoing cargo ships. He'd like to see refineries built in the West Bank and southern Israel, and perhaps even in the Sinai Desert, if a deal could be made with the Egyptians, which I suspect it could."

"Under the right circumstances, I think we'd be open to such ideas," said Doron, cautiously optimistic at what he was hearing, but still waiting for the political cards to be played a few days hence.

"Excellent," said Bennett. "And is it fair to say the PLC would look favorably upon such options as well, once they were fully briefed on the president's proposals?"

"I think that's a fair assumption," Sa'id concurred, adding cryptically, "given the right circumstances."

Sa'id too was wary. He was betting everything on such a deal. Indeed, he was gambling his very life. The list of people lining up to assassinate him the moment they found out where he was had to be growing by the minute, and the mile. But if the warlords and jihadists were willing to sacrifice their lives in pursuit of war, Sa'id had decided in the last few days that he was willing to sacrifice his life in the pursuit of peace. Palestine did not need another Arafat or ayatollah. She didn't need a Saddam. She needed a Sadat, an Arab leader with the courage of his convictions, a man willing to die so Palestinian children and grandchildren would not have to.

At the same time, Sa'id was also willing to waive all prospects of financial gain from such a joint venture now that he was prime minister. He had already asked the PLC and Galishnikov to research how he could give up his financial stake in PPG and the Medexco joint venture, without giving up the ability to direct the company's involvement in this peace process. If he turned control over to his deputies or board of directors, they could turn on him and refuse to allow PPG to participate in such an IPO or peace deal. But he didn't think they would. They were all longtime friends. They'd been dedicated to Sa'id and his company from its earliest days as a start-up in the Gulf.

But Sa'id knew the hearts of men. He knew money and power were temptations few could resist. It warped their loyalties. It tempted their allegiances. He was living in a house of mirrors now. He wasn't sure whom he could trust, or how even his closest friends would react to him now that he was suddenly the man at the top of the greasy pole. So even now, Dmitri Galishnikov—an Israeli, a Jew, but perhaps Sa'id's closest friend in a world gone mad—was in his room down the hall trying to come up with a solution.

Any way one sliced it, Sa'id knew he was about to forfeit billions of dollars in personal wealth. It wouldn't be easy for the youngest of six children, born penniless in the West Bank town of Ramallah under Jordanian occupation. But that was a long time ago. Sa'id was now a very wealthy man. Yes, he had always dreamed of becoming a billionaire, and now such a dream was within his grasp. But this was more important. He had no choice. He had to send his fellow Palestinians—and the Arab world—a message: there could not be even the appearance of corruption or impropriety in the new government of the new Palestine. So as soon as possible, he would sign away his fortune. The real question was, would he ever sign a treaty, or would it all be for naught?

39
★ ★
★

IT WOULD TAKE most of the evening to do a proper autopsy.

Several days would be needed to identify the body. And they didn't have several days. A conference call was hastily organized between the president, the director of the FBI, the secretary of homeland security, the national security advisor, and senior New York officials, including the mayor, the governor, and both United States senators.

The evidence was sketchy and thus far inconclusive. But the tension in the city and throughout the country was palpable. They couldn't afford to be wrong. A bombing in Times Square would have incalculable consequences within the United States and around the world.

It was an agonizing decision, but at a few minutes before 10 a.m., a vote was taken among the participants. The conclusion was unanimous. All New Year's Eve events in New York were canceled. The governor would call out the National Guard to provide additional security in Manhattan and the boroughs. And the president would talk to the mayor of Washington about canceling events in the nation's capital as well.

★ ★ ★

Bennett now turned to McCoy.

"Erin, why don't you go over some of our projections of what could be possible if an adequate agreement was struck by both sides."

"I'd be happy to, Jon. Thanks. Prime Minister Doron, our assessment is that Gaza, the West Bank, and the Sinai would very likely become the new Saudi Arabias of the Mediterranean. In that sense, we mean their competitive advantage may best be in focusing on the actual drilling, refining, and industrial development of the petroleum.

"There's going to be a tremendous explosion of new jobs, particularly for young men building roads, buildings, and industrial facilities, putting in water, sewage, electrical and communications infrastructure, and the like. Large portions of this will be well suited for the Palestinian labor force, not to mention Egyptians and Jordanians, though that would, of course, take a great deal of thinking through to make sure no Palestinians are cheated out of jobs that should more rightfully be theirs and that there are no security problems related to foreign workers coming into Gaza and/or the West Bank. But you can see where we're going with this."

"I can," Doron agreed, not bothered by discussions that were still, obviously, in the conceptual stage. "What do you see for Israel? You've got my wheels churning, I must say. But I'm curious what you're thinking."

"Well, I appreciate that. I think Jon and I would say that Israel seems best positioned to become the new Silicon Valley and Switzerland of the Mediterranean basin. You've got tremendous potential—especially with all this influx of capital—to continue emerging as one of the world's great high-tech, banking, financial-services, and health-care capitals. You're already operating well ahead of other countries in the region, more on par with Europe and the United States, and this could very well put your high-tech industries into the stratosphere.

"We haven't got specific numbers on it, but I think if you input all these numbers into an economic model for Israel, you'd see inflows of capital into your country that had nothing directly to do with oil or gas or anything petroleum related, per se, but began flowing simply because people began to believe that peace really was at hand and that Israel was ready for exponential growth. It's not been surprising for you guys to grow six to eight percent a year in real terms. I think it's fair to say that under many of these scenarios, you guys would be growing in double digits for much of the next decade, if not longer."

The room was silent for a few long minutes. Bennett and McCoy glanced at each other, but said nothing. They glanced at Sa'id. The man was still stone-faced and motionless.

Doron, meanwhile, leafed through his briefing book, nodding and occasionally underlining something that caught his eye. "I see you've got a section on Jordan here," he finally said. "Can you give me the executive summary?"

"Jon?" McCoy asked.

"Hey, go right ahead," Bennett responded. "You're doing great."

McCoy appreciated that more than Bennett knew, but she tried not to tip her hand. Bennett had been doing most of the talking, and would be for the next few days. But she'd done most of the legwork to get to this point, and it was nice to have an opportunity—however brief—to make her case.

"Well, fair enough. The bottom line is that Jordan is in an incredible position to benefit from the president's Oil for Peace proposal. The Hashemite Kingdom, of course, already has a peace treaty with Israel. It's got a large labor pool that could be hired for all kinds of infrastructure projects. Moreover, with the right strategic plan, it could very well become the Palm Springs or Phoenix of the region, focusing on tourism, resorts, luxury spas—that kind of thing."

Doron looked across the table at Sa'id. "And golf?"

Sa'id was surprised by the question. "Perhaps—yes, maybe even golf."

"The king would like that, wouldn't he?"

"Yes, I suspect he would." Sa'id laughed.

McCoy then directed the two men to page 114 of their briefing books, while she put a new PowerPoint slide up on the wall. She and Bennett and their team had crunched more numbers, and these were astounding.

McCoy explained that if all things went as well as expected, every Israeli and Palestinian could, two or three years from this moment, be holding Medexco stock worth somewhere between a half a million and a million dollars per family. If the region remained peaceful and people held on to their stocks after the holding period, they could very well be sitting on several multiples of that.

For now, Doron said nothing. His face betrayed nothing. He just looked at the numbers, jotted some notes, and kept flipping through the pages. Bennett and McCoy were dying to know what he was thinking. But they would soon enough.

Doron could do the math. He knew the average Palestinian family currently earned less than $1,500 a year, while the families of suicide bombers had gotten checks from Saddam Hussein's regime for at least $25,000, sometimes more. Iraq's cash-for-terror machine had just been shut down by the Americans, thank God. But the Iranians already seemed to be moving into the vacuum with full force. He knew that nearly half the men in the West Bank—and upward of 70 percent of men in Gaza—were unemployed, and he knew all too well that idle hands were the devil's workshop. What's more, the exploding birthrates in the territories meant five out of every ten Palestinians were under the age of fifteen.

The bottom line, thought Doron: the West Bank and Gaza were ticking demographic time bombs. Teeming masses. Youthful passions. Filthy housing. Cramped quarters. Few jobs. Low wages. Seething resentments. And poisonous anti-Semitic messages preached every day in overcrowded Palestinian schools and every Friday in hundreds of mosques to thousands of weary, angry souls. A quarter of a million Muslims turned out every week at the Al-Aksa Mosque on the Temple Mount alone. They were told there was no hope for a better life other than permanent revolution against the Jews. Why should they believe any differently?

Something had to change. Israel couldn't live the way she was living. There was no way she could remain a Jewish democracy ruling over millions of Palestinians. And there was no way she could remain an island of prosperity in an ocean of poverty and misery. Something had to give. Maybe Bennett was right. Perhaps the immediate prospect of more jobs, better jobs, good pay, health-care benefits, new schools, new apartments, pools and community centers, and stocks and bonds and personal investment accounts that would turn many into millionaires—combined with the prospect of a state they could call their own—maybe such a package really could be a strong enough inducement for Palestinians to break with the past and make peace with Israel. Doron hoped so. He really did. But he'd lived in the Middle East long enough to know how dangerous mirages are to thirsty men—false gods offering false hope. And you cannot drink the sand.

"Well," Bennett concluded, "we've given you a lot to chew over."

"You have indeed," said Doron. "And I appreciate not only the imagination and creativity you've brought to the table but the careful, and I might say extensive, detail you've put into this. It's a very impressive proposal, and I'm looking forward to going over this briefing book in great detail. I'm sure that I'll have a lot of questions."

"And we'll do everything we can to answer them as best we can," said Bennett.

"I'm sure you will."

Doron now turned to Sa'id and looked him in the eye. "Mr. Prime Minister, I want you to know that I appreciate your willingness to participate in these meetings on your holy day. Your gesture has not gone unnoticed."

"Neither has yours," Sa'id responded. "Neither has yours."

★ ★ ★

FOX broke the story first.

Nadir Sarukhi Hashemi heard the story on CNN a few minutes later. New York was canceling all New Year's Eve festivities. So were Washington, D.C., Chicago, and L.A. Over the course of the next thirty minutes, cancellations began coming in from cities and towns throughout the United States. No one wanted to surrender the night to terrorists. But given all that was happening, the risks simply seemed too great. Nadir hoped to Allah there was another team in play, if not several. But his orders were clear. He couldn't stay in Arkansas. He had to get to Atlanta and Savannah, pick up his weapons and supplies, and get in position. He'd already let too much time go by, and his sense of shame was almost overpowering.

★ ★ ★

Bennett sat alone on the couch in his room.

He was numb. Overwhelmed by the president's call and the prospect that his mother had been kidnapped, Bennett's emotional circuit breakers had simply shut everything down. Normally, his mind would start racing. He was a strategist, so he'd strategize. He'd make lists. He'd make calls. He'd work the phones, gathering more information to process and analyze and assess. But now he just stared at the phone. His breathing was calm. His pulse was normal.

If anything, he had the sudden urge to run. For a jogger as obsessive-compulsive as he was, missing a single day wreaked havoc with his body, mind, and soul. Every morning at six, he was pounding the pavement. Five miles at least. Ten miles if he could. More on weekends. Back in New York, it wasn't unusual for him to rack up fifty to sixty miles total every week. It was time to get alone—away from the phones, away from the e-mail, away from the stresses of deals and deal makers—and let everything go.

But he'd been locked in underground bunkers for the better part of a week. He hadn't laced up once. He'd barely tasted fresh air. Nor could he now. It was still raining outside. And what was he going to do, run through the mountainous streets of Gibraltar with a bulletproof vest on and a dozen Navy SEALs surrounding him?

There was a knock at the door. He could barely gather enough strength to answer it. So he didn't. But the knocking continued. He kept ignoring it, but it wouldn't go away. Then the door clicked open. It was McCoy.

"Hey, I just heard—how're you doing?"

He looked at her a few seconds, but didn't say anything. The smell of Jack Daniel's said it for him. She had no idea where he'd gotten it from. But the bottle was half empty and there wasn't a glass in sight.

McCoy whispered something to Tariq and the rest of the detail standing post outside Bennett's room. Then she came in, shut the door, and sat down on the couch beside him. It was quiet for a little while. Neither said a word. They just sat together, listening to the windup alarm clock sitting on the nightstand beside Bennett's bed.

Normally, the silence would have been awkward for both of them. More so for Bennett. But it wasn't today. It felt good to have someone sit with him, and he was glad it was her, glad she'd thought of coming down to be with him.

"It's funny, McCoy," he said. "My dad was a newspaper man all of his life. Loved it. Delivering papers on his bike every morning, rain or shine. Working on the school paper. Going to S.U.—Newhouse. All those years with the *Times*. 'Course, he couldn't have cared less about me. Dragged my mom and me all over the world so he could get *the story*. Gotta get *the story*. Spent his whole life getting *the story*."

Bennett closed his eyes. "My dad knew details about every single kid of every single member of the politburo. Every one of them—birthdays, hobbies, how they were doing in school, favorite Olympic sport—you name it, he knew it. It was incredible. And it's not like this was easy stuff to get. It was the Soviet politburo, for crying out loud. But it didn't matter.

He'd stay out all night, gone for weeks, talk to anyone he had to talk to, all to get a little more buried treasure to put in his story. Gotta get *the story*. It's all about *the story*."

He leaned against the back of the sofa and stared up at the ceiling. "Ask me how many term papers of mine he ever read."

McCoy didn't say anything. She knew Bennett didn't really want an answer.

"The guy's a two-time Pulitzer prize winner and never read one of his own kid's term papers."

It was quiet again for a few minutes.

"And my mom never said anything. She hated what that job did to my dad. She hated all that time he spent on the road. But she hated confrontation more. She never told him to quit. She never told him to spend more time with us. She just kept everything to herself. Sometimes I wonder why she ever married him."

"To have you," said McCoy, nudging him with her arm.

Bennett shook his head and took another swig from the bottle in front of him. "I was a mistake. My dad never wanted to have kids. My mom, she wanted like six or seven or twenty—I don't know. She wanted a lot, but little munchkins running around the house wasn't exactly *conducive* to the life of a *New York Times* foreign correspondent. . . ."

Bennett closed his eyes again. "But here I am, smack-dab in the middle of the biggest story in the world, a story my dad would've given both his arms to get, and he's not even here to see it. And there's my mom—a woman who believed the only two times your name should be in the paper was when you're born and when you die—and there's her name and picture splashed across the front page of every paper in the world."

There was silence again for a few minutes.

"I can't do this anymore, Erin. I thought I could, but . . ." He put the bottle down and toyed with the Harvard class ring on his finger. "My dad's dead. I missed his funeral. Missed Deek's funeral. Practically everyone I've met in the last few days is dead. Some died right in front of me. I've almost been killed more times than I can count. You've almost been killed. And now my mom . . ."

He stopped and stared at the bottle of Jack Daniel's. "You know, McCoy, I said a little prayer the other night. Yes, I did—I actually asked for God to do something to help us all out—help you, help my mom, keep us safe . . . and don't I feel like a moron now."

McCoy wanted to put her arm around him, then thought better of it and held back.

"I'm tired," Bennett said quietly. "I'm so tired. . . ."

"I know."

"I didn't sign up to lose everything. . . . I just . . . I'm done, I can't do this anymore."

She got down on her knees in front of him, took his face in her hands, and looked into his eyes, wet and bloodshot.

"Jon. Jon, you're tired. You're drunk. You've been through hell. Now this with your mom—I know how you feel. Believe me. I lost my dad, my mom—it's hard. It just is. I know. But let me tell you one thing, Jon Bennett—you were born to do this deal. Don't ask me why. I've got no idea. But I'm telling you, my friend, you're here for a reason. And you're going to wake up tomorrow morning and take a lot of aspirin, and then you're going to make your case to Sa'id, and you're going to keep putting one foot in front of the other until you get this thing done."

"Erin, really, I need to go home. I need to . . ."

"And what? Sit around watching TV, worrying? Come on . . ."

"No, but I—"

"Jon, listen to me. *Listen* to me."

Bennett tried.

"Ever since you hired me, I've been totally amazed by you—amazed how you can find buried treasure, how you can see a deal before anyone else does, how you can negotiate so everyone feels like they're getting what they want. Jon, this is it. This is what you've been getting ready for your whole life. And now you're here. I watched you with Doron today. He likes you. He responded to you. You're painting a picture for him. He can see it, and I think he just might buy it. And I don't know anyone else who could have done that. I couldn't have; that's for sure. Honestly, I don't think the president could have done it either. You've got a gift, Jon. And you've got a moment. The only question is, what are you going to do about it?"

Bennett was listening. He was also studying every contour of her face, as though he was trying to burn it into his memory forever.

"I'm scared of dying, Erin," he said, his hands beginning to shake again. "I'm scared of losing you, losing my mom. I'm scared of being alone. . . ." His voice trailed off.

"I'm scared too," she said, searching his eyes for something she could hold on to. "And I'm not saying it's easy. We both know better. But, Jon, that's what makes it exciting. That's what makes it worth doing—because it's hard, because it's never been done, because people think it *can't* be done. And we should show them they're wrong."

"Or die trying?"

"Maybe—maybe, I don't know. I don't want to die. But I'm willing to if that's what it takes. It's just that whatever price we've paid so far—and it's been high, too high—but it's all worthless if we don't see it through to the end. Right? Jon, look, I want to see you do this deal. I think you might be the only one who can, and I want to see *you* make it happen. I want to *help* you make it happen. Not because it's going to make us rich, or win us his-and-hers Nobel Peace Prizes, or get our names splashed across the headlines, or whatever. I just think it's the right thing to do. I think it's going to help a lot of people you and I will never meet. And I think that's a good thing. I don't know if we're going to make it. But I sure as heck don't want to quit before I give it my best shot. Do you?"

The question hung in the air unanswered. At least out loud. McCoy looked into Bennett's tired eyes and smiled. She'd seen what she needed to. She kissed him on the forehead, eased the bottle out of his hands, and headed for the door.

"I'll make sure the guys bring you a little dinner. Then get some sleep, okay? We've got a big day tomorrow."

40

BENNETT AND McCOY met for breakfast at nine.

They reviewed the game plan and the latest directives faxed in from the NSC and State. It was mostly last-minute guidance on wording and negotiating tactics from previous Arab-Israeli meetings.

The professionals at Foggy Bottom were almost apoplectic that Bennett and McCoy were beginning to conduct the actual peace talks without a senior American diplomat present. So Bennett suggested that later in the week, after the memorial service for Tucker Paine and the slain DSS agents, the president send over Ken Costello, the under-secretary of state for political affairs, and Marty Benjamin, director of the Policy Planning Staff, to assist. The president agreed. He'd also have Deputy Secretary of State Dick Cavanaugh begin a round of off-the-record meetings with Arab foreign ministers to sketch out the administration's thinking of the post–Saddam Hussein, post-Arafat world.

The four principals met at 1:00 p.m. in the same private dining room they'd used the day before. Doron said his government would do anything they could to help the FBI find Bennett's mother. Sa'id gave Bennett a long embrace and repeated the prayer he'd been praying all night and morning for Mrs. Bennett's safe return. He noted that his wife and four teenage sons had been safely airlifted out of Ramallah and were now in the United States under the 24/7 protection of the U.S. Secret Service. And he described the live, New Year's Eve call-in interview he'd done on Al-Jazeera, updating people on Operation Palestinian Freedom and urging fellow Arab leaders to do everything in their power to persuade the rogue Palestinian forces to lay down their arms and begin the New Year in peace.

After about forty-five minutes, all four were done eating and moved over to the more comfortable chairs. Bennett thanked both men for all they were doing to achieve peace and for agreeing to meet again. He thanked Prime Minister Doron particularly for agreeing to meet on the Jewish Sabbath. And he noted President MacPherson's appreciation that they were willing to meet in secret, without aides, without massive diplomatic delegations, in an NSA facility built in a tunnel deep inside the Rock of Gibraltar. It wasn't easy for any of them, he conceded. But it was the right thing to do.

"Gentlemen, the author Isaiah Berlin once wrote that the world is divided into two camps. The Fox knows many things, observed Berlin, and scurries after them all. The Hedgehog knows one big thing and stays focused like a laser."

McCoy didn't know where he was going with this.

"In our case," Bennett continued, "the Fox is the man easily distracted by centuries of hatred and mistrust and by decades of previous deals, many of them unworkable, some of them unwise, and all of them unconsummated. The Fox is easily fixated on issues that should not be—cannot be— solved first, and may not be solved for many years to come. He is perpetually chasing his tail, going around in circles, making himself and all who watch him dizzy, and frustrated and despondent that anything of lasting value will be achieved. The Hedgehog, on the other hand, sees the big picture, refuses to be sidetracked, and does not let the perfect become the enemy of the good. I propose we follow the way of the Hedgehog.

"The president considers the peaceful resolution of the Arab-Israeli conflict a top priority. We'll help you strike agreements on final borders, refugees, water rights, and the status of Jerusalem. But that's Phase Two of our Oil for Peace proposal. Phase One is about agreeing to a three-year transition in which both sides create a terror-free zone, build political and economic infrastructure, commence oil-and-gas operations, and begin to establish a free and vibrant Palestinian democracy committed to a peaceful two-state solution."

Bennett took a sip of coffee and continued. "Obviously, we now have a new situation in the disputed territories. My government has made no determination at this early stage in Operation Palestinian Freedom of how long U.S. troops might remain. But the president is open to the possibility of our forces serving as a buffer between Israel and the Palestinians to prevent suicide bombings, rocket attacks, and the like."

There was an awkward silence for a few moments. The riptides of history were already pulling them out to sea.

"I am open to this," Prime Minister Sa'id offered. "But it must be said up front that ending all occupations—by the Israelis or the Americans— must be central to these talks, as well as an acknowledgment by Israel of full Palestinian sovereignty over the pre-1967 boundaries."

Bennett could see Doron shift in his seat. This was it. They were in it now, and playing for keeps.

"And we need a firm timetable," Sa'id continued. "President Carter promised us a fair resolution at Camp David. President Bush did so at Madrid. Then there was Oslo, and the Road Map. We were supposed to have a Palestinian state by 2005. Now here we are. It is the first day of *2011*. And we have nothing. We are like your Charlie Brown cartoons, like Charlie, Lucy, and the football. Someone always pulls away the football at the last moment, and we land flat on our backs. We are losing confidence in this game."

"Mr. Prime Minister," said Bennett, "I appreciate your goals, and your candor. I don't want to recount the entire history of failed negotiations or either side's failures to keep their promises. But the president has instructed me to say this, and to say it as plainly as I possibly can."

Bennett paused and looked Sa'id straight in the eye. "Palestinians do not have a state today because the Palestinian leadership has thus far refused to give up its ambition to have *all* the land of Israel. Refused to give up the strategy of armed conflict to achieve that goal. Refused to clamp down on terrorist networks that attack innocent Israeli civilians. And refused to accept any of the previous political deals that have been negotiated. The president understands full well that the Israelis have often mistreated the Palestinians and subjected them to all kinds of human-rights abuses. He doesn't condone or excuse such behavior. But he believes, and it is the position of my government, that it is ultimately the fault of the previous Palestinian government that your people do not have a state."

Sa'id couldn't believe what he was hearing. Neither could Doron.

"In 1947," Bennett continued, "the League of Nations came up with the Partition Plan, essentially dividing the Holy Land in half. Israel said yes. The Arabs said no. And five Arab nations invaded, seeking to throw the Jews into the sea. In the summer of 2000, at the second Camp David summit, Prime Minister Barak offered Chairman Arafat eighty-seven percent of the West Bank and Gaza. Previously, no Israeli prime minister had ever offered more than forty or fifty percent, I believe, and it struck many in Washington as a very generous offer."

Doron wanted to add "Too generous," but he held his tongue.

"But Chairman Arafat wanted more," Bennett continued. "He negotiated all the way up to ninety-seven percent of the land, and half the Old City of Jerusalem. Barak agreed. But what did Chairman Arafat do? He rejected the deal outright. Then he went back to Ramallah and set into motion the Al-Aksa intifada, a wave of terrorism and suicide bombings that left thousands of Israelis and Palestinians dead and wounded."

The tension in the room was palpable.

"My government will not dictate the terms of an agreement. It doesn't matter to us what percentage you two agree upon. Indeed, the whole point of our Oil for Peace proposal is to shift the terms of debate away from how much *land* each side is giving away to how much *wealth* each side can acquire if a deal—*any deal*—is agreed to and lived up to. Israeli foreign minister Abba Eban once said, 'The Palestinians never miss an opportunity to miss opportunity.' President MacPherson is adamant: this had better not be another opportunity missed."

*　　*　　*

New Year's Eve was over.

There were no bombings to report. The most dramatic incident had occurred at three minutes after midnight local time. Three men were in a Cessna trying to fly from Toronto to Rochester, skimming the waters of Lake Ontario at barely a hundred feet. Spotted by a Coast Guard cutter, they were warned repeatedly to identify themselves and turn back. When those warnings had failed, two F-15E Strike Eagles flying combat air patrol intercepted the aging Cessna and shot it down just minutes before it reached Greater Rochester, home of such industrial giants as Kodak, Xerox, and Bausch & Lomb.

Investigators were still picking through the crash site. It was unclear whether the men were planning a kamikaze attack—the plane was filled with cases of explosives—or perhaps were planning to land at a small, private airstrip where they'd meet other operatives, or set out on their own.

As best they could tell, the feds had busted up at least nine terror cells trying to penetrate U.S. borders over the past week. Fourteen men and three women were now in federal custody, and seven more men were dead after battles with federal agents on the borders or in the air.

☆ ☆ ☆

"Jonathan, I resent your premise," Sa'id stated calmly.

"Fair enough. But it's not my premise," Bennett responded. "It's the president's."

"Nevertheless, it is entirely unfair. It suggests that we must make all the concessions, not the Israelis."

"The president isn't blaming you personally, Ibrahim. He's blaming Chairman Arafat and his regime—the very regime that is now out there ripping themselves and your people to shreds. It's a fair analysis, and it happens to be true."

"I am sorry you feel that way, Jonathan."

"I don't *feel* that way. Those are the facts."

"Look, Jonathan, I want a state. Chairman Arafat wanted a state. Abu Mazen wanted a state. My people want a state. Period. Not tomorrow. Not next year, or in three years, or three thousand years from now. We want a state. We want to rule ourselves and live in dignity. That is all we have ever wanted. A state and peace to raise our children. Please don't insult me by saying the last half century of violence was all our fault."

"Ibrahim, it wasn't *your* fault at all. It wasn't the fault of the Palestinian people. But look, it's just not true that Arafat and his regime simply wanted a state and peace to raise their children. That's what *you* want. That's what *most* Palestinians want. But that's not what Yasser Arafat wanted or he would have taken Barak's deal.

"Mr. Prime Minister," Bennett now asked Doron, "didn't your

predecessor, Ariel Sharon, agree to a two-state solution? Didn't he say the occupation couldn't continue?"

"He did."

"And what about you?"

Doron took a deep breath. He hadn't expected being put on the spot so soon. A Palestinian state terrified Doron. Not for ideological or religious reasons. Doron's concerns were entirely security related.

A state meant sovereignty. The right to establish an army, air force, and navy. The right to build airports. The right to buy weapons and make treaties and conduct military exercises and so forth. Sa'id seemed like a reasonable person. But who would succeed him? What if the next Palestinian prime minister—or the next after him—cut a deal with Syria? or the Saudis? or Tehran? What then? What recourse would Doron's successor have if he gave away so much so soon? Still, Doron knew the negotiations could very well be over before they really started if he couldn't give Sa'id a private assurance that a three-year transition would eventually have a payoff to something more substantial.

"With caveats about secure borders and assuming the terrorists were eliminated and other Arab states were willing to end the embargo against Israel—with all those caveats built in—yes, my government is not opposed to a two-state solution."

There. He'd said it. Now the question was, did Sa'id believe it?

★ ★ ★

"Director Harris, it's for you."

FBI Director Scott Harris was huddled with Homeland Security Secretary Lee James, Secret Service Director Bud Norris, National Security Advisor Marsha Kirkpatrick, and their senior staffs in the White House Situation Room. The president and First Lady were still asleep in the Residence. Those gathered for this meeting had been up most of the night, overseeing the most extensive antiterror campaign in U.S. history, grabbing only an occasional catnap in their offices.

But this call was urgent.

"It's Harris. What've you got? . . . You're sure? . . . All right. Thanks."

He hung up the phone and turned to the others. "Autopsy report just came in."

"And?" asked Kirkpatrick

"It's not Ruth Bennett."

"They're sure?"

"Dental records."

"Which means . . ."

"You got it," sighed Harris. "She's still out there somewhere."

* * *

The principals reassembled after a fifteen-minute break.

McCoy handed each man a five-page, single-spaced, typed, and sta-pled document. It was marked "Confidential" and "Eyes Only." But it had been vetted before the trip by the vice president and his policy and politi-cal team, each member of the NSC—particularly the CIA, Defense, and the State Department Policy Planning Staff—as well as by three former secretaries of state.

Bennett suggested he simply give each man an overview and save the substantive discussions for Monday after they'd all had some time to think it over and discuss it with their advisors. Both men agreed.

A U.S. PROPOSAL FOR PEACE AND PROSPERITY

The United States offers "A Proposal for Peace and Prosperity" between Israel and the Palestinian Authority.

We do so in the spirit of United Nations Security Council Resolution 242, passed on November 22, 1967. This calls for the "withdrawal of Is-raeli armed forces from territories occupied in the recent conflict."

Resolution 242 also calls for the "termination of all claims or states of belligerency and respect for and acknowledgment of the sovereignty, territorial integrity and political independence of every State in the area and their right to live in peace within secure and recognized boundaries free from threats or acts of force."

Bennett began by stating for the record that Resolution 242 (and its corollary, Resolution 338) had served as the basis for all previous Arab-Israeli negotiations and should continue to do so. He reaffirmed that the president would commence discussions with other countries in the region to enter peace talks with Israel, and that Morocco and Pakistan were already showing a surprising degree of interest.

Then he dropped the bomb. He noted that the resolution called for an Israeli withdrawal "from territories occupied in the recent conflict," not "from *all* territories occupied." The distinction was important—land for peace, but not necessarily *all* the land for peace.

"My government accepts that there will be controversy on this point," said Bennett. "And I don't want to bog down on this point right now. It's something for the final status negotiations, not this Transition Period. We simply want to acknowledge up front that we're aware of this controversy and sympathetic to both sides' points of view."

Sa'id wasn't happy that Bennett had brought it up at all, but for now he let it pass.

Grateful the land mine he'd just stepped on hadn't yet gone off, Bennett continued.

> To this end, the U.S. proposes:
> Phase I—a three-year Transition Period
> Phase II—final status negotiations
> Phase III—signing/implementation of a final Peace Treaty

Bennett now began outlining the proposed guidelines for the Transition Period.

A. Coordinating Body

A Coordinating Body, headed by the United States—in consultation with those Arab States who recognize the State of Israel and NATO—will be responsible for assisting the Palestinian prime minister and the Palestinian Legislative Council in the planning and formation of a brand-new, democratic government structure. The new government will be known as the Palestinian Administrative Authority (PAA), to distinguish it from its predecessor.

Every measure possible will be taken by the PAA and the United States government to prevent anyone with ties to terrorism from participating in the new Palestinian government.

U.S. military and security forces, at the discretion of the president of

*the United States, will not leave the territories in question until the
PAA is deemed by the president of the United States as ready, willing,
and able to operate effectively and prevent terror attacks against Israel or
elsewhere.*

Neither said a word. Again, Bennett continued.

B. Administrative Authority

*A Palestinian Administrative Authority will be established in the areas
under Palestinian control. The PAA will be responsible for administer-
ing the day-to-day lives of the Palestinians in matters such as the economy, police and law enforcement, education, housing, religion, culture,
communications, and other sectors.*

*The employees of the PAA will be Palestinians who have not been
involved, directly or indirectly, in any terror activities.*

*The PAA will operate for a Transition Period of at least three years.
During this Period, Ibrahim Sa'id will remain the prime minister, and
the current members of the Palestinian Legislative Council will remain
in place.*

*During this Period, the required democratic structures and condi-
tions will be created so as to enable the sides to enter into permanent
settlement negotiations at the end of the Period.*

*At the end of the Period, free and open elections will be held in these
areas. The elections will be administered and overseen by the Coordinating Body, in order to ensure that they are being held in accordance
with accepted democratic standards. Only after such elections will final
status negotiations be concluded.*

For now, neither Sa'id nor Doron registered an objection or asked a
question.

Sa'id's interim appointment was for only eighteen months. But he'd
insisted upon democratic Palestinian elections as part of his agreement to
accept the prime ministership, and the PLC had readily agreed, so that
wasn't likely to be a problem.

So far, so good. But it was the next section that would set off the fire-
works.

* * *

Washington's focus was now on the FBI field office in Buffalo.

Special Agent George Polanski took a call from Dorothy Richards, Ruth Bennett's sister, from her farm in Lackawanna, just south of Buffalo. She was sorry for calling so early, but she was worried. Mrs. Richards explained that she and her husband had attended a New Year's Eve party at a neighbor's. It was their first time out of the house since Ruth's disappearance, and they were hoping to let off a little steam. They'd just gotten home and found two voice-mail messages. Both were from their grown children, one in San Diego, the other in Austin, Texas. But when they'd checked their "call log," they found two calls from the 212 area code in New York City. Both were from the same phone, but the number wasn't one they recognized. The caller ID system had been blocked from the other end.

Was it Ruth? Was it her kidnappers? Was it a ransom call they'd missed? They had no idea. Cursing themselves for not being home to get the calls, they wrote down the number and called the FBI field office, as they'd been instructed to do if anything unusual came up.

Polanski immediately dispatched agents to the Richardses' farm to take a full statement and tap their phones. A colleague began running a trace of the 212 number. Simultaneously, Polanski called the FBI Operations Center in Washington to brief them on the newest development. Nine minutes later, his phone was ringing off the hook.

"Polanski."

"Special Agent George Polanski?"

"Yeah, who's this?"

"This is the White House operator. Please stand by for the president."

Polanski couldn't believe it. He cradled the phone on his shoulder and began rummaging through his desk. He found his bottle of Tums and popped it open. It was empty.

Suddenly the president was on the line. "Agent Polanski?"

"Yes, sir."

"This is Jim MacPherson. How are you today?"

"Busy, sir. And you?"

"I'll bet you are. As you can imagine, I'm taking a special interest in this case. What can you tell me about this phone call to the Richardses' farm?"

"Not much sir, I . . ."

Polanski's partner was shoving a yellow legal pad in his face with some scribbles he could barely read.

"Wait, hold on a moment, Mr. President. . . . I may have something. . . ."

"Take your time, son."

"Yes, sir—I . . ."

"What is it?" MacPherson demanded.

"You sure this is right?" Polanski asked his partner.

"Agent Polanski, what have you got?" the president asked again.

"Sir, we just ran a trace on this number. . . ."

"Whose phone is it?"

"Mr. President, it's . . ."

"It's *what*?"

"Sir . . . it's . . . it's Jon Bennett's cell phone."

41

BENNETT HESITATED.

But there was no getting around it. So he braced himself, and dived in.

C. Security and Terror Prevention Arrangements

During the Transition Period, the United States will continue to be responsible for overall security, as well as for the freedom of passage in the entire area from the Jordan River to the Mediterranean Sea.

The United States will assist the PAA in recruiting, hiring, training, and deploying police and law enforcement officers. The employees of the new PAA security forces will be Palestinians who have not been involved, directly or indirectly, in any terror activities or the civil war.

The United States will also assist the PAA in establishing an independent judiciary, including the recruitment, hiring, training, and oversight of judges, prosecutors, and public defenders, all for the purpose of establishing the rule of law and ensuring fair, speedy, and just trials and all manner of legal procedures.

For security purposes, Israel will have the right to set up transition zones and buffer zones—in cooperation with U.S. forces and PAA leaders—using any appropriate method, to prevent the renewal and resurgence of terror activities.

It sounded innocuous enough, but Sa'id was furious.

"Absolutely not—that is *completely* unacceptable," he said instantly and a bit louder than he'd meant to. "Of course I accept Israel's need for security. But that last part is nothing but a thinly veiled cover for Doron's illegal and immoral 'security fence' between our two peoples. We are absolutely and unequivocally opposed to such language, and I can tell you right now, Jonathan, that this is a deal breaker for us."

Bennett had been warned in a conference call a few days before with Deputy Secretary (and now acting Secretary of State) Dick Cavanaugh to expect precisely this reaction. But Sa'id was even more heated than Bennett had expected from an old friend.

It was true that between Israel and the West Bank, the government of Israel was already building a wall some 20 feet high and 220 miles long, including around the 30-mile perimeter of Jerusalem's municipal boundaries, effectively cutting off East Jerusalem from the rest of the West Bank. This would be combined with a sophisticated network of underground and long-range electronic sensors, unmanned aerial vehicles, trenches, land mines, guard paths, and checkpoints reminiscent of Checkpoint Charlie between East and West Berlin during the cold war.

Eighty-five miles were already complete—at a cost of some $2 million a mile—but Palestinian officials were going ballistic. "This is a Fascist, apartheid measure being done, and we do not accept it," Arafat had told the Israeli newspaper *Haaretz*. "We will continue rejecting it by all means." Mohammed Dahlan had echoed the apartheid theme, telling the Israeli daily *Yediot Aharonot* that "this fence will be a fence of hate. The 'whites' will be in Tel Aviv and the 'blacks' in the West Bank."

Doron wasn't about to be swayed.

"A security fence is absolutely nonnegotiable," the Israeli prime minister said quietly. "Look at all the suicide bombers. Look at what is happening in the territories right now. I simply cannot allow Israeli citizens to be vulnerable to such violence day after day after day. A fence does not solve every problem, but it solves many of them. We should have finished it a long time ago."

"No, no, I am sorry, no," Sa'id responded, careful to control his passion. "You are constructing the Berlin Wall. No matter what you call it, it becomes a de facto political boundary. And after you spend a billion dollars on it, are you going to take it down? Of course not. A fence creates facts on the ground that affect the final status. So it is either one or the other. Either we negotiate our boundaries now, and probably get no-where, or we negotiate a Transition Period, and no fence."

"Whoa, whoa, gentlemen," Bennett broke in. "You've got problems with this section. That's fine. I promise you we will take all the time it takes to work our way through that minefield. But not today. That starts Monday. Fair enough?"

It was a serious stumbling block. But they could certainly wait another few days. Both men nodded, reluctantly.

★ ★ ★

Now it was the president who hesitated.

Bennett was in the middle of sensitive negotiations at a critical mo-ment. The last thing MacPherson wanted to do was interrupt whatever momentum the peace talks were beginning to develop, or further distract an already beleaguered Bennett as he guided the two prime ministers through the plan.

Still, they needed Bennett's input. Did he have his cell phone with him on the "Mount of Olives"? It wasn't his White House phone. That had a 202 area code number. It was his GSX phone. Why was he still using it? Had he called his aunt? Twice? Why hadn't he left a message? Or did someone else have his cell phone? And if so, why?

A check of phone company records and Bennett's LUDs—line-usage details—indicated that some calls from the cell phone had been made from Germany. That had to be while Bennett was there in the hospital. Other calls had been made from Orlando. That had to be the two days Bennett was visiting his mom after getting out of the hospital and back to the States. After that, not a single call had been made for almost three weeks until the two calls to Buffalo. Had Bennett given the phone to his mother?

They needed answers and time was critical. If Ruth Bennett was still alive, the cell phone might now be their only hope. If she wasn't, the phone could lead the feds to her killers. Scott Harris—standing in the Oval Office with the president, vice president, Marsha Kirkpatrick, and Lee James—could see that MacPherson was agonizing over the decision. He tried to take off some of the pressure.

"Mr. President, if I may?" said Harris.

"Please, Scott, by all means."

"Let's allow Jon to keep working undistracted for now. My people can work this thing from several angles. We won't call the phone until we talk to Jon and find out what he did with the phone. Perhaps we can regroup in a few hours. Is that fair?"

The president looked around to the others. All nodded agreement.

"Fine. Let's meet back here this afternoon. Scott, you pick the time. Coordinate through Marsha. Now, where are we with the suicide bombers?"

Homeland Security Secretary Lee James took that. "So far, so good, Mr. President. You know the stats. No attacks yet and lots of people scooped up. Moreover, it appears that when our special forces in Iraq took out those two carloads of people on the border of Syria—"

"You mean when we caught Daoud Juma?"

"Exactly—best we can tell at this point, most of the men in the two cars that were blown up by Hellfire missiles were fedayeen heading for the U.S."

"You mean we got a bunch of suicide bombers and didn't even realize it?"

"That's the current thinking."

"But there could still be some out there."

"Well, sir, from all the interrogations—remember, we've got a lot of people in custody right now and we're working them pretty hard—anyway, from all these interrogations, we think we may have gotten all of the bombers but one."

"Really?"

"Don't quote me on that. I don't want that out in the press. But yes, we think we've gotten all but one."

"And this lone bomber—do you think he's already in the country?"

"Impossible to say. But I think we've got to go on that assumption."

"So what do we do to find him?"

"If it is a *him*," added Kirkpatrick.

"Well, sir, whoever it is had to have slipped into the country within days if not hours of your order to close the borders from any new people entering, and the arrival—or attempted arrival—of the other bombers."

"Assuming it's not a sleeper agent," noted the president.

"Right. But nothing we've gleaned from the bombers in custody would indicate that they're using sleeper agents for this mission," James responded. "There may be some here, providing weapons, explosives, what have you. But they don't appear to be ready to blow themselves up."

"Okay, assuming you're right, it's still like finding a needle in a haystack, isn't it?"

"Well, assuming we're right, at least we've got the time frame narrowed down to a few hours or a few days before we went to Threat Condition Red. So what we're doing right now is rechecking—by hand—the identity of every single person who legally entered the country during that time frame, double-checking to see if they are who they said they are, and if any names ring a bell with us, the CIA, Interpol, the Israelis, you name it."

"And if this guy—or gal—got into the country illegally?" asked MacPherson.

It was a question none of them wanted to answer.

☆ ☆ ☆

Oblivious to events back home, Bennett pressed on with his presentation.

D. Development of Democratic Life

The Coordinating Body, together with the PAA, will formulate new educational programs, curricula, and textbooks for all levels that inculcate values of peace rather than of terror, and will eliminate those educational programs that encourage and praise terror.

Freedom of political, social, and religious association (which is not based on terror) will be established as a means of building a democratic political structure, which will support free elections and be responsible for the day-to-day administration of the civilian life of the residents.

Freedom of speech and press will be guaranteed, restricted only by a prohibition of direct or indirect support of terror.

Agreement with and adherence to these principles will be an essential prerequisite for all economic and other assistance which will be given to the Palestinian Administration Authority.

Doron liked what he saw, though he was careful not to show it. Sa'id too was pleased. How he was going to get all this passed by the legislature, however moderate they claimed to be, was a different question. But that was a fight for another day.

Another diplomatic land mine was about to go off, and Sa'id could feel it coming.

E. Dismantling of Refugee Camps

The Coordinating Body, immediately upon the establishment of the PAA, will work in close coordination to build normal apartments and homes for those in the refugee camps, and then dismantle the camps altogether. Arab countries, with the assistance of the United Nations, will finance this effort.

In the first stage, the refugee camps in the West Bank will be dismantled, followed by a second stage in which the refugee camps in the Gaza Strip will be dismantled.

F. Evacuation of Jewish Settlements

The Coordinating Body, immediately upon the establishment of the PAA, will work in close coordination with the government of Israel to evacuate Jewish settlements in the West Bank and Gaza Strip. The evacuations will commence no later than six months after the signing of this agreement by Israel. The Israeli prime minister will publicly support such evacuation, and his government will assist the Jewish residents of these enclaves in relocating them to new homes within the State of Israel.

Israeli police and/or military forces will be given safe, temporary passage to such settlements to assist in their orderly evacuation.

The Coordinating Body will assess the value of these settlements— their land, buildings, infrastructure, and relocation costs—and establish their fair market value.

The PAA will have the option to purchase said settlements at their fair market value within two years of their evacuation, or they may put them up for auction, available only to current residents of the PAA areas.

Both men held their fire. Now was not the time.

Doron couldn't wait to see the Palestinian refugee camps dismantled and new apartments built with Arab and U.N. money. That should have been done decades ago.

But as Bennett and McCoy could see, Doron took serious exception at the suggestion that he should evacuate every Jewish settlement in the disputed territories. And he was supposed to *sell* those settlements to the Palestinians? It was political suicide. He could see dismantling some. But all? There was no way, and the Americans knew it.

Nevertheless, Doron calmly made a few cryptic notes in the margins, and nodded for Bennett to proceed. There was no need for alarm, he reminded himself. Americans were playing poker, and Israel had a full house. Israel still controlled the land, and possession was, after all, nine-tenths of the law.

☆ ☆ ☆

The Viper snaked his way north on I-95.

Atlanta and Savannah were finally behind him, though they'd not gone as planned. He'd expected to get his share of explosives at the first stop, and a cache of weapons at the second. But at the last moment, his Al-Nakbah control agent—a sleeper from Saudi Arabia, working for a midsize life-insurance firm near Atlanta—had called an audible.

Given all the extraordinary security precautions in place at the moment, getting into Washington, D.C., as an Italian businessman working for Microsoft might not be easy, but it was possible. But not with a trunk full of weapons and C4 plastic explosives. Bomb-sniffing dogs and new portable explosive detectors were being used at all the checkpoints in and around the capital, and the control agent concluded it simply wasn't worth the risk. The good news: two other Al-Nakbah sleepers were living in D.C. If he could get into the city, someone would bring him "supplies." All he needed to do was pick a "soft" target and be ready to move.

Nadir Hashemi was bleary-eyed and exhausted. He popped down another two amphetamines and washed them down with lukewarm coffee. He could do this, he told himself. He just had to stay focused.

He thought about the story he'd read online this morning. The British foreign secretary had denounced the wave of suicide bombers trying to penetrate the United States, but added, "When young people go to their deaths, we can all feel a degree of compassion for those youngsters. They must be so depressed and misguided to do this."

Compassion? Nadir wanted no compassion from the British, or the

Americans, or any of the infidels destroying both of his homelands. *Depressed and misguided? Who was this guy to speak when he didn't understand the first thing about the fedayeen or Al-Nakbah?* Nadir didn't see himself as depressed or misguided. Just the opposite. He wasn't headed to Washington to commit *intihar*—suicide—but *istishhad*, martyrdom. He wasn't acting out of hopelessness and despair. He was driven by an overwhelming desire to cast terror into the hearts of the imperialist oppressors in the capital city of the new Roman Empire.

Martyrdom bombers weren't misguided, Nadir reminded himself. They were achieving the highest level of jihad. They were holy fighters earning respect on earth and rewards in heaven. And this was it. Washington was just a few hours away, and so, too, was his departure for paradise.

★　★　★

This section needed serious work, thought McCoy.

G. Creation of Oil for Peace Economic Infrastructure and Progrowth Strategies

Immediately upon the signing of this agreement, the government of Israel and the PAA will approve all necessary licenses for the Medexco joint venture and promptly take all necessary steps to expedite the joint drilling and production of petroleum off the shores of Israel and Gaza.

The government of Israel and the PAA will take all necessary legal and legislative steps to protect private property rights and eliminate or reduce all tax, tariff, and regulatory burdens that hinder economic growth and development, with particular attention to taxes, tariffs, and regulations that impede the creation and expansion of small business.

The president of the United States will encourage the Congress to promptly pass a "U.S.-Palestine Free Trade Agreement" that is consistent with the "U.S.-Israel Free Trade Agreement" of 1985, and the "U.S.-Jordan Free Trade Agreement" of 1995.

The Coordinating Body will assist in the creation of secure and transparent Palestinian banking and monetary systems, free enterprise zones, and the building of necessary economic infrastructures.

At a later stage, in tandem with the progress of the Transition—and

*in coordination with Israel—Palestinian workers will be permitted
to apply for new Israeli work permits to work inside of Israel.*

It was the heart of the Oil for Peace strategy.

The president wanted a deepwater seaport in Gaza; airports in Gaza
and the West Bank; and a network of highways, bridges, and/or tunnels
linking the West Bank to Gaza. Back in Washington, McCoy had argued
that they should spell out such ideas in the document. Bennett had resisted. These were details, not fundamentals. There were tougher issues
to solve, and they couldn't risk letting the Transition Period negotiations
bog down.

H. Negotiations for Permanent Peace

*After three years—and at the conclusion of free, fair, and democratic
elections—the State of Israel and the elected representatives of the Palestinian people will negotiate the terms of a permanent peace.*

*Both parties agree up front that such negotiations will be conducted
in accordance with United Nations Security Council Resolution 242.*

*The United States will assist in every possible way to bring both par-
ties to a just and lasting resolution of the conflict.*

It was almost 4:00 Saturday afternoon Gibraltar time—10:00 a.m.
back in Washington—when Bennett and the principals finished for the
day. Bennett took a sip of bottled water and sat back in his chair. McCoy
finished her cup of coffee and tried to size up what had just happened. No
one had stormed out in protest. Not a bad day.

Just then there was a knock at the door. Tariq entered, walked over to
Bennett, handed him a note, and whispered something in his ear.

Bennett went white as a sheet.

42
⋆ ⋆
⋆

"HAVE A CAPABILITY, comrades, but appear not to."

The words seeped out of his mouth and hung over the room like the thick, pungent smoke of his Cuban Cohiba.

"Make use, but appear not to. Be near, but appear far. Or far, but appear near."

Yuri Gogolov stared out over Tehran on this bright but quiet Sunday afternoon. The storms were gone. The rains had stopped. At least for a few days. He and Mohammed Jibril were doing their best to get comfortable in their new home, after the "untimely demise" of Jibril's personal driver. The plush penthouse apartment of the director of Iran's counterintelligence service wasn't Gogolov's first choice. Too high profile. Too likely to be monitored by the West, particularly by the Americans. But it would have to do for a few more days, until Jibril could make the necessary arrangements to get them back to Moscow, or perhaps St. Petersburg.

As they waited for the latest news from the several fronts they'd opened in recent days, they dueled each other over a chessboard hand-carved and painted almost a hundred years before by Jibril's great-great-grandfather, Salim Jibril. Gogolov was, of course, the undisputed grand master. But chess ran in Jibril's blood, and for now, at least, he was pressing the offensive and hoping to make this arrogant Russian squirm, even for a moment.

"When strong, avoid them," Gogolov continued. "If of high morale, depress them. Seem humble to fill them with conceit. If at ease, exhaust them. If united, separate them. Attack their weaknesses. Emerge to their surprise."

Jibril slammed his bishop down, taking one of Gogolov's knights, his eyes gleaming with delight. "Check."

Gogolov stopped staring out over the city, smiled ever so faintly at Jibril, then looked down at the board. Next he casually slid his queen diagonally two spaces. In so doing, he defended his king. But that was not all.

"Checkmate," he said quietly, drawing hard on the Cohiba.

Jibril—a gaunt, wiry man with quick black eyes and thin black hair—sat in disbelief. He'd never lost a chess match in his life. Now he'd lost three—in a row.

"Enough of your Sun Tzu and child's games," snorted a heavyset man by the window, nursing a bottle of vodka and staring blankly at a minaret across the street. "This is a time for work, not for play."

Gogolov laughed. "Relax, Zhiri, you'll give yourself an ulcer. Everything is on track, my friend. Everything's in order."

It was true. Even now, four Al-Nakbah assassin teams were mobilizing. Securing planes. Renting speedboats. Getting weapons. Purchasing ammunition and smuggling explosives into the assembly points. And Al-Nakbah intel operatives around the world were doing everything possible to track down the location of Doron and Sa'id. Jibril had sent out a coded e-mail saying a friend needed a new chess set. He was missing "two kings" and looking for precise replacements. Anyone with suppliers who knew anything about chess and might be helpful in tracking down these "two kings" was requested to contact him at once. Prices were negotiable, but time was of the essence.

Gogolov wasn't worried. Spread around enough money and the truth could always be bought. Besides, they weren't relying solely on Al-Nakbah's sleepers and "suppliers." The intelligence networks of the Saudis, Syrians, and of course, the Iranians all had their ears to the ground. So did the Libyans. Khaddafi's spy network in southern Europe was extraordinary, as was his new alliance with Al-Nakbah. Khaddafi was restless. He'd been out of the game too long. Reagan had scared him off. Now MacPherson was ticking him off. He wanted back in, and he was ready to play hardball.

With so many people looking, they'd pick up something soon. If not through their own sources, then maybe through the media's. Marcus Jackson's front-page story in this morning's *New York Times* was extraordinary. "Point Man for Peace Conducting Covert Talks." Gogolov had already read the entire story online, twice. It was a little thin on hard facts. But it was full of speculation and nondenial denials that the Israeli and Palestinian prime ministers and the architect of President MacPherson's peace plan were holed up somewhere in the Middle East or southern Europe, talking a deal.

According to two Israeli Knesset sources, Doron hadn't been seen for three days, going on four. Sa'id had shown up on Al-Jazeera television New Year's Eve, but he'd done the broadcast by satellite and it was unclear, even to the broadcast engineers, from where the signal had originated. An unnamed Saudi diplomat in Riyadh, meanwhile, was quoted as saying flatout that "the United States is conducting a covert peace process under the cover of war in Palestine." A senior European Union Parliament member was quoted as saying "such rumors of covert peace talks, without E.U. and U.N. participation—if true—would be troubling, to say the least."

The White House, according to Jackson's story, refused comment, but they weren't outright denying the substance of the story. Press Secretary Chuck Murray said simply, "Military operations in the Holy Land are our prime focus right now. Our forces are there as peacemakers, and obviously the U.S. government is committed to doing whatever we can to end hostilities and bring both sides back to the table. Beyond that, it's all just speculation."

Secrets were hard to keep in the information age. But soon enough, they'd know the truth.

"So relax, Zhiri," Gogolov insisted, lighting up another cigar. "It'll happen when it happens. Until then, why don't you come play our little Mohammed a game of chess. He can't beat a master like me. Maybe he'll have a chance with a drunk like you."

✯ ✯ ✯

They could see the twin engine coming in on final approach.

It was an hour late, but at least it was here. Traffic on Winston Churchill Avenue, the main thoroughfare from the Frontier—the border crossing with Spain—into the small city of Gibraltar came to a halt as crossing gates went down, lights began to flash, and every driver and pedestrian was warned that another plane was about to touch down.

The airport that serviced the Rock wasn't the world's busiest, or its safest. The numbers told the story. It was true that Prince Charles and Princess Diana had flown into Gibraltar on the way to their honeymoon cruise on the royal yacht *Britannia*. But they were the exception. Of the 6 million tourists who visited each year, fewer than a hundred thousand came by plane. Locals claimed no atheist had ever landed here. Perhaps someone could be an atheist when he or she got *on* a plane bound for Gibraltar, people would say. But nobody who'd ever encountered the fierce crosswinds and harrowing approach into a runway jutting a half mile into the Atlantic and traversing directly across the peninsula's busiest street ever got *off* that plane without thanking God for surviving the landing.

Even from this distance, they could now see the distinctive orange-and-purple letters of the FedEx logo, and both silently hoped their "package" was unharmed. The Sunday sky was overcast and chilly. Two new storms were brewing—one was coming down the coast of Spain from the North Atlantic; the other was sixty or seventy miles eastward over the Mediterranean. They were poised to make an unusually harsh winter even worse, but forecasters said Gibraltar should have at least a few days of respite until the new fronts moved in, and Bennett and McCoy were grateful. They needed to be outside for a while. They needed some fresh air. And they were looking forward to seeing Dr. Eliezer Mordechai again. He'd been a good friend and a wise mentor for them both. He'd been an invaluable asset in helping them understand how best to negotiate with his fellow Israelis. Better yet, he said he was "bearing gifts from afar," whatever that meant.

Bennett and McCoy sat alongside the tarmac in the back of a black, armor-plated Chevy Tahoe, not far from two navy Seahawks waiting to take the SEALs back to their base at Rota, Spain, when this mission was done. Tariq was at the wheel of the Tahoe, scanning the environment from behind his aviator sunglasses. Four more agents from ST-8's Gold Team watched over them and their surroundings from a minivan twenty yards away. Sa'id and Doron were still safely inside the "Mount of Olives." It wasn't time to let them outside. Not just yet.

Fifteen minutes later, Bennett, McCoy, and Dr. Mordechai were sitting inside a café halfway up the Rock. They ordered fish and chips and asked the former Mossad chief all about his trip and his health while their security team took up positions inside and out of the restaurant.

"In the spirit of peace and friendship, allow me to offer a toast," McCoy said, holding up her glass. "To Dr. Eliezer Mordechai, who absolutely, positively had to be here overnight—and *wasn't*."

The three clinked glasses. Mordechai and McCoy had a good laugh. Bennett seemed far away, worried about his mother, worried about the impact Marcus Jackson's front-page story in the *New York Times* was going to have on the peace process.

"Thanks for coming," McCoy offered. "We really appreciate it."

"Not at all," the old man replied. "It's my pleasure. I'm sorry for the delay."

"Don't worry about it. Actually, today's a good day. We've given our two 'friends' the day off to consult with their 'friends,' so for the first time in too long, we've got a little time on our hands."

Mordechai nodded his appreciation to McCoy and then turned back to Bennett. "Good, good. Now, Jonathan, what's the latest with your mother? I've been worried."

Bennett's already gloomy expression darkened further. His pain was barely contained under the surface, and Mordechai could immediately sense it wasn't a topic he wanted to discuss, especially after the update he'd received the night before.

Fortunately McCoy could see it as well and graciously stepped in. "Someone's using Jon's old cell phone—the one he used at GSX. They made two calls to his aunt in Buffalo on New Year's Eve, and now they've electronically withdrawn several hundred dollars from Mrs. Bennett's checking account."

"How would they have gotten the phone? And the PIN number?"

"We have no idea. Jon forgot the phone at his mom's house when he was visiting there for a few days, after coming back from the hospital in Germany. He asked her to look for it, but she never found it. She doesn't have a cell phone herself. hasn't ever used one or wanted one. And she almost never withdraws large amounts of money from her checking account."

"Can't the FBI track the cell signal?" asked Mordechai. "We do it all the time."

"They're trying. But apparently, whoever's got the phone is pretty smart. They're keeping it off until they make a call. All the calls have been very quick, none more than a few minutes. And the FBI doesn't want to call the phone directly for fear it might tip off the terrorists, *if* it's in the hands of terrorists."

Mordechai could see Bennett's discomfort intensifying, so he shifted gears. "Hey, how about that gift I promised you?" he asked, reaching into his briefcase and pulling out a gift-wrapped package about the size of a shirt box.

"Gifts are good," said McCoy as she cleared away some plates and glasses to make room. "What have you got?"

Mordechai slid the package over to McCoy to do the honors, as Bennett was staring blankly out the window.

"A file?" McCoy blurted out, not bothering to hide her disappointment. "You got us a file? You know we've got these in America, Dr. Mordechai."

"You don't have this one." The old man grinned.

Intrigued, she glanced around the room. It was almost three in the afternoon. The place was nearly deserted. Sure no one was watching, she opened the brown folder. The first page was a spreadsheet in Arabic.

"What's this, your income taxes?" she quipped.

"Keep reading."

She did for a few moments, and a few pages, then looked back up. "How'd you get this?"

"I have my sources," he said, lighting up his pipe and taking a few puffs.

"I know, but really, how'd you get this?"

Sweet smoke filled the air around their table. Bennett turned back from the windows and looked at McCoy, then at Mordechai. "What are you guys talking about?"

The former Mossad chief had both their attention. Now he was ready to talk. He took a few more puffs on his favorite pipe, then leaned forward and began to whisper. "You asked me to follow the money, right?"

"Right."

"So I did."

"And? What'd you find?"

"It's worse than we imagined."

"What do you mean?"

The story Mordechai proceeded to tell sent chills down their spines. On the first night of Operation Palestinian Freedom, U.S. forces, at the suggestion of Israeli intelligence, had raided two seemingly innocuous warehouses in central Ramallah. Both were owned by Yasser Arafat and the Palestinian Authority. Neither seemed to have any strategic significance. But the gun battle to secure both facilities had been fierce, and now Washington knew why. Inside was a treasure trove—top-secret files of Arafat's dealings with other Arab and Islamic countries and organizations, including banking records, financial spreadsheets, phone records, written and electronic correspondence, memos, as well as transcripts of meetings and phone calls.

The files had been airlifted by helicopter to a secret IDF base near the Sea of Galilee. There, U.S. and Israeli officers began copying and cataloguing everything. The process would likely still take another week or two, Mordechai said, after which everything would be returned and put back in its place. In the meantime, however, Arab-speaking linguists and intelligence analysts were beginning to translate what appeared to be the most important documents.

"They've uncovered a money trail you wouldn't believe," said Mordechai.

"Try me," said Bennett, now fully engaged.

"For starters, just take a guess at how much money since 1998 the Saudis have pumped into the hands of Yasser Arafat, his henchmen, and the other Islamic extremist groups in the territories to conduct 'martyrdom operations' against us."

"I have no idea. A hundred million?"

"Not even close."

"*Five* hundred million?"

Mordechai shook his head.

"A *billion*?" asked McCoy, incredulous.

"That's what we thought," Mordechai admitted, "a billion and change."

"Not true?"

"Not even close."

"Well?"

"You ready for this?" Mordechai asked, then pulled out a pen and began writing on a clean paper napkin: 15,442,105,150 Saudi riyals.

"What's that in real money?" asked Bennett.

"No pun intended?"

"Very funny."

Mordechai smiled, then wrote down the translation—$4 billion U.S.

Bennett couldn't believe it. He just stared at the figure for a few moments, then looked at McCoy. She, too, was stunned.

"You're telling me the Saudis gave the Palestinians four billion dollars since 1998 to wage war against Israel?" asked Bennett.

"That's what I'm telling you."

"All to Arafat?"

"No, some went to the Palestinian Authority. A lot of it went directly to the PLO, Fatah, Hamas, and Islamic Jihad—before we destroyed them a few years ago—and more recently to Al-Nakbah, which is slowly picking up the pieces left behind by Hamas and Islamic Jihad. Most of the money, though, does seem to have gone through Arafat and his henchmen. The unifying factor was an organization's willingness to conduct, facilitate, or condone jihad—including suicide bombings—against Israeli civilians."

"How did it all work?"

"We're still piecing that together," said Mordechai, pulling several documents from the file. "Since the Six Days' War in '67, the Saudi government as well as many wealthy Saudi individuals have funneled money to the Palestinian leadership through a number of so-called charitable organizations. The first and oldest is the Popular Committee for Assisting Palestinian Mujahedin. A second and more recent one is called the Support Committee for the Al Quds Intifada and the Al-Aksa Fund. And there are others. Since the late nineties, the Saudis have dramatically stepped up their giving and earmarked large amounts of it to the families of suicide bombers and others killed or wounded in operations against Israel. They say it is for humanitarian purposes, for families grieving over their losses. But each family gets a check for five to ten times their normal annual income. It is clearly a payoff for families to brainwash their children to give themselves up for the cause while they get the cash."

Bennett and McCoy sifted through the documents, skimming the English translations and trying to grasp the magnitude of what they were looking at.

"It's not easy to move huge amounts of cash like that," McCoy observed.

"Apparently it is easier than we thought. The records seem to indicate that vast amounts of Saudi funds were wire transferred from a bank in Jiddah to the Palestinian Authority Treasury Department. We've even uncovered the main account number."

"How come nobody's told Erin and me about this yet?"

Mordechai scooped up a forkful of fish and considered how to answer that.

"They think you have enough on your plate. They don't want you focused on anything but making peace."

"So why are you telling us now?" asked McCoy.

Mordechai said nothing. He took another forkful of food and poured himself another cup of coffee. Bennett could see the mischievous twinkle in his eye.

"Dr. Mordechai seems to be sending us a little message," said Bennett.

"Oh, really?" said McCoy. "And what's that?"

Bennett looked over at Mordechai and raised his eyebrows, but the mystery man didn't take the bait.

"Please, go right ahead," said Mordechai. "You are doing fine."

So Bennett continued. "Making peace, according to the good doctor, isn't simply about cutting a deal, good as that might be. It's time to follow the money—and cut it off."

McCoy looked back at Dr. Mordechai. "How's he doing?"

"He is getting warmer."

"All right, Jon, carry on."

Bennett wiped his mouth with a napkin and took a few sips of water. "If I'm hearing him right, he's saying the suicide bombers and other terrorists on the front lines are largely motivated by ideology, religious and political. They want to do something heroic, something they'll be remembered for," Bennett continued. "But Dr. Mordechai doesn't believe their leaders—the men who send these bombers into battle, the men who are more than willing to sacrifice hundreds of their own countrymen while they themselves live in walled compounds, surrounded by dozens of bodyguards, driven around in bulletproof limousines—such leaders aren't driven purely by a cause, certainly not the glory of Islam. They're driven by old-fashioned greed."

"So the whole Palestinian liberation movement is corrupt?" asked McCoy. "Nobody's fighting for the good of the cause?"

"I did not say that," said Mordechai.

"Then what are you saying?"

Bennett was tracking with Mordechai, so he continued. "Dr. M. here isn't saying there aren't plenty of foot soldiers willing to die for the cause. There are. But for the old guard running the show, the war against Israel and us is now a multibillion-dollar business. Which means that if our little peace deal has any chance of working over the long haul, then we've got to get a whole lot more serious about pressuring the Saudis to cut off the cash."

"True," said Mordechai. "The Saudis are a very serious problem. But it is not just the Saudis. The Iranians are doing the exact same thing, and far too few people are paying attention. Think about it. They are directly across the Persian Gulf from the Saudis and the United Arab Emirates. They have massive reserves of oil and gas. And what are they doing with all that money? Building a modern society? Educating and employing their young people? No. The mullahs want to rebuild the Persian Empire. And with Iraq out of the way now, they just may have a shot. They are buying weapons from the Russians, who are so broke they will sell to anyone for the right price. They are buying nuclear power plants from the Russians. Why? Because they need nuclear power? Of course not. They are sitting on some of the richest petroleum reserves in the world. No, the Iranians are building nuclear bomb factories, and the Russians are helping them. While they are at it, they are building a new worldwide terrorist network as well. Once they helped fund Hamas and Hezbollah and the rest. Now it looks like they are funding, housing, and aiding Al-Nakbah, a terror network that I am beginning to think may be more dangerous than all of its predecessors."

"Al-Nakbah? Why's that?" asked Bennett.

"You have seen the transcripts of the interrogations of your old friend Stuart Iverson?"

"No. Have you?"

Mordechai gave him another mischievous smile.

"What are you talking about?" asked Bennett, astounded. "How could you have possibly seen the transcripts? There are only a handful of people in the world who even know we cut a deal with him, much less that he's actually talking."

"I guess I am one of them—the president cut Iverson a deal a couple of days ago. Took the death penalty off the table. Now he is singing like the Dixie Chicks."

McCoy couldn't believe it either. Who was this guy? "All right, so what's he saying?"

"He is painting a portrait."

"Of who?"

"Of Gogolov and Jibril—their personalities, their motives, their objectives—unlike anything we have ever seen before. These guys are scary. But they are also smart. They are playing both sides of the street. Ostensibly they are an independent organization, started to wage jihad against the Russians in Chechnya. But they have expanded—metastasized. Jibril is working his Iranian connections. Gogolov is working his Saudi connections. And it is working, better than we realized."

"What else?" asked Bennett.

"From what I can see, we have all been missing the forest for the trees. We are all focused on Iraq and this civil war and cutting this peace deal, and we should be. Don't get me wrong. These are important battles in the war on terror. But it is now clear that there is something else going on here. Another evil is growing in the shadows—Gogolov and Jibril—Al-Nakbah. They are planning something. I don't know exactly what it is. I am not sure if Iverson knows exactly. But it is worse than anything we have seen so far. Their fingerprints are everywhere. And what is beginning to worry me is that if we don't deal with this threat head-on—and soon—the consequences could be catastrophic."

43

***

"SIR, WE GOT a hit."

"Talk to me."

"Bennett's cell phone—it just went live."

"I need a location."

"Hold on. Hold on."

"Come on, come on. Let's go."

"Just a second—the computer's triangulating the cell towers right now."

"Come on, come on."

"Give me a second, sir, we've almost got it."

It was just before eleven o'clock Sunday night in New York. The voice of the senior ELINT officer was secure, thanks to the bureau's digitally encrypted wireless network. Still, it was muffled. He could barely be heard over the roar of the helicopter as the surveillance team maintained its round-the-clock vigil over Manhattan. Still, the message got through and a bolt of adrenaline shot through the entire team.

The lead chopper pilot contacted FBI Operations in Washington. A minute later, Scott Harris burst into the room and got the update from the senior watch officer on the night shift. Forty-five seconds after that, the location came through.

"Sir, you're not going to believe this."

"Come on, let's go, let's go."

"It's Greenwich Village, sir."

"What?"

"That's what the computer says—Regency Towers—penthouse suite."

"You've got to be kidding me."

"No, sir. That's what it says."

"Son of a . . ."Harris speed-dialed Special Agent Neil Watts, his Joint Task Force commander. "You getting this?"

"Just did."

"You think it's legit?"

"I don't know what to make of it."

"No chance it's a mistake?"

"I doubt it. Has anyone been there before?"

"Once. At the beginning. Looked secure so we never went back."

"Is there a security system?"

"No. We checked."

Harris didn't have time for recriminations. His mind raced through his options, and his troops were waiting for their orders.

"Just give us the word, sir."

"You got it, just as we war gamed. Nobody goes in till I give the order. Clear?"

"Clear."

"Good. Let's just hope it's real."

Two minutes later, the FBI's Hostage Rescue Team was airborne. Forty-five seconds later, so was the NYPD's SWAT Team Two. Twenty-four heavily armed men sliced through the icy-cold air as four Blackhawk helicopters banked hard to the south.

"You still got the signal?" Commander Watts asked as they approached the perimeter.

"Strong and clear. Definitely the penthouse."

"Have they made a call?"

"They're checking voice mail."

"You're serious?"

"I am."

"Guess we should've left a message."

"Very funny, sir. I think they'll get our message—loud and clear."

"What about ground units?"

"On their way, sir. We've got two unmarked bureau cars—four agents—sixty seconds out. Tactical Unit is inbound from Wall Street. ETA about two minutes. And you'll have a hundred more cops there in less than five."

"Good. Cut off the streets in a four-block radius—and no sirens."

"Don't worry. No sirens."

Watts assessed the situation. They had to be idiots to be there. Unless it was a trap. How many did they have with them? And how well armed were they?

"Watts, it's Scott Harris. How soon?"

"My guys are ready, on the perimeter. Everyone else is moving into position."

"What's the plan, Commander?"

"We can surround the place or we can storm it right away. It's your call."

"What do you recommend?" asked the FBI director.

"I don't know yet."

"Come on, Watts, give it to me. What's your gut telling you?"

Watts exhaled. He honestly didn't know. He always preferred taking his time, gaining as much intel as possible, and planning a raid in precise detail. But this was different. If they were really dealing with suicide bombers, negotiations weren't going to work. The minute the bad guys knew they were surrounded, anyone in the apartment—including the hostage, if there *was* a hostage—was as good as dead. Storming now would give Hostage Rescue Team maximum tactical surprise. But there were no guarantees.

Another radio crackled to life.

"Tactical is on the scene, sir. Permission to set up?"

"Do it—just be careful," said Watts, straining to see the building through high-powered binoculars from a half mile away—any closer and the roar of the choppers would give them away.

"Come on, Watts; give me your best call," ordered Harris.

"I don't know, sir. I . . ."

"Watts, I've got the president on the other line."

Watts couldn't see the building clearly enough. He'd be getting a live audio and video feed momentarily from agents sneaking up the stairwells.

But they had fifteen flights to climb and that still might not give him enough information. He was out of time.

"*Storm it,*" Watts said finally.

He just hoped like crazy he was right.

"Fine. Put your men on notice. I'll talk to the president."

Every minute that ticked by felt like an hour. But it also brought more data. The first audio probe agents attached to the front door indicated a television was on somewhere in the penthouse suite. No voices. No footsteps. And still no outbound calls had been made. Snipers took up positions on the roofs of four adjacent buildings as plainclothes agents began evacuating lower floors of the Regency Towers, as quickly and carefully as possible.

The president didn't agonize over the choice. If the on-scene commander wanted to go in, he wouldn't second-guess him. Everyone knew the stakes. Everyone had trained for this moment. And everyone knew the president would have to call Jon Bennett the minute the operation was over, regardless of how it turned out.

Harris relayed the message to Watts. Watts passed it on to his men. It was a go.

"Okay, guys, on my mark."

Twenty-four commandos rechecked their weapons. The Blackhawks gained altitude—a thousand feet, two thousand, three thousand, and climbing. When they reached five thousand feet, the lead pilot guided the rest of the choppers over the strike zone, then gave Watts the thumbs-up.

Watts sucked in some air and clicked on his radio. "*Fox Five, Fox Five—go, go, go!*"

The Blackhawks dived for the roof. Coming in fast and high would minimize the chance of being heard. But it was still a risk. Snipers readied their weapons. SWAT Team One waited outside the penthouse doors. Medical teams huddled in the lobby, ready to triage any casualties. Each Blackhawk now leveled off, each on its own predesignated side of the building.

Watts gave the signal. "*Fire, fire, let's go, let's go.*"

Suddenly, all power in the building went down. FBI snipers unleashed a fusillade of tear gas and flash bombs. The night erupted with explosions. Windows shattered. The penthouse filled with smoke. The Hostage Rescue Team and SWAT Team Two fast roped from the Blackhawks. They burst in through the windows. SWAT Team One blew off the front door and stormed in from the hall. Thin red beams from laser sights criss-crossed through the noxious fog as the commandos hunted their prey.

More agents rushed up the stairwells and elevators. Watts could hear the chaos from his command chopper, hovering over the roof. Harris demanded answers, but there were none to give. Not yet. The drama inside was still unfolding.

Watts ordered the searchlights on. Each chopper lit up the tower and trained its video camera on the scene. Harris could now see what was happening—outside at least—and immediately ordered the images cross-linked via secure fiber-optic trunk lines to Langley and the White House Situation Room, where the president and his senior advisors were huddled and waiting.

And then, suddenly, all went silent.

Watts waited, his heart pounding. Harris held his breath. The silence was eerie. Then a radio crackled back to life.

"Chopper One, this is Black Leader. Over."

"Black Leader, go ahead."

"It's done, sir—we've got her."

"You've got her?"

"Affirmative."

"You *sure*?"

"Yes, sir—same as her picture."

"Is she alive?"

"Yes, sir—unconscious—knocked out by the gas—but she should be okay."

"Thank God."

"Yes, sir."

"And the others? How many were there?"

A flash of static garbled the transmission.

"How's that, sir?"

"I said the others—the terrorists—how many were there?"

"None, sir."

"What's that? Say again."

"None, sir. The place is empty—it's just her."

* * *

Bennett hung up the phone.

It was three minutes after six Monday morning, Gibraltar time. He'd been up since just after four, and he still couldn't believe it.

She was safe—in stable condition at an undisclosed hospital. Under the watchful eye of a dozen FBI agents. The lead story on every TV network. Front-page news around the world again. But she was safe, and he'd just talked to her, and that was all that really mattered to him now.

Bennett turned off the lamp beside the bed and closed his eyes. The whole thing was unbelievable. There'd been no kidnapping. No Al-Nakbah terror cell. His mom hadn't even known the world was looking for her. She'd just wanted to get away for a while. Far away. Someplace where no one would call her. Where no one would bring over flowers. Where no one would stop by to "see how she was doing."

Ruth Bennett had simply wanted to be alone. Where it was snowing and the trees glittered with Christmas lights and she could lock herself away and hide. Where she could ignore the news and turn off the phones and watch *Miracle on 34th Street* and *It's a Wonderful Life* and get lost in a sweet and simple—albeit imaginary—world of good friends and happy endings. So she'd hopped on a train—she'd always hated to fly, despite her late husband's jet-setting—and headed to the Big Apple to spend a week at her son's place. She had his spare key. He was out of the country. What harm could it do?

The ATM card? Of course she'd used it. Back in Florida, she'd used most of the cash she had on her to pay for the train ticket to New York. She always paid cash. Once she got to Manhattan, she'd needed some cash to buy milk and bread and few groceries. With Jon in Israel and Germany and Washington and back to Israel, the place had been empty for a month, after all. *The cell phone?* Yes, that was her. She'd found it on Christmas Day as she did some housecleaning and tried to keep her mind off being all alone. But Jon had given her his voice-mail number and password in case she found it. So she'd taken it with her, just in case. *The two calls to her sister—why hadn't she left messages?* "Jon," she'd said, "you know me. I hate answering machines. They're so impersonal. I just figured I'd call back."

Why hadn't she kept the cell phone on all the time? Just trying to conserve the battery. She didn't have the charger. *Hadn't she gone out?* Too cold. *Hadn't she read a paper or watched the news?* Of course not. That's exactly what she was trying to avoid. *Hadn't anyone seen her?* She had no idea. "You know New Yorkers, Jon. I was one of them for twenty-five years. Nobody makes eye contact with strangers. And certainly not all bundled up in weather like that."

The whole thing was so ridiculous, so anticlimatic, thought Bennett. Yet it was also surreal. For days, the world had followed the hunt for the suicide bombers and the hunt for his mother hour by hour, hanging on every detail. But had they really overreacted? The police? The media? Had he? No, Bennett thought. No, they'd been reacting to the moment.

The country was at Threat Level Red, for crying out loud—its highest alert status—and the threats had been real. They still were. The whole world had seen the suicide bombing in Gaza live on TV. They were all watching wall-to-wall coverage of the civil war in the Holy Land. Everyone was following the hunt for suicide bombers headed to America. The gun battles on the borders. The plane forced down over Rochester. A body floating in the East River.

With all that, how could the FBI, let alone the media, *not* react? How could they ignore the serious possibility that the mother of a senior aide to the president had been kidnapped by terrorists? In the context of what they were all going through, everyone assumed the worst. It wasn't an overreaction. This was life in the age of terror.

Still, what was the world coming to? Was it now a crime to disconnect for a few days from voice mail and cell phones and pagers and BlackBerrys—or, perish the thought, not use them at all? Was it a crime to use cash, not a credit card that told every cop exactly where you were, exactly what you were buying? Was taking a week to get away and hide to rest and read and think and turn off the news and not read the paper such cause for suspicion? Was going missing from the world for a few days now a federal offense?

It felt that way. In part because evil was seeping into the windows, under the doors, through the vents. People sensed it, and they were scared. The country was on edge. Go missing for a few days and the world could change forever.

* * *

Nadir Sarukhi Hashemi pulled off I-95 North and headed for D.C.

As he came up Route 395, he hit a backup of cars trying to cross the 14th Street Bridge into the city. Every car was being stopped and searched by the police at the checkpoint a few hundred yards before the bridge, and every officer was armed with a submachine gun and a variety of instruments capable of detecting metal, radiation, biological and chemical toxins, and a full range of explosives.

As Nadir pulled up to the orange cones, he was asked for his driver's license and registration. He gave the officers all his rental papers and his fake Italian passport.

"Mario Iabello—that you?" the officer asked, staring at the photo and Nadir's face.

"Afraid it is," Nadir said with a slight Sicilian accent. "Of course, they say if you look as bad as your passport photo, you're too ill to travel."

The officer wasn't amused, especially not standing outside on a bone-chilling January afternoon. He gave the passport to another officer, who called the number in to the FBI and DHS to check against their watch lists. At the same time, he asked "Mr. Iabello" if his fellow agents could check through the contents of his car. Mr. Iabello readily agreed. He had nothing to hide. All they would find was luggage and a trunkful of software. After a few more questions, and a thorough search, the lead officer wished Mr. Iabello a pleasant stay in the nation's capital, and waved him through.

Easing the gas pedal down, he moved forward across the bridge, silently thanking Allah. He couldn't believe it. Again, he was in.

* * *

It was nearly four o'clock Monday afternoon when Bennett woke again.

He'd sleep all day if he could, and almost had. His physical and emotional systems were verging on overload again. But there was a peace process to attend to. The *New York Times* story speculating on covert peace talks had everyone rattled. The precise location of the "Mount of Olives" might still be a secret, but the code name wasn't. Nor was their mission.

The White House was getting a barrage of questions, as were the

Israeli and Palestinian governments. This was complicated by new battles in the West Bank and Gaza, the bloodiest to date. Twenty-six Palestinian gunmen had been killed overnight. Nine more on the DIA's most wanted list were taken into U.S. custody. But five American Rangers were dead and sixteen were wounded. The White House was going to have to issue a statement soon. Bennett's team had to get as much done as they could before their cover was completely blown.

Bennett took a shower, got dressed, and popped his head out the door to ask one of the guys on his security detail where McCoy, Doron, and Sa'id were. They weren't answering their phones. Even Galishnikov wasn't answering his phone.

"They're all in the dining room, sir. Been there most of the day."

"Doing what?" Bennett asked with a yawn.

"Yelling about a security fence, I guess. I don't know for sure, Mr. Bennett. I've been here standing post since eight this morning."

Bennett and his four-man detail headed down to the dining room, where he couldn't have been greeted more warmly by the two prime ministers and McCoy. Mordechai and Galishnikov were sitting in on the session as well. Yes, they'd been duking it out all day over the security fence, but they'd shifted to talking about the prospects of a Medexco deal. Now they were ready for a break and grateful Bennett's mom was safe and sound.

"This calls for a celebration," Galishnikov boomed, glad to be back with everyone after being asked to stay in the background a few days until the Doron-Sa'id relationship warmed up. "Let us all go out for some dinner."

"Always thinking with your stomach, Dmitri," quipped Sa'id. "That is what I like about you."

"That is a great idea," Dr. Mordechai added. "And I know just the place—the Top of the World restaurant, they just opened it last fall on the summit of the Rock. Great food. Incredible view. You can take the cable cars up there. And I am paying."

"Well, well, now we're talking," said Bennett, surprised by how relieved he felt to be doing anything but haggling over the peace plan tonight. "When do we leave?"

As the men chatted for a few minutes, McCoy stepped to the door to consult with Tariq, overseeing all security operations. McCoy and Tariq, in turn, huddled with the Israeli Shin Bet team there to protect Doron. It only took a few moments. The unanimous answer was no. Not tonight. It would be impossible for them to secure the route and the restaurant and the food for the two prime ministers in just a couple of hours. After all, among other things, they'd need to clear the place of all employees so no one would recognize Doron or Sa'id. Perhaps they could arrange things for the next night. But tonight was off.

McCoy relayed the news to the group. Doron and Sa'id said Tuesday night would be fine. They could yell at each other all day, then cap off the night with a lovely dinner on top of the world. Mordechai asked if it would be a problem for him to take Bennett, McCoy, and Galishnikov up there tonight, just to check things out. Tariq thought about it for a moment, consulted with the others, and agreed it would be fine. He'd just need to send a protective detail with them.

"So, Dr. Mordechai, that mean you're paying both nights?" asked Bennett.

The old man laughed. "In your dreams, Jonathan. You were almost a billionaire. Why don't you pay tonight?"

"*Nyet, nyet, nyet,*" Galishnikov cut in. "I will be a billionaire soon. The least I can do is buy dinner for a few ugly old friends, and for the lovely and beautiful Miss Erin."

They all laughed again. It was settled. Tariq said he'd have the cars ready in fifteen minutes. That was good enough for Bennett. He was ready for a night on the town. All he needed to do before dinner was stop off at a few gift shops along the way to pick up something for his mom.

★ ★ ★

"*You've got mail.*"

Mohammed Jibril was restless. He deleted most of the garbage in his in-box. It was a mishmash of different stuff from operatives and informants around the world. But none of it was what he was looking for. Just as he was about to log off, an instant message came in. It was from Harrods in London. Jibril's stomach tightened.

The gift shop in Gibraltar may have found the item you were looking for. . . .

Please IM back or call our toll-free secure number if you're interested. . . . Time sensitive . . . product may not be in stock for long.

The gift shop in Gibraltar? That was the cutout man they'd used to transmit messages to Khalid al-Rashid, the Arafat security chief who'd set the whole last week in motion. He had no idea what the guy's name was. But it didn't really matter. How would they know anything about . . .

Jibril froze.

Please remind me . . . which product are we talking about again?

He pressed *Send* and waited. A few seconds later, the reply popped up.

Hand-painted chess set for your friend . . . understand he lost his two kings . . . our supplier in Gibraltar thinks he's stumbled upon just what you wanted.

Jibril just stared at the screen.

need 100 percent confirmation . . . are you sure?

supplies limited, came the reply. *cost triple what we quoted you before. . . . must be wire transferred by day's end.*

Jibril had no problem with that. If they really had what he thought they had, he'd have paid them ten times their asking price.

have to check with my friend . . . but latest price quote shouldn't be a problem . . . but how can I know you have precisely the two kings he's looking for?

Again he hit *Send*. This time the reply took longer. Almost a minute. Jibril was dying for an answer. Should he resend his last message? Had it not gone through?

Beep.

There it was.

my supplier is sure . . . the knight just walked into his store not ten minutes ago with a queen and some pawns . . . bought a gift for his mother . . . actually paid with a credit card . . . couldn't believe it . . . will fax copy of the transaction if you'd like.

Jibril pushed away from the computer. This couldn't be accurate. Jon Bennett was on Gibraltar? With Erin McCoy and a team of bodyguards? A thousand thoughts flooded into his mind. It could be a mistake, or a gift from Allah. He had to confirm it. But how? The Libyans, perhaps. They had an operative on the Rock, some woman who ran a travel agency, if he remembered correctly.

If it was true, if Bennett was there, then Doron and Sa'id had to be there as well. But for how long? Given the leak to the *New York Times,* they could be leaving any minute. Especially if Bennett was buying gifts to take back home. If they were going to strike, they'd have to strike fast. Jibril typed in one final message. He was already taking a risk staying on-line for so long.

if we wanted to have some friends drop in and see the merchandise, could you help us?

that might be a problem. . . .

how much more of a 'problem' are we talking about?

Another delay. Jibril couldn't take it. Two minutes later, the IM came back again.

my supplier says a new price of five times our original quote would do. . . .

The middlemen on Gibraltar were greedy. But not nearly greedy enough, thought Jibril. They had a deal, he wrote back. The money would be in their account by morning. Then he logged off and got dressed. First he'd track down the deputy chief of Libyan intelligence. It was still early in Tripoli. Then he'd wake Gogolov.

44

THE VIEW WAS BETTER than Mordechai had promised.

The food was better than Galishnikov had expected. The maître d' was British. The wines were French. The food was Italian and North African. The chefs were Moroccan and Sicilian. The atmosphere was quiet and intimate. And every sixty minutes, the rotating restaurant took you on a 360-degree tour around the Med.

To the north, they could see the sandy beaches of the Spanish Costa del Sol and another storm moving their way. It was still fifty or sixty miles out. But it wouldn't bother them tonight. They opened a 1967 burgundy and Galishnikov said a toast to Ruth Bennett's health and a speedy and safe reunion with her son. Soon they were working on their salads and looking southeast toward the Er Rif Mountains of Morocco. Mordechai kept them spellbound with tales of hunting Russian and Libyan spies through the alleyways of Casablanca as a junior Mossad agent.

Neither Israeli kept kosher, so steaks and lobster tails were served all around. It was the clearest evening on the Rock in weeks, and despite the storm clouds behind them, they could still enjoy a breathtaking sunset. The conversation meandered, and after a while Bennett was looking at the sparkling lights of the city of Gibraltar, now shutting down for the night. He could see the commercial ports below them, the blinking strobe lights of the runway, and the narrow roads zigzagging up the mountain. He could see the cable-car station where they'd arrived, and silently hoped

Tariq would insist on driving them all down the Rock at the end of the night. He wasn't sure he was ready for another wind-battered adventure. He'd had enough adventures for one lifetime. But he could picture bringing his mom up here one day. Gibraltar was one place she'd always wanted to go and had never been. She'd never survive the flight. Maybe they could take a cruise.

★ ★ ★

Gogolov hated being woken up.

But he softened when he heard the news.

The "Mount of Olives" was the Rock of Gibraltar. How fitting, he thought as he cleaned his glasses and dressed for a long night. A NATO stronghold. A joint U.S.-British espionage base. Another example of failed treaties and the arrogance of Western imperialism. And a perfect target for his assassin teams, already poised to strike.

★ ★ ★

They finished their steaks and three waiters cleared the table.

Galishnikov ordered a tray of French pastries and a bottle of the best brandy in the house for his friends, a bottle of their best vodka for himself, and a pot of Turkish coffee for any weaklings among them. The bill had to be quickly approaching seven or eight hundred dollars, thought Bennett. But this Russian simply didn't care. And why should he? He was with his friends. They were all alive and in one piece. And he was about to become the richest man in Israel.

"So, Dr. Mordechai," Bennett began after everyone had been served.

"Please, Jonathan, how many times must I ask you to call me Eli? All my friends call me Eli. Why won't you?"

"Because you're practically old enough to be my grandfather."

Everyone laughed, but Bennett was ready to be serious, and Mordechai could tell. So could McCoy. The only thing Galishnikov was serious about, at the moment at least, was polishing off his bottle of Absolut.

"Okay, Eli," Bennett continued, "here's my question."

"Fire away, my boy."

"What in the world is going on?"

Mordechai was a bit taken aback by the intensity of the question. So were McCoy and Galishnikov.

"What do you mean, Jonathan?"

"I mean, what in the world is going on, Eli? Things are out of control. Kamikazes, snipers, anthrax—suicide bombers? What is this? We've got a war in Iraq, a Palestinian civil war, people trying to blow up the Temple Mount. I mean, I don't know, I just . . ."

"It's scary, isn't it?"

"Yes!I It's scary. One minute I'm working on Wall Street. The next minute I'm in the middle of something . . . I don't know what I'm in the middle of. Everyone I know is getting killed. I can't sleep. I thought I almost lost my mom . . ."

Bennett finished off his brandy and stared out the window at the lights of a jet in the distance. Galishnikov poured him another glass.

"You used to run the Mossad," said Bennett, turning back to Mordechai. "You're a pretty smart guy. So tell me—what's going on?"

* * *

Jibril couldn't believe it.

Colonel Khaddafi wasn't simply promising to help. He was dramatically upping the ante. Yes, he had an agent on Gibraltar who ran a travel agency. Yes, she would be activated immediately. But there was more that Libya could do, if she were needed. Much more.

Jibril didn't know quite what to say, except thank you. It was a generous offer, to say the least. Almost too generous. He said he'd have to discuss it with Gogolov and get back to the colonel as quickly as possible. And then he did. Gogolov, too, was stunned. This could change everything.

* * *

"Jon, do you believe in the supernatural?"

"I don't know. Why?"

"Angels, demons, Sodom and Gomorrah?"

"Eli, really, I don't know what you're talking about."

The old man was always full of surprises, but Bennett respected his experience and his wisdom.

"Sure you do. I am asking if you believe that there is an unseen battle going on all around us—a cosmic showdown between good and evil. That there is an all-knowing, all-powerful force in the universe that can enter time and space, that can alter the course of human history, that can destroy the living and raise the dead."

"You're asking if I believe in God?"

"No, no. Not just God. A God who is at war with evil. A God with a plan and a purpose. A God who has the awesome, fearsome power to achieve that plan and accomplish that purpose."

Bennett looked at McCoy, then to Galishnikov. He wasn't sure where this was going. "I don't know, Dr. Mordechai. I mean, I work at the White House, not the Vatican. The whole God thing is a little above my pay grade."

Mordechai said nothing. Neither did McCoy or Galishnikov. It was as though all the molecules in the room were suddenly rearranged. He didn't know why, or how, but Bennett suddenly felt embarrassed. He could feel the blood rising behind his neck and ears. He just stared into Mordechai's eyes for what seemed like an eternity. They were somber and sober and serious—and they weren't backing down.

"I don't know," Bennett said finally, quietly. "I don't know what I believe."

"Then I suggest you figure it out—quickly."

"Why?"

Dr. Mordechai let the question hang in the air for a moment. "Because that is the answer to your question."

"I don't understand."

"Jonathan, I have spent my whole life lurking in the shadows, cultivating sources, paying off informants, desperately hoping I would find my enemies before they found me. Why? Because I wanted someone to put a bullet in my head? No. Because knowledge is power. Because what you don't know can kill you. Because the more you know about your enemy, the more likely you are to outlive him."

The old man took out his pipe and a package of tobacco. "When the FBI wants to know what the mob is up to, what do they do? They send in a Donnie Brasco, right? When the KGB—or now the FSB—wants to know what the CIA or FBI is up to, what do they do? They recruit an Aldrich

Ames or a Robert Hanssen, right? On Wall Street they call it insider trading. It is illegal. In the intelligence business, it is a matter of life and death. But in the nineties, the CIA stopped paying off 'unsavory characters' as sources. Why? It is a long story. The point is, America went dark. You stopped being able to see inside the mind of evil. You let evil go unchecked. And you paid a terrible price. You got September eleventh. And you got Saddam Hussein without any weapons inspectors. Now, which is really worse? Paying off a greedy Iraqi scientist to tell you how and where he is helping Saddam build the bomb, or having to bomb Baghdad and kill a whole lot of people?"

No one said a word. Morechai lit a match and took a few puffs, letting the smoke gently curl upward toward the ceiling fan above them. "My business is all about sources. So is yours. Who you know and what they know. Maybe you cannot stand your sources. Maybe you wish they would all keel over and die. You know what? It does not matter. It does not matter what we think about a source. The only thing that matters is whether that source is credible, whether he or she is telling you the truth, even if the truth is ugly, even if the truth does not make sense. Right?"

Bennett nodded.

"Good. Now I am going to tell you what you want to know. I am going to tell you why all hell is breaking loose. But I am going to cite you a source you may not like. That is not the point. The point is, does the information make sense? Is it credible? Is it true? If it is not, don't worry about it. Blow it off and move on. But if it is, then you have a decision to make: what are you going to do about it, and how long are you going to wait?"

* * *

Nadir pulled up in front of the Willard InterContinental.

He waited for one of the valets to park his car and another to help him with his suitcase, briefcase, and laptop. He tipped them both generously, then went inside to check in. In a few minutes, he'd fire off an e-mail to his contact. By tomorrow morning, he'd have exactly what he needed. Tonight he'd go for a long walk and get the lay of the land.

"Will you be paying by credit card?" the clerk asked.

"Yes, please," he said, pulling out an American Express Gold Card.

It was all Nadir could do to suppress a smile. *Put it all on the card,* he thought. *He'd never be around to pay it anyway.*

★ ★ ★

"Fair enough," said Bennett. "So what's the answer?"

Mordechai took a sip of brandy, stared at his pipe for a moment, the sweet smoke filling the air, then looked back at Bennett and continued. "We are not living in normal times, Jonathan. We are now living in what the Hebrew prophets called the last days."

"What does that mean?"

"I will give you an example. Remember the story of the Dead Sea Scrolls?"

"No."

"Erin?"

"The little boy throws a few rocks in some caves, looking for his sheep, and hears a bunch of pottery break. Turns out the caves are the hiding place for hundreds of ancient biblical scrolls."

"Exactly. And part of those scrolls contained the book of Isaiah, almost three thousand years old, written exactly like what is in the Bible today."

"Okay, I'm with you."

"So here is what Isaiah said in chapter 2," Mordechai continued, from memory. " 'In the last days the mountain of the Lord's temple will be established as chief among the mountains; it will be raised above the hills, and all nations will stream to it.'"

"Meaning what?"

"Meaning three thousand years ago, Isaiah said the Temple would be rebuilt in the last days. Daniel said the same thing. So did Ezekiel. In chapter 37 he predicts the rebirth of the modern State of Israel after centuries of neglect. In chapters 38 and 39 he references peace and prosperity in the land of Israel, as well as a bunch of other events I will not go into now. In chapter 40 onward, he talks in great detail about the Temple yet to come."

"Okay, okay," said Bennett. "I got it. I got it. But there is no Temple. Are you saying you support what the Temple Mount Battalion was trying to do?"

"No, of course not. What those guys were trying to do was terrorism, pure and simple. Nobody should try to force the hand of God. I am just saying there are a whole lot of people out there—Christians and Jews alike—who believe we have entered some new phase of history, and the Temple is coming. And this is why."

Bennett took a deep breath and tried to process that. "Fair enough. Go on."

"The same thing's true about Babylon. Is it a wealthy, powerful city right now? No. But watch out. The prophets say Babylon will rise from the ashes. 'O great city, O Babylon, city of power,' says the book of Revelation. Babylon will have 'riches and splendor' and 'great wealth' and 'the merchants of the earth' will grow 'rich from her excessive luxuries.' But Babylon will also become 'a home for demons and a haunt for every evil spirit' and 'she will be consumed by fire, for mighty is the Lord God who judges her.' Jeremiah says the same thing in chapter 51: 'The Lord will carry out His purpose, His decree against the people of Babylon. You who live by many waters and are rich in treasures, your end has come. . . . Before your eyes I will repay Babylon and all who live in Babylonia for all the wrong they have done in Zion.' "

Bennett shifted in his seat and leaned across the table toward Mordechai. "Fine—Babylon, the Temple, that's all well and good. But none of that proves we're in the last days right now. That's what I want to know. What's going on *right now*?"

45

★ ★
★

"REMEMBER THE BUSH administration's Road Map to peace?"

Mordechai put down his pipe.

"Of course," said Bennett.

"The Scriptures lay out a road map to the last days, complete with signs that will tell us when we get there."

"A road map, huh?"

"That is right."

"Okay, I'll bite. What are the signs?"

"First, the world will hear of 'wars and rumors of wars.' We will see 'wars and revolutions.' 'Nation will rise against nation, and kingdom against kingdom.' We will see 'great earthquakes' and 'famines and pestilences in various places.' Persecution will be rampant as the 'gospel of the kingdom' is 'preached in the whole world.' At the same time, 'many false prophets will appear and deceive many people.' There will be all kinds of strange signs in the skies. 'Men will faint from terror, apprehensive of what is coming on the world.' "

"Okay, go on."

"Israel—described throughout the Jewish Scriptures as the fig tree— will be restored and in full bloom. 'Jerusalem will be trampled on by the Gentiles until the times of the Gentiles are fulfilled'—that is, until the last days when the Jews retake control of the Holy City, and Jews from all over the world start streaming back to their homeland. And 'when you see these things happening,' the Bible says, 'you know that the kingdom of God is near'—even 'right at the door.' "

"Really," said Bennett, intrigued, but not quite sure what to say. "Really."

"And you think we're passing all those road signs?"

"Don't you?"

Bennett laughed. "I don't know. I didn't even know they existed until two seconds ago."

"Well, think about it, Jonathan—'wars and revolutions' and 'kingdom rising against kingdom.' Just look at the twentieth century."

"Yeah, but, Eli, come on, man has always had wars and revolutions."

"World War I, the war to end all wars? The Russian Revolution. World War II. Hiroshima and Nagasaki. Six million butchered by Hitler, and that is just counting the Jews. The rise of the Evil Empire. Twenty million slaughtered by Stalin alone. Half the world enslaved by Communism. Korea. Vietnam. Pol Pot. All the Middle East wars. China and India. India and Pakistan. The rise of nationalism. Tribal warfare in Africa. I could go on and on and so could you. Of course there have been wars and revolutions throughout time. But never anything on the scale we saw in the twentieth century."

Bennett considered that for a moment, but wasn't ready to concede the point. "And what was another one, earthquakes? You can't just say because we've had a few huge quakes in the last few weeks that we're living the 'last days.' "

"Fine. Do the research."

"What do you mean?"

"I mean ask the U.S. Geological Service. They say there are five hundred thousand earthquakes every single year. A hundred thousand that can be felt. A thousand that do serious damage. At least a hundred registering 7.0 or higher on the Richter scale. That is a serious earthquake almost every four days. And the more urbanization occurs, the more damage a quake can do, the more people a quake can kill, the more costly these earthquakes are. In 1990, almost forty thousand people died in a quake in Iran. In '76, a quarter of a million people died during a massive quake in China. The '94 earthquake in Northridge, California, was the most expensive in American history so far. Caused forty billion dollars in damage. Got the picture?"

"I guess so."

"You could say the same thing about 'famine and pestilence.' Just look at Africa. Ethiopia, Somalia—hundreds of thousands of people died of starvation. And disease? We have ten million AIDS orphans in Africa alone, and the numbers are climbing every day. Are we supposed to do nothing? Are we supposed to say, 'Oh well, it's just a sign of the End Times' ?"

"No. Of course not."

"No. Of course not. We gave to help people who are dying, suffering, what have you. But my point is this: number one, the *magnitude* of these problems, and number two, the *convergence* of all these signs and events in the same century and right up to the present moment—that gives us all the evidence we need. That, and the fact that for the first time in over two thousand years Israel is suddenly a country again, and Jerusalem is suddenly under Jewish control, just as predicted. That is what clinched it for me."

Bennett noticed that Galishnikov had suddenly stopped drinking, though his bottle was still half full.

"Maybe it was 1948," Mordechai continued. "Maybe it was '67. I don't know. At some point some kind of cosmic clock began ticking. A prophetic countdown is under way, Jonathan, and for better or worse, we are right in the middle of it."

"What does that mean for our peace plan, you know, a few years down the road?"

"Believe me, Jonathan, you don't want to know."

* * *

MacPherson stepped into the Situation Room.

He was on crutches now, aided by Special Agent Jackie Sanchez. It was the first time out of his wheelchair since the attempt on his life in Denver some five weeks ago, and he was still a bit shaky. But it was progress, and every bit counted.

The NSC principals brought with them a lengthy agenda, including updates on developments in Iraq and Operation Palestinian Freedom. The good news: they'd retaken the PLC headquarters and broken through to the PLC legislators holed up in the communications center, most of whom were fine, though suffering from malnutrition and minor dehydration. The bad news: there was still a suicide bomber on the loose.

The president demanded an update.

"Sir, we've got the list of legal border entries down to 2,903 people," said DHS Secretary Lee James. "Of these, we've whittled the list down to 169 people that our investigators are taking another look at."

"Based on what?"

"A whole range of reasons, sir. All of them seem to have their papers in order. We're just double-checking their flight and hotel information, rental car records, the businesses they work for—that kind of thing."

"You got all the manpower you need?"

"We've set up a Joint Task Force Command Center at the NAC. We've got almost fifty investigators in there right now. They're in constant contact with all the field people. I'm pretty sure we'll be through all the names by noon tomorrow."

MacPherson clenched his fists under the table. It was taking too long.

☆ ☆ ☆

It was late and the foursome needed to get back.

Galishnikov reviewed the bill. Bennett's head was swimming.

"Dr. Mordechai—I mean, Eli," McCoy began. "I really appreciate all you said tonight. I just have a quick question before we go."

"Sure, what is it?"

"Well, weren't some of the verses you were citing from the New Testament?"

Galishnikov's head popped up. So did Bennett's.

"What?" the Russian asked. "Is that true?" He gave the headwaiter his credit card and turned back to the group.

"Most of it was from the Jewish Scriptures," said Mordechai. "But yes, it was Jesus who laid out the 'road map,' the signs of the last days, in the Gospels."

"Jesus?" Galishnikov blurted out. "But you're Jewish, for crying out loud."

"So was Jesus," said Mordechai, now cleaning out his pipe.

"But I don't get it," said Bennett, genuinely curious. "What's the former head of the Israeli Mossad doing going around quoting Jesus?"

Mordechai looked around at the group. "It is all about sources, my friends. And I told you already, there is only one question that counts: is the source telling the truth? If he is not, cut him loose. But if he is, you had better hold on tight and listen good, because the stuff he gives you could save your life."

* * *

Jibril sent instructions to his men in the field.

They had only a few hours to make final preparations. Later that day, the first team would take off from the island of Malta, in the middle of the Mediterranean, not far from Libya. They'd fly a westerly course in a Learjet owned by a Lebanese shipping magnate. The second team would leave from Cairo, flying northwest on a Citation occasionally leased by the Syrian oil minister when he vacationed in North Africa with his mistress. The third team would use speedboats rented in the Spanish enclave of Ceuta on the coast of Morocco. The fourth team would take off from Paris in a Gulfstream V, newly purchased by a Saudi sheikh. Their flight plan would take them to Málaga, on the southern coast of Spain. They'd refuel there, supposedly drop off a few corporate clients, then head to Gibraltar for a few days of rest and relaxation.

That was the cover story, anyway. Bland and routine.

* * *

Bennett stared into the darkness.

It was almost two in the morning on Tuesday. His team had been back from dinner for almost four hours, and he still couldn't sleep. The pains in his stomach weren't subsiding. He got up, stumbled into the bathroom, and took another a handful of ibuprofen and antacids. Then he splashed some water on his face and climbed back into bed.

A new stack of faxes from the White House and directives from the NSC and State Department were waiting for him. But he had no interest in reading them. All he could think about was the conversation with Mordechai.

He kept chewing it over piece by piece. The guy certainly had a lot of secrets. His years in the Mossad. The house in Jerusalem. One of the most highly respected men in Israel, yet a covert Christian. But was he right? He'd been right about a lot. He did his homework, and there was no question something was different about him. It wasn't just his knack for knowing things nobody else seemed to, or his gentle, relaxed manner—a bit counterintuitive for a man who had killed more people than Bennett could count. There was something else.

Bennett couldn't quite put his finger on it, but it intrigued him. McCoy had it too. So did the president. It was a sense of peace, a sense of purpose that he didn't have. These people weren't afraid. They weren't scared of the future. They chose life, but they weren't scared of death. They seemed to know exactly where they were going and who they were going to see when they got there. And the more Bennett spent time with them, the more he thought they just might be right.

Mordechai certainly wasn't the kind of person to base his faith on some slick-talking television evangelist or touchy-feely emotional experience. He knew all the arguments for and against, and he'd come out for.

"I just started studying the source documents," Mordechai told the three of them just before they left the restaurant. "I started reading the Jewish prophets to see what they said to look for in the Messiah. I found out that Micah said the Messiah would be born in Bethlehem. Honestly, I had never known that. Isaiah said the Messiah would be born of a virgin, and live in Galilee. I had never read that before."

Neither had Bennett. His parents hadn't even owned a Bible when he was growing up. And they'd been in Moscow. It wasn't like he was going to stumble onto one.

"Daniel," Mordechai went on, "said after the Messiah was 'cut off,' Jerusalem and the Jewish Temple would be destroyed by an occupying power. David said 'evil men' would kill the Messiah in a merciless fashion, and that his hands and feet would be 'pierced.' Isaiah said the Messiah would be 'pierced for our transgressions' and 'crushed for our iniquities.' He said 'the punishment that brought us peace was upon him, and by his wounds we are healed.' He also said the Messiah couldn't be held down by the grave but would live again and 'prolong his days.' I could go on and on. But look, I am no rocket scientist. I just looked at the picture the prophets were painting, and I said, who does that look like?"

Then Mordechai said something Bennett couldn't shake. "One day I was reading a parable that Jesus told His disciples. He said the kingdom of God is a like a treasure hidden in a field. When a man found it, he hid it again, and then in his joy went and sold all he had and bought that field.

And it hit me, Jonathan. I was that man. I knew the truth. I had found buried treasure. But what was I going to do about it? Walk away? Ignore it? Or follow Christ whatever the cost?"

Bennett kept thinking about that. He had a million questions. He wanted to research everything Mordechai had said in great detail, and in time he would. But the more he thought about it, the more he realized he didn't need anything else to make a decision. He was ready.

He slipped out of bed and got down on his knees. He didn't know why exactly. It just seemed humble, reverent—not qualities with which he most identified, but maybe the right thing to do. And there in the darkness he cut a deal with God. He'd believe that Jesus died on the cross and rose from the dead. He'd follow Him with everything he had. He just wanted to know two things: that he was forgiven for every stupid thing he'd ever said or done, and that he was going to heaven if he never lived to see another day.

There was no flash of lightning. No angels singing hallelujahs. But in his heart Bennett knew the deal was done. He had his buried treasure. And he could sleep.

46
★ ★
★

GOGOLOV'S FORCES were now on the move.

It was Tuesday, January 4, and the first to make contact was the gift shop on Gibraltar. It was just after five in the morning there, and something was afoot.

Nothing was being reported on local radio or TV or in the newspapers. But police activity was definitely increasing. A few extra officers at the airport. A few more undercover cops patrolling the summit. And something was stirring at Devil's Tower Camp. Lights had been on all night. Vehicles were moving in and out.

Jibril was concerned. DTC was the base camp for the Royal Gibraltar Regiment, the British army forces assigned to maintain security on the Rock, as well as provide a daily ceremonial guard outside the governor's residence. Together with a squadron of Royal Marines, the regiment's three infantry rifle companies were an impressive defensive shield. So far as Jibril knew, no exercises were planned so early in the New Year. But why all the commotion? On the plus side, "Gift Shop" had learned that a party of four had dined at the Top of the World the night before, spending eight hundred dollars. The name on the credit card: Dmitri Galishnikov—Ibrahim Sa'id's Israeli partner.

The next contact came at 6:00 a.m., Gibraltar time. The Libyan travel agent had a lead. She'd just gotten into the office and found a message on her answering machine from four very irate Brits on holiday. Their dinner reservations for Tuesday night at the Top of the World restaurant had suddenly been canceled with no explanation. They were told the restaurant would simply be closed all day, with apologies. They could come back the next night at a discount.

Jibril briefed Gogolov. It wasn't much to go on. But it might have to do. One possibility was that Doron and Sa'id were heading up to the Top of the World for dinner that night, and the activity they were picking up was preparations for their first night out of the "caves." Another possibility was that Doron and Sa'id were going to fly out of the Gibraltar airport that night, and security teams were simply sealing the high ground to prevent Stinger missile attacks from the summit. Still another possibility was that none of this had to do with anything and it was all just wishful thinking.

Gogolov didn't hesitate. They were never going to get perfect intelligence. This was a circumstantial case, at best. But it was pretty good. This was it. He could feel the adrenaline surge through his body like a narcotic. It was D-day—again.

* * *

Bennett and McCoy waited together in the dining room.

It was now just before 8:00 a.m. in Gibraltar. Doron and Sa'id would be down for breakfast in a few minutes. A long day of haggling over security fences was ahead. To be or not to be; that was the question. McCoy was dreading it. Bennett, on the other hand, seemed in unusually good spirits, chatting up a storm about how the Turks had built a fence along the Green Line in Cyprus in 1974 after the last major war with the Greeks. It seemed to have worked.

"Maybe we should be reconsidering our position," said Bennett, with a bit too much enthusiasm for so early in the morning. "The Israelis have a fence around the Gaza Strip already. Do you realize not a single suicide bomber has ever come into Israel from Gaza since there's been a fence? They've all come from the West Bank. Maybe there's something to that."

McCoy just looked at him. "What's with you?" she asked between yawns.

"What do you mean? Nothing—why?"

"I don't know. You just seem different. Chipperer."

" 'Chipperer'?" Bennett teased. "You're just making up words now?"

"Hey, give me a break. I'm exhausted. All those faxes and memos. Good grief. I didn't get to bed till four."

"Ouch."

"What about you?"

"Slept like a baby."

"Woke up every few hours and cried, huh?"

Bennett laughed, then got up and went over to the buffet table. "No, I actually feel pretty good. Hey, how about some coffee?"

McCoy looked at him quizzically. "You sure you're all right?"

Jon Bennett had never offered to make *her* coffee.

⭐ ⭐ ⭐

The weather was brutal as the Citation lifted off from Cairo.

But they'd hit clear skies soon enough. The team headed south for a while, then banked westward and climbed to thirty thousand feet. The pilot and copilot still weren't exactly sure how their flight plan had been cleared to cross Libyan airspace, but they weren't asking any questions. Their mission was to cross the Sahara, hit the Atlantic, then loop around and come back through the Strait of Gibraltar. Barring anything unforeseen, they would easily reach their target by 5:00 p.m.— just on time.

⭐ ⭐ ⭐

One by one, the speedboats left Ceuta.

Not together, of course, nor in the same direction. They left casually—every hour or so, in order to keep anyone from getting suspicious. Not many boats were heading out into such choppy waters. The winds were picking up, and the sky in the east looked particularly nasty. But the Al-Nakbah teams weren't completely alone, to their relief. Ferries to and from Algeciras and Tangier continued to run, and there were always a smattering of fishing trawlers willing to head out in any weather.

Each driver maintained strict radio silence. They were right under the shadow of the NSA's Echelon system, after all. But none of them would need a radio today. Everyone knew what the signal was. When it happened, it'd be impossible to miss.

* * *

The morning's negotiations didn't make much progress.

But Bennett wasn't discouraged. At least they were talking.

The group took an hour-long break at eleven to allow both sides to touch base with their advisors back home, then gathered again for a working lunch. It would be a short workday, he told them. They'd be done by three that afternoon and have ninety minutes or so to themselves before they boarded the motorcade to the summit. Dinner was set for five. The storm wasn't expected to hit until eightish. But they should be back by then.

"Everything all set?" Bennett whispered to McCoy as they sat down for lunch.

"Yeah, just talked to Tariq," she said. "The advance team has been there all morning. Everything looks good."

"Great. The Brits up to speed?"

"They know a few American VIPs are going up there tonight. They don't know who. But yes, they're being very helpful."

"Does the Gibraltar governor even know we're here?"

"I doubt it—not unless Downing Street told him. We certainly haven't."

"Fair enough. What's for dinner?"

"I don't know. It's a surprise."

* * *

A G5 took off from Charles de Gaulle.

It cleared the outskirts of the sprawling city, then banked southeast toward the French Alps. Once at their cruising altitude they'd hit the gas and raced for Málaga, Spain. They knew they were heading into rough weather, but they were ready for more than a little rain. Their tanks were topped off with fuel and their fuselage was packed with explosives.

* * *

A Learjet lifted off from Malta.

The team was excited. They'd been training for months and they'd finally been green-lighted for a mission. The pilots, on the other hand, were anxious. They were flying under instrument flight rules and under tremendous pressure to get into position on time. There was no way they were going to be able to approach Gibraltar directly.

A massive storm was dead ahead and could hit the Rock by nightfall. Winter storms weren't unusual, but the violence and intensity of the storm they saw building on their radar unnerved them. Eight minutes off the island, they refiled their flight plan. They'd try to go south and hug the coast of North Africa. If they were lucky, they could outflank the storm, bank right, and approach via Algeciras. They just hoped Jibril knew what he was doing. They were all willing to die. They just wanted to take someone with them.

★ ★ ★

Hours passed.

It was now 10:32 a.m. in D.C.—4:32 p.m. in Gibraltar. The holidays were over. The temperatures were beginning to climb back toward freezing, and people in Washington were cautiously going back to work and school. The nation was still at Threat Level Red and security was tight. Checkpoints were still up on all roads and bridges leading into the capital. Avenger antiaircraft missile batteries still surrounded the Pentagon. Police helicopters still patrolled the skies while F-16s roared overhead.

All morning long, the phones in the Executive Office of the president had been ringing off the hook, and now a busy day was about to get busier. Muriel Clarke, the president's executive assistant, checked her caller ID. It was Homeland Security Director Lee James's AA on line 5.

"Hey, Margie, good morning—missed you last night."

"No, Muriel, it's Lee. Where's the president?"

"Oh, sorry 'bout that—uh, he's in the Oval with the economic team."

"I need to talk to him."

"You're coming over in a little while, aren't you?"

"No, you don't understand—I need to talk to him *now*."

★ ★ ★

The day had gone too fast for Bennett.

It hadn't gone fast enough for McCoy. She was looking forward to dinner with Doron and Sa'id and glad Mordechai and Galishnikov had been invited along. But she was tired. The past few weeks were taking their toll, and she was glad they'd be back by eight—eight-thirty at the latest. Safe inside a mountain. Protected from the storms. Nothing else to do but lock her door and take a nice, long, hot bath.

The phone beside her bed rang. It was Bennett. It was time.

★ ★ ★

The president took the call.

"Lee, what have you got?"

"Italian passport—name's Mario Iabello. Says he works for Microsoft as a software salesman out of Rome. Problem is, Microsoft has never heard of the guy. And the passport turns out to be a fake."

"All right. So you got him?"

"Not quite."

"What do you mean?"

"He passed through Tijuana last week, right before we shut down the border."

"Okay. So where is he now?"

"He's in Washington."

"Microsoft Washington?"

"No—here—*our* Washington. The Metro Police cleared him across the 14th Street Bridge yesterday afternoon."

"I can't believe that. He's here?"

"Somewhere."

"How could he have gotten in with explosives or weapons?"

"We don't think he could have. Best guess—he's got a sleeper here in the city with pre-positioned weapons, possibly C4."

"What are you thinking? Car bomb?"

"I don't know. He rented a car in Mexico City, then switched it in San Diego. One of my guys is talking to the rental agency right now."

"Do we have a license plate?"

"We do. D.C. police took it down last night—routine procedure."

"What about a photo?"

"Yes, we've got the one on the passport."

"Is this guy in our system?"

"No—not in ours, not in the FBI database, Secret Service, or the CIA.

We have no idea who he is. But, Mr. President, right now he's our prime suspect."

"And he's here."

"Yes, sir. The Joint Task Force is putting everyone on alert—all federal law enforcement, obviously, plus the Metro Police, Park Police, Capitol Hill Police—you name it. With your permission, we'd like to give this guy's name and photo to the media immediately. It'll raise the panic level, sir, but getting the public on the lookout for this guy could make all the difference."

"Do it."

"We also need to shut down the city—airports, train stations, buses, bridges—no one in or out. Lock down the schools. And we propose assigning police units to every school and every government building."

"Lee, do what you have to do—*just get this guy.*"

* * *

News Channel 4 broke the story first.

The local NBC affiliate cut into the expanded hour of *Today* with a four-color photo of "Mario Iabello" and the chilling news. According to the Department of Homeland Security, Mr. Iabello was now wanted in connection with multiple violations of immigration law, should be considered armed and very dangerous, and was likely to be in Washington, D.C., at that very moment.

* * *

"Mr. President, it's Bud Norris at Secret Service."

"Go ahead, Bud. I've got you on speakerphone."

MacPherson huddled in the Situation Room with Bob Corsetti, Marsha Kirkpatrick, and the NSC's top counterterrorism specialists. All operations in the White House were being shut down, and the grounds were swarming with heavily armed agents on high alert.

"Mr. President, I can report that Checkmate is safe. He's currently airborne, and en route to Location Six. Megaphone is at the Capitol. He's being taken to a secure underground facility. All other protectees are in the process of being taken to secure facilities as well. The Capitol's shut down and being reinforced with extra security even as we speak."

"Good, thanks—Lee, are you there?"

"Yes, sir, I'm here."

"And Scott Harris—you on the line too?"

"Yes, Mr. President, I am."

"Good—I'm told we'll have the videoconference system back up in a moment. But, Lee, let's start with you. What've you got?"

"Mr. President, we've just talked to the agency that rented Iabello's car."

"And?"

"All their cars have antitheft devices installed at the factory. We've got the frequency and the tracking codes, and they're helping us to hunt it down right now."

"What do you mean—LoJack, that kind of thing?"

"Exactly, sir—a low-frequency homing device. We should have it in the next few—"

The secretary's voice cut off.

"Lee, you still with us?" asked MacPherson. "This thing still work?"

"Yes, Mr. President, I'm still here—someone's bringing me the location right now. Hold on."

You could hear a pin drop in the Situation Room. Nobody said a word, though members of the VP's national security staff were now slipping in as well. The TV sets lining the walls were all on mute. But every picture was the same—Mario Iabello—the suicide bomber who got away.

"Come on, come on," said the president, barely under his breath.

Suddenly the secretary was back on the line. "We've got it, Mr. President—the car is at the Willard."

"But . . . that's across the street."

47

★ ★
★

WITHIN MINUTES, the hotel was surrounded.

News helicopters weren't flying. All non–law enforcement aircraft over D.C., Virginia, and Maryland were grounded instantly. But this was Washington. News cameras were everywhere. So were satellite trucks. In their homes and offices across the country, Americans watched the unfolding drama in horror. Sirens filled the air. Secret Service SWAT teams took the lead. They were, after all, based out of the Treasury Building not fifty yards from the Willard's front door. FBI Critical Response Units poured in as well, as did agents and bomb-squad technicians from at least six different agencies.

★   ★   ★

Marcus Jackson's wireless phone began beeping.

Jackson cursed under his breath. He was sitting alone in the Starbucks around the corner from the Old Executive Office Building. Hard at work on his laptop, sipping a latte and trying to get a little work done, it was tough enough to concentrate with all the sirens outside. Something big was going down. But he was a political reporter. Let someone else chase ambulances. He reached into his briefcase, grabbed his phone, and turned it off. Sure enough, it was the assignment desk in New York.

Get a life, boys. The Times *has other reporters. Call someone else.*

The front door jingled. Jackson looked up and smiled. The man in a bulky green winter parka didn't smile back. He just glanced around the nearly empty store and left. Jackson shook his head and went back to the story on his laptop.

★　★　★

The Willard didn't have aboveground parking.

So close to the White House and major landmarks, there simply wasn't room. All vehicles receiving valet parking were kept underground. This posed additional dangers. If they sent a bomb-squad unit in to find the car, Iabello could be waiting—in the garage or nearby. He could detonate the bomb with a remote switch and potentially bring half the block down with him. But they didn't have much choice. Finding the car and defusing the bomb in time might be their only option. If they were lucky, they'd be able to storm Iabello's room and catch him by surprise. But maybe he was watching the news.

Maybe he wasn't in the room at all.

★　★　★

Now his pager began going off.

Jackson couldn't believe it. He rolled his eyes and grabbed the little black box off his belt. He checked the number—his editor again—911. He hit the button on the top and again there was quiet. No peace, but at least a little quiet. Jackson scooped his phone out of his bag and powered it up. It beeped again. Six messages. Already? He'd had it off for only a few minutes. He hit speed-dial two and got his editor.

"Jackson, where have you been?"

"I'm getting some coffee, working on a story."

"Forget the story—haven't you heard what's going on?"

"No, what?"

"The feds are tracking down a suicide bomber in D.C."

"What?"

"I've been trying to call you. Why aren't you at the White House?"

"I'm at Starbucks."

"Well, get over there. Murray's about to brief and we've got no one on point."

"Isn't Eicher back?"

"No. He's in St. Louis for the Senate race."

"Fine," said Jackson, shutting down his computer and packing up his stuff. "What have you got? What do we know already?"

"You on your wireless phone?"

"Of course."

"Good—get moving. I'll e-mail you the FBI release and this guy's mug."

"Fair enough."

"And Jackson . . ."

"Yeah, boss?"

"Watch your back."

★   ★   ★

Tariq and his advance team triple-checked every detail.

The Top of the World was cleared of all employees so no one could be around to identify the two prime ministers. Every square inch was swept for explosives, weapons, and bugs. The kitchens were being scrubbed down. Special food was brought in. All systems looked good. All but the weather. The storm was moving in a little too fast. It wasn't cause for cancelation, just concern.

Tariq radioed back to the security detail inside the Mount of Olives. There'd be no cable-car ride tonight. They should take the principals up the service road. The decoy motorcade should come up first, arriving at 4:50 p.m.

The real "package" should hang back a bit, arriving around 5:15 p.m. instead.

★   ★   ★

"Mr. President, my guys are in—we got the car."

It was Bud Norris in the Secret Service Op Center. He sounded breathless.

"And?"

"Nothing—no bomb, no weapons, nothing."

"What about *him*?"

"SWAT Team Three just stormed the room. Nothing, just a suitcase and some personal effects. Iabello wasn't there."

"Then where is he?"

"We don't know, sir."

"Then rip that place apart until you find him—you hear me?"

* * *

Beep, beep, beep.

It was Jackson's phone. He had mail.

He raced across 17th Street and flashed his White House press pass to a team of Secret Service SWAT members taking up positions on the corner. They went through Jackson's bag and searched him with a handheld metal detector and a handheld explosives detector. Then a uniformed officer personally escorted Jackson to the northwest gate to be searched all over again.

As he waited in line behind three other reporters, Jackson checked the message from his editor. With a few clicks of his phone, he opened the e-mail and photo and his eyes went wide.

Jackson's hands began to shake.

Four agents turned toward him.

He'd just seen this guy. Mario Iabello. Five minutes ago, maybe ten. This was the guy—the guy in the parka who had just done the U-turn out of the Starbucks.

* * *

"You've got mail."

Jibril's stomach tightened. His eyes immediately shifted from the CNN coverage of the crisis in Washington to the laptop beside him.

* * *

"Mr. President."

It was Secretary James. The videoconference system was up again.

"I'm here—what've you got?"

"Marcus Jackson just told one of our agents he thinks he saw this guy, Iabello."

"Where?"

"At the Starbucks near the OEOB."

"When?"

"Ten minutes—maybe a little more."

"And he's sure?"

"Sure enough—we're deploying units right now."

"Are the choppers up?"

"They are—we're flooding the zone in a ten-block radius in every direction."

"He could be anywhere."

"That's true, Mr. President. He could be anywhere."

But Norris suddenly cut in from the Secret Service Op Center. "Mr. President?"

"Yes, Bud."

"This guy's too close—a block from the White House, maybe less. We need to move you downstairs—*now*."

* * *

Jibril checked the message.

It was Gift Shop on Gibraltar. He was on the roof of his building with binoculars, pretending to fix his television antenna. He could see a motorcade heading up the Rock to the Top of the World restaurant—two sedans up front, followed by two minivans. That was it. That was them. It was beginning to drizzle, the note added. Visibility was worsening. But they'd be there in less than ten minutes.

* * *

The Viper wasn't used to the cold.

He'd grown up in Baghdad and the deserts surrounding it. He was used to 120 in the shade. Not the winter wonderland of Washington, D.C. But he had the parka and he drew the hood tightly around his face. Then he plunged his hands back into the pockets, grabbed the ignition switch again, and picked up the pace.

* * *

Jibril looked over at Gogolov and nodded.

Gogolov nodded back. Jibril picked up the satellite phone and began calling each pilot. Yes, the NSA would pick up the calls. But it didn't matter. The whole thing would be over in an hour. He and Gogolov would be on a plane out of Iran in less than five hours.

* * *

He crossed the street and began moving toward the hill.

Toward the ring of American flags, snapping smartly in the bitter January winds. There were a lot of cops, but most of them were on the far side of the Washington Monument. They were huddled around the row of yellow school buses parked near the souvenir stand and the bathrooms, feverishly herding children out of the monument's elevators and back onto the buses. But he could make it. He couldn't run. He couldn't draw attention to himself. But if he kept moving briskly, he could make it.

* * *

The second motorcade began to assemble at the entrance of the cave.

Six Gold members of SEAL Team Eight piled into the lead minivan. Doron and three Shin Bet agents climbed into the back of the first Chevy Tahoe, while two SEALs up front prepared to drive and monitor communications. Sa'id and a team of five SEALs climbed into the second Tahoe, while Bennett, McCoy, Galishnikov, and Mordechai squeezed into the back of a red VW Bug.

"Sorry, Mr. Bennett," said the NSA's chief of security. "It's all we've got left. We're not used to so much company."

Normally, Bennett would have been ticked off. But not today. Nothing could bother him today. The security chief thanked him for his patience and wired him up with a radio earpiece and wrist microphone for the drive up.

"Bug One ready to bug out," Bennett joked. "Let's get this show on the road."

* * *

He was almost there.

He began climbing the hill. He pulled back his hood for a few moments to get a better view. He'd never seen the Washington Monument before. Just in pictures. It was huge. It was beautiful.

He could feel his heart pounding in his chest. He thought about his mother, about her dreams for a Palestine liberated from the Jews. If she hadn't already been in paradise, the thought of American troops in Hebron and Jericho would have killed her for sure. He thought about his father. What would he think when he heard the news? Would he know it was *his son? Nadir had mailed a letter to him—and one to the president—just before he left the Willard. How long would it take before they were delivered?*

The letters might take some time. But the message he was about to deliver would be the blast heard round the world. Jihad was here—in America—land of the infidels and the home of the oppressors.

He ripped off his hood and began to jog. He didn't care who saw him. He couldn't wait. He was ready to die, ready for the whole world to know that . . .

Nadir suddenly froze in his tracks as a Cobra helicopter gunship rose over the hill dead ahead. He turned to bolt left, toward the yellow school buses, but another Cobra was now staring him in the face. He turned right—another. Around—another.

"Mario Iabello, put your hands up," boomed a loudspeaker on one of the Cobras. *"We have you surrounded. You have nowhere to go."*

He was trapped, and still a good hundred yards from the buses, from the children and the cops and the monument itself.

"Do not take another step or you will be fired upon."

He could hear sirens screaming in the distance.

"Take off your jacket."

Police cars of all kinds were racing across the grounds toward him, coming from all directions.

"Take off your jacket now."

The voice echoed across the city, down toward the White House a half mile or so behind him, down toward the Capitol at the other end of the Mall.

"I repeat, take off your jacket now."

This was it. He could see the buses screeching away from the curb, surrounded by police cars. Another few seconds and a hundred pistols and rifles and machine guns would be pointed at his head. There was no way out but one.

"Mario Iabello" began to unbutton his coat—slowly, one button at a time. One sleeve came off. Then the other. Then the entire parka came off, and all eyes focused on the custom-made vest—packed in a circle around his waist were a dozen twelve-inch bricks of C4—and the long red ignition cord he carefully removed from the lining of the coat. Four Co-bra gunships hovered, ready to pounce. Four pilots flicked off the safeties on their front-mounted machine guns, ready to fire.

And then Nadir Sarukhi Hashemi raised his face to the sky, shouted *"Allahu Akbar!"* and pulled the trigger.

★ ★ ★

The massive explosion was blinding, even on television.

Gogolov and Jibril couldn't believe what they were seeing. They'd done it. They'd accomplished what they set out to do. It didn't matter that the Viper was the only one to die. He'd died in a fireball in the heart of the enemy's capital. America would never be the same. Nor would Al-Nakbah.

"You've got mail."

Jibril could barely pull himself away from the television. The images were mesmerizing and soon they'd be gone. Soon the coverage would shift across the Atlantic. He just hoped none of his team did anything to knock out the satellite uplink stations on the Rock. It was a show the whole world had to see.

The newest message was from Gift Shop. What? Another motorcade was heading up to the summit? Had they been wrong? Had they moved too fast? Jibril grabbed the satellite phone and speed-dialed the G5. But there was no answer.

★ ★ ★

Bennett's motorcade was less than half a mile away.

Their headlights were on, and their windshield wipers were cranked up to the highest setting. The storm was coming in faster than expected, and so were the lights of the business jet. The lead driver in the package saw it first and realized immediately what was happening.

"Incoming," he shouted as he slammed on his brakes and veered to the side of the road, hoping not to get clipped from the Tahoe right behind him.

Bennett hit the brakes too and pulled the wheel hard to the left, barely missing the back of Sa'id's vehicle ahead of him. He knew he should slam the VW into a K-turn and start racing for cover. But he couldn't look away. None of them could.

The jet was coming in fast and hard from their right. It was a Gulfstream, and it was heading straight for the restaurant. For a split second, Bennett froze. He couldn't believe what he was seeing. He suddenly thought of Tariq and the advance team. They were about to perish in a firestorm meant for him. Bennett wanted to scream but couldn't. All he could do was watch as the plane slammed directly into the restaurant and set the summit ablaze.

Bennett could feel the anger rising fast. Every friend he had was dying in a war he couldn't stop. Now it was Tariq Abu Ashad, his guardian angel since Gaza Station. The guy was a saint—quiet and unassuming but one of the toughest and nicest guys Bennett had ever met. He was a Palestinian in love with America, and an American in love with Palestine, and now he was gone. Bennett slammed his fists on the dashboard. He fought to choke back the emotions forcing their way to the surface. But there was no time to mourn. The SEALs in the minivan were screaming at him to move.

"Go back, go back—let's go, let's go, let's go."

The chatter on the radios was deafening. Bennett could see all the taillights ahead of him turn white. He jammed his stick shift into reverse and hit the gas. All the other cars in the package were turned around, but Bennett didn't have time. He was now doing forty driving backward down Signal Station Road on the Rock in the rain.

"Sa'id, Doron—are they okay?" McCoy shouted over her radio.

The answer came back immediately from both Tahoes. The prime ministers were rattled but safe.

"Devil's Tower, Devil's Tower, this is Gold One, do you copy?"

"Gold One, this is Devil's Tower—what's going on?"

"Code Red, we have a Code Red. A kamikaze just took out the restaurant. We're coming back to you—repeat, coming back to you. Stand by one."

"Roger that, Gold One—we'll seal the cave behind you."

"Get CENTCOM on the line and tell him we're under attack."

"You got it, Gold One, we've already—"

Bennett couldn't tell what had happened. Was the transmission cut or did the watch commander simply stop talking?

"Jon!"

Bennett had never heard McCoy scream like that. He couldn't stop, not yet, but he could see what she was seeing. Not a hundred yards off the mountain to their right, another jet—a Citation—was screaming in at what had to be five hundred miles an hour.

A split second later, the plane slammed into the British military command post and the entrance to their living quarters. Another fireball lit up the darkening sky. The explosion mixed with booms of thunder. Sticks of lightning crackled on the horizon, and Devil's Tower was off the air.

48

"MR. PRESIDENT?"

MacPherson was still trying to process the explosion at the Washington Monument, but it was General Mutschler at the NMCC.

"What is it, General?"

"Gibraltar Station is under attack."

"What?"

"Two kamikazes—one took out the restaurant; the other took out the British military command. A third plane just touched down at the airport—it's unloading a team of terrorists. There's heavy fighting going on right now. Mortar shells are coming in from speedboats out in the harbor."

"What about Bennett and others?"

"They're still on the mountain—two main roads are cut off by fire. There's only one left."

★　　★　　★

"Jon, look out!"

They were fast approaching a hairpin turn, but their wheels were in the gravel and there was a thousand-foot dropoff less than three yards to their right. Bennett was still driving backward and even Galishnikov was terrified of plunging over the side.

"I got it. I see it. Hold on—Gold Three, I'm making this turn. Follow my lead."

Bennett slammed on the brakes again and pulled the wheel hard to the right. The red VW spun out, and Bennett struggled for control. They were sliding toward the edge.

"Jon . . ."

Bennett could feel the muddy gravel underneath them and adjusted back to the left. It was just in time. They could suddenly feel solid road again, and Bennett jammed the stick shift into second, then third. Both Tahoes and the minivan spun out on the turn as well, but everyone made it and now Bennett was on point, picking up speed as they blew south down Charles the Fifth Road. Seconds later, they hit the next hairpin turn and barely made it. Now they were heading east down Queen's Road doing sixty. That's when they first saw the billows of smoke coming from the airport.

"Gold One, this is Bennett. You there?" Bennett couldn't remember his own code name, if he even had one. And he didn't care.

"This is Gold One—I'm right behind you."

"I'm just trying to get us off this mountain. But what do I do then?"

"Head for the Governor's Mansion. They have a safe house there."

"How do I get there?"

"I'll tell you when we get closer."

Bennett came to another hairpin turn and downshifted quickly. He broke left and was now coming down Old Queen's Road. Then a fast, hard right, and another hard left. A few minutes more and they'd be in the heart of the city.

"Gold One, this is Frontier Six. Over."

It was a Brit Bennett hadn't heard before.

"Frontier Six—go."

"It's on fire. I say again—the Governor's Mansion is on fire."

"What? What happened?"

"Attacked by RPGs a few minutes ago—guys in speedboats out in harbor."

"What's your status?"

"Not good. We've got a wicked firefight on our hands."

"How many?"

"Eight, maybe ten guys. Took us all by surprise—we saw the explosions at the summit and I sent most of my men up there."

"What's all the smoke down your way?"

"They just blew up their plane on the runway, they did. Nothing can get in or out."

Bennett needed options. He needed someplace safe to get his team. But where? Everything he knew was gone. He needed time to think, but they were moving too fast. They were doing seventy toward a short tunnel when two shots erupted from their right. The first missed but the second sliced the front windshield, shattering it into a thousand pieces. It was safety glass so none of it went flying, but suddenly Bennett couldn't see.

"*McCoy* . . ."

He had no idea who was shooting at them. He hit his high beams in the tunnel and prayed no one was in his way. McCoy reached over and rolled down his window. Bennett stuck his head out into the driving rains and tried not to lose control on the next series of turns. He had no idea where he was. He was moving through alleys and parking lots, desperately trying to reach Main Street, the Queensway, anything that would get him out of these narrow lanes and deadly zigzags that were going to kill all of them if a sniper didn't take them out first.

"Gold One, this is Bennett again."

"Go."

"Now what do we do?"

The SEAL Team commander thought about it for a fraction of a second. There weren't any good options. His instincts told him to get this team as far from Gibraltar as possible. It was a risk. He didn't dare take a boat. Not with terrorists out there in speedboats. They could sprint for the frontier, blow through the border, and drive to Rota. But that would take hours. And there was an intense gunfight at the Frontier.

"Gold One, come on, let's go!" Bennett shouted. "I need an answer— *now!*"

"Make a break for the airport, Jon."

"What? Are you crazy?"

"Jon, we don't have a choice. We need to get you guys out of here now."

"We've got no plane. The runway's on fire."

"Jon, shut up and do what the man says."

It was McCoy. The VW went silent. So did the radio traffic.

"These guys know their stuff," McCoy continued as Bennett sped into the city along deserted streets gushing with rain. "The SEALs can fight their way onto the airstrip. There's two Seahawks there. We can use those."

"And who's gonna fly them?"

"Hunt and Brackman are both pilots—they flew together in Desert Storm."

"And then what?" asked Bennett, trying to calm down. "This storm's right on top of us. We go up in this and it'll kill us for sure."

"Have some faith, Jon. We'll blow up that bridge when we get to it."

☆ ☆ ☆

MacPherson pressed General Mutschler for details.

"What do you have to back them up?"

"We've got a rapid-response team at our base in Rota, Spain. They're almost completely socked in by the storm coming down from the north— and they're completely on the entire other side of Spain, on the Atlantic coast. But we're sending them anyway. They'll be in the air in the next few minutes."

"What else have you got?"

"We've got another team of SEALs out on the *Kennedy*. They're closer. Visibility is practically nil—less than half a mile at this point—but it's possible."

MacPherson was furious. "General, I don't have to remind you what's at stake here. Now I want you to get these guys out. I don't care how you do it—just do it."

☆ ☆ ☆

"All right, Gold One, take the lead—we'll follow you."

Bennett eased off the gas a bit and let the minivan roar ahead. They were on Smith Dorrien Avenue, coming around a curve onto Winston Churchill. They'd be at the airstrip in less than a minute and it was going to be a fight to the death.

McCoy readied her Uzi and handed her Beretta to Bennett. "When we get there, pull behind one of the Seahawks. I'll jump out and lay down some covering fire. You get Mordechai and Galishnikov into the chopper and watch my back. When you guys are ready, shout. I'll be right behind you."

The package now crossed the tarmac, and everyone in the VW gasped at the devastation. The burning wreckage of the Learjet was front and center, and the airport terminal was engulfed in flames. Machine-gun fire erupted from their left.

"Point Man, this is Prairie Ranch, do you read me?"

It was Marsha Kirkpatrick in the Situation Room.

"Roger that—what've you got?" Bennett shouted into his microphone as he tried desperately to steer clear of the firefight.

"Hang in there. We've got a rescue team coming in from Rota—ETA about fifteen minutes."

"Negative, negative—we're under heavy fire—we can't wait that long."

Bennett cut right, barely missing a tanker trunk in the middle of the tarmac, still running and apparently abandoned in the fight.

"Jon, look out!"

It was Mordechai.

"Where? What is it?" yelled Bennett, unable to turn his head or risk crashing.

Now McCoy saw it too. *"Get down, get down—RPG."*

Bennett didn't know where it was coming from. He didn't want to know. He just ducked as low as he could, hit the gas, and raced for the Seahawks.

The RPG missed them by inches. It slammed into the fuel tanker, unleashing yet another explosion. The force of the blast blew out all the windows of the VW, but they were finally there.

Bennett grabbed his microphone again. "Gold One, we don't have time to wait for a rescue—get us out of here now."

"Roger that, I'm right behind you."

Bennett pulled behind the lead Seahawk, grabbed McCoy's 9 mm, and started helping the two Israelis out of the backseat. The SEALs took up a blocking position and returned fire. Tracer rounds crisscrossed the tarmac as sergeants Hunt and Brackman powered up the choppers and prepared for liftoff.

Bullets whizzed by his head and three or four more explosions went off, though Bennett quickly lost count. Before he realized it, McCoy was slapping him on the back and yelling at him to jump into the sixty-four-foot bird or get left behind. Doron, Sa'id, and their protective details, as well as Mordechai, Galishnikov, and another handful of SEALs, were already locked and loaded and ready to go. The rest of the SEALs would take the second chopper. Bennett scrambled in with the others and McCoy jumped in last.

She put on a headset and gave Bennett his own to block out the noise and communicate with the others. Sergeant Hunt completed their preflight check. Two SEALs took up their positions by the .50-caliber machine guns mounted in the doors and opened up on the terrorists now firing at them.

"Look out, look out."

It was one of the SEALs. Bennett couldn't see what was happening. But he could hear it. Someone was firing at them at close range. The .50s opened up and blew the guy away, but not before six rounds riddled the back of their Seahawk.

"We're hit, we're hit—go, go, go."

Both Seahawks gained altitude and began pulling away from the airport. The question was, which way should they go? The Seahawk's onboard color radar showed the storms pelting the coastline and interior of Spain, making the route to Rota treacherous at best. The worst of the storm was now over the Rock itself. Thunder boomed above them and lightning was flashing all around them. Heading out to the aircraft carrier actually seemed the marginally less dangerous course of action, but it was a crap shoot either way.

"It's your call, Sergeant," Bennett said. "Just get us out of here."

Hunt climbed into the raging storm and made his decision. "Freedom One, this is Striker One Six," he told the USS *John F. Kennedy.* "We are airborne. Our feet are dry, but we are coming to you. Over."

"Striker One Six, this is Freedom One—negative, negative—be advised weather our way is extremely dangerous."

"Look out," yelled Galishnikov. *"RPG—left side."*

Every head turned. They could see the white contrail heading straight for them. The Seahawk banked hard to the right. The RPG sliced past their left window, missing by inches. Now the pilot pulled straight up into the lightning and fog. Everyone was holding on for their lives, but now the gunfire didn't seem as terrifying as the weather.

"Freedom One, this is Striker One Six, you do not understand—we have the package. I repeat—we have the package. We are under heavy fire. We have no other options. We are heading your way."

49

MACPHERSON AND HIS TEAM tracked the drama from the Sit Room.

With the suicide bomber crisis over—at least for now—there was no need to be in the Presidential Emergency Operations Center, the blastproof bunker three stories under the White House. They'd be safe where they were. A steward brought in coffee and sandwiches, but no one was hungry. They were listening to a live, secure feed, cross-linked from the Pentagon.

"Can I talk to them, Bennett and McCoy?" MacPherson asked.

"Not yet, sir," said Defense Secretary Trainor, patched in via videoconference. "Let's give them some time to get their bearings and battle that storm."

*   *   *

"Freedom One, this is Striker One Six again. Do you copy?"

Hunt tried to establish contact with the *Kennedy*, still nearly fifty nautical miles away. Nothing. He checked his radio equipment and made some fast adjustments. "Freedom One, I repeat, this is Striker One Six. Do you copy?"

It took a moment. Then a hiss of static and a garbled voice came crackling back.

"Striker . . . Six . . . Free . . ."

"Freedom One, please repeat. Say again, please repeat."

More hiss and static—then a clear channel.

"Striker One Six, we're launching two F-14s to watch your back."

That was more like it.

"Roger that, and thanks, Freedom One. Our feet are wet. We're coming home."

Bennett stared out the window of the Seahawk. They were just four hundred feet above the angry whitecaps, trying to stay under the thick fog without crashing.

No one said a word for the next few minutes. They simply surrendered to the sounds of the whirling rotors above, the crashing waves below, and the deafening thunder exploding all around them. The chopper continued rocking back and forth, occasionally dropping a good twenty-five or thirty feet in a split second.

* * *

Two F-14 Tomcat Interceptors went to full power.

Seconds later, they catapulted off the pitching deck of the *Kennedy*, one after the other, racing from zero to a hundred fifty miles an hour in just three seconds. It was no night to fly. The pilots didn't even know who they were risking their lives to escort home. But orders were orders and they were pros.

* * *

The Seahawks were now just thirty miles from the *Kennedy* battle group.

But they were absolutely being mauled by the storm raging around them. The winds were gusting upward of sixty to seventy knots. Massive sheets of rain were moving horizontally. Bennett forced himself not to look out the window at the snaking bolts of lightning and the massive black waves.

Suddenly, warning lights and buzzers filled the cockpit. Hunt checked his instruments and his radar. Then McCoy saw his head jerk back. They had company.

"Freedom One, Freedom One, this is Striker One Six. We are being painted. Some bogey just locked on to me. What is going on?"

Painted? Bennett's eyes opened instantly and he sat up. Someone out there in the darkness had just acquired tone and was preparing to fire their missiles at them.

"Striker One Six, we just picked up two MiG-23s. They're coming fast and low from the south-southeast."

Bennett couldn't believe what he was hearing. MiGs inbound on their location? Why? Who were they? It didn't make sense. He leaned into the cockpit to see the blips on radar. Sure enough, they were sitting ducks.

Mordechai leaned over with his assessment. "Libyans."

"You sure?" said Bennett.

"I am sure."

McCoy agreed. So did the SEALs. It was the only explanation.

"Freedom One, where's that cover you promised?"

"Striker One Six, they're inbound hot. They should be there any moment."

"We might not be—"

Beep, beep, beep, beep, beep.

"They fired. One of the MiGs just fired!" yelled Hunt. "Missile in the air!"

Hunt immediately deployed countermeasures and pulled back on the yoke. The Seahawk climbed to three thousand feet, then went into a hard dive as Bennett and the others hung on for their lives. Just before they crashed into the waves, Hunt banked hard right, then hard left, then pulled up and broke right again. Everyone looked left as a Russian AA-10 air-to-air missile sliced by at Mach 4, missing the Seahawk by less than a yard. Even Galishnikov was terrified now, and he lost everything in his stomach on the floor.

Beep, beep, beep, beep, beep.

"They've locked on again!" Hunt yelled. "They've got tone."

They'd been lucky but he wasn't sure he could pull an evasion like that again.

Just then the two F-14s raced by—one to the left, one to the right. A cheer went up in both choppers and Bennett could hear the radio traffic as both pilots locked on to their bogies.

"I've got tone," said the lead.

A moment later, his wingman did too.

"Fox two, fox two."

"Fox two, fox two."

Sidewinder missiles exploded out the sides of the F-14s. A fraction of a second later they could feel the concussion of two massive explosions. The MiGs were history. Everyone breathed a sigh of relief—everyone but Bennett. They weren't out of this storm yet. They still had to land.

* * *

Bennett could see the landing lights on the *Kennedy*.

The navy's last conventionally powered aircraft carrier, the USS *John F. Kennedy* was a thousand feet long, twenty stories high, and weighed more than eighty thousand tons. But the waves below were now cresting at thirty to forty feet. Even at three-quarters of a mile out, Bennett could see the four-and-a-half-acre flight deck pitching wildly back and forth, between fifteen and twenty degrees at least, making it impossible to stand on the deck, much less land on it.

But the Seahawks didn't have a choice. They needed to get down, and fast.

Bennett watched Hunt wipe the sweat from his face and ready himself for the task ahead. He could hear the confusion of chatter over the radio as the chopper moved into position over the rolling carrier deck. He had no idea how they were going to get down. Even if they did slam the Seahawk down on the deck clean—and at the right moment—what was to prevent them from being thrown overboard and crashing upside down twenty stories below?

The windshield wipers on the Seahawk must have been going Mach 2. It didn't seem to matter. Still, Bennett could see a member of the *Kennedy* crew on the flight deck, crawling on his belly toward a mechanical contraption just below them. He was carrying a huge pole with a hook at one end. He wore a helmet and goggles, a waterproof suit, and an orange life vest with a whistle and strobe lights attached. He also seemed to be attached to a lifeline of some kind, though Bennett couldn't tell for sure. Whatever—the guy was either the gutsiest man he'd ever seen or the stupidest.

"*What are you doing?*" shouted Bennett.

"*Not right now, sir,*" Hunt yelled back, focused like a laser on a procedure he'd trained on at Lakehurst but had never actually done in combat conditions.

Beep, beep, beep, beep.

Bennett's eyes scanned the instrument panel. It couldn't be another MiG, he thought, not here. He was right. It wasn't a MiG. It was fuel. Hunt looked at the gauge. It was almost on empty. He tapped it slightly. The needle went down, not up. It didn't make sense. They'd had full tanks at liftoff. How could they possibly have . . .

The gunfire on the tarmac, Hunt thought. The fuel lines must have been hit. With everything else going on, he hadn't noticed. But now they were running on fumes. He radioed the *Kennedy* and told them their situation. With both prime ministers onboard, Hunt's chopper was going to be the first down anyway. But now they were out of fuel and out of time. They had to get on the deck and fast.

"Roger that, Striker One Six. Fire when ready."

The Seahawk hovered over the carrier, fighting against the crosswinds to stay steady. Hunt punched a button and fired a huge, thick cable down toward the deck. It whipped about wildly in the wind and Bennett had no idea what was going on.

The man below strapped himself into the mechanical contraption, and lifted the pole into the air. A huge gust of wind almost ripped him off the deck, but the safety tether did its job. *Was this guy completely nuts?* If a bolt of lightning didn't fry him, the static electricity being generated by the two fifty-four-foot rotors had to do it for sure. Twice, the pole seemed to explode in sparks and smoke. The guy never let go. A moment later, he successfully hooked the Seahawk's cable, grounded it, connected it to the mechanical contraption, and scrambled for safety.

"McCoy, what's going on?" Bennett shouted. If he was about to meet his Maker, at least he wanted to know why.

"They're hooking us into the RAST system," McCoy shouted back.

"What's that?"

"Recovery, Assist, Secure, and Traverse—it locks us into the deck of the carrier. Now the pilot's going to throttle up, and try to pull away."

"Pull away? What for? We need to land this sucker and get inside."

"We will. But the carrier does all the work for us. The cable is attached to a huge machine down below, the bear trap. It's going to mechanically pull us down onto the deck and lock us there so we can't be washed overboard."

Bennett could hear the engines revving up. *"Then why pull up and away?"*

"*'Cause if the cable snaps, we need enough power to get airborne again—fast.*"

"Or what?"

"*Or we die.*"

Beep, beep, beep, beep.

Everyone jumped. Bennett scanned the instrument panel. It was the low-fuel warnings going off again. They were out of time. But it couldn't be helped. This was the only way down.

Hunt went to max power and pulled his yoke back. Bennett and the others grew silent. They could feel the Seahawk fighting to pull away and the carrier's retracting cable trying to pull the twenty-three-thousand-pound chopper to the deck. The crosswinds were surging against their sides, buffeting them in every direction as Hunt tried to hold steady. The rain and fog were so thick they could barely see outside. All they knew was that they were getting closer. They could feel the intense tug-of-war, machine raging against machine. And then—suddenly—they felt metal smash against metal and the huge metal claws lock on.

They were down. Hunt shut down his engines. One by one, they crawled out of the chopper doors, clipped themselves onto a safety line, and dropped down onto the greasy, oily deck—down onto their bellies, holding each hook for dear life as the carrier swayed from side to side like a child's seesaw at the park. Hunt led the way, to show them how. Sa'id went next, followed by his security detail. Then Doron and his Shin Bet agents. Mordechai was next. Then Galishnikov, followed by McCoy, at Bennett's insistence. The rest of the SEALs brought up the rear.

It was slow going for all of them. Bennett could see nothing. His face was raw from the driving salt rains. He could barely breathe. The surging winds seemed to suck his lungs dry. He looked back and saw the other Seahawk making its approach.

Inch by inch, Bennett made his way across the deck. He crawled toward the LSO—the landing safety officer—and the flight deck director, both screaming instructions to him he couldn't even begin to hear amid the raging storm.

His knuckles, clutching the freezing metal hooks in front of him, were white as ghosts. But ten terrifying minutes later, the "point man for peace," the "two kings," and what was left of their team made it to the end of the line.

They were safe. They'd been to hell and back. But they were safe.

EPILOGUE

✶ ✶ ✶

"Mr. Speaker, the president of the United States."

The Capitol erupted.

Both chambers, both parties—ambassadors from all over the world—stood and applauded the president longer and harder than any ovation Bennett or McCoy had ever heard before. The air was thick with emotion, with a sense that they were all witnesses to something dramatic and historic and almost miraculous.

He couldn't believe he was here—in the president's box for the State of the Union. With his mom on one side. And Erin McCoy on the other, more beautiful than he'd ever seen her before. With Dmitri Galishnikov and the SEALs in the row behind him. With the First Lady in the row in front of him—standing beside Israeli prime minister David Doron and his wife, and Palestinian prime minister Ibrahim Sa'id, his wife, and their four sons.

Exactly three weeks before, they had landed on the *Kennedy*. And now they were in the United States Capitol. With the world watching. With U.S. combat operations in the West Bank and Gaza now complete and successful. With a three-year transition accord signed that very afternoon at the White House. With Doron and Sa'id receiving a hero's welcome. With a sumptuous state dinner planned for the following night. With Yuri Gogolov and Mohammed Jibril now number one and number two on the FBI's Most Wanted List, and the Libyan Defense Ministry still smoldering.

The president's speech was magnificent. Shakespeare had outdone himself. Peace was finally at hand. At the moment, anything seemed possible. And it was surreal. There was no other way to describe it. Simply surreal.

A motorcade took them all back to the White House. The president and First Family invited them all up to the Residence for a post–State of the Union party, and Bennett asked Galishnikov to escort his mom. He had a few things to attend to. He'd be right up.

"Pssst, Erin, come with me," said Bennett, as he took her by the hand and led her out to the colonnade by the Oval Office.

"What are you up to?" McCoy asked. "You've been acting strange all night."

They walked out to the Rose Garden, covered with snow and twinkling with lights. The air was soft and cool, no wind, not even a breeze. Out in the distance, McCoy could see the Washington Monument. It was still there, still standing strong, unmoved by the violence of the last days.

"I'm not real good at this," Bennett said, conceding the obvious. "But here goes. I know we've been so busy with everything at Camp David and the State of the Union and all, but I was just wondering . . ."

He hesitated.

Jon Bennett could cut billion-dollar deals and Middle East peace treaties and drive a VW down the Rock of Gibraltar doing forty in the rain, but somehow this seemed hard.

"You were wondering what?" asked McCoy.

"I don't know. I'd just thought, if you weren't doing anything Saturday night, that, perhaps . . ."

"Perhaps . . ."

"Perhaps you'd let me take you out to dinner somewhere—anywhere you'd like to go. You don't have to commit to marriage or anything. Just a nice dinner, you know, to say thank you for all I've put you through."

McCoy couldn't help but laugh. "A suicide bombing, a siege in Gaza, a war on Gibraltar, and a helicopter ride from hell? Yeah, dinner and a movie really ought to cover it, Bennett."

Bennett laughed too, and gently wiped away a snowflake from her cheek. "Well," he said, "at least it's a start."

IS IT TRUE?

* * *

To learn more about the research used for this book—and to track the latest political, economic, military, and archeological developments in Israel, Jordan, Iraq, and other countries described in *The Last Days*— please visit:

www.joelrosenberg.com

You can also sign up to receive Joel C. Rosenberg's
free e-mail newsletter,
>> FLASH TRAFFIC <<.

ACKNOWLEDGMENTS

To my incredible wife, Lynn—my hero and best friend. You constantly amaze me with your grace and discernment, your kindness and stamina. I don't know how I'd survive without you. Every day we walk together I learn something more wonderful about you. I love you so much. Thanks for loving me and doing this adventure together. We're living our dreams, and this is just the beginning. To Caleb, Jacob, and Jonah, my prayer warriors and "traveling buddies." I love being your dad. I love seeing your faith, hope, and love growing day by day. Spain, Morocco, Gibraltar, Jerusalem—who knows what's next!

To everyone in our previous acknowledgments, especially our families, friends, and kindred spirits from Syracuse, Washington, McLean, and Frontline. To our November Communications compadre, "John Black John Black," thanks for all your "air support" and wisdom! To Dan ("Duncle") Rebeiz, welcome aboard; Marcus and Tanya Brackman; the "Posse"; our Spain '03 team; the Stahls; the Rose family; Shirley O'Neill; and the team at *World* magazine. Thanks for your faithful friendship and for making us part of your lives.

Special thanks to Rush Limbaugh and Sean Hannity. You sent *The Last Jihad* into the stratosphere and our lives into hyperspeed with your passion and enthusiasm. We couldn't have been more surprised or had more fun. And many thanks to Steve and Sabina Forbes and Bill Dal Col for your enduring friendship and tremendous encouragement. We're still so humbled and grateful. God bless you guys!

To those who've been so generous with their time, research, and insights, including Allen Roth, Steven Schnier, and their colleagues; Ambassador Dore Gold; Mey Wurmser at AEI; Jim Phillips and Ariel Cohen at Heritage; and to so many Palestinian and Israeli sources who wish to remain anonymous.

To everyone who put together such wonderful book events for us over the last year, and have blessed our lives in so many ways, including Stanley and Gay Gaines; Janet Westling and her family; Bridgett Wagner at Heritage; Jeff Taylor; Nancy Streck, Steve Scheffler, and their team in Iowa; David Keene, Diana Banister, and everyone at CPAC; and even the kind folks who invited me to do the "Pat the Bunny" readings on that beautiful Saturday afternoon—thanks so much!

To Greg Mueller, Leif Noren, Keith Appell, Mike Russell, Peter Robbio,

Suzanne Bakri, and the wonderful team at Creative Response Concepts for everything you did for me.

To Tom Doherty, Bob Gleason, Linda Quinton, Elena Stokes, Brian Callaghan, and the stellar team at Tor/Forge Books. You guys are absolutely amazing. Thanks so much for all you did to make *The Last Jihad* a best seller and for giving me the opportunity to do what I love. I couldn't be more grateful.

And to Scott Miller at Trident Media Group, the best agent in the business. What an amazing year—who woulda thunk it? Thanks again for your wisdom and candor, your willingness to go the extra mile, and most of all for your friendship. Let's hope there's more to come.

October 2003

JOEL C. ROSENBERG

Joel C. Rosenberg is the *New York Times* best-selling author of *The Last Jihad, The Last Days*, and *The Ezekiel Option*, with more than one million copies in print. As a communications strategist, he has worked with some of the world's most influential leaders in business, politics, and media, including Steve Forbes, Rush Limbaugh, and former Israeli prime minister Benjamin Netanyahu. As a novelist, he has been interviewed on hundreds of radio and TV programs, including ABC's *Nightline, CNN Headline News*, FOX News Channel, The History Channel, MSNBC, the *Rush Limbaugh Show*, and the *Sean Hannity Show*. He has been profiled by the *New York Times*, the *Washington Times*, and the *Jerusalem Post*, and was the subject of two cover stories in *World* magazine. He has addressed audiences all over the world, including Russia, Israel, Jordan, Egypt, Turkey, and Belgium, and has spoken at the White House.

The first page of his first novel—*The Last Jihad*—puts readers inside the cockpit of a hijacked jet, coming in on a kamikaze attack into an American city, which leads to a war with Saddam Hussein over weapons of mass destruction. Yet it was written before 9/11, and published before the actual war with Iraq. *The Last Jihad* spent eleven weeks on the *New York Times* hardcover fiction best-seller list, reaching as high as #7. It raced up the *USA Today* and *Publishers Weekly* best-seller lists, hit #4 on the *Wall Street Journal* list, and hit #1 on Amazon.com.

His second thriller—*The Last Days*—opens with the death of Yasser Arafat and a U.S. diplomatic convoy ambushed in Gaza. Two weeks before

The Last Days was published in hardcover, a U.S. diplomatic convoy was ambushed in Gaza. Thirteen months later, Yasser Arafat was dead. *The Last Days* spent four weeks on the *New York Times* hardcover fiction best-seller list, hit #5 on the *Denver Post* list, and hit #8 on the *Dallas Morning News* list. Both books have been optioned by a Hollywood producer.

The Ezekiel Option centers on a dictator rising in Russia who forms a military alliance with the leaders of Iran as they feverishly pursue nuclear weapons and threaten to wipe Israel off the face of the earth. On the very day it was published in June 2005, Iran elected a new leader who vowed to accelerate the country's nuclear program and later threatened to "wipe Israel off the map." Six months after it was published, Moscow signed a $1 billion arms deal with Tehran. *The Ezekiel Option* spent four weeks on the *New York Times* hardcover fiction best-seller list and five months on the Christian Booksellers Association best-seller list, reaching as high as #4.

www.joelrosenberg.com

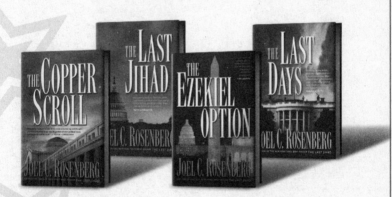

A crisis in the Middle East...

A hotly debated presidential campaign...

The threat of an assassination...

And as pressure mounts to build the Third Jewish Temple in Jerusalem, the world is forced to take sides.

* * *

From the *New York Times* best-selling author Joel C. Rosenberg comes another heart-pounding international thriller...

DEAD HEAT

COMING SOON!

* * *

ISRAEL DISCOVERS MASSIVE RESERVES OF OIL, GAS

In August 2005, while on *The Ezekiel Option* book tour, I had lunch in Dallas with Gene Soltero, the president and CEO of a company called Zion Oil. I had never heard of the MIT-trained economist and petroleum engineer before, but took a liking to him immediately. Balding, with short tufts of gray hair over each ear, and small, wire-rimmed glasses, Soltero was a soft-spoken man in his sixties who looked more like a professor of management at some college in the American Midwest than a treasure hunter in the Mideast. But he had quite a story to tell, and a lot of questions for me.

On a recent visit to Israel, an investor in his company had picked up a paperback copy of *The Last Jihad* in Ben Gurion International Airport, read it on the plane home, and gotten so excited about it that he had emailed Soltero and everyone else in the company urging that they read it too. Why? Because in the novel, an American company working with a team of geologists and petroleum engineers in Israel discover massive reserves of oil and natural gas in the Holy Land, making all of them rich and changing the geopolitics of the region forever. Except to Soltero and his colleagues it wasn't fiction. It was their lives.

As Soltero explained it, all the top executives in the company quickly read *Jihad* and *The Last Days*, in which a Wall Street strategist turned White House advisor puts together an "Oil For Peace" plan whereupon the U.S. will underwrite the billions of dollars necessary to develop the new petroleum find if the Israelis and Palestinians will stop the violence and find a way to work together. The more Soltero and his colleagues read, the more intrigued they got. *How had I come up with such an oil and gas storyline? Did I know about all the biblical prophecies that said Israel would, in fact, discover oil in "the last days"? More to the point, did I know just how close their company and others were to seeing these prophecies come to pass?*

We agreed I would tell my story and then he would tell me his.

THE PROSPERITY PREREQUISITES

When I began writing *The Last Jihad* series, I did base it on prophecies in the Book of Ezekiel which indicate that there are two things that must occur before Israel's "last days" showdown with Russia and Iran. The first "prerequisite," as it were, is that that there must be a period of calm and stability in Israel before the "war of Gog and Magog." The second is that Israel must build up significant wealth. But the truth is I had no idea at the time just how much detail the Scriptures contained with regards to the discovery of oil in the promised land, and thus I had no idea how close to reality my fiction was going to be.

The "prerequisites" come from Ezekiel 38:8 and Ezekiel 38:11-13, which read: "After many days, you [dictator of Russia] will be summoned; in the latter years you will come into the land that is restored from the sword, whose inhabitants have been gathered from many nations to the mountains of Israel which had been a continual waste; but its people were brought out from the nations, and they are living securely, all of them. . . . And you will say, 'I will go up against the land of unwalled villages. I will go against those who are at rest, that live securely, all of them living without walls and having no bars or gates, to capture spoil and to seize plunder, to turn your hand against the waste places which are now inhabited, and against the people who are gathered from the nations, who have acquired cattle and goods, who live at the center of the world.' Sheba and Dedan[1] and the merchants of Tarshish[2] with all its villages will say to you [the Russian dictator], 'Have you come to capture spoil? Have you assembled to seize plunder, to carry away silver and gold, to take away cattle and goods, to capture great spoil?'"

In the next chapter, I will discuss the "peace prerequisite." But as Soltero and I talked, I focused more on the "prosperity prerequisite."

Ezekiel 38 clearly indicates that prior to the Russian-Iranian attack:

The Jews have poured back into the land of Israel

The Jews are settling and in the process rebuilding the ancient
    ruins and "waste places" of Israel—that is, there is a building
    boom under way

The Israelis have become wealthy enough to acquire silver,
    gold, cattle and other material "goods"

Israel is so wealthy that even the Saudis and those who live
    in the Gulf states can see that Russia and her allies covet
    Israel's treasures

A look at Ezekiel 36:11 provides yet another clue: "I will increase the number of men and animals upon you [land of Israel], and they will be fruitful and become numerous. I will settle people on you as in the past and will *make you prosper more than before*. Then you will know that I am the Lord." (New International Version, emphasis added) That would be quite a development, I thought. After all, when Solomon was king of Israel, he was one of the wealthiest men in the world. Yet Ezekiel was saying that modern Israel would be wealthier still.

In *The Coming Peace in the Middle East,* Dr. LaHaye had considered a number of ways that Israel could become so peaceful and prosperous. Among them: "Suppose that a pool of oil, greater than anything in Arabia . . . were discovered by the Jews in Palestine. This would change the course of history. Before long, Israel would be able independently

---

1 Ancient names for modern-day Saudi Arabia and the Gulf states.
2 Historically southern Spain, though it could refer more generally to Europe or the Mediterranean states.

to solve its economic woes, finance the resettlement of the Palestinians, and supply housing for Jews and Arabs in the West Bank, East Bank, or anywhere else they might choose to live. Even if something besides oil were discovered, it would have the same far-reaching effect if it were able to produce high revenues."[3]

When I first read that, I nearly laughed. *Oil in Israel?* Wouldn't that be nice? Israelis have long complained that if they are really the chosen people, why in the world didn't God resettle them in Saudi Arabia? As the late Prime Minister Golda Meir once put it: "Moses dragged us for forty years through the desert to bring us to the one place in the Middle East where there was no oil!"[4] But the more I thought about LaHaye's theory, the more it seemed just like something God would do—unveil a dramatic plot twist near the end of the story.

Interestingly enough, though, when LaHaye and Jerry Jenkins wrote the first *Left Behind* novel in 1995, they chose to make the Jews of Israel wealthy not through the discovery of oil, but through the discovery of a unique chemical that could make not just Israel's deserts bloom but help any country suffering from famines and other agricultural insufficiencies. When I read *Left Behind*, I was surprised. It was (and still is) certainly possible that God could use a stunning scientific discovery like the LaHaye-Jenkins character Dr. Chaim Rosenzweig invents to bring great wealth to Israel. But I couldn't help but think that it seemed more likely that the Lord would use oil than fertilizer.

And then in the fall of 2000, as I was working for Sharansky and Netanyahu, the *New York Times* published two headlines that riveted my attention:

GAS DEPOSITS OFF ISRAEL AND GAZA OPENING VISIONS OF JOINT VENTURES

New York Times, SEPTEMBER 15, 2000

ARAFAT HAILS BIG GAS FIND OFF THE COAST OF GAZA STRIP

New York Times, SEPTEMBER 28, 2000

---

3 LaHaye, p. 105.
4 Cited in "Moses' Oily Blessing," *The Economist*, June 18, 2005.

Wrote reporter Bill Orme: "Drilling deep below the seas off Israel and the Gaza Strip, foreign energy companies are discovering gas reserves that could lift the Palestinian economy and give Israel its first taste of energy independence. Industry experts, including those on this giant platform, say the Palestinians and Israelis will both profit if they can work together in a high-stakes partnership. They need each other for the efficient development of these offshore reserves, since neither side alone can fully afford the billion-dollar investment in pipelines and pumping facilities that is being sketched out, experts say."[5]

What's more, experts had calculated that Israel had "some three to five trillion cubic feet of proven gas reserves," and according to Yehezkeel (Ezekiel) Druckman, Israel's Petroleum Commissioner, "there may be more." At current prices, Orme reported, "the value of the strike was estimated [at between] $2 billion to $6 billion, depending on pressure, quantity and other variables."[6]

Ezekiel? Israel? Proven reserves? Billions? As I explained to Soltero, when I read those words the hair on the back of my neck stood up. True, the stories spoke "only" of natural gas, not a massive oil strike. But what if Druckman was right? What if this was only the beginning? What if there was more where that came from?

By the time I sat down to write *Jihad*, I had decided to add a fictional oil strike—discovered by a fictional American investment company working with a fictional Israeli company called Medexco, run by a fictional Russian Jewish petroleum engineer named Dmitri Galishnikov. I did so not because I believed that the Bible *specifically* predicted it, but because it suddenly seemed plausible, and I wanted this thriller to seem as realistic as humanly possible. Little did I know.

BLACK GOLD

Just days before Jihad was published in November 2002, a curious headline flashed across the news wires: "Israeli Geologist Drills for Oil

---

5 William A. Orme, Jr., "Gas Deposits Off Israel and Gaza Opening Vision of Joint Ventures," *New York Times*, September 15, 2000.
6 William A. Orme, Jr., "Arafat Hails Big Gas Find Off The Coast of Gaza Strip," *New York Times*, September 28, 2000.

Based on Biblical Guidance." The article told the story of Tovia Luskin, an Orthodox Jew born and raised in Russia who became so convinced by studying the Bible that there was black gold buried under the sands of the Jewish State that he moved to Israel, conducted extensive research, launched a limited partnership called Givot Olam, and came to the conclusion that "there are 65 million barrels of oil" in Central Israel alone.[7]

There was just one problem. Tovia Luskin was wrong. A year later, just before *The Last Days* was published, the news broke that Luskin and his colleagues had discovered oil reservoirs at their Meged-4 drilling site in Central Israel holding not 65 million barrels but *100 million barrels*.[8] A few months later, came even more stunning news: new testing had revealed that the Givot Olam site contained not 100 million barrels but upwards of *a billion barrels*, leading the Associated Press to report, "an Israeli oil company has made the largest oil find in the history of the country," and driving their shares on the Tel Aviv Stock Exchange up by thirty percent.[9]

People e-mailed me from all over the country to see if I had seen the stories and to ask me yet again if my novels were coming true. But the gusher of headlines about the activities of Givot Olam and Zion Oil had only just begun to flow.

NATURAL GAS, OIL FOUND IN DEAD SEA

Jerusalem Post, APRIL 1, 2004

ISRAEL STRIKES BLACK GOLD

ARUTZ SHEVA, MAY 4, 2004

OIL BARON SEEKS GUSHER FROM GOD IN ISRAEL

REUTERS, APRIL 4, 2005

---

7 Ross Dunn, "Israeli Geologist Drills For Oil Based on Biblical Guidance," VOA/Israel Faxx, November 20, 2002.
8 "Oil Traces Found East of Kfar Sava," *Haaretz,* September 12, 2003.
9 "Israeli Oil Company Claims Oil Find Valued At US$6 Billion," Associated Press, May 4, 2004. Luskin told reporters that he believed "about 20 percent [of the reserves] are commercially exploitable," though he cautioned that much more testing had to be done and said "the company would need to raise between US$20 million and US$50 million to develop the find." See also Amiram Cohen, "Givot Olam Drills Afresh At Kfar Sava," *Haaretz,* November 23, 2004, which notes: "Based on rock properties of the Meged 4 site, Givot Olam calculated that each square kilometer of the oil structure contains approximately 5 million barrels of oil, which translates into a total of 980 million barrels of oil at the site."

IN ISRAEL, OIL QUEST IS BASED ON FAITH

Wall Street Journal, MAY 1, 2005

HIS MISSION: SEEK AND YE SHALL FIND OIL

USA Today, MAY 19, 2005

A VISION OF OIL IN THE HOLY LAND

Newsweek, JUNE 13, 2005

MOSES' OILY BLESSING: WILL ISRAEL FIND OIL?

The Economist, JUNE 18, 2005

SEARCHING FOR OIL IN ISRAEL

CBS NEWS, SEPTEMBER 20, 2005

IS ISRAEL SITTING ON AN ENORMOUS OIL RESERVE?

WorldNetDaily, SEPTEMBER 21, 2005

The story in the respected London-based *Economist* magazine particularly caught my eye. "In the 1980s, John Brown, a Catholic Texan cutting-tools executive, and Tovia Luskin, a Russian Jewish geophysicist and career oilman, both had religious epiphanies. Mr. Brown became a born-again Christian, while Mr. Luskin joined the Orthodox Jewish Lubavitch movement. Soon after, each found inspiration in chapter 33 of the Book of Deuteronomy, in which Moses, nearing death after guiding the tribes of Israel to the border of the promised land, leaves each tribe with a blessing."[10]

"The most lavish," the article continued, "goes to Ephraim and Manassah, the two tribes descended from Joseph (he of the technicolour coat). Their land, says Moses, will yield the 'precious fruits' of 'the deep lying beneath, of the 'ancient mountains' and of the 'everlasting hills.' In this text Mr. Luskin saw . . . 'a classic description of an oil trap.' Where geological sediments are bent into an arch, the boundary at the top between an older layer (the 'ancient mountain') and a newer one

---

10 "Moses' Oily Blessing," *The Economist*, June 18, 2005.

can trap oil—the 'precious fruits.' Mr. Luskin named his company Givot Olam—'everlasting hills.' Mr. Brown had a more mystical revelation . . . that pointed to the same area: the biblical territories of Ephraim and Manassah, between today's Tel Aviv and Haifa. He registered his firm as Zion Oil."

Given my own Russian Jewish heritage and born-again Christian faith, I was intrigued. I tracked down Luskin at his office in Jerusalem and chatted with him by phone about all the headlines he was generating.

"Listen, news is not my profession," Luskin told me, clearly preferring science to public relations. "I'm a professional person looking for oil in a very professional way. . . . Since 1993, we've raised $50 million. We've drilled three wells and all three wells encountered oil. It's a big oil field. We're not producing yet . . . but we're on the way [and] we're learning more and more as we go."[11]

Luskin, a graduate of Moscow State University with a degree in geology and a love for oil exploration, told me he left Russia in 1976 and moved to Canada where he worked for Shell Oil and other petroleum companies. Later he worked for oil companies in Indonesia and Australia before emigrating to Israel with his family in 1990.

"Were you raised as a religious Jew in Russia?" I asked.

"Of course not," Luskin replied. "I became observant in Australia when my older kids went to [religious] school, I basically went, too. . . . Initially, I came to the idea of looking for oil in Israel from reading the *Chumash*, the first five books of Moses. This was the first thought [I had about it]. And then I came to Israel and started studying the geology here. . . . I collected a lot of data. I bought data with my own money, and also I had some information about oil exploration in [the mid-1980s] in Syria. When I got the Israeli geological data it was striking in that it was very similar to the Syrian Basin, which seemed to me to extend down to Israel, which turned out to be exactly right. And then before I came to Israel I wrote to the Lubavitcher Rabbi and asked for the blessing for the project, and he answered me, and I came."

"So how close are you to commercial production?" I asked him.

11 Interview with Tovia Luskin, March 22, 2006.

"We are about to start a new well," he said. "Hopefully this well will take us to production stage. . . . Eventually, we will probably need to drill around 40 wells."

OIL AT ARMAGEDDON?

Sitting with the president and CEO of Zion Oil, the man John Brown had hired to bring his "mystical revelation" to fruition, I began drilling him with my own questions.

What exactly had gotten him involved in such risky and speculative hunt for oil in the Holy Land? What exactly were these prophecies upon which he and Brown and Luskin were basing their companies? And what did he believe the future held?

Soltero, who has worked in the oil and gas business for more than four decades and served on the board of the Independent Petroleum Refiners Association of America, explained that he joined Zion Oil not long after Brown had founded the company in 2000 because Brown had such a compelling way of looking at Israel through the third lens.

It seems that in 1981, Brown visited a church in Clawson, Michigan. There he heard a sermon by the Rev. James Spillman who had written a 79-page book called *The Great Treasure Hunt*. On the back cover of that book were printed three questions:

Would You Like to Know:
- Where the greatest treasure in the world is buried?
- Why will Russia attack Israel?
- The secret behind the battle of Armageddon?

Yes, Brown thought, *I'd like to know the answers to those questions,* and he listened carefully as Spillman made his case.

In his book, Spillman argued: "Biblical prophecy describes an event in which the armies of the world, led by Gog and Magog, would invade Israel 'to take a spoil.' What could Israel possibly possess in the last days that would make it such a prize for conquest that the world's armies would meet there to fight for the spoils? . . . Countries don't invade their neighbors for pomegranates and olive oil, but they do go to war over another kind of oil. Petroleum. . . . The problem, however, is that Israel is an oil poor country. Fifty years of oil exploration and production in Israel have produced about 20 million barrels total. That's a little over two days of the oil production coming out of Saudi Arabia. Armies will go to war over oil, but not two days worth. But what if a significant about of oil were discovered in Israel, a really significant amount?"[12]

That night, Spillman made a similar case to Brown and the rest of the assembled congregation, and then walked them through a series of Old Testament passages, describing God's ancient promise to unlock enormous wealth and treasures for the children of Israel in "the last days."

> **GENESIS 49:1**—"And Jacob called unto his sons, and said, 'Gather yourselves together, that I may tell you that which shall befall you *in the last days*.'" (King James Version translation of the Bible, KJV)
>
> **GENESIS 49:22**—"Joseph is a fruitful bough . . . *by a well*." (KJV)
>
> **GENESIS 49:25**—"From the God of your father who helps you, and by the Almighty who blesses you with blessings of heaven above, *blessings of the deep that lies beneath*, blessings of the breasts and of the womb." (New American Standard Bible, NASB)
>
> **DEUTERONOMY 33:13**—"Of Joseph he said, 'Blessed of the LORD be his land, with the choice things of heaven, with the dew, and *from the deep lying beneath* . . .'" (NASB)
>
> **DEUTERONOMY 33:19**—"They will call peoples to the mountain; there they will offer righteous sacrifices; for they will draw out the abundance of the seas, and *the hidden treasures of the sand*." (NASB)
>
> **DEUTERONOMY 33:24**—"Of Asher he said, '*More blessed than sons is Asher*; may he be favored by his brothers, and *may he dip his foot in oil*.'" (NASB)

---

[12] Spillman's son, Steve, recently updated the book. See James R. Spillman and Steven M. Spillman, *Breaking The Treasure Code: The Hunt For Israel's Oil* (Medford, Oregon: True Potential Publishing), 2005 (original copyright 1981), p. 3-4.

DEUTERONOMY 32:12-13—*"The Lord alone guided him,* and there was no foreign god with him. He made him ride on the high places of the earth, and he ate the produce of the field; *and He made him suck honey from the rock, and oil from the flinty rock."* (NASB)

ISAIAH 45:3—"I will give you *the treasures of darkness and hidden wealth of secret places,* so that you may know that it is I, the Lord, the God of Israel, who calls you by your name."(NASB)

As Soltero explained it, John Brown was electrified. He went home and carefully studied these Scriptures, and many others Spillman had laid out, asking God to help him understand them and know how, if at all, he could be involved in finding such a treasure. For the next two decades, Brown traveled back and forth to Israel, learning everything about the oil and gas business he possibly could, meeting everyone in the (tiny) industry that he could, studying maps, researching locations, cross-checking with the Scriptures, and praying for wisdom all the while. By April of 2000, he finally felt he knew just enough to begin a company, and launched Zion Oil with the help of an Israeli lawyer named Philip Mandelker, using the following mission statement:

> Zion Oil & Gas was ordained by God for the express purpose of discovering oil and gas in the land of Israel and to bless the Jewish people and the nation of Israel and the body of Christ (Isaiah 23:18) I believe that God has promised in the Bible to bless Israel with one of the world's largest oil and gas fields and this will be discovered in the last days before the Messiah returns.[13]

The company was soon awarded a license by the Government of Israel to explore for oil and gas on 28,800 acres in Northern Israel, and it was during this time that Brown turned to Soltero and Glen Perry, formerly with ExxonMobil, now Zion's Executive V.P.

---

[13] Spillman, 2005 edition, p. 134-135.

"John had learned a lot about the oil and gas business," Soltero told me. "But he knew his understanding of the Bible was just the first step. He also needed experienced professionals well versed in the technical aspects of exploration to make this thing work."

"And how is it going?" I asked.

"We were recently awarded an expanded permit to explore some 219,000 acres in Northern Israel," Soltero told me. "We've been drilling for the past several months and the initial results are very exciting. For legal reasons, I can't say more right now. But let's just say it's possible that your novels have vastly understated how much oil is out there."

As he described where they were drilling, I realized it was just a few miles from the Jezreel Valley and the ancient city of Megiddo.

"Wait a minute," I said. "Are you telling me you think you've found oil under Armageddon?"

Soltero just smiled. "I wish I could say more, but right now I can't," he demurred.

In talking to other oil experts in Israel and the U.S. over the next few months I was able to confirm that there is, in fact, both oil and natural gas under the region known in the Bible as Armageddon, where the Scriptures say the final cataclysmic conflict of history will occur. Just how much is there remains unclear as I write this. There is more testing to do, and many technical challenges abound before any of it will be commercially viable to pump and refine, challenges that Tovia Luskin and his team are encountering as well, despite having already found a billion barrels of oil not far away.

Still, Soltero and Brown are clearly excited by the prospect that they are on the verge of something historic, and prophetic. What's more, former Israeli Petroleum Commissioner Ezekiel Druckman has joined Zion's board, and the company had gone public, filing on January 26, 2006 with the Securities and Exchange Commission for an Initial Public Offering to raise more money for more drilling and research.

What intrigues me is that they are not alone in their efforts to examine Israel's economy and geology through the third lens of Scripture.

"Zion is actually one of six companies to drill in Israel where the founder was originally inspired by Old Testament Biblical passages to take an initial look, and then turn the exploration management over to oil and gas professional," Mandelker, Zion's lawyer, told me when I met him and his colleague Glen Perry in Tel Aviv in the fall of 2005.[14] And several of them are beginning to see promising results.

Will one of these companies hit the big one? Will they all? Will someone else? The truth is we cannot know exactly who, or exactly when, because the Bible does not tell us. Nor does the Bible tell us for certain that the oil will be discovered in full *before* the rest of the Ezekiel 38 and 39 prophecies unfold. It does tell us that oil will be found in "the last days," and it says Israel will be wealthy before the Russian-Iranian coalition attacks. That much we can take to the bank. Thus, expect to read future headlines like this one, "Israel Discovers Massive Reserves of Oil, Gas."

Still skeptical about a small, resource-poor country suddenly finding "black gold, Texas tea" like an episode of *The Beverly Hillbillies*? Then consider the curious story of Equatorial Guinea. For centuries, the tiny country on the Western shores of Africa (tucked in between Gabon and Cameroon) was as poverty-stricken as one can possibly imagine. Until 1995, that is. That was when they discovered oil. Lots of oil.

The country's proven oil reserves have gone from virtually nothing to over 1.2 *billion* barrels. Production has shot from 17,000 barrels per day in 1996 to over 371,000 barrels per day in 2004. Foreign investment is pouring in. The economy has been averaging 15-20% growth per year. In 2005, the economy grew by over 25%, and little Equatorial Guinea is now the second richest country in the world on a per capita basis, after Luxembourg.

Not nearly enough of this oil wealth is actually winding up in the hands of the people. Much of it is winding up in the hands of the country's president and his elite circle of friends and advisors. But still, the

---

14 Author interview with Philip Mandelker, November 14, 2005. Among the other companies that recently have been pursuing oil and/or gas exploration (some with a Biblical perspective, but not all): Avner Oil Exploration, based in Israel; BG (formerly British Gas), based in Great Britain; Delek Group, based in Israel; Ginko Oil Exploration Ltd (which estimated in 2004 that there were some 20 billion barrels of oil in the Dead Sea basin), based in Israel; Isramco, based in Texas; Ness Energy, Inc., based in Texas; Lapidoth Israel Oil Prospectors, based in Israel; Modii Energy, based in Israel; and Sdot Neft, based in Israel.

whole little-country-hits-the-big-one scenario certainly has to make one stop and think. If miracles can happen in sub-Saharan Africa, could they not happen in the Holy Land, too?

ISRAEL, HOME OF MILLIONAIRES

That said, let's be clear: Israel has already become enormously wealthy over the last six decades, and far wealthier than her immediate neighbors. Finding oil would simply be icing on an already impressive cake.

Despite a population of only seven million people, for example, Israel is now home to more than 6,600 millionaires, defined as people with a liquid net worth of more than one million dollars. Of these, there are some seventy multimillionaires, individuals with liquid assets of $30 million or more. Of the top five hundred wealthiest people in the world, six are now Israeli, and all told, Israel's rich had assets in 2004 of more than $24 billion, up from $20 billion in 2003, according to a report published by Merrill Lynch.[15]

Today, Israel has become an economic powerhouse and one of the world's high-tech leaders and a magnet for foreign investment. "Israel is like part of Silicon Valley," Microsoft founder Bill Gates said on his first trip to the country in October 2005. "The quality of the people here is fantastic. . . . It's no exaggeration to say that the kind of innovation going on in Israel is critical to the future of the technology business. So many great companies have been started here."

No wonder, then, that foreign direct investment in Israel in 2005 alone hit a record $10 billion, up 67% from 2004, the second highest growth rate in the world. Or that more Israeli-based companies and companies started by Israelis are listed on NASDAQ than from any other country. Or that Intel, whose next-generation chip was designed in Israel, broke ground in February 2006 on a new $3.5 billion microchip factory and research and development facility in the town of Kiryat Gat, and reported that it now has more employees in Israel than it does in Silicon Valley. Or that Google announced in 2005 it was

---

[15] Shlomy Golovinski, "Israel, The Home of the Millionaire," *Haaretz*, June 15, 2005.

opening new research and development facilities in Israel. Or that over the past decade, more than $8.7 billion has poured into Israeli venture capital funds. Or that an Israeli professor, Robert Aumann of Hebrew University in Jerusalem, won the 2005 Nobel Prize for Economics.[16]

And it is not just high-tech successes that Israelis are experiencing today. Israel now leads the world in exports of industrial oils, fertilizers and polished diamonds. In 2005, the tiny Jewish state placed 8th worldwide in per capita exports. Tourism, too, is surging since the end of the war in Iraq, climbing 26% in 2005, and up 78% in the number of first time visitors. Such a list of economic achievements could go on and on.[17]

That is not to say Israel does not still struggle with poverty, unemployment and underemployment. It certainly does and these are challenges her leaders must constantly and compassionately address. But Israel has made extraordinary—and some would say miraculous—economic gains since 1948 and has become dramatically wealthier than any of her immediate neighbors.

What's more, Israel is poised for explosive economic growth, quite apart from future oil and gas discoveries. Ben Gurion International Airport has been expanded and modernized. New highways and light railways are being built. Inflation, which raged at 100% or more a year in the early 1980s, was a mere 1.2% in 2004. Interest rates are historically low. The exchange rate has been stable. And after a serious recession in 2001-2002 due to the global economic downturn combined with the Al-Aksa intifada (a.k.a., "Arafat's War"), growth is surging again, hitting 4.4% in 2004 and 5% in 2005.

In June 2005, I attended a $1,000 a plate dinner with Benjamin Netanyahu at the St. Regis Hotel in New York. The evening was part of a fund-raising event for Israel's leading free market reform think tank, the Israel Center for Social and Economic Progress, run by Daniel Doron, who has been a friend and mentor of mine on all things Israel since the early 1990s. It was going to be held on the Monday night after the release of *The Ezekiel Option*.

---

16 See "Investing In Israel" and "Venture Capital In Israel," Updates, Israeli Ministry of Industry, Trade and Labor, www.moit.gov.il, accessed March 15, 2006.
17 Ibid.

That night, Netanyahu, who was then serving as Ariel Sharon's Finance Minister, talked about the sweeping changes enacted during his tenure—deep tax cuts, privatization of state-owned industries, banking deregulation, and so forth—and the remarkable economic growth that had resulted. But he insisted there was much more to come.

"In ten years, Israel could be one of the ten richest countries in the world," Netanyahu explained, noting that nine of the top ten wealthiest countries in the world are small countries with less than ten million people each, and that many of them were not on the list at all a decade or two or so ago.

Ireland, for example—a country roughly half of Israel's size, with about four million citizens—was barely a blip the global economic radar for most of the 20th century, Netanyahu observed. By 2005, however, the "Emerald Tiger" had a roaring, low-tax economy and was ranked the eighth richest country in the world in GDP per capita.

"There is absolutely no reason why Israel can't soon become one of the most successful countries in the world," Netanyahu concluded.[18]

Looking back, I am grateful for the opportunity to attend that night. For whether he meant to or not, Netanyahu had just confirmed that Ezekiel's promise of a dazzling economic future for Israel in the last days was rapidly coming to pass.

---

[18] The Israel Center dinner was held on June 27, 2005. See www.iscep.org.il for details, accessed on March 15, 2006.